CONTENTS

CHAPTER 1: The Forge   3

CHAPTER 2: The Arena   15

CHAPTER 3: Jabs   25

CHAPTER 4: Lion VS Wolf   36

CHAPTER 5: Evolution I   45

CHAPTER 6: Poor losers   50

CHAPTER 7: The Temptress   59

CHAPTER 8: Elemental Affinity   68

CHAPTER 9: Dinner   81

CHAPTER 10: The Duke's Manor   88

CHAPTER 11: Early Payback   100

CHAPTER 12: Secrets   111

CHAPTER 13: Release   127

CHAPTER 14: Guardian   132

CHAPTER 15: Reunion   137

CHAPTER 16: Weapons of War   150

CHAPTER 17: You Need What?   157

CHAPTER 18: We're Running out of Time?   166

CHAPTER 19: We Already have Plans   174

CHAPTER 20: Swindling swindlers   183

CHAPTER 21: The Bad Pack   201

CHAPTER 22: The Road to Munich   206

CHAPTER 23: Dangerous Times   217

CHAPTER 24: Doors   231

CHAPTER 25: Bang-Bangs for Less   246

CHAPTER 26: Time to go   260

CHAPTER 27: Arrival   273

CHAPTER 28: Start the Hunt   287

CHAPTER 29: Into the Zoo   301

CHAPTER 30: My Worth   316

CHAPTER 31: Mighty Stag   322

CHAPTER 32: Old Loves   331

CHAPTER 33: Not Everyone is Bad   344

CHAPTER 34: Through the Funhouse Mirror   353

CHAPTER 35: Space Invaders   364

CHAPTER 36: Into a Routine   374

CHAPTER 37: The Plot Thickens   388

CHAPTER 38: Approaching the End   393

CHAPTER 39: Coward's Bravery   402

CHAPTER 40: One Snake, Two Heads   413

CHAPTER 41: Done Your Part   421

CASSIUS LANGE

COPYRIGHT © 2023 BY

Cassius Lange

PUBLISHER'S NOTE:

This is a work of fiction. All names, places, characters, and incidences are either the product of the author's imagination, or are used fictitiously, and any resemblance to actual people, alive or dead, events or locations, is completely coincidental.

ISBN:

9798394032936

1st Edition – 2023

CHAPTER 1: THE FORGE

Our wolfpack spent several days at the ruined manor in the woods, searching the bunker and crumbling structure above for more treasures. Unfortunately, beyond the food in the bunker and some old clothes, everything else was worthless.

Hera and Prometheus left on the second day, after a lengthy conversation about how we should prepare for what lay ahead. In the end, it made more sense to separate, and approach our needs from two different angles. They would make the trek back to the cabin to collect the girls, while Ajax and I stayed behind. The big man had some exciting plans, involving the metallic remains of a dead alpha wolf, and a specially trained smith in Zurich.

Although I was excited about seeing Layla again, it wasn't optimal sending the two off into the wild by themselves. So, we did what any reasonably merc team with a relatively tame but savage wolf would do, we sent Omega with them.

The time alone with Ajax helped me identify how much the big guy had changed. He was still an absolute beast of a man, strong and dependable, but something had shifted in him. His mood became darker, and I struggled to guess what was on his mind.

Two theories emerged. One, that it started with the wolf pelt cloaks. It was possible that part of the wolf king's personality remained and was...polluting him. And the second was considerably more complicated.

Ajax admitted that he was from Glarus and knew some of the people and dealings in the area. With the atrocities that happened after the collapse, I had to conclude that he saw or experienced some truly horrible things.

The big man spent the first night after Prometheus and Hera left wrapped in the cloak. He even had the wolf head perched on top of his own, complete with black face paint. I admired the commitment and how the whole look pulled together—his burly physique wrapped in the powerful wolf's charcoal-and-black fur, with his face covered in alternating black and gray stripes.

I didn't see the need for face paint but did chuckle as he troubled himself with the application. Damn, he was a perfectionist.

My own cloak was similar, but not quite as glorious. Then again, it could also have something to do with the man beneath it. I was darned near half the big man's bulk and half a head shorter. Whatever the case, it kept the cold wind at bay, which was what truly mattered.

"I wish we'd known about that house with the bunker!" I said, letting a bit of my irritation bleed forth.

Ajax chuckled but continued to pick his way through the woods, bending over smaller trees as he went.

"What is the old phrase?" the big man asked. "Hindsight is keener?"

"Something like that," I grunted as a bent sapling snapped up and almost hit me in the face.

It wasn't just that we'd had to bury and hide our loot in the woods to keep it safe, but since our meeting with Kruger, men had been following us at a distance. I was relatively sure they were there on Alfred's orders, as they weren't uniformed men of the Protectorate, but slippery rogues in black and gray clothes.

We finally gave them the slip when we'd doubled back, climbed a bluff overlooking the city, and hid for several hours. I heard them pass below, whispering confusedly, then traipsed off in another direction. To be safe, Ajax and I stayed there until dusk, before moving again.

"Patience is a virtue some men do not possess," Ajax chuckled. Yes, he'd laughed about it, but I'd struggled to keep him still. Normally our peacemaker, he'd wanted to jump the men and hide their bodies.

"Try explaining that to Alfred and Kruger," I'd whispered, considering they were already investigating the death of their second missing noble. He'd harumphed and crossed his arms over his barrel chest.

Moving through the night, I took Prom's job of patrolling our perimeter, then set up at a safe distance and waited until dawn. We approached the burial site as the sun rose, the light quickly burning away the mist.

"Still got your spade?" Ajax asked with a barely concealed smirk.

I slipped off my backpack, let it hang on a nearby tree, then rummage through my stuff. I worked carefully in the early morning light, as to not cut or prick myself on all the sharp tools I had accumulated. Several moments later, I pulled the small folding shovel free and held it out toward Ajax. He chuckled and crossed his arms over his chest.

"Oh, so you think I am going to dig?" I asked, squinting at my large counterpart. "Pull your weight, big guy. Besides, you're bigger and stronger. It will take you half the time."

Ajax cleared his throat but didn't uncross his arms.

"I'm your elder, and your better. Of course, you'll do it."

I quietly crossed my own arms over my chest, replicating his stance.

"You? Better? Why don't we fight to settle it?"

He snorted and shook his head. "I'd beat you bloody, welp. Then I would have to carry the bones and your broken body back to the city."

"Then it is settled," I said and tossed the shovel at him. "I will not dig without a fight, and you don't want to carry us both back to the city."

"Ugh...what?" he stammered but lashed out with cat-like reflexes and caught the shovel. I smiled, took two steps back, and looked around.

"Are you sure this is the spot? None of the ground is disturbed."

"See those trees over there?" he asked, pointing at a pair of matching aspens. "Not only is the one on the left marked, but in a few minutes, when the sun fully rises, their shadows will overlap and show us where to dig."

"So, that is cool," I admitted. "Why didn't anyone tell me?"

Ajax unfolded the spade and locked it open.

"For starters, your memory. But we've been using this kind of trick for years now. It just makes sense, especially in a world where everyone else wants to take what we've got."

Following Ajax, I stepped off to the side and watched as the sun crested the horizon. Bright, golden light spilled over the hills and trees, bathing everything around us.

Two long shadows formed as the light hit the trees, but as the sun rose, they slowly moved, until finally forming an "X" on the ground. Ajax pointed, grinning, and then tossed me the spade.

I caught the shovel, and realizing the folly of arguing further, dropped to my knees and started digging. He joined me a few moments later, after letting me believe that he was only going to supervise. Ajax laughed, unfolded his own spade, and pitched in.

We started to work, but the humor of our initial exchange melted away. Ajax's awkwardness returned, but he refused talk about it. It bothered me that he didn't feel comfortable confiding in me but didn't want to anger him by pushing the issue.

It just compounded my own issues, as after the dream in the bunker, I seemed to have hit a new plateau in my own memory recollection. I knew my name, felt confident in who I was, and even revisited the memories of the convergence, but that was it. Nothing new had surfaced.

"Absorbed anything yet?" Ajax said, a short while later.

"Meaning?"

"Some things came back to you in your dream, right? Has it made the politics, the secrets, the fighting to stay alive, hell, even the freaking wolf make any more sense? Everything happened so quickly, and we never even had a chance to sit down and process what happened."

I tried to hide my surprise, as Ajax finally seemed to be bringing it up. Perhaps this meant he was finally able to unload what had been troubling him.

"Yes and no," I said, studying his face. The wrinkles had deepened around his eyes, making him look a bit older, but I couldn't tell if that was age or stress. "It was like I dislodged a bunch of stuff and it broke free. Now it just tumbles nonstop in my mind. I'm left to worry about a woman, a home, and world that isn't part of my life anymore."

"That sounds maddening," he grunted, and pulled a large scoop free from the hole.

I worked, waiting to see if he would continue, but the silence took over. It took us a short while, some grunting, cursing, and a chipped spade, but we finally managed to dig our stuff up. I stored the two fangs and the needle in my pack while Ajax pulled out a pair of thick bags and started piling Ivory's bones inside.

Even when caked in dirt, the silvery bones had a proud shine and gleamed in the sunlight. A barely perceptible angry muttering tickled the back of my mind, but I pushed it away. Ivory was stirring, his perpetually foul mood only deepened by our excavation of his remains.

"You...*monsters*," he hissed, a moment later. "We would only have eaten you, but...you insist on parading around with my remains even after my death!"

"I will craft the most beautiful hammer with these!" Ajax said, as if privy to Ivory's lamentations.

He stuffed the rest into a duffel but held a smaller bone out to me. Ajax swung the black duffel bag over his shoulder with ease, as I cursed and struggled to lift mine aloft.

"You are a burden, even in death," I muttered, and Ivory sniggered. He may have been offended by how we handled his remains, but he loved the fact that I had trouble carrying him around.

"It was more spread out on our way here," Ajax whispered, adjusting the straps on his shoulder. "Four of us shared the weight, but now? Man up and bear the weight."

There it was again. He was grumbling, but definitely not speaking to me. Was he just speaking to himself? My mind spun as I silently wondered if his cloak hadn't somehow given Ivory the power to slip into his thoughts.

"*And they aren't that heavy! Tell him to stop making such a big deal about it. I will...I will rip his throat out! Let me at him!*" Ivory snarled a moment later, seemingly answering my question. If the alpha really could inject himself into Ajax's thoughts, he likely would have gone straight to the source.

"Can you imagine having metal bones!" Ajax said, finally turning to me. "I would kill for a set, you know? Yes, I would be heavy, but nothing would be able to break my limbs."

"Don't tempt me, or I might try to stick one of these bones inside you while you are sleeping," I said, throwing him a wry grin.

"That, my boy, would definitely start a fight!" he laughed, and together we started walking.

We took our time on the hike back, stopping regularly to set down the bones and rest. It was our second break when I felt a strange sense of dread wash over me. Alfred's men were about, that much was clear, although we couldn't see or hear them. With silent hand signals, Ajax and I formulated a plan, backtracked, and took a detour south.

It took us a good hour longer than it had to, but we managed to avoid Alfred's spies. The guards watched us when we finally approached, grunting and straining under the weight. Ajax's face was red, and he was sweaty, so I knew I had to look just as bad. Luckily, and likely due to Gruber's assistance, we were allowed into Zurich unmolested.

Once inside the city, we moved silently through the alleyways and darkest corners, only traveling on the busy streets when we had no other options. We played the part of disinterested mercenaries, and for all the pedestrians knew, that's what we were. They didn't need to know that we caried a treasure of unimaginable wealth in our bags.

It was an exhausting walk to our destination, the better part of an hour avoiding traffic and moving through crowds, while fighting to avoid attention. Ajax pointed to a building on the east side of the city, easily half a mile beyond the Limmat river. It appeared to be a workshop of some kind, perhaps a smithy.

The first thing I noticed was the smell of smoke and blue-gray haze hanging over the building. We finally approached, finding a cozy, two-story stone building. A large chimney sat on the right side, belching a healthy stream of smoke into the air. A rusted iron fence surrounded the yard, and the windows were barred, making it one of the most heavily fortified buildings I'd seen.

"That was...hell!" I cursed, dropping the heavy bag next to me as we finally came to a stop.

The bones landed with a loud thud and rattled, kicking up a small cloud of dust. I stretched my arms and back, then rubbed my aching shoulders. It felt like it would take me hours to unwind the knots that had formed in my muscles, but if Ajax could work his magic on the bones, then all the pain would be worth it.

"Stop grumbling, you big girl," Ajax said and slapped my aching shoulder.

I pushed him away and glared, but he just laughed even harder.

"Fine. I'll tell you what. Later, I'll take you to the riverside. They are famous for their message parlors," he offered, throwing me a sideways wink. "If you're lucky and pick the right girl, she might give you a happy ending!"

My growing smile faltered. He didn't just say that, did he?

"Ajax! Shit, man, I thought I was the pervert here, but no. It sounds like you the one who needs to pick 'the right girl'."

"Oh, I usually pick well," he said with a shrug, then hefted his bag off the ground.

I laughed as we moved together through the gate, closing it behind us. The smell of smoke and metal hung heavy in the air as we entered the shop. The ring of metal against metal echoed from deeper inside the building, which served like a beacon, pulling Ajax in.

"Mike?" Ajax yelled as he walked through a doorway and into a brightly lit room.

The clanging stopped and I heard a dull thump before someone responded, their voice hoarse and ragged. I formed a mental picture of someone who had worked too long in a hot, dry space.

"You know better. If you're stupid enough to interrupt my work, then you best have brought me something to drink."

"Would a swift kick in the shorts suffice?" Ajax asked.

The other man said something I couldn't quite understand. They both laughed.

"I Just wanted to drop some stuff off for tomorrow, old friend. But I know your rule. I will bring the good stuff with me when I visit again."

Ajax moved aside, finally giving me a glimpse of a stout, broad-shouldered man standing over an old, battered worktable. He wasn't overly tall, but like Ajax, he was powerfully built. His face was artificially aged as well, as long burn scars interrupted his beard, and one particularly spectacular scar transected his right cheek.

He pulled off a heavy leather glove and held a hand out to Ajax, who clasped his wrist and shook it happily. Before I saw them shake hands, I could have sworn they were going to start fighting. Was that what old friendships meant?

"You haven't been by in ages. Last time you brought the kid with you," Mike said.

His voice sounded even drier to me now, until he slid a hand into his apron and produced a small canteen. He unscrewed the lid, put it to his lips, and took a long pull.

"Yeah, things have been—hectic," Ajax replied, absently.

"Isn't it always? Anyway, it's good to see those beauties again," Mike said and nodded to my blades.

I smiled and nodded, liking him almost instantly. He had a way about him that made me feel welcome and safe, despite the fact that we'd just met.

"Sorry, Mike, this is Takemi. Tak, this is Mike."

I offered the stout man my hand and he grasped me, wrapping his thick fingers around my wrist. I copied the gesture but couldn't match the man's considerable strength.

I looked down at the greeting, then with a cocked eyebrow turned to Ajax.

"Has your man never shaken a hand before?" Mike asked.

"Ahh!" Ajax gasped. "No. Takemi took a hammer to the skull during our last battle. It almost caved his head in. As a result, he has struggles to remember much of anything."

I noticed that he didn't bring up that I wasn't from Europe originally, but realized it was probably for a reason. Mike nodded, but the color drained from his face.

"I heard about a massacre, but I didn't realize it was your group!"

I let go of the big man's wrist and looked down at my arm, then splayed my fingers. "I woke up during the battle in a tent. My arm was shattered, my skull fractured, and I had no clue who I was. A little came back, but not all of it."

I looked away, a little embarrassed that I didn't remember him, but thankfully the discomfort passed quickly.

"It looks like you've recovered," Mike observed.

Recounting the experience made me realize how lucky I'd been. I had survived something not many would, so who was I to squander this opportunity?

"Hell, Takemi's more dangerous now than he was before. Maybe that crushed skull unlocked some hidden potential!" Ajax said with a hearty laugh, then slapped my right shoulder. "He's terrifying, I tell you."

Mike nodded thoughtfully, smiled, then held his hand out again.

"So, let's do this again, since we're meeting for the first time, again. Greetings, Takemi, I am Mike!"

* * * * *

I argued with Ajax after we left Mike's workshop, as he insisted on taking me to riverside. To my credit, I stayed strong for a few minutes, until my back tweaked, and I relented.

Luckily, riverside turned out to not be the seedy, redlight district I had feared. In reality, it was a beautiful row of buildings lining the stone riverwalk.

We entered the third building down, where a bright-eyed older woman greeted us, then led us back to a well-lit sunroom in the back. Following her instructions, I disrobed and crawled onto the table. A young woman entered a few moments later, and without word, started my massage.

"I've got knots in muscles I didn't know I had," I whispered as the young lady worked deeper and harder.

Knot by knot, my masseuse worked her way down my body. Pleasure mixed with pain, but they eventually blended into a euphoric trance that I'd never thought possible. It was beyond relaxation.

I thought Ajax was joking when he offered to pay for a

massage, or worse, he was trying to trick me into joining him in some racy brothel. It turned out he hadn't been lying—about it being a fit, and the best massage I would ever receive.

"Told you," Ajax chuckled, after snorting himself awake. He'd fallen asleep not three minutes into his own massage.

The room was old but nicely appointed. Small, spindly tables held boxes of radiant crystals, while chests of drawers covered the back wall, their open shelves practically bursting with jars of medicinal ingredients.

Ajax grunted and sighed as his masseuse manhandled him. She leaned in, putting her weight into one elbow, and worked to release his bound muscles.

Whereas the girl working on me was young, Ajax's masseuse was in her late fifties and sizable in her own right. Her ash-colored hair was pulled into a conservative ponytail, and she wore red silk, the fabric embroidered with a large golden dragon curving all the way around and down her legs.

They used delightful, scented oils, before placing warmed healing stones on our backs. They were hot, just shy of being painful, but worked magically to release the rest of my tension.

I noticed there was more to the two than him just being a customer. He'd either come here often and was familiar with the parlor, or he knew the lady in private. I didn't know which of the two amused me more, though. Especially when he jokingly asked the receptionist to bring on the pain. It had made the woman blush and giggle as Ajax lifted his eyebrows at her suggestively.

"What next?" I asked, as my girl finally removed the hot rocks from my back. She'd wiped the excess oil away and excused herself. "We're not exactly flush with cash right now."

He waved me off, as the older woman moved her more violent attention to his legs.

"Talk later...let me...enjoy this," he grunted and winced. "I could do for a little longer...without your voice."

I rewarded his snarky comment with an almost five-minute-long rambling session of nonsense. Besides, I didn't understand how he could enjoy the violent, almost physical assault he was enduring.

When Ajax turned away from me and started snoring again, I took the hint and returned to my thoughts. No sooner had I closed my eyes than Ivory stirred in the back of my mind.

"Enjoying yourself, hairless ape," he hissed. *"Why are you wasting time like this? You should be growing stronger, or hunting, building your skills to survive what's coming."*

"This is not the time, Ivory," I replied. *"Besides, all you seem to do is bitch and complain."*

"Then release me from this accursed pedestal so I might do more! I can't even feel my legs anymore! This is animal cruelty, I tell you! Barbarism!"

I shook my head and very nearly responded out loud. How weird would that look? In truth, very.

"I didn't know a wolf soul could even feel pain. Did your legs fall asleep? Are they all tingly?"

"Ugh. It is very uncomfortable."

I considered that if I gave him a little more freedom, he might be more inclined to help if the need arose. Then again, I also had to consider that he might try to harm me in some way. I would have to be cautious.

"We'll talk about it next time I visit the mind palace. But for now, can you let me relax?"

"...take care of him, alright?" Ajax said.

I missed the first part of their conversation but took interest at once.

"He's been through a lot—got his ass kicked and had his head caved in. I'm just trying to help a...struggling friend."

"Of course," the woman replied, her voice far softer and sweeter than I expected. "He seemed to like Miko. She is very good with her hands."

I pretended to be asleep then, grunting quietly. I heard the woman tsk and Ajax chuckled.

"Okay, next time. But for me...?"

CHAPTER 2: THE ARENA

Pretending to be asleep only thrust me from one uncomfortable situation into another.

I heard Ajax's masseuse whisper and my big counterpart giggle, the noise disturbingly out of place for such a fearsome warrior. Then I heard the stopper pull free from a bottle of oil, heard his towel pulled away, and unfortunately, I couldn't block out what happened next.

I pretended to startle awake when they nudged me some time later, after far more oily slapping and grunting than I was prepared to endure. But I kept it to myself. After all, the big man had gone far too long without a little affection.

It was dark outside by the time we exited the parlor, the streets lit by flickering lanterns. The sides streets were lit mostly with candles and oil-filled braziers, but on the busier thoroughfares glowing crystals were set in tall holders. There were more pedestrians out and about than I'd anticipated, too. Then again, as Ajax reminded me, Zurich was a city of pleasure. And those distractions were easiest found at night.

He navigated me through the streets, weaving through more crowds than I could ever remembering seeing in one place.

"Where are you taking me?" I asked for the third time, after failing to rub the sleep from my eyes. It was true, I hadn't really fallen asleep—to my detriment, but the relaxing atmosphere had done a number on me. The scented candles and incense mixed with the scented oils and the massage put me in a hyper state of relaxation.

"I remember a certain someone who used to gamble every now and then," Ajax said, throwing me a sidelong glance.

"Gambling? What kind of gambling? Horse races? Because I don't really like cards."

"Horse races!" the big man bellowed and tipped sideways. "You are such an American. No, there haven't been horse races since the collapse."

"I'm drawing a blank here," I said.

"Blood sports!"

"Really?"

He noted my response, because...well, he'd always been able to read me like an open book. The fights I'd been in lately were so violent and vicious that I couldn't imagine why anyone would volunteer for anything remotely similar.

"Are there...many people who want to fight?"

"It's not what you're thinking, Takemi. Yes, some contestants are weapon experts, but most are pugilists, scrappers, or martial artists. The fights are usually no-holds-barred and full-on brawls, so with that said deaths can occur, but are not the point. They are not death matches."

I quickened my pace to keep up, as if longer strides and obvious excitement carried him forward. I struggled to wrap my head around what he'd just said. How did they structure fights so they were even remotely fair? Not every martial art was made the same, just like weapons, with reach, style, composition, and design.

Put me in a ring with a boxer or a scrapper and allow me to use my blades, and I would carve them up. There would be no contest. On the other hand, put me in that same ring and take away my blades, and I likely couldn't compete as well.

"It's a martial arts contest, not a death match," Ajax said, as if able to hear my silent musing. "Occasionally the contestants will be real warriors, although they are not allowed to use their weapons in the ring. Other than that, the rules are loose. Break noses, legs, arms, whatever…as long as you aren't killing on purpose."

Somehow, I had a feeling that he wasn't just telling me about the arena, and that before the night was through, I would find myself in a fight.

"As long as there are no war hammers smashing guys in the head, I'm game," I muttered to myself. "Have you ever fought?"

Ajax shook his head as he walked me through the crowds, then the big man abruptly turned down what looked like a mostly deserted alley. A single door sat at the far end, with a light glowing overhead, highlighting two heavily armed men.

We approached the guards, who seemed to be actively ignoring us. I hovered just behind my large friend and sized them up—big, muscular men, with calloused knuckles, and hard eyes. They weren't just fighters. They were killers.

"Two tickets," Ajax said, handing the one on the left some money. The man grunted something, counted the cash, and stepped aside. I watched quietly, taking everything in.

"Are you knowing the rules?" His English was poor, and his German accent thick. He accentuated the first syllable of each word, as if punching it with his tongue.

"We do," Ajax replied simply. "We won't cause any problems."

"Good. Enjoy evening."

The steel door behind the man slid open then, swinging just enough to let us pass. It closed behind us, the noise echoing loudly in the dark space.

A short passage lay ahead, dropping into a gloomy stairwell. Ajax led, winding down the circular descent deeper into the underground. I focused in on the big man's shoulders, but the repetitious nature of the winding stair hit my head and stomach. After just a few moments, I was nauseous.

We went down and down, the air growing cooler and dark, until the rust-streaked concrete gave way to painted, white walls. Ajax stepped off at the bottom into a small passage, the air tinged with a thick layer of haze. It hung at eye level, forming halos around the caged industrial lights.

We emerged from the tunnel into a massive basement space, with rows of chain-link fence barricading a recessed arena ahead. The ceiling rose high above, the white concrete walls featuring alcoves and balconies providing unobscured views of the arena below. The space was packed with people, lining the fences. Some women sat on men's shoulders, while figures as small as children had climbed the chain link, clinging high above the ground for a better view.

The Arena itself was set into a deep crevice. Rows of tables were spread around on platforms extending outwards, so the entire floor looked like an inverted pyramid.

People in the crowd muttered angrily as we passed, moving onto a metal stair to descend toward the arena. Three tiers of fences appeared, but it wasn't until we were on the second level that I fully saw the arena floor. Two combatants were already fighting.

We stopped at an empty table in the second row and settled into seats. It was a good spot, allowing for a clear view of the pit. The two men fighting could not have presented a starker contrast. One wore a white martial arts Gi, the heavy fabric spattered with blood, while his opponent wore just a pair of khaki pants. Several footprints marred his bare chest, while a dark bruise covered his ribs.

Ajax watched for a moment as the two fighters circled, exchanged a few halfhearted blows, and circled again. My big counterpart snorted, clearly unimpressed by the performance. I turned back and watched. Yes, the fighters looked tired, but it also appeared that they had been beating the shit out of one another for some time. Why did he find them lacking?

The answer came soon enough as the two fighters clashed. The man in white kicked out, connecting solidly with his opponent's side. The man in khakis reeled under the blow but came back in with a desperate counter-attack. His left hand hit the martial artist in the shoulder, while his follow-ups connected with his chest, and face.

It was a blur of movements that seemed impressive at face value, but to my trained eye, it was all speed and no power.

The crowd cheered from the assault, but they didn't understand what was really happening. It was more of a show than a real fight. If it had been Ajax or I in there in place of either fighter, the bout would already be over.

Another thought came to mind as we watched. Were they just ordinary men? Or cultivators? If so, they were working hard to look as weak and slow as possible.

"Why are these guys in the ring? I thought you said this place would be more brutal," I asked, speaking up to be heard over the crowd.

"They're probably just a warm-up bout. What's with the lack of patience? Got somewhere to be?"

People muttered and laughed around us, and a sideways glance confirmed that it was directed at me. Had I said something funny or offensive? Perhaps spoken too loudly? But it became clear that it wasn't just my words, but rather how we looked.

"Fucking dirty bastards!" a man to our right slurred, his accent and drunkenness making him hard to understand. "Wearing animal skins…like some kind of…kind of…animal! I wonder who they robbed to get the entrance fee?"

Ajax tensed and his eyes met mine before we turned as one to the offending table. Three men sat there, with two of the occupants wearing rich clothing with gem-studded rings and necklaces, the jewels gleaming in the dim light. The third and final man was different. I could sense a great deal of power and danger emanating from him. Weapons. He was certainly carrying weapons.

Ajax met their disdainful gazes with a smirk, then shook his head and turned away. The two nobles turned to one another, obviously enraged from his dismissal. The men shifted, their seats groaning, and looked right at me.

Not wanting to cause too much trouble, I did the only thing I could, and tried to diffuse the situation.

"Sorry lads, I'm not into men," I said, loud enough to carry to the tables around us. "You might try the dark alleys outside. Maybe you can find someone to keep you company there."

Chairs scraped against the floor as people either stood or turned our way. I seemed to have gotten a lot more interest than intended, as the crowd trained their attention on us, not the fight. The ball was in their court now and everyone waited to see how they would respond.

Red-faced and embarrassed, the noble in the middle rose to his feet. He shoved his chair, knocking it over, then kicked it out of the way for emphasis.

"What did you say, barbarian filth! What did you just say?"

Oh boy, he was angry. And not just mad, but the irrational, "I'm about to make bad decisions" variety. His face turned a dark shade of red and his angry voice, which had formerly been reasonably deep, rose several octaves. He squeaked when he tried to talk.

Ajax rolled his eyes, chuckling quietly to himself, then kicked me under the table.

"Ahh, excuse me, kind lady. I thought I was arguing with a man," I replied casually, and turned back toward the arena. I turned back after a moment's pause, gave the man a quick once over, and snorted. "But still, you really aren't my type!"

The crowd around us burst into laughter. The noble stood there, his feet firmly planted to the ground. I not only suggested that he was propositioning me, but then I openly called him a woman—and an ugly one at that.

A vein throbbed on his temple and his eyes bulged with

anger. He fell so completely into rage that I didn't know how to respond. And truthfully, I don't think he did either.

"How—how dare you!" he spluttered, after finally finding his voice. "Do you know who I am? W-W-Who you just insulted? I could…I should…if you wish to die, there are much easier ways to go about it. You should show respect to your betters!"

The second well-dressed man sitting at that table finally spoke up, although he mumbled so badly, I couldn't understand what he said.

"Betters? What would that look like?" I asked, then turned to Ajax. "Can you point one of them out to me…if we see one?"

"Swine! He is the second son of Baron von Bauer!"

The second man said it with pride, his chest swelling and his chin rising. I shrugged dismissively.

"Who?" I asked.

"Is he the…?" Ajax started to ask, "No. I can't remember the name."

Confusion swept in, replacing a bit of their rage. Confusion that we didn't know who the Baron's son was? Or that we weren't showing him any respect? Fuck that, I had no respect left for nobles after what we'd seen. I wanted them to know that I didn't know who he was, but also that I didn't care.

"Why should I care?" I said. "We've been out there, in the wilds, beyond the protective walls of the city. You know what your nobility means out there? Let me tell you. Nothing. People live and die. It is that simple. And you nobles don't use your power, your wealth, or your influence to change that. So, no. I don't know who he is. Nor do I care."

My words were ice cold, but they were honest.

"The Baron is one of the most powerful men in Munich!" the second man screamed, as the first, the nobleman's son, twitched.

The floor went silent as those who hadn't been watching us took notice. He seemed satisfied with the effect, although the baron's son just looked twitchy and wrathful. The third man, obviously their bodyguard, just looked uncomfortable.

"But you're not in Munich, friend," Ajax said coldly, accentuating the last word. "You are in a city where a lot of people have lost friends and family thanks to the arrogant pricks in Munich." The big man finally turned to face them, the feet of his chair scraping loudly against the ground.

"I suppose he is right," I dropped a hand on Ajax's shoulder.

The two angry men actually nodded, blinking in surprise, yet their bodyguard's discomfort seemed to deepen.

"Yes, well—"

I didn't give him time to finish.

"What I meant to say was this, and listen carefully, okay?"

The bastard even nodded. I chuckled, but just managed to keep from laughing loudly.

"You're not in Munich. How safe do you think you are? Most of the people here hate you for what your leaders have done. What would happen if we stopped you from leaving this place alive?" I let my right hand come to rest on the handle of my wakizashi hanging at my side.

The baron's son blanched, as all the color bled from his face.

"I'm sorry. Did I scare you? Did you just soil yourself?" I asked.

The young man stepped back, almost falling over the chair he knocked over earlier, and sprawled into his guard's lap. A chorus of laughter erupted all around us, as even the fighters interrupted their bout to see what was going on.

The young noble extricated himself from the bodyguard's lap, the crimson flush returning to his cheeks. Once he'd regained his feet, he rounded on the man.

"Are you going to just sit there? What is my father paying you for?"

The bodyguard looked around nervously and finally rose

to his feet, approached the noble, and leaned in, whispering something in his ear. I focused, and with Ivory's heightened sense of hearing, just managed to make out what he said.

"I'm here to protect you, liege, but if you start a confrontation here, all three of us will end up dead. Now sit down and stop causing trouble. Those men are fucking mercenaries!"

The noble's face paled again but his eyes flicked to me, his disdainful look not wavering.

"You're joking, right? Why do you think they're impressive? With their...fur cloaks?" He shook his head, but the bodyguard leaned in, and again we listened.

"Those cloaks aren't from normal wolves. I'm certain that at least one of them was from a grade three beast, maybe even four. Do you really want to take the chance? The chance they weren't rich enough to buy something like that? If they fought and killed a beast like that, we've got no chance."

The noble opened his mouth to argue, but no sound came out. He opened it for a second time but seemed to think better of it. Quietly, he picked his chair up off the ground and sat. He leaned into his friend, and the bodyguard, their voices again dropped to a whisper.

"Which one is the grade three beast?" the noble asked. The bodyguard half turned and eyed us, then leaned back in.

"The big guy. The other one is similar but not quite as large. It might be a grade two or a weak grade three."

Ajax smiled proudly as I shook my head. The bastards were actually sizing us up by grading our cloaks.

"Dick," I muttered, and his smirk turned to a grin.

"I told you!" Ajax muttered, "When you finally grow into a man, we can swap!"

I looked back to the nobles, but quickly lost interest and turned to the arena. The two fighters were now barely standing and thoroughly beaten, bruised, and soaked with sweat. More than a little blood covered them and the ground beneath them, too. Ajax and I stood as the crowd erupted into cheers, honoring the two men and their performance.

"This place is alright with me!" I said, slapping Ajax on the back.

CHAPTER 3: JABS

The crowd settled and the fight resumed. The two fighters, evidently wary of letting the bout go on too long, circled twice, and appraised one another.

The fighter in white kicked at his opponent's leg, but at the last second pulled back, pivoted, and did a roundhouse kick instead. The feint worked and the heel of his foot connected with the bare-chested man's shoulder, staggering him.

It wasn't a bad move, but he'd cocked it up. If he'd aimed a little higher, then he might have caught the man in the chin, or further in, and hit his collarbone. I had seen men suffer broken clavicles during fights. It usually laid them low.

Shaking off the strike, the bare-chested man danced right, faked left, and rushed in, trying to take the martial artist before he could recover his balance. He grabbed the man's head and wrenched it down, bringing his knee up at the same time.

Cheers erupted from the crowd as the knee connected, the martial artist's nose crunching loudly. Blood splattered over the mat, staining the man's Gi as well. The scrapper tried to press the advantage, but even with a broken nose, the martial artist broke free.

The bare-chested man slid in and jabbed with a left and

then a right, peppering the wounded man's face and nose. He defended with his arms, slapping a few weak punches away, but the scrapper pivoted right and swung a strong right hook, breaking right through the man's defenses and slamming into his jaw.

"Did you see that?' Ajax roared, clapping excitedly. "This bout is over, I tell you. Over!"

"Not so fast," I cautioned, and threw him a wink. I knew from ample experience that you should never count a trained fighter out.

The bare-chested man circled, flexing and shadowboxing, as he played to the crowd. They roared appreciatively. Some men jumped up and pumped their fists, sloshing their drinks. I spotted several women in the crowd across the arena that lifted their shirts, flashing the fighters. The scrapper noticed and roared his approval. All the while the martial artist circled and waited.

Desperate to impress the women, the scrapper pumped his fists and moved in again, a wide, confident smile now on his face. He snapped two quick jabs, the attacks left intentionally short. When he reared up and threw his strong cross, the martial artist retreated. Sensing victory, the scrapper advanced and swung wide.

I grabbed Ajax's arm as the martial artist reacted, snapping his elbow up to block, while striking hard with his right. The movement was so fast I almost didn't see it, only heard his lead foot slap the mat.

Staggering back, the scrapper clutched at his throat.

The strike evidently was strong enough to collapse his windpipe, but the shock and pain were enough to put him entirely on the defensive. A round-house kick sealed the deal, knocking him out with deadly precision.

"Well, fuck!" Ajax muttered in surprise.

"What did I say?"

I joined in on the cheering, as the victor turned, bowing to the audience. His nose was a mess and every time he bowed, it dripped a healthy spatter of blood onto the mat.

When the cheering died down, the winner climbed out of the ring and made his way up the steps. He wobbled, his legs obviously unsteady. A pair of uniformed men rushed in from the side and helped guide him to a chair.

Two more uniformed men rushed into the ring and attended the loser. They checked his pulse, lifted his eyelids to check his pupil response, and more. A moment later they waved off to the side, and two more men appeared with a stretcher. They eased him onto the stretched and carried him out of the ring.

"Are you ready for more?" a strong, energetic voice yelled from overhead. I lifted my gaze to the balconies, trying to track the speaker.

The crowd responded, cheering and clapping their hands. Ajax and I joined in, cheering for more action.

"That's right. Raise those voices!" the speaker continued. *"Ladies and gentlemen! Tonight we have a special treat in store for you, an old favorite! The fist that shattered a thousand chins, and the chin that broke a thousand hearts!"*

The crowd erupted, cheering and screaming, and in response the temperature seemed to rise. I had no idea who was about to fight, but the other guests seemed to know, and that became infectious. Before long, Ajax and I were standing, clapping, and screaming with them.

"That's right! Appearing in our next match is our very own favored son, Zurich born and bred!"

The crowd grew louder, chanting a name.

"Leo!"

"Leo!"

"Leo!"

"That's right! Leonardo Lienhard! Leo the Lionheart!"

The ambient light from glowing crystals dimmed, before a magnified spot of light hit one of the four doors on the far wall. A man sauntered into the arena, the Swiss flag printed on the side of his shorts. He strutted around, gyrating his hips, and the women responded, screaming, and calling his name. The lewd suggestions and catcalls continued, especially when Leo turned, showing that he had a white cross on his ass.

"Is that a target on his ass?" I shouted, leaning into Ajax.

Several angry stares flashed our way from nearby tables.

Ajax flashed me a disapproving frown, then eyed the crowd around us. Was he disappointed in their response? My comment? Or that I was letting loose and having fun? It appeared that with or without memories, I was a lightning rod for trouble.

He leaned in closer and spoke in a barely audible whisper.

"You want to make some money and crystals? You would likely be healed before the girls get here."

The announcer continued, but I wasn't paying attention. My mind latched onto Ajax's question and spiraled down that rabbit hole. We needed to start cultivating in earnest, and how better to prepare than winning a bunch of crystals?

"They open the arena up to a challenger from the crowd," Ajax whispered.

I sat, not wanting to draw more attention to us, but leaned in to my counterpart.

"Let's see if he's any good," I whispered as the second fighter entered the arena. A wolfish smile crept up my face.

It was...a woman and boy did she look fit. She wore tight-fitting shorts and a sports bra-style top. Her arms and legs were impressively muscular, but it didn't make her less feminine. I did appreciate her skin tone, which shone light brown in the crystals glowing overhead.

The crowd responded to her differently. A smattering of applause erupted, but there were no cat-calls or lewd comments, at least not like I expected.

Judging by her face, the woman meant business. She watched Leo, her eyes narrowed, and jaw clenched. I liked her intensity, but liked her long, black hair more. It was pulled together in a single French braid down her back.

"How long is her hair?" I whispered. "And it's so dark."

"Zaäbar! My chocolate goddess!" a man yelled below, waving at the woman from the first ring of seats. The way she responded told me everything, as her head snapped around.

Without warning, the female fighter leapt over the ropes, jumped up and out of the arena, and ran at the man's seat. Before anyone could react, she grabbed the man by the throat and lifted him out of his chair.

"What did you just call me?" she growled, my extra-sensitive hearing serving me well.

The man swallowed hard and tried to speak, but it appeared that she was holding his throat too tightly. Thoroughly interested by the building drama, I slid forward in my chair, hoping to hear, or see, more.

In a flash, the female fighter's hand shot out, her fingers latching onto the man's family jewels. He gasped, yelped, and started to splutter and shake, as his ears and neck turned red. Then she seemed to squeeze and twist, and the man gave a shrill, strangely feminine cry.

"I c—called you my ch—chocolate goddess."

"I have tolerated you bastards calling me Zaäbar but let me make myself perfectly clear! My skin is not chocolate, or coffee beans. If I hear that out of your mouth again, I am going to come back over here, and twist those shriveled berries right off your body. Understood?"

She didn't shout, but she also didn't need to. I found that I liked her instantly. Sure, she came off as a little hotheaded and potentially violent, but considering I hung around with mercenaries and a wild wolf, that didn't seem like much of a problem.

Then again, she was likely angry from having to deal with narrow-minded and racist bastards... often. I couldn't give two fucks what color her skin was. We all bled red, after all. I was interested in watching her fight. She finally released the heckler's balls and crawled back into the arena.

Zaäbar stood in the middle of the mat, while Leo walked circles around her, a smug smile on his face. Her expression didn't tell me much either, as they both didn't seem to like the other.

"Who should we bet on?" I asked, hooking an arm over Ajax's broad shoulders. The big man watched, chewing his bottom lip, and grumbling to himself.

I found myself rooting for Zaäbar, but for more reasons than I initially realized. Yes, she was attractive, and feisty, and likely fighting against great odds, but she was also facing what looked to be a rather pretentious noob.

Leo's short blond curls, blue eyes, and smug smile notwithstanding, he acted like every prissy, pampered royal I'd met. I kind of wanted to smash his face in, on the off chance that he was related to someone who was…well, someone.

Was I jealous of all the fanfare? Not particularly. I just really didn't like the blatant favoritism going on here.

"These Swiss pricks…" I started to say to Ajax but caught myself before I could go too far. He was Swiss, and not every one of them was a self-righteous asshole like Alfred.

Before Ajax could reply, the announcer spoke, drowning him out.

"*Tonight, we have a clash between two S-ranked former champions of the Second League!*"

The crowd started chanting and stomping their feet, at least those sitting on the ground floor and around us.

"Do they really have to make so much noise?" I muttered, crossing my arms and glaring at the ring. A headache was already forming.

"I've watched Leo fight before, Tak. Yes, he's a showy bastard, but he is blindingly fast and ruthless. I've only ever heard of her, but she has killed three men so far. Most probably annoyed her first or thought she'd be a push over. Ya know? On account of her being a girl."

"She looks more like a woman to me," I replied, elbowing him in the ribs.

I watched the two fighters circle each other, wondering how hard it had to be for a woman to climb the ranks. It would have been hard for anyone not from Zurich to succeed, but for someone like her, that stood out from the pale hair and eyes crowd...well, you could say the deck was likely stacked against her.

"I don't want to bet on either of them," I admitted.

"Oh? I am torn, as well," he replied and leaned in. "But I know which chocolate cookie I'd like to win."

"Why...do you need another massage? You're still practically glowing from the last one."

Ajax snorted and pointed at the ring just as the announcer started counting down.

"Wagers are closed! The bout will begin in three. Two."

A piercing, high-pitched voice rang out then, cutting through the chatter.

"Kick his ass, Viv!"

I probably wouldn't have noticed it if the voice hadn't been so shrill. It appeared that we weren't the only ones rooting for Zaäbar, or Viv, or whatever her name was.

"Go!"

Zaäbar moved like lightning, unleashing a furious barrage of attacks toward Leo. Most turned out to be feints, to set him up for a vicious kick.

Leo deftly blocked most of the attacks and jumped back but couldn't dodge the kick. He danced sideways and back, swinging wide to push her back. But I noticed a wince when he shifted his weight between legs.

How much damage had she caused with that one kick? Leo's arrogant smile was gone now, replaced by a determined grimace, which devolved into an angry scowl. He was probably realizing that he couldn't afford to play around with Zaäbar. Her bite matched her bark.

"He's a fool," I muttered.

Ajax grunted in agreement. After all, anyone going into a fight should expect their opponent to be dangerous.

That meant triple for cultivators: firstly because of their strengthened bodies, second their skills, and lastly, their fighting experience. Anyone hunting monsters would have a trick or two up their sleeve.

The crowd hooted and yelled, while a small contingent chanted for Zaäbar. My headache was starting to build, and the crowd wasn't helping. It was arguable if the crowd knew anything about fighting. Wouldn't that be a kick in the nuts? A beloved local fighter like Leo lose? And to a woman? Oh, I would pay to see that!

A group of people screamed and hollered to our left, throwing insults and fists into the air with equal abandon.

"What's their problem?" I nodded toward them.

"They probably have a lot of money riding on Leo. So, if he loses, they lose big."

Ah, that would do it. Selfishness—not exactly a foreign emotion to me, as everyone struggled with it. As far as the angry people in the crowd? It was their own damned fault, especially for betting on the flashy fighter.

I smiled as Zaäbar effortlessly dodge and parried Leo's kicks and jabs. He wasn't bad, if I was being honest—fast, with good technique, and what looked like good reach and torque generation. His attacks also looked precise, but he was hobbling on his left leg. The smug prick let her strike first and was already fighting from a deficit.

"What is Second League?"

"A division for fighters who have formed two veins," Ajax replied, his eyes glued on the fight.

My respect for the fighters went up a notch as Leo unleashed a hail of kicks and punches. Zaäbar blocked the first three, dodged the fourth, but caught a kick to her thigh. Without missing a beat, the woman countered, unleashing an equally violent barrage.

They were fast, precise, and knew how to bring the pain. Any one of their serious blows would have killed an ordinary man, I was sure of it.

Zaäbar landed another blow to Leo's shin, and he almost fell. When he squared back up with her his limp was more severe. Words were exchanged—Zaäbar pointed and laughed, and Leo shouted something back.

I laughed as Leo's mouthguard shot out of his mouth and landed on the mat.

"What are you laughing at?" the royal snot next to us asked. Disgust was written all over his face.

I ignored the jab, focusing on the fight and their movements, trying to predict what would happen next. Could I have blocked her attacks? Would I have been fast enough to counter Leo?

Without weapons, maybe. Maybe not. That might have been my own brand of arrogance speaking, though. I hadn't seen either of them fight with a weapon yet. And then it dawned on me: they were trained for bare-handed fighting.

Zaäbar swung in with a right cross and caught Leo in the jaw. He staggered back from the blow, a collective groan growing from the crowd. Unlike the majority, I cheered and raised my fist in support.

"Go, Zaäbar!"

The crowd around me didn't appreciate my zeal for Leo's opponent. That was fine. Life was full of disappointment. They might as well find that out sooner rather than later.

Zaäbar looked in my direction, and I could see a flash of confusion in her eyes before they snapped back to Leo, who tried to take advantage of her momentary lapse of focus.

They grappled, wrenching and twisting on one another for a moment, before Zaäbar drove a knee into Leo's wounded leg. Her face twisted in a feral snarl as she captured his wrist and twisted. Leo buckled under her strength, moving with the move instead of letting her break his wrist. A heartbeat later, his face met the ground.

"Yield!" she yelled, holding him in the armlock, his face pinned against the mat.

She wrenched on his wrist, using her weight for

leverage. Leo groaned and cursed. The crowd groaned with him, obviously angry their money was about to fly away. I tensed, preparing incase things became heated.

Zaäbar suddenly released her hold and Leo rolled away. The crowd gasped as their champion rose to his feet, flexing his wrist and rotating his shoulder. He grimaced, assessing the damage. I didn't think it was his shoulder that was hurt, more likely his ego.

"Torn rotator cuff? Maybe a broken wrist," Ajax muttered, his gaze locked on the action. I nodded before realizing he wouldn't see my reaction.

"Maybe both. Did you see that knee strike? She caught him right in the ribs. He's going to struggle to come back from that."

Zaäbar moved in again, but Leo slapped her hands away and rolled for distance. Then he did something odd. He reached into the pocket of his shorts. To the average spectator, it might have looked like nothing, but to my trained eye, I saw it differently. His shorts were tight, which meant the pockets were small, but there might have been enough room for a crystal.

Zaäbar cried out as Leo's hand snapped toward her, scattering what looked like dark dust right into her eyes. She cursed and flailed, pawing at her eyes.

"What was that?" Ajax roared, and together we rose to our feet.

A moment later my heightened senses took over and I caught of whiff of something on the air. It bit at my nose, burning in both nostrils.

"That was pepper," I gasped. "He threw pepper in her eyes! The cheating bastard!"

Half of the crowd roared, while the minority, of which I seemed to fit, yelled in outrage. Leo rushed in and Zaäbar covered up, dropping her elbows to protect her ribs, and using her hands to shield her face.

She tried to block and counter when he got close, but I

could tell that she could barely see. Leo dodged and blocked with ease, playing with her. I balled my hands up into fists as his mocking smile returned.

Showcasing his impressive speed, Leo overwhelmed Zaäbar with quick jabs. She staggered and fell under the onslaught. Sensing victory, the blonde followed her to the ground, punching again and again.

"You cheating scumbag!" I screamed, moving forward. The movement sent the table flying over the handrail and down to the next level, where it crashed to the ground. People yelled and cursed, turning angry glares our way. Luckily, I'd caught Leo's attention, too.

He looked right at me and smiled, his front teeth smeared with blood. Then slowly, he brought his knee down on Zaäbar's throat. She slapped at him, fighting, and gasping for air.

"Scumbag?" he called. "Why don't you come down and say that to my face?"

CHAPTER 4: LION VS WOLF

I stepped out from around the table and moved toward the arena, pausing on the steps to the lowest tier. The angry prick leaned toward me, lifting his knee off Zaäbar's neck.

"Douchebag," I said.

Leo eyed me, his cheeks glowing a darker shade of red.

"I would say you hit like a girl, but that would be offensive to your counterpart, Zaäbar, because up until the point where you started cheating, she was kicking your ass."

Leo tried to smile, but his expression faltered. Murder flashed in his eyes.

"Sorry. I didn't realize you were deaf, but yes, I just called you a cheating piece of shit!"

I watched gleefully as his face darkened. He rose to his feet, his attention purely on me now. Zaäbar was all but forgotten.

"If you say one more word, I will kill you where you stand!"

"One more word!"

His eyes flared as he rushed towards me, but just as he jumped over the ropes, a pair of black-uniformed guards intercepted him. If he had attacked me while I was fully armed and armored, I would have cut him in half, but I wasn't sure how the Protectorate would feel about that.

"You should thank them, they just saved your life!" I yelled.

I dropped my hand to the pommel of my wakizashi, and Leo's eyes narrowed. He seemed to finally notice that I was armed. His rage dissipated.

I grinned as he blanched, then winked at him for good measure.

"Do you have the balls to face me in the pit?" he screamed, pushing away from the security guards.

"Balls?" I replied with a snort. "Why would I need balls to fight a cheater like you? Maybe you should consider a new career. Comedian? Bathroom attendant?"

He sneered and took a breath to respond, but I waved him off, and started unbuckling my sword belt. It swung free and I passed the blades to Ajax. He grinned, but I couldn't tell if he was proud or upset. Did he want to be the one to knock some respect into the spoiled shit?

I stripped out of my armor, first releasing the harness that would usually hold my Nodachi, but that oversized monster was currently stored under my bed back in the cabin. I dropped the Kevlar and polymer weave armor on top of the wolf cloak.

Stripped to just my pants and shirt, I removed my boots and socks. Leo paced in front of the ropes, but I took my time, drawing it out as long as possible.

The crowd whispered and murmured all around me. I knew what they wanted or had a fairly good guess. The match had been a good one, but Leo brought it to a screeching halt with his cheating antics. I called him out on it, and now presented them with an entirely new set of circumstances.

I walked up to the ring and ducked inside, then sauntered past the arrogant little shit. He flexed and snapped his head forward, trying to get me to flinch, but when you'd faced the kind of odds that I had, you developed a steel will.

Leo was shorter than I'd figured from my seat above. Interesting. And not that it meant much as size didn't have much bearing on a fight between trained combatants. But considering his attitude, I'd figured he was a colossal giant with the world poised beneath his thumb.

He danced backwards and shadowboxed the air, a smug grin plastered on his face. I stretched as two guards helped Zaäbar out, her legs wobbling beneath her. Zaäbar looked to me once she set foot outside the ring, her expression full of confusion. I simply smiled and gave her a nod.

My anger was bleeding away, which left me contemplating the situation. Fuck. I was about to go toe to toe with another S-ranked two-vein cultivator. With my bare hands. And against someone who trained extensively with the sole purpose of beating the crap out of people like me.

Ajax and the girls kept telling me I'd always been a hot-headed person, but I spent copious energy since waking to prove them wrong. Evidently, I couldn't hide from who and what I truly was. The only unarmed combat I'd engaged in since waking in the battlefield tent was to beat the crap out of a squad of so-called elites. But that had been reflexes—my body taking over. Could I rely on that now?

The crowd erupted all around us, cheering for Leo as he bounced on the ropes. He looked at me and smiled, clearly enjoying the applause. I watched and smirked. Leo sneered and jumped back to the mat. Clearly, I was somewhat of an enigma —anyone in the know would have rightly been afraid to fight him, and yet I openly mocked and challenged him.

"Challenger!" the announcer yelled. "We need to know your name."

"And where to send your body when I'm done!" Leo laughed.

"Call me Wolf," I said, unwilling to give them my real name or my nickname. Besides, I didn't want to lend too much credibility to their charade. "Wolf versus the Lion!"

The noble from Munich was suddenly quite brave as he

shot out of his seat and shouted.

"He's got a mangy mutt-cloak! He's nothing but a dog! Call him 'dog'!"

The audience laughed and began to chant.

"*Mutt!*"

"*Dog!*"

I shook my head but didn't rise to their petty provocations. When the room finally calmed a little, Leo hit me with a smirk.

"Well, Dog? Oh, sorry. Can I call you that? Can I call you 'Dog'?"

I shrugged.

"Why would I care what a small...cheater calls me?"

The audience gasped at my comment and Leo didn't wait for the announcer to start the fight. He lunged right at me, his speed even more impressive up close. I deflected the jab with my forearm, the blow reverberating up my shoulder and making my arm go numb. I pushed some ether down my limbs, the pain quickly fading.

He followed up with a hook, but I dodged the blow and stomped for his toes. I threw a jab at his face, then rounded to the right with a spinning elbow strike, hitting him in the solar plexus. I ducked and jumped back for distance. Leo barely missed with his counter, a strong kick aimed at my neck.

I squared up and moved sideways, snapping my hands out to keep my muscles loose. Leo circled, his look of surprise worth every moment. He'd expected me to be a pushover.

Raising my hands, I tucked my elbows in against my ribs, covered my face, and moved in. I focused on my breathing, relaxed my facial muscles, and envisioned my attacks. This would be a real test for this arrogant little shit. And myself for that matter.

I hit him with a one-two combo, jabbing with my left fist and following it up with a slightly more powerful straight. I saw a hint of glee on Leo's face as he concluded that I was a boxer and noticed him adjust his hips just enough so he could kick.

I smiled and prepared.

<<Enhanced Strength>>

The skill activated, enhancing my muscles to the full extent of its capabilities. I braced, preparing to take the blow head-on. I wasn't disappointed as his foot connected with my thigh. The attack was strong, but it didn't move me.

Using my regained memories, I hooked my left leg behind his right ankle, and sent him tumbling to the mat. Leo landed awkwardly, as he didn't appear used to having fighters take him to the ground. Either way, he landed on his right arm, and something snapped loudly. I winced, wondering if it had broken.

A gentleman would have let him get to his feet. A gentleman might have considered it dishonorable to take advantage of a man who couldn't fight back, but I was no gentleman. Besides, I was dealing with a man that threw pepper in someone's face and then knelt on their neck. Who was I if I couldn't teach him a lesson?

I stomped on his ankle, doing my best to cripple him. Leo twisted his body and rolled, trying to gain distance, and protect his wounded limbs.

I leaned in close and whispered.

"How does it feel to be on the losing end?"

Jeers and shouts echoed all around us, but I tuned them out. They called me a dog, insulted and degraded me. But that was all they *could* do.

Leo tried to roll away but I planted a kick in his side. He slid several feet back from the force of my blow. Overkill? Sure, but that's how pompous pricks like him learned best. Kick them until the message sank in.

Beating on Leo got boring, but I realized that I couldn't risk killing him, especially if I couldn't make it look like an accident. Was he really a two-veined S-rank? Because my memories and experience told me he should have been far stronger and faster. No, maybe it wasn't just him. Zaäbar was on his level, which could only mean that I was undervaluing my own strength.

I resolved to recheck my stats when we got back.

Wanting to get it over with, I grabbed Leo and wrenched him around, and twisted his good leg. He cried out and the audience joined him, but the protests were getting louder. They were also starting to throw things at the arena.

"Does this count as my win?" I yelled, turning toward the referee. "Or do I need to keep hitting him until he's pulp?"

Zaäbar could have surrendered, but she was stubborn. Leo hadn't surrendered either, so by the same right, I could keep beating on him until he did. But that was the fundamental difference: he was 'royalty' or at least famous, and I was an unknown...a dog. Or a wolf, to those that truly knew me.

"Y—yes! The winner of our main fight is—" he paused for a moment as if trying to remember my name. His gaze flicked toward Ajax, who loomed large and impressive in the stands, still wrapped in his wolf cloak. "—Fenris! The monstrous wolf!"

The audience responded—a healthy mixture of cheers and boos. There were some cheers mixed in with the jeers and shouts. Ajax was the loudest among them. And beside him was the royal from Munich. If looks could kill, I would have keeled over right there.

The name the referee gave me tickled a memory and I subconsciously tried to think of what it meant. Maybe mythology? Fuck it, I would ask someone later. Probably Ajax.

I climbed out of the ring, not bothering to bow to the crowd. Ajax clapped me on the back the moment I sat down, his mouth pulled up into a lopsided grin. I put on my socks and boots just in case we needed to leave quickly.

"You just won us 200 crystals, Tak."

I looked at him in surprise and then shook my head.

"What idiot bet you that much?"

I looked past him to our grumpy noble friend from

one table over. Question answered. Now they had even more reason to hate me, but hate and anger were fickle emotions, and I'd shown them we weren't to be fucked with.

As I finished dressing and putting my weapons back on, I finally noticed that Leo had been removed from the ring. A bloody smear marred the mat where they'd dragged him out.

"Think they're gonna come at us for this? I know you've been setting this up one way or another," I whispered.

"Probably," he chuckled. "I really can't take you anywhere. You are like a trouble magnet."

"Says the guy that set me up. Now feed me and I will consider forgiving you. Am I the only one who's feeling the need for Swedish Meatballs right now?"

"That was low! Even for scum like you!" our nobleman friend from Munich said, after gaining a bit of strength.

"Yeah, Tak! That was really low!" Ajax said with a shrug, then got up ceremoniously.

"Speaking of low," I said and turned to the nobleman. "How do you feel about making a wager?"

His eyes narrowed on mine as he licked his lips.

"What kind of wager?" he asked, his German accent thicker than before.

"It is Bauer, right?" I asked but didn't wait for him to confirm. I seemed to remember that he was a son of a Baron or Duke, but the specifics weren't important. "You see, I have a sword here, and your bodyguard has one, too. How about I wager you a hundred crystals that I can disarm your bodyguard in...three moves. Is that the kind of action that interests you?"

The young nobleman snorted and slapped his open palm on the table, the vein on his forehead pulsing angrily. For a moment, I thought he might drop dead from a stroke.

"Preposterous! He is a top-tier bodyguard, and you've just fought against an S-Rank fighter in the arena! Honestly, mongrel, how much further do you think you can push your luck?"

I held eye contact, refusing to look away. The young nobleman nodded and pulled a small bag from his jacket, only to have his hotheaded counterpart fly off the handle.

"Honestly, you can't possibly...he's a...your father will..."

Baron Von Bauer's son dropped a hundred crystals onto the table between us, then nodded to his man. I grinned, gently tapping the pommel of my katana.

Bauer's bodyguard didn't appear happy with the arrangement but didn't voice his displeasure out loud. He pulled his coat off, revealing carbon steel body armor. It glimmered in places where the synthetic coating had worn off. The man pulled his saber free, twirling it expertly in the air before him.

"Herr Bauer," I said, remembering the word Ajax used before. "Why don't you count down? Or give the go-ahead?"

I channeled some of my ether forth and activated both of my skills, increasing my strength and speed twofold. No one noticed anything as there was no sonic boom or bright light, no indicator when they were activated.

"Go!" the young nobleman said, his lips pulling into a wide smile.

I lunged, bringing my katana down in an overhead arc. He raised his saber to block but buckled under my blow. The saber almost dropped from his hand, but he kept his grip. I slashed again, this time my blade striking closer to his face. The blow pushed his sword arm down. He braced, locking out his elbow and wrist, but he'd prepared for all of my pressure to come from over top, not the wakizashi he wasn't expecting. My shorter blade hit his saber at the handguard, dislodging it from his hand without spilling a drop of blood.

"Wh—what just—how?" the bodyguard stammered. Bauer frowned.

"How can you stand for this? Did you see that?" Bauer's young and equally hotheaded counterpart raged, his cheeks were now as red as the nobleman. Honestly, I'd generally ignored the young man up to that point.

"That attack was *barbaric*," Bauer said, eyeing me curiously. Although he looked disappointed, he didn't necessarily look angry. "I'm not quite...happy with this outcome if you will, but I'm a man of my word." He got to his feet, then motioned for the door. "Take your crystals and leave."

CHAPTER 5: EVOLUTION I

I trotted along through the long weeds, two of my pack crashing into the underbrush behind me. Pale Fox and Short Tooth chattered to one another, then growled something at me. Alpha wasn't with us. Unfortunately.

Pale Fox was my least favorite of the pack. Short Tooth was female, but she was strong. I could respect that. But the fox was quiet and sneaky, and I feared that he was always looking to steal my food.

He was also wary of me, even though a long time had already passed, and I growled at him plenty, to let him know that he was pack. I did my best to ignore their noise, but they were loud and poor wolves.

I missed Alpha and Deer Eyes, the two strongest of the furless wolves. They didn't fear me, and regularly gave me food. Burned meat. And rubs. And hugs. I liked their attention. I really did.

I didn't know why Pale Fox and Short Tooth were backtracking, but we were traveling down the path we'd taken a moon ago. Were they going to feed their pets? The two females? If they were as tame as I thought, they wouldn't be able to hunt their own food, so that made sense. But if that was the case, I could have stayed and cared for them. Or maybe I would have eaten them. No! Alpha seemed to like his mate. He would be mad at me if I ate her. He mounted her exclusively, so that told me all I needed to know.

I snorted, dropped my nose to the ground, and searched for scents. The furless wolves passed as I slowed, my gaze tracking on the she-wolf, Short Tooth. She seemed to notice and turned toward me. I growled and yipped, jumping on my front legs. Then I circled them both.

I had fun teasing Short Tooth. She was so twitchy and seemed to genuinely want to understand me.

The two furless wolves began to grunt at me. Stupid wolves! They growled so weird. It wasn't like I couldn't communicate, but they were just too dumb to make wolf noises. All they did was grunt, hoot, and wave their pale paws in the air.

I tasted a familiar scent on the back of my tongue, flicked my tail at her as I dashed ahead, and did my best to send her a mental grin. I knew she wouldn't understand it, but I wasn't an uncouth beast like they were. I was loyal to the pack and smart. They would see that, like Alpha did, in time.

I sighed blissfully as I leapt and ran, enjoying the freedom of being able to run like a wolf! I caught the scent again—prey—turned to Pale Fox and growled. He howled quietly, understanding, and nodded.

With a hungry thrill shooting through my body, I accelerated into a full sprint. The scent of deer rose off the ground and plants around me as I tracked. The hunt filled me with energy and made my body stronger. I wasn't the weak outcast like when Alpha found me. My new pack accepted me, and thanks to them I was growing stronger.

I felt the two different energies flow through me, gathering in my chest as I ran. They flowed and swirled around each other, then merged around my beating heart. It felt so good to use the energy properly unlike my foolish pack. How could wolves be so different?

Something was wrong. The energy inside me suddenly surged and turned to fire, like the heat the furless wolves used to burn meat. The fire filled me, pushing outward through my fur. I slowed my gait, then stopped, and looked down at my paw. One moment it was there, and the next, it was almost transparent.

I yelped in alarm and pawed at the ground, then bit myself. My paw was still there, but…A deep puddle formed on the ground, its surface shimmering in the sunlight. The ground beneath the puddle seemed to bend and twist in strange ways. I touched it with my paw, fur coming away slick but cold, as if it were water from the cold time, when frozen flakes dropped from the sky.

Would my furless pack be able to see me? Would the strange energy hide me from their eyes? Oh, yes! I would be able to play them for fools! The joy! And not just that, I'd be able to stalk prey without them ever noticing me. I couldn't mask my scent, but I could use the wind to my advantage.

I crouched low and pushed through the tall grass. The trees and shrubs all swayed in the breeze, their leaves and flowers perfuming the air. And through it all, I could still smell my prey. A clearing sat directly ahead, with a large stone bluff rising up behind it.

A bleating cry echoed from the clearing ahead, the energy in my chest flaring in response. A wave of power rushed into my muscles. My fur stood on end and hardened. That was new. It had never happened before, but I felt as if I could even take a blow from my pack's bright claws!

Pale Fox and Short Tooth crouched somewhere behind me, their noises far quieter now. They were excited, too. I could feel it.

Anxious to make a kill, I leapt from cover and moved in fast. But everything was wrong. I locked my front legs and jumped to the side, pulling off my attack as something large stood up. It smelled like a wolf but was so much larger, with thick brown fur and a massive head. Its mouth pulled open, and it roared.

A deer lay at the monster's feet—my prey—its neck torn open.

The dead deer was large, with branching antlers. Steam rolled off the blood pooling around its body.

I snarled and growled, snapping my jaws so the large beast knew I wasn't prey. Pale Fox and Short Tooth ran in and finally saw the large monster. They pulled their bright claws and barked loudly, pointing at the monster.

"Bear! Bear!" Pale Fox cried.

I lunged at the creature, the bear, as my furless wolf friend called it. It roared and swiped at the air, its claws as long as Alpha's bright blade.

Pale Fox and Short Tooth tried to retreat, to move away from the bear's kill, but the large beast dropped down to all fours and charged. Afraid for my pack, I circled around behind the bear, and as it reared up over Short Tooth, I lunged and snapped my teeth into its hind leg.

I bit down as hard as possible, my teeth punching through thick skin and muscle, and pulled. The bear roared and jerked, trying to rip the leg free. I pulled with all my strength, but the massive beast was too big for me to move.

The bear reared up and swung around. I released my hold and jumped back, the monster's claws almost catching me in the head. If those claws hit me, I'd be in trouble, despite my new and improved fur.

I backed off and snarled, showing the bear my teeth. It spread its arms appearing even larger, and roared, the noise bristling every bit of fur on my body. It was a bear, as Pale Fox called it, but it was like a wolf—a really big, strong one. Its eyes glowed red and I struggled with the impulse to bow my head.

No! I was not that weak wolf anymore. I had a new alpha and he helped me become strong. There was no way I would back down. I would show Alpha how strong I was.

With fur bristling, I snarled as loud as I could, and lunged. Pale Fox and Short Tooth were there, too, their bright blades gleaming in the light.

The bear roared and swiped at me, but I ducked the claws and lunged in. My teeth missed the monster's flesh but snapped together loudly. The bear cried and swiped again. Too close to dodge, the massive paw hit me, the strength behind the blow rolling me over several times.

I felt the pain and heat but sprang back to my feet. Pale Fox and Short Tooth cut at the air with their bright claws, holding off the creature back. I charged, coiled my legs, and jumped onto its back. My jaws snapped in again and again, tangling in its thick fur, but sinking into the flesh beneath.

The bear spun and raged, but I bit and clawed, until I finally lost my grip and fell free. I landed, caught my balance, and reared up on my hind legs, snarling and snapping.

The bear growled, but the air was full of fear now. It dropped to all fours but the glow was leaving its eyes. We had showed it that we were not weak or afraid, that we were strong wolves.

The bear looked from me to Pale Fox, and then Short Tooth, whose bright claws stood ready to cut its flesh. I growled a final challenge to the strong beast—to back down, to submit.

To my shock, the bear lowered its head, and sat.

CHAPTER 6: POOR LOSERS

"Gentlemen! Can I have your attention, please?"

I'd barely left the ring when the Baron's son called for attention. Ajax stiffened and the rowdy crowd quieted. I knew we were in trouble before the stuffy little prick even continued.

The fact that he was sitting on the ground floor had been bothering me. Why wasn't he sitting up in the private rooms above? I pushed the thought aside. There were so many possibilities, I would only be wasting my time trying to guess.

I climbed the stairs to leave but froze as someone shouted from the crowd. It was in German, so I didn't know what it meant, but the anger and emotion behind it hit me like a cold bucket of water. Ajax reached back and tried to pull me along, but I resisted.

"Don't stop, he's only going to cause trouble. We need to leave. Now."

I nodded and jogged up the stairs, my head turned to listen in on what he was saying.

"I will pay any man or woman one hundred crystals for their heads! No, per head!"

Needless to say I stumbled at that, stopping on the stairs.

"Sore loser!" Ajax yelled, his voice booming through the

large space. "Anyone looking to collect on that contract will lose more than their head. So, consider that!"

The crowd went quiet for a moment, then erupted in a raucous cheer. A jolt of fear shot up my spine as Ajax and I both sprinted up the stairs. I mean, yes, I'd been meaning to dish out some punishment since they called me a dog, but that didn't include fighting off an entire crowd.

It took us a good minute of climbing and cursing to reach the top of the stairs and the door. Before I could even reach the handle, Ajax's hand landed on my shoulder. I pulled it open, stepped aside, and let Ajax pass. It only made sense. I didn't know the city, and if I led, it would only slow us down or get us hopelessly lost. Besides, I was faster than him, so I could always fend off attackers and catch up.

"Stay right behind me," Ajax grunted, as he pulled his hammer free and rushed past the two guards.

They grunted something as we ran up the tight stairwell, going around and around. I got dizzy, but that faded as we stumped into the cool, fresh air.

The guards outside let us go, and I thanked whoever it was that stayed their hand, be it God or their experience in dealing with thugs. They were just doing their jobs, and I wouldn't have reveled in the idea of cutting them down.

Ajax led me through a twisting maze of streets and alleyways, never even looking back over his shoulder. We moved with ground-eating speed right into a narrow alley on the right, then ahead and left into a dead-end street. He cursed and looked around, grinned, and used his hammer to break down a particularly rickety looking wooden fence.

"I knew it was this way," he laughed and charged through.

"Aren't those people going to miss their fence?" I asked and followed him through.

"Maybe, but they can be rebuilt. And that one was already fit for falling over."

I'd already lost track of how many turns we'd made, and

by the time we finally arrived at the bank of the river I was completely lost.

"You don't expect us to swim across that…do you?" I asked, watching the dark water whisk by.

The river wasn't so wide that I was afraid of drowning, but both banks would be a nightmare to climb. Steep concrete walls lined the sides and rose almost three meters above the waterline.

"Hey, if you want to swim across feel free, but I was planning on walking over the bridge," Ajax laughed, pointing off to the left.

"We really shouldn't dawdle—"

He didn't even get the chance to finish his sentence before we heard footsteps rapidly approaching. I spun on my heels and studied the group of men. They slowed to a walk as they spotted us and fanned out. Most looked to be out of breath, while a few even had their hands on their hips. It both told me they were no cultivators, and highly likely skipping cardio day at the gym.

There were ten men total, hardly a terrifying force considering what Ajax and I had already been through. They spread out, forming an irregular semicircle around us, with apparently no thought to strategy.

We didn't have anywhere to go but into the river, so we took a few steps closer to gain ground behind us. If they knew what was good for them, they'd retreat. I hoped they were just running on bluster, because if not, I wouldn't hesitate to defend myself. Although, I didn't enjoy the idea of killing weak, unarmed men.

"Finally, some blood," Ivory cackled in my mind.

"Bad doggy!" I snapped back. *"You don't speak for days on end, and suddenly now you want to chat?"*

"Yeah, well that's what happens when you're stuck in this cramp, crappy little space. And just so you know, your insults hold no power over me, hairless ape. Now, why don't you show me if you've learned anything."

"Learned anything..." I scoffed.

"Don't make this difficult," a short man said, and pulled a cudgel out from behind his back. He tapped the weapon against his offhand, the weapon causing a soft, thumping sound.

I had to resist the urge to roll my eyes and tell him to shove it where the sun didn't shine, but then thanked him mentally for drawing me away from Ivory.

The wolf had a way with words—a poetry, if you will, and his chosen language was hate and animosity. With each passing day, the captured wolf spirit sounded more human, and less like a wolf. Of course, I didn't tell him this. I figured that would just push him over the edge.

"Difficult? Us?" Ajax laughed and bent backwards. "If you lot didn't want a difficult life, then you shouldn't spend your time trying to kill people for money, you fools! Didn't you see my friend here bastardize Leo? And you think you've got a chance against the two of us?" Ajax hollered.

He sounded surprisingly cheerful, and I found his mirth infectious. A grin formed on my face as my right hand went for the katana on my left hip. My hand tightened around the handle, itching to draw the sharp blade.

"Who said anything about killing anyone?" the short man asked.

If I hadn't heard the Baron's son earlier, then I might have believed him. The accent being on the word *might*.

"That...*guy*," I said, refusing to acknowledge the royal prick, "offered the crystals for our heads, not for a tap on the shoulder."

His face twitched to one of his counterparts and they abruptly started laughing.

"A hundred? Hah! He paid double that just to take you two on!"

The short man charged, his companions following suit. The fastest man in the crew was barely two meters away when I snapped my katana free and cut upwards at an angle, slicing clean through his right elbow. Light gleamed off my blade, blood sprayed, and the man screamed. He slumped to his knees and I kicked out, catching him right in the face.

Another man tripped over the first, falling right over on his face with a loud *crack!* The spectacle gave the rest of the gang a moment of pause.

"You'll die for that!" a third man roared.

"For your friend tripping over an unconscious man and knocking himself out?" I asked.

He charged.

I sidestepped his awkward attack and cut hard, my sword biting deep into his shoulder, cutting clean through his collarbone.

"Three down," I yelled, as the wounded man fell away, clutching at his shoulder. "The loser pays for food!"

"What? You can't set the terms after we've already started! That's cheating!" Ajax growled, then smashed his fist into the short, smug man's face. He wasn't quite so talkative with my big friend's fist in his mouth.

I turned as another man moved in my peripheral vision. He'd crept around to the side and was trying to catch me unaware.

<<Blazing Strike>>

Energy pooled and formed inside me, the move coming together like a blossoming flame. I saw the man approach, slow as he was, and made a split decision. Instead of cutting his head off, or cleaving him in half, I decided to prove a point and targeted the thick pipe in his hands. My blazing strike hit home, the pipe exploding in a shower of sparks, metal fragments, and heat. The force knocked the wielder unconscious.

I grunted as something heavy struck my back, staggering me forward. Either by luck, strength, or skill, I didn't fall over. I clenched my jaw and turned just as my attacker raised his wooden cudgel again. It was the short, mouthy man. Evidently Ajax's punch to the mouth hadn't silenced him after all. Stupid move.

A smug smile formed on his lips. Why? Who knew with guys like this. But hey, if Ajax's considerable fist relocating his teeth hadn't driven home our point, then maybe a double dose of steel would.

I pulled my shorter sword free and lunged, bringing both blades up in a cross slash. He tried to block with his cudgel but missed badly. His guts spilled out as he landed face-first on the cold, hard ground.

I looked up to search for my last two opponents and was more than a little pleased to see them backing away. They didn't seem so eager to play now. Idiots. If only they could have seen reason before steel met blood, everyone could have gone home.

Perhaps they had families. Or, maybe watching their friend's guts spill onto the ground sobered them from their blood lust. Greed had almost gotten them killed. Fools. Idiots!

"Run, little piggies! Or join your friends," I howled and brought both swords to bear. The remaining men turned tail and ran.

I turned to Ajax and saw three of his opponents on the ground. The remaining thug was trying to find an opening in his defenses, and not successfully, mind you.

I worked around from the side, letting the last man see my blood-stained blades. As soon as he noticed, I stepped aside, making sure he could see what happened to his mouthy leader.

"You will pay for this," the last man cursed as he stepped away from me. "I will come back with more men!"

I sighed.

"You could have just run away. Now you're going to have to..." I nodded to his right.

The man turned his head, just in time to see Ajax's hammer swing in. It struck him in the side, knocking him clear off his feet. Silence filled the street around us.

I wiped the blood from my blades, then sheathed them in their scabbards. Hooking the toe of my boot under one man,

I flipped him over, then checked his pockets. There were some coins and a handful of crystals inside. When I found nothing else, I moved on to the next.

It took us a few minutes to check the dead men, before coming to a live one. It was the first guy, the one whose arm I'd removed at the elbow.

"Where is the rest?" Ajax asked, kneeling next to him. He held out a big hand, a small pile of crystals sitting in his palm. "Your mouthy leader said he paid twice what he offered."

"He only—paid a deposit!" the man gasped, clutching to his bloody stump. The poor bastard had already lost a lot of blood, and no amount of crystals was going to bring his arm back.

"You should have asked for more and then just run with it," I said, leaning in closer so he could hear me over the river. "Your greed has cost you and your friends everything. Don't put this on us."

"This is mercy," Ajax whispered, easing his stiletto through the dying man's heart. He gasped and slumped forward, his last bit of strength bleeding away.

Ajax shook the blood from his short weapon and stood, clearing his throat. Our eyes met for only a moment, but it was long enough that we agreed on what to do next.

In total, there were only ninety crystals between them along with a few hundred copper and silver coins.

I stomped my foot and turned on the spot, then started to pace.

"What?" Ajax asked.

"That bastard thought that we were worth so little! He talked the whole group into throw their lives away, and for what? Less than a hundred crystals and some scattered coins?"

"I'd say these men probably already had the coin on them, Tak," he said, without a hint of humor.

"Even worse," I whispered.

* * * * *

The next morning, I woke to a world of pain. I felt as if I'd been run over by a truck—my body was a mass of purple and green bruises, especially the arm I'd used to block Leo's punches and kicks. My right leg sported an almost black bruise from where I'd been kicked.

I was angry with him for a moment, but then I remembered what I'd done in return. Leo got what he'd deserved, and then some.

After crawling out of bed, I spent some time stretching, meditating, and then my usual regiment of physical exercises. They helped with the stiffness and pain and would encourage faster recovery.

When I finished, I dressed, slipped on my sword belt, and then went to find Ajax. He wasn't in his room, which meant one of two things. Either he'd slept somewhere else or was already up and cooking a meal. I was hungry, so the second option worked for me.

Winner winner chicken dinner.

My search led me to the kitchen, where I found Ajax. He'd already prepared several plates with pancakes, eggs, bacon, ham, cheese, some fruit and vegetables I'd never seen before, and freshly squeezed orange juice.

I grabbed a plate and sat next to him. He cast me a sidelong glance, grunted something unintelligible, then picked up what looked like a stein of beer, and proceeded to down half of its contents. Shit, the guy was a monster.

"What's the plan for today?" I asked in between bites and a sip of juice.

He took another bite and chewed thoughtfully before responding. I waited, noticing how much the big man resembled Omega when he was chewing on a bone.

"I need to make myself a new hammer and then sort out the knives."

I nodded, then took a bite of pancake. Evidently, this wasn't going to be a boring day after all. Maybe I would even learn something new if I accompanied him. And speaking of knives, who didn't enjoy some alone time with a blade and whetstone?

"Sounds fun. Do we go right after breakfast?"

He shook his head, stuffed another bite into his mouth, and chewed.

"We need to go to Baden first."

I watched him for a moment, my confusion deepening. Nothing linked up in my memories—the name "Baden" or otherwise.

"Is that a place?" I asked, after nudging him with an elbow. "Got a girl there? Or is it another one of mine? With my memory the way it is, who knows how many of them I have stashed all over the place?"

"No," he grunted, not pulling his eyes off his plate. "I have a friend there. She...ugh, doesn't know I'm here."

"A female friend, huh?"

"Yeah, but it ain't like that. Do you remember the tailor who made our cloaks? She's his niece. And no, she's not one of yours. So, you'd best purge that idea out of your head now."

The look in his eyes suggested she was a lot more to him than he was letting on. I was starting to get to know the real man, layer by layer. It only made me more curious.

CHAPTER 7: THE TEMPTRESS

A short while later and we were standing by a large stone pier. It was old, that much was clear, as the stone pilings had crumbled to the point where the rebar inside was showing. The result was long, rusty streaks running down toward the water.

Several vessels were docked, each about thirty meters or so long. Apparently, I'd made it across the ocean in one similar...if not slightly longer. The thought made my stomach churn just a bit, as I envisioned riding out the waves in what was a relatively modest craft.

The river was wide and surprisingly muddy, as the silt was churned up from regular boat traffic. I watched the water, which made me think about fishing. From what I could tell by my fractured and incomplete memories, I liked fish. Perhaps not for breakfast, mind you, but that didn't mean I couldn't enjoy a round of fishing. With all the conflict lately, I could use some downtime and a good fishing rod!

"Why are we here?" I asked, unsure of what to expect. He'd mentioned something about going to Baden to see his niece.

Ajax laughed and shook his head.

"You need to learn to read between the lines. We'll be riding one of those, you fool."

The closest boat was painted white with a black stripe running along the top of the hull. A large red stack extended out of the stop of the boat, a gentle stream of smoke issuing forth.

"What—is that thing?" I asked curiously.

He shrugged and pushed me toward it, his large hand easily wrapping around my shoulder. I hated when he did that, as it made me feel like a child in need of guidance.

"This is a steam barge. One of a handful that still run without any electricity. At least in Zurich."

"I see, and I mean I know what a barge is, but you know, I haven't seen anything running on steam since waking up. Was just surprised, I guess."

"And that, my friend, is exactly why we're taking the barge. We could have taken the bridge and then a cart. It would be almost as fast, but I wanted you to enjoy the ride. Thought it might just jar loose some more memories."

He was right. I did appreciate seeing the steam barge as I liked new things. Well, it looked rather old but still, well-maintained. It remained to be seen how good it ran, or how enjoyable the ride down river would be.

We were among the last passengers to board, not that there were many people ahead of us, but Ajax seemed to be in no particular hurry...about anything. I felt wobbly on my feet as soon as we were onboard, but I tried to hide it by pushing ether into my legs and arms. I held on to the railing and tried to enjoy it as much as I could. Ajax seemed to see right through me.

"You already look green. Do you get seasick so easily?"

I shrugged. "Maybe? I think I will feel better once we're moving," I said, then added, "I hope."

"You hope," he muttered and looked out over Zurich. We were only about thirty minutes out on foot, so the city was still all around us. "It's like this because the boat is still docked. You are right, once we set out, it should stop rocking so much."

I nodded and just focused on breathing. Seasick? I was on a fucking river! Man was this humiliating. I could fight off giant, ether-bastardized creatures, and fight duels, but I was about to be done in by a rocking boat on a river.

Ivory snickered in my mind, letting me know just what he thought of me. Great. And to add insult to injury, now I was being ridiculed by a dead wolf! Luckily, I was right, and once the boat set off my stomach settled.

"Thank goodness for that," I breathed.

"You've been slacking," Ivory said, his voice thick with condescension. I couldn't feel any emotion radiating off him, however, which was strange.

"I've been busy earning crystals," I replied with a mental thought. *"I'll start once we're back."*

I sat down next to Ajax on a bench. He unfolded a small wooden table from the wall between us and snapped his fingers. A waiter appeared moments later, after leaving the cabin's small bar.

We ordered drinks and food, but it wasn't until we finished and sat back for cups of coffee that I fully appreciated why Ajax wanted to travel by boat. It provided us with a different kind of downtime, one that forced us to sit back, talk, and enjoy the ride. I appreciated it, even though a small part of me felt it was a bit wasteful.

The river widened once we cleared the city, affording us an unparalleled view of the countryside. The alps framed it all in, their peaks already covered in snow. One mountain—I didn't know its name—was haloed in clouds, which lit up like fire as it passed between us and the sun.

Birds chirped and dove for fish, some deer appeared at the riverside for a drink, and I thoroughly enjoyed the hell out of it. Best of all, I felt safer now that we were out from under Zurich's oppressive shadow. If at least for a little while.

We enjoyed the journey, though it didn't take nearly as long as I'd hoped. Only a few hours after departing, we arrived.

I watched Ajax for a moment before standing. He sat, chin perched on his palm, gazing at the distant horizon.

"You look at peace for the first time in...well, as long as my shitty memories go back," I said.

Ajax cleared his throat and turned his gaze my way.

"I need change, Kenji. All the fighting, the uncertainty, all of it. It's just getting to me," he admitted.

I nodded, understanding his point. I had the benefit of brain damage to wipe most of my bad memories away. Unfortunately for him, they were still pretty fresh.

"We'll disembark," Ajax said, almost giggling. "I have always wanted to say that. Anyways, we'll get off here and then travel the rest of the way by road. It'll be another half-an-hour by foot."

I nodded, silently wishing it was just another thirty minutes by boat. Walking felt like a bit more work.

It was not quite noon when we arrived in a small, alpine village. We passed through without stopping and continued on to a modest wooden cabin. It looked well-maintained and lavish, with a wooden patio and wicker furniture outside.

"You go first. I'll just stay out of the way," I said and settled in next to the railing.

Ajax sucked in a deep breath, held it for a moment, and then let it out, before stepping up to the door. He knocked twice, and then twice more. The silence stretched after that, until a young woman finally appeared at the door. She opened it a crack at first, then threw it wide and jumped at Ajax.

"Rupert!" she squealed. "What are you doing here?"

I tried not to laugh, but Rupert? I'd heard the old man slip up when we first arrived in Zurich, but I'd never imagined that the big man's name was Rupert. Ajax grumbled and cast me a sidelong glance but returned the girl's hug.

"The cat's out of the bag, Rupert," I whispered.

The girl hugged him again before finally stepping back and noticing me.

"Takemi," she said, her eyes filled with questions.

Apparently, she knew me, but as it had become my new normal, I didn't remember her. How many times would I have to go through this?

I offered her a warm smile and she returned it. She didn't look much older than twenty-five, maybe a little less. Her bright blue eyes hadn't been dulled by loss or time, and her blonde hair bounced in delicate ringlets. Shit, just how young was she when I first met her?

"About that, Stef. Takemi had his head caved in and lost his memories a couple of months back, so—"

Caved in? Delicate.

"But true. Hahaha!" Ivory chimed in.

"So, he doesn't know who I am?"

Ajax nodded and her face fell.

"You're not pulling my leg, are you?"

"Unfortunately, no. He didn't even know who I was," the big man replied.

I cursed my shitty luck. She seemed to notice and waved it all away.

"Don't worry! Now you can get to know me all over again," she giggled. "And if you're wondering, I'm not that young. Besides, I like my men a bit meatier than you!"

"Funny. That's what you told him the first time you two met," Ajax chuckled and shuffled on his feet uncomfortably. He refused to look me in the eye after that.

"Cradle snatcher," I whispered and winked at him.

Ajax spluttered incoherently, but Stef saved the big man.

"Oh, no. Uncle Rupert has always been a perfect gentleman. In fact, it has often made me wonder if he prefers men."

I honestly had no idea how to respond to that, so I avoided the comment entirely. This girl could probably give Layla a run for her money, a battle of two sharp wits and even sharper tongues.

"Oh, and because I see the gears turning, I am twenty-four years old and every bit the adult. If you call that cradle-snatching, then perhaps I can direct you to some care homes where you might find ladies that are more to your liking."

Ajax burst out laughing as I shook my head. Again, I didn't know how to respond, which appeared to be a growing trend. Was I slow, or just in a rut?

"Stef, please," he begged. "I was friends with your dad for years and I've known you since you were a little girl."

She smirked, and her eyes seemed to sparkle. It was in that moment that Stef looked like a predator, and Ajax was her intended prey.

"Rupert, it's not like he would disapprove, if he were still alive. You know he saw you as a brother!"

I laughed uncomfortably and backed further away. Stef spun on me, her eyes narrowing to slits.

"Don't, Takemi. You are the last man to pass judgement. I have heard plenty of stories about your exploits. We love who we love."

"Before he died, he made me promise to take care of you," Ajax said, intervening.

The back of Ajax's neck had turned pink, and his face was joining in. Poor man.

"Precisely! And I have to say, you really aren't taking good care of me right now!"

I stepped back and down the stairs, slowly, as not to catch the hunting predator's attention. Ajax heard the stair creak and turned to me, silently begging for help, but I did what any self-respecting warrior would do—I turned and fled. He was on his own.

* * * * *

Stefanie offered to make us food, but we declined, stating that we were in a hurry. She gathered her belongings and joined us on the barge. Ajax was desperately trying to keep some distance from her, even pushing me to stand between them, but the more he moved the more determined she became to corner him.

She simply wouldn't listen to his excuses, and I don't think it helped that she persisted in calling him uncle, either. Hell, if I was in his shoes, that probably would have tripped my "warning bells" too. I had to admit that it was funny seeing the fearless warrior crumble under the young woman's advances.

I leaned forward and whispered to Ajax when Stefanie wasn't looking.

"We'll call this payback for Layla, *Uncle* Rupert."

Ajax turned and glared at me, but then his gaze drifted off into the distance, as if he was trying to recall something. Perhaps he was trying to remember what he'd done to me that was really so bad. Then realization dawned and I knew he remembered the bar and how he set me up after I lost my memories.

"What did Takemi say? It's not nice to whisper when in other's company," Stef said, noticing us.

Her voice drew the attention of several other people sitting nearby, but they lost interest and moved to different seats. I shook my head, turned to watch the scenery slide by and sighed. Watching Ajax...or, Rupert assaulted by a tenacious young woman just made me miss Layla even more.

"Takemi didn't say anything meaningful," Ajax muttered, as Stef pushed into his side.

"Oh, now I want to know that much more," she replied and threw me a wink.

She seemed confident that I was on her side. Honestly, I wasn't sure. I could understand where Ajax was coming from, but she really did seem to care for him. And hey, how was a man with my kind of memory supposed to pass judgement on anything? They had history and a real connection. Just a short time ago I would have given my left arm for a little of that.

The boat trip passed peacefully after that, as Stef finally wore away at Ajax's resolve. He sat and talked quietly with her, and for the time being that appeared to be enough. By the time we arrived back in Zurich, Stef held Ajax's hand in a death grip and all but skipped along, leading us to her uncle's shop.

The young woman charged in and before the door even closed behind her and started yelling.

"Uncle Finn, I am here! Rupert brought me to see you!"

A familiar face poked out from behind a doorway, before the old man appeared and gathered Stef up in his arms. Admittedly, the uncle thing gave me a moment of pause, as I wondered if he was truly an uncle, or the Ajax kind.

"Uncle Finn! Tell Ajax that he's still being silly and that daddy wouldn't have minded if we hooked up!"

I watched as the man sighed and shook his head before stepping away from the little temptress and flashing us a warm smile. He suddenly looked a few years younger.

"I'm sure he wouldn't have minded, Steffi. Ajax is a good man, but what you do not understand is that he can't give his permission."

Stef's eyes bulged in anger, and I got the feeling she wanted to stamp her feet. She proved me wrong by showing more self-control than I thought her capable of.

"See, Rupert! Even Uncle Finn thinks you are a good man. What more do you need?" Stef asked, her voice rising in both pitch and volume.

I settled against the wall by the door, thoroughly enjoying the spectacle. At first, I'd struggled with what aversion Ajax had to the girl, but the longer I was with her, the more I understood. She wasn't just energetic, but practically nuclear. If she wasn't yelling, then she was probably dancing, or pulling on someone. Good gracious, she made me tired just watching her.

Ajax looked at Finn with pleading eyes, but the tailor seemed content to stay neutral. Good for him.

"Stef, it is because Ajax is a good man that he has kept you at arm's length. You wouldn't want him to break his promise to your late father, would you?"

Stef growled. It was a noise that Ivory would be proud of, as well.

"None of you understand!" she screamed, ran past Finn,

and disappeared into the back room. "Father wanted me to be happy, not alone," she said, appearing one last time. Tears had welled up in her eyes. In the next moment, she slammed the door shut again.

"Give her time, Ajax. Hopefully, she will move on from this infatuation," Finn said, hopefully. Although, he didn't look nearly as confident as he sounded.

"She's been like this since her father died six years—" Ajax started but trailed off.

"I know," Finn replied and looked away. "Rest his soul. We all miss him. We really do."

"...Alright. Well, tell her I will come by later if the two of you feel like going to the Gazebo," Ajax said, making for the door.

Finn's eyes lit up and he rubbed his hands together.

"Are *you* paying?"

"Ha!" my big friend laughed. "I don't need to. An idiot is."

CHAPTER 8: ELEMENTAL AFFINITY

We retreated to Mike's smithy, where I paced for a while, watched the two men work, and then paced some more. Eventually, I found a stool and sat.

I leaned against the wall and closed my eyes, directing most of my focus on the ether coursing throughout my body. Once I did that, I became aware of wisps of it naturally pushing and flowing out of the environment around me, so I pulled it in, circulated, and stored it.

It was a tolerable way to keep my mind off the aches and pains from the brawl the night before. Unfortunately, processing ether did weird things with my memory. And that is not to say it unlocked new ones, but it latched onto recollections—both new and old—and cycled them through my brain, like a strange old movie played out of order.

The dojo reappeared in my mind, the wood structure dark and foreboding in the dream. Beth was there, arguing with...me. Ken, Kenji, a man she loved, but was angry with. I'd done bad things for bad people, all in the name of supporting her.

I tried to banish the recollection, as I'd already seen it dozens of times, and the pain and betrayal on her face was too much to bear. I couldn't do anything to change it now, and it hadn't led me to any new breakthroughs, so it just felt less than productive to dwell there now.

Loud banging noises came from inside the smithy, the sharp staccato ringing of hammer on metal punctuated by Ajax and Mike's voices. They were having fun. The air was hot, too, tinged by the tang of hot stone and metal. They were smelting and refining the metal bones for his hammer.

"Damn!" Mike cursed, "Es ist immer noch nicht heiß genug!"

"Bah!" Ajax growled, and the air filled with the sound of bellows opening and closing.

"Heisser! Heisser!"

"Ich Weiss," Ajax cried, his German thick. "I've never seen metal with such a high melting point before."

The ether curled and pushed through me, my dream gaining substance and potency. Beth and I were in the dojo again, arguing and yelling. I drew harder on the ambient ether, hoping it would help me break through to continue the memory and just maybe, heal more of my fractured mind.

I saw Beth pick up the katana, but Mike and Ajax's voices intruded on the dream. The ether flow inside me wavered and I felt my focus slip.

"Sheisse, that's why we cannot smelt this, Rupert. Es ist tungsten! Tungsten!" Mike growled, as something heavy slammed down onto a workbench.

The blade flashed and I felt the distant bite in my stomach. The moment was approaching, when I would pull my bleeding body out of the dojo as I tried to follow Beth. That was when the ether would soak into me. When everything would change. If I could just pool a large enough mass of energy, perhaps I could push through the darkness that followed.

"Sei kein groll," Ajax grumbled. "That is good, no? Tungsten is strong!"

"We call it wolfram here. The problem is it has a melting point over twice that of steel. I cannot get that kind of heat in a smithy this small," Mike explained.

I pulled and massed the ether, infusing it into my body and mind, trying to empower my dream. Beth's car door slammed, and I heard her drive away. The ether was soaking into my wound as the cloud invaded the world around me. But the darkness was crowding in.

No! Stay with it, I thought, fighting to push through. I wanted to know more. To pull the rest of puzzle pieces together and finally feel complete. Footsteps entered the room and I heard Ajax and Mike talking.

"This is not going to work," Mike said. I heard him unscrew his flask.

"Yeah, and here I was thinking it was a good thing," Ajax muttered. "If there only was a way to smelt it."

The ether spun like a chaotic storm in my center, making my chest, arms, and legs buzz with violent potential. But the dream was fading out. I could feel something beyond the darkness, as more memories hung tantalizingly beyond my reach. With an angry and disappointed gasp, I opened my eyes.

"Damnit!" I cursed.

"Still fighting the dreams?" Ajax asked. I nodded and pushed back up onto my stool.

"I thought it was an issue of ether manipulation, so if I could pool and control enough of it, then I could force my way deeper into the memories."

"And it was not," Mike said, matter-of-factly. I nodded, fighting to hide my anger and disappointment.

"And what of you? How goes your project?"

"We can't smelt the Wolfram," Ajax explained, although I already knew. "We cannot get it hot enough to melt."

"I am simply not equipped for that kind of smelting," Mike added. "I don't think anyone is, for that matter. Perhaps the royal forge? But good luck getting in there."

I sighed, knowing very well that Ajax would jump completely into the smelting, smithing, and forging project if left to his own devices. And it wasn't that he was without self-control, but he appeared determined to complete the challenge. Ajax scratched his scruffy beard and let out a deep sigh. An idea formed in my mind, inspired by my failed memory breakthrough, no less.

"What about ether?" I asked.

"What do you mean?" Ajax asked, straightening.

"Well, what if we used ether to help during the process?"

Ajax simply shrugged, his shoulders and face falling afterwards. He looked spent, both physically and emotionally. The big man did not like being left without answers, or failing, for that matter.

"Perhaps the metalworkers at the royal forge would know. But for us, way out here, that is still a mystery," Mike explained.

"Yeah, yeah. You can figure it out, for now, I am tired of heat, and banging, and failure," Ajax grumbled.

"I'll tell you what, little wolf. If you can somehow smelt those bones with your ether, I will treat you to another massage."

"Deal," I said and pushed off the stool, glad for the challenge. "But this time, alone, so I can enjoy the...quiet. Oh, and I don't want you to be the one giving it, either."

Ajax let out a bark-like laugh and slapped Mike on the shoulder.

"Did you hear that, Mike? Come, let us get a getränk. My throat is dry and I am thirsty."

I walked the two men outside, but while they headed for the pub, I settled on a wooden bench in the yard. Taking a cleansing breath, I looked down at the paw. It was warm outside despite being close to the fall season, but not too much to be unpleasant.

The wolfram bone, or tungsten, as Ajax called it, was incredibly heavy, despite its size. I studied it for a moment, before tapping into the mass of ether I'd used to try and breakthrough in my dream. It swirled into the bone but accomplished nothing. No matter how hard I tried, the ether didn't do anything to the metal, save for swirling around happily inside before rushing back into my hands.

"The abomination was right, you really are as dense as a rock," an arrogant voice cackled in my mind.

"Angry hound," I thought back. *"If you have something helpful, then say so. Otherwise, I am not in the mood for your insults."*

I was fairly confident, or let's say hopeful, that the wolf spirit had an idea, otherwise he wouldn't have deigned to stoop to talk to me. Ivory was like that, looking down at me from a high pedestal. Literally.

"You have an open metal affinity channel, and yet you are pawing around with fire. Honestly, how did your kind ever elevate itself to the top of the food chain?"

"Simple," I whispered, "We developed tools to account for our inherent weaknesses."

"Pale, hairless monkeys, beating things with sticks. That is all I see."

Despite his attitude, I knew deep down inside that Ivory wanted to be helpful.

"A metal affinity?"

"Ugh. Yes. Naturally. You can use that affinity, but you need to 'mean' to. I can't believe that I have to explain this to a supposed higher being, but here I am. The channel is inside you and contains the potential for that affinity. If you concentrate, you can connect it to your ether, through your veins, and manipulate the element at will. If you are strong enough, that is. And hounds are domesticated beasts, watered down through generations of in-breeding. I am an apex predator—the embodiment of instinct, purified by ether. Remember that."

"Okay, dead apex predator. Thank you for your help."

Ivory grumbled and snarled, picking up on my sarcasm, but went quiet as I tried to focus. I used my left index finger, gathered some ether from inside, and pushed it out to my hand. It was much harder to do in practice.

I tried nearly a dozen times from start to finish with no success. The idea of tapping into an affinity I didn't know I could use, ended being a tiring and ultimately frustrating experience.

Mold the metal, I thought, as I worked. Yet, it didn't...work.

"Move, metal," I whispered, after pooling ether into my finger yet again. Nothing happened. Talking to the metal bone in my hand felt preferable to the chaotic, frustrated thoughts swirling in my mind.

I reset, cleared my mind, and tried again for what felt like the thousandth time.

"Change, metal..."

"Be metal..."

"Commune with metal..."

A dull ache settled in my hand as my fingers grew tired. The soft tissue behind my eyes was growing tired as well, as the early signs of a headache formed between my ears.

"Reach out to the metal. Try and be one with it. That is how it works for us. It is natural, not some forced words," Ivory said, forcing his way into my thoughts once again.

"I am already holding it."

"That is not what I mean, you dense, poo-flinging primate! I mean, reach down inside, and let your affinity connect with the metal. It is there, all the time, but its voice is obviously quieter than the rocks tumbling around inside your skull. So, if you can, quiet your mind!"

"Okay, that is actually helpful. The name calling is mean and hurtful, but still helpful. Would it hurt you to be nice?"

"It just might. Maybe someday, after the sting of being hunted and killed by such lower lifeforms fades, we can be best friends and frolic in fields of flowers together."

"That sounds kind of nice. Promise?"

"I'd sooner chew off my own legs and let my stumpy carcass roll down a hill and into the river."

"Okay, we'll come back to that later," I said, and did as he

suggested. *"...but I could use your stumpy carcass to bait a really big hook and catch some monstrous fish!"*

"Ugh. Go bang rocks together."

I pushed as much from my mind as possible—thoughts of Layla, the frustrating dreams, the tumultuous uncertainty of what would happen to us in Munich, and more. It was a hard task, as actively pushing the thoughts away just made me think about them even more. So, instead, I focused on the black—the patches of missing memories wedged between everything else. It was in that darkness where I found my quiet mind.

Wisps of ether started swirling inside me, infinitesimal currents of power I otherwise might not have felt. There was more than one, but that was all I could tell, and they were different. I squeezed the bone in my hand and felt one of the small wisps respond.

I fed the ether toward the wisp and felt it grow stronger. It was like a voice without sound, a part of me looking for a nudge. So, I gave it one.

The wisp grew stronger and forced its way up my arm, until my finger started to pulsate. I pressed it down against the paw and let the ether move into the piece of wolfram. The cold, dense surface instantly changed, bending, and becoming malleable to my touch.

I opened my eyes, only to discover that I had formed a perfect, finger-shaped depression in the hard metal.

"Hey, he did it!" someone said, as a shadow loomed over me.

I looked up to find Mike and Ajax standing above me, evidently just returned from the pub. Ajax's eyes were wide with excitement.

With the two men watching, I repeated the process, first finding the quiet of my mind, and then empowering my affinity.

Ether flowed into my hand, and I carefully molded the wolfram, shaping it into a small ball. It took time and patience, as the metal would move, but absorb my ether while doing so. Once finished, I held up a fairly round metal sphere, then tossed it to Ajax.

The big man deftly snatched it from the air and tossed it from one hand to the other. I could almost see his mental gears turning as he tried to rationalize what I had done. That was when the penny dropped, and his bushy beard split into an almost child-like grin.

Grabbing another bone from his bag, Ajax rushed over to me, passing the small ball of metal to Mike as he walked past.

"How?"

I accepted the bone, fell into my process, and formed a small dent in the metal. It became easier every time I did it, as if I was forming a stronger relationship with the affinity.

"Show some respect. That metal was me. It should not be thrown around like some...toy!"

I winced at Ivory's irritable response. It was loud and strong but jarred something loose in my head. We'd gone to kill the wolf so the Duke could get his hands on the metal affinity *core*. So, having killed Ivory, I claimed the ability to shape that metal.

Wow, my head is a mess. Why is this a revelation?

"Because you are poo-flinging monkeys."

"Truthfully, I don't touch feces. I'm a bit of a clean freak."

Ajax snapped his fingers in front of me.

"Huh? What?"

"What? Where did you just go? Your eyes were open but there was no one home behind them," Mike said.

"Sorry. I was thinking. It is kind of a dangerous thing for me," I said, laughing. It was true, in more ways than one.

"Tell us. How did you do that?" the smith asked.

"It is just the proper application of ether."

"Because look," Ajax said, bending and twisting the bone in his hand. It moved and molded as easily as if made of clay.

The big man rushed over to the two stacks of wolfram bones. I watched him select a large bone, perhaps a femur, and then went to work. His brow furrowed in concentration as he tried to push ether into the metal and bend it...physically. Of course, nothing happened, as he did not possess the right affinity.

Deciding to pay him back for our uncomfortable message time, I remained quiet, barely concealing my smirk. After several more attempts, he bashed the ground with the bone, and turned with a glare.

"You are an insufferable dick, Takemi. Just a bit of ether, you say. That is all, you say," he grumbled.

"This is quite enjoyable to watch. Now you know how I felt watching you try to use fire to melt those bones," Ivory snorted. *"It's not as if you'd kill yourself by trying to smelt it, but I couldn't watch you any longer. Appreciate me!"*

I snorted. They didn't know about Ivory, so I acted as if I was responding to Ajax's frustration.

"Snorting, heh?" the big man grumbled. "The more time goes on, the more you look and act like that damned wolf you let follow you around. Come along now. Be civilized, Takemi, and tell me how you did it!" Ajax snapped.

"Sorry," I said and leaned toward him. "The secret is that you need to have a metal affinity."

His face fell, and I understood why. Without a rare affinity like metal, he was relegated to the helpless position of watching and waiting.

"And you have metal as your affinity?" Mike asked.

"I do," I said. "Is there anything I can do to help?"

"Ausländer," Mike said, under his breath, then straightened. "Yes. Can you bind two pieces of metal together, we need a blank large enough for the head of a hammer."

"Sure, let me see what I can do," I offered and moved over to the bag. I knelt down and picked up two pieces that looked to be about the right size if put together, then concentrated. Using ether and my affinity I made both pieces malleable, and once done, tried pushing them together. Unfortunately, they didn't stick.

Okay, so this wasn't going to be as easy as I'd originally thought. I approached it like clay, where two pieces could be pressed together while wet. These, however, were wolfram bones.

"You could try using more brain cells than it takes to breathe but wait—this is you we're talking about."

"That is less than helpful, Ivory. If you can't stop being such a prick, I might just leave you up on that pedestal forever."

"Grrr. I think you underestimate how much noise I can fill your head with. You do not want to test me."

"I don't want to stick you on that pedestal any more than you want to be stuck on there," I said, trying to defuse the situation.

It was true, the alpha wolf was an ass, a jerk, and a hobo invading the tranquil palace of my mind, but he was also a knowledgeable being with loads of experience to tap into. Unless we found mutual ground, I'd be condemning my mind to be a neverending battleground.

A question popped into mind. Why…would a wolf know how to work metal, anyway?

"I'm going to sit here and growl until you figure this out."

I held the two chunks together and pushed some ether into the first, then tried to wind the same strand through the second to bind them together. It didn't work.

"Shit," I cursed, and tried again.

This time I held them together, wound ether into the first and then threaded it through the second, but before it could snap back around, I pulled it free, wound it around, and formed a perfect loop. The edges of the metal shimmered before liquifying. Then they merged. Just like that. The metal hadn't even heated up, and yet they felt securely fastened together. Weird.

"You're ignorant, but you can't help that. Allow me to enlighten you just this once."

"Go ahead."

"You used ether instead of heat to alter the bonds of the

metal, making it soft at mere room temperature. Since they were touching, once the ether pulled free, the metal solidified, binding them together into a single piece."

I lifted the now conjoined piece of wolfram and Ajax accepted it, his grin widening.

"More," he said, handing me bone after bone. "Bigger."

I worked for a long while, forming a solid chunk of wolfram longer than my forearm and almost twice as thick. The damned thing weighed more than I did by the end, so I had to bend over and work on it on the ground. What's more, it looked as if it had swollen in mass, if that was at all possible. Had I somehow made the metal expand?

Mike grunted and hefted the sizable chunk off the ground, then carried it in the shop. Ajax lifted the bag of bones and followed, with me close on his heels.

"Can you do a few more?" Mike asked, as he dropped the chunk onto a workbench. "I need some that is thin, so I can roll it into a shaft for the handle!"

He needed to do what now? Ajax knelt down next to me and clarified, using less blacksmith talk. I formed a picture in my mind and selected a piece, then went to work.

I took a large bone, formed it into a ball, then started to push it flat. Once that was complete, I pulled at it, stretching the ends. Once I was done, I stopped to rest. Ajax dropped my pack next to me, as I'd accidentally left it outside. The stilettos and the spider's ice spike fell out.

After taking the sheet of wolfram to Mike, I returned to my seat, pulled out a smaller bone, and picked up the ice spike. I didn't think that I'd be able to bind the two materials together, but the ice spike would make a fantastic weapon, if only I could craft it a handle.

I tried to form the chunk of metal into another sheet, then *attempted*, badly, to wrap it around the spike. It was that moment when I understood that I knew almost nothing about weapon crafting. It was true that I knew how to maintain and care for my swords, but making a new one? Well, that was foreign territory.

"What're you aiming for?" Mike asked, standing next to me. I'd been so engrossed in the process that I didn't notice him approach.

"Not sure," I admitted and held the strange amalgamation of ice spider and metal wolf bones up between us. "It should make a good dagger. That is, if I knew what I was doing."

He gave the long, thin needle-like spike an appraising glance and whispered to himself for a moment.

"Zhe way I see it, you've got two options for this thing, Takemi. First—make a short rapier out of it, and second, a long stiletto. Or a dirk."

"Truthfully, I've got all the swords I need, and I'm not overly fond of fencing. I gravitate towards kendo and bushido. You know? Hard, fast cuts, and violent strikes."

"Then a stiletto it is," he said, patting my shoulder.

"If you leave it with me, I could work on it for you. I'll need you to make some more workable metal though."

"Deal," I said, "Just be careful. If you touch the sharp tip, it will freeze your skin solid. You should have seen the spider we pulled it off of. Very nasty."

"I believe it," he said, carefully accepting the spike. "Do you want to wrap the handle in leather, or are you going to use the metal to form a custom handgrip?"

Well, damn! I hadn't thought about either of those options, but if I had to choose, then I would almost definitely go with a custom grip. Although leather was soft and didn't necessarily get as slippery when wet.

"Custom?" I asked warily, making it a question as well as statement.

He motioned for me to get Ajax's bag of bones.

"No need to choose now. If you don't like the metal handle, you can always wrap it afterwards. Or, make a grip that you can take on and off."

"Good. Find me two more little bones, then you're going

to need to bind them together for me and I will shape it. All you'll need to do next is to form the grip you want," Mike instructed and moved back to his workbench.

We worked together for the better part of a half hour, molding the pieces of wolfram together. Mike worked with his tools but talked me through everything he did. I watched the small handguard come together and then the handle. Mike had me grab the handle once we made the metal soft, my fingers pressing lasting indentations as I squeezed. I set it down, but accidentally bent the handguard.

"Shit," I whispered. "The metal is still so soft."

"So, change it back," Mike said, and crossed his arms over his chest.

"*See? You're kind of capable. Just please, make sure you don't kill us,*" Ivory said.

"*Is there a way to shut you up?*"

"*Not really. You should be glad I'm helping at all. I will consider making fun of you as my payment in trade.*"

"*At least you're not asking for steak.*"

"*How would I eat it?*"

I snorted again and coughed to cover it.

"*You could always ask Omega how it tastes, you know? He has become a big fan.*"

"*You are truly a vile creature! I am going to sleep now! Don't wake me up unless we're in imminent peril. You know what, never mind. Just don't wake me up. I would rather perish in my sleep.*"

"*Fair enough. You have earned yourself some goodwill. And as promised, I will figure out how to release you from the pedestal.*"

"*Fine. In that case, good luck,*" Ivory muttered, as his voice faded into the back of my mind.

CHAPTER 9: DINNER

Per Finn's request we got cleaned up and went out to eat later. The restaurant, it turned out, held a two-Star Michelin rating before the collapse and the quality had not decreased by much. And there I was, sitting at a table draped in silk, with glowing candles for light, wearing my armor. Like a tool.

The Maître-D gave me an entertaining look, especially when Ajax and I handed him a pair of Wolf cloaks. He eyed the wolf head hoods, complete with fangs and held them out to arm's length. Suffice it to say, it almost came to a scuffle when he treated the cloaks without much respect.

We stood out like sore thumbs, while Finn and Stefanie had changed into what I could only describe as finery. He was a tailor, after all, and she his niece, so it wasn't a surprise. In comparison, Ajax and I looked like your stereotypical mercenaries. Sure, the new lightweight, high tech armor Omega found for me in the ruined manor looked nice, but it was still riot gear.

"Perhaps we need to reconsider the elements of our wardrobes...if we're going to stay here for long," I whispered, leaning into Ajax.

"If we stay at all," he replied.

At one point I thought they'd deny us service, but when Ajax flipped the waiter an ether crystal and said it was just a deposit, the staff's demeanor changed. And it wasn't like we were low on crystals. I had over two hundred of them myself, and I knew my big friend had just as much.

I watched in amusement as Ajax continued his dance with Stefanie. And by dance, I don't mean a romantic, side by side sidle to a slow song. I mean, he was trying to keep his distance, and thanks to her tenacious nature, doing a piss-poor job of it.

I decided to be a good friend and sat next to Finn, making sure that the seat next to Ajax was empty. This, of course, brought me all manner of dirty looks. Stef gave me plenty of smiles, and regularly kicked me under the table. I couldn't tell if she was just being flirty, or violent. Or, if her version of flirting was violent. Yikes.

"Thank you, uncle. You're such a gentleman."

I buried my face in the menu, trying to hide my barely restrained laughter. It was a moot point in the end, as the freaking menu was printed in German. Luckily, there were small pictures next to some of the items, so that helped. Still, I wanted to make sure I didn't mess up, so I waited for Ajax to finish fending off Stef's most recent bout of aggressive flirtations.

"I can't read any of this," I whispered.

Stef tittered and shook her head.

"I never understood why so many Europeans were raised bi-lingual, but you Americans could barely speak one language," she said, letting her accent thicken.

"Oh, most of us were bi-lingual. Some tri-lingual," I said, setting the menu down. "I spoke Japanese when growing up, as that was all my grandparents spoke. But I spoke more English as I got older. Then I learned some Spanish. But my specialty was bad English. I can speak that really good!"

Stef laughed, loudly, the sound drawing most of the room's attention to our table. Ajax looked like he wanted to melt into the floor.

"Don't worry about that, I will order for you, Takemi," the big man offered.

"Will you order for me too, my Rupert?"

My Rupert? I thought, as I watched the young woman bat her eyelashes. Oh boy, Ajax was in trouble.

Ajax's cheeks flushed and he disappeared behind his menu. Sometime later he reappeared, cleared his throat, and motioned the waiter over.

When the waiter finally arrived, Ajax ordered a long string of dishes, although he did it in fluent French, not German. Even the waiter seemed impressed.

Two pages of notes later, he finally walked away, nodding to himself. I barely understood a single word Ajax had said but couldn't deny that it sounded...pretty. French was decidedly softer on the ears than German.

"Uncle?" Stef asked sweetly as she looked over at Finn.

"Yes, meine hübsche Nichte?"

"Have you thought about what we talked about earlier?"

The old tailor sighed and seemed to deflate. He rubbed his face, looked to Ajax, and then back to the girl.

"He is almost twice your age, mein Schatz. I cannot make him accept you."

I took a sip of wine and leaned back in my chair, trying to distance myself from the conversation. I knew it was only a matter of time before she tried to draw everyone at the table into the issue.

"Alter spielt für mich keine Rolle," Stef grumbled, shaking her head. "I don't care about something as stupid as age. I am not some starry-eyed teenager. I am twenty-five—a woman, and I know my own mind."

"Yes, you are," Ajax interjected. "But you must consider that I have known you since you were a baby. I have changed your diaper more than once, fed you from a bottle, and held you while you slept. That is how I will always see you, my dearest friend's baby girl."

Ajax's logic was sound, and I understood where he was coming from. Changing how you see someone isn't an easy task, especially when bound to such strong bonds.

"Why won't you let me show you, Rupert? Let me show you that I am not that little girl anymore." She leaned forward and ran a finger down his chest, and in response, Ajax's cheeks turned a shade of purple.

He turned my way and shot me a glance, pleading for help. Except, I didn't know *how* to help him. Stef seemed completely set on the notion, and who was I to try and dissuade her? Or could I, even if I tried?

"You have said that you are lonely lately—" I started to say, hoping to ease the conversation into another direction, but before I could finish, Stef pounced.

"You're lonely? But you don't have to be. Please, why can't you see that? I am here. You can be yourself with me. Just please, consider it. For me?"

"Can we talk about this later?" Ajax pleaded.

"I don't understand why we can't talk about this now," she hissed and leaned forward. "You are gone for months at a time, and when you finally do come home, you avoid me."

I watched Ajax's eyes drop to the table, and when he didn't respond, I knew he was trying to protect her from the truth. The things she didn't want to consider.

"He is a soldier, a mercenary, and sometimes he works for the worst kind of people. He can't take you with him because it is dangerous out there. And what he doesn't want to tell you is this. We don't form strong relationships with people because there is a strong chance that they will become leverage. We have seen it happen. And if the wrong people find out, they will hurt you to get to him. Ajax keeps you safe by keeping his distance."

The anger in Stef's eyes bled away, but she shook her head.

"I am willing to accept the risks," she started to say, but Ajax shook his head.

"In Vaduz, a pair of soldiers from a premier military unit tried to assault Takemi's lady, Layla, and her sister. If he hadn't been there, well, it would have been bad," Ajax said. "Life is already dangerous enough, but when attached to those like us, it just messes with the odds."

Two waiters appeared, breaking the uncomfortable tenor of our conversation. They laid out two trays before us, covered with an assortment of tiny plates. My heightened sense of smell took over, as each and every dish assaulted my senses.

"Ajax," I said, taking it all in. My mouth was watering.

"Dig in, brother."

I surveyed each plate, struggling with where to begin. Ajax stuck a fork in what looked like asparagus wrapped in bacon, dipped it in a thin line of dark sauce, painted onto the plate, and took a bite. I almost started drooling just watching him.

The plate next to that looked like gnocchi, but I also spotted stuffed mushrooms, what looked and smelled like crab dip, and some sort of cheesy, soufflé. I went for the crab dip first, scooping out a conservative portion with a small bit of toast.

Chewing hungrily, I fought the urge to groan loudly. It was also a struggle to chew with my mouth closed. Evidently, eating and living in the wilds, with animal companions, no less, can make a man a little uncivilized.

"What do you think?" Ajax asked, looking up from his plate. "It is good, no?"

I moved onto one of the stuffed mushrooms next, taking a large bite before responding. It was earthy and warm, but cheesy, with a subtle but not understated heat. What I thought were peppers, turned out to be tiny filaments of ether, expertly wound into the food.

It was impressive how subtle it all was, as I had to stop and focus on my stomach even to detect it all.

"I have never had food like this," I admitted.

"Not many have, anymore. You will find this food more restorative than a week's worth of quality sleep. Eat your fill and enjoy!"

It turned out that the little plates were merely the appetizers, as the waiters brought us no less than six more courses. Each was small, but very different. By the end of the meal, I'd identified two problems. One, that I'd eaten entirely too much. And two, that I wasn't sure how was I supposed to go back to normal food ever again.

"Why haven't you infused ether into our food?" I asked, after wiping my mouth and settling back in the chair.

"Takemi, you are funny," Ajax said, after taking a drink.

"Funny. How?"

"Everything is simple to you. 'Ajax, why haven't you simply infused ether into our food before'? 'Ajax, why can't we just do whatever we want'?"

"Okay, to be fair, I asked a lot of those questions *because* I might have sustained a brain injury and lost my memories. But," I said, holding up a finger, "I am getting better."

"Yes, you are. But just a little," he chuckled. Finn and Stef joined in, and I threw my napkin at the big man.

"It isn't as simple as just infusing ether into the food while cooking," Ajax explained, gesturing to the spread of dirty plates. "They grow most of these fruits and vegetables using crystals. Even the animals are either hunted in the wild or raised on ether-rich food. That, in part, is why this place is so expensive. They have taken ether and integrated it into their farming and their livestock. Genius, really."

I honestly had no idea.

"And we got all of this for five crystals?"

He snorted and rubbed his belly. "Six per head."

I winced at the cost, but then remembered the night at the arena. This meal was paid for by the foolish noble who'd hired a bunch of incompetent thugs to kill us.

Raising my glass, I smiled at Ajax.

"Then we give thanks to the Bauers from Munich! For

they have filled our bellies with this magnificent feast!"

"Wait," Finn asked, lowering his glass and leaning in. "You didn't make an enemy of them, did you?"

I shared a knowing look with Ajax before we nodded.

"Unfortunately for him, he lost three hundred crystals betting against us in the arena."

"Fortunate for us," Ajax interjected. "And then we beat up a bunch of goons he sent after us."

Finn groaned, set down his drink, and then rubbed his face.

"They are an incredibly influential family in Munich. But they also possess strong ties here in Zurich, as well. As in... with the wrong kind of people."

"I guessed as much. Once he opened his mouth."

"What were you two doing in the arena?" Stef asked. "Only the wrong sort goes there."

"We just wanted to watch the fights," Ajax said, defensively. "In the end, Takemi had to get his hands dirty! He mouths off too much for his own good."

Stef rolled her eyes while Finn watched me, his eyebrows raised.

"I don't take insults well," I admitted. "He was a stuffy bastard with a bad attitude. It was about time someone put him in his place. But it is true, I am working on taming my hotheaded tendencies."

"Some of these families haven't been challenged for decades, Takemi," Finn said, after taking a drink, "So, that is probably wise. They have a long reach, and longer memories."

"Point taken," I said, as the waiters arrived with desert.

CHAPTER 10: THE DUKE'S MANOR

Dark clouds moved in later—the churning, charcoal-colored variety that threatened thunderstorms. We hid in the shadows, using our newfound concealment as we stood outside the late Duke Manfred's manor. We'd been laying low for hours by the time the clock tower struck twelve times. Midnight. And yet, there was still no sign of any trackers, pursuers, or the usual bastards and ne're-do-wells that randomly made our lives miserable.

With our patience finally exhausted, we moved in. The guards on duty weren't the finest I'd seen, but they weren't bad either. The problem? They didn't seem overly concerned with keeping people out of the manor, and it's not like the duke was inside for them to guard. They walked lazy patrol routes, occasionally shining flashlights into dark corners like they were simply going through the motions. And yet, as lackadaisical as they appeared, they were also incredibly punctual, which led me to believe their apathy might have been for show.

The wall towered above us, easily five meters tall. It was mortared together granite blocks and to my surprise, knowing the late Duke, very...ugly. For a nobleman overly concerned with status, etiquette, and outward appearances, I had expected something with more pomp and flash. Hell, even the pink stone they used in Tuscany and the south of France would have been better. A wrought-iron gate would have also been more attractive but wouldn't have given the manor anywhere the same privacy.

We used the wall's design and the guard's lack of vigilance against them. I scaled the wall easily using my **Enhanced Strength** skill, my fingers digging into the mortar between stone blocks.

I pulled myself over the top, just enough to peek over the edge. After making sure there weren't any guards patrolling nearby, I gave Ajax a thumbs up and I swung myself over the top and dropped to the ground on the other side.

I landed hard but absorbed the impact with my legs. It helped that I was now many times stronger and more durable. If I'd been a normal person, I probably would have at least broken both of my ankles.

I looked around, then struggled through a twinge in my knees as I moved to hide behind some bushes to my right. I leaned against the wall and gave myself a once over. My legs were fine, but my knees hurt like a bastard. Okay, so I was stronger, but by no means indestructible. Perhaps long drops off stone walls were something I should avoid for a while longer.

I turned and waited for Ajax to join me, intermittently turning to watch for approaching guards. I had barely time to catch my breath before Ajax dropped to the ground like a bowling ball. He rolled to his feet and grinned as I pointed to the much smaller inner wall. Beyond that sat a row of bushes and tall grass, then a walking path to the manor itself.

We crept silently along the wall, working to watch in front and behind us. Ajax and I communicated with nods and grunts, falling back on our wilderness habits. Footsteps sounded to our right with almost no warning, and I went prone. Ajax froze behind me.

Two separate voices filled the cool night air as two men walked casually along the stone path, making their rounds. They walked at a steady pace, chatting quietly in German. I listened intently, hoping to catch certain keywords —specifically the Duke's name.

The two men stopped to smoke not far ahead, the smell of cigarettes lazily wafting toward us. Ajax and I crept forward to keep an eye on them. Their backs were turned toward us, so I caught the big man's attention and mimicked a cutting motion across my neck. He shook his head, so I made a hammer strike motion and gave him a goofy face. He chuckled but pressed his index against his lips. Fine, we waited.

The two men finished and moved on, hiding the cigarette butts in a hole in the wall.

"...Und sie trug nicht einmal unterwäsche," one man said.

"Sie sind enttäuscht?" the other responded, and the two moved away, chatting and laughing.

"They are talking about a girl who doesn't wear any undergarments," Ajax explained.

"Commando?" I asked, "very nice. I approve. What about us?"

"We go inside and steal some shit. That pompous prick owes us that much."

I nodded and waited for him to move past and lead the way. We'd gathered some intel already. First, we talked to several former servants to get the lay of the grounds. Then, we used two of the taller buildings in the area to confirm our route and watch the guards.

Ajax hugged the wall and moved. I followed close behind, keeping an eye out for patrols while marveling at how quietly my big friend could move. We were lucky and didn't run into anyone, and as we'd planned, immediately spotted the lit outline of a large wooden door.

Ajax dropped to his knee and looked around, ensuring the area was clear before moving for the door. He ducked under two windows without looking, but I wasn't quite as trusting. I peeked inside to make sure no one was there, waiting for us. He stopped ahead and next to the door, reached into a pouch on his belt, and pulled forth a sizable ring of keys.

Ajax tried three of them before the lock clicked and the door swung open. I followed him and closed the door behind us, sliding the lock back into place. Part one—success.

Lanterns hung from the walls around us, but not all were lit. The few that burned left the shadows long, especially in the corners. Unless someone looked in through the windows at the right moment and caught us in the bright pools of light, we'd be mostly invisible.

We moved through the small entrance chamber and into the lobby, where the manor's true decadence shone. Lavish decorations covered every wall—paintings, sculptures, armor, weapons, and relics, while a single seating area occupied the center of the large space. Leather sofas had been arranged in a half-circle, just across from a grand fireplace. Expensive rugs covered the stone, but one in particular caught my eye. It was a beast pelt, specifically of a massive white bear.

"He died as he lived," I muttered, and Ajax nodded as he moved quietly to the front door. The lock clicked loudly as he turned the bolt.

"Come on."

The wooden floors were exquisite, the hardwood shining in the limited light. And yet, they made it oh so difficult to move quietly. Our footsteps echoed, and with a look of horror, Ajax stepped on a soft spot and the boards creaked.

"Closer to the walls," I whispered, and gestured for him to move away from the center of the hall.

Hugging the walls helped a little, but we still made some noise. I hated it—the echoes, the glossy reflections, and the wide-open space with nowhere to hide. It gave me the unshakable feeling that someone would appear around a corner at any moment.

If anything, the paintings, and tapestries only grew

more ornate the deeper we went into the palatial house. I had to hand it to the Duke, he knew how to live. Unfortunately for him, his house of treasures didn't help him survive the wilds, not to mention treacherous family members and hired swords. And those were lessons I'd carry with me for a long time: never underestimate people.

Ajax tapped my arm and then pointed at the staircase on the left. I nodded and followed, making sure I kept enough distance so I could respond if something popped up or if he needed to retreat. He reached the top of the stairs first and scanned the hallway. We waited for several moments, listening to the house, but it was disturbingly quiet. Even as houses went, this one felt almost preternaturally still—almost dead.

Ajax slunk across the hallway and entered the first room, disappearing inside. I followed but checked the room next door. It was a gym with some weight machines on one wall, a heavy bag hanging in the center, and some cardio on the opposite wall.

"Hey—" I started to say as I crept into the room to meet up with Ajax.

The word froze in my mouth as loud footsteps reverberated through the hallway behind us. I half turned and gently pulled the door shut behind us. The steps sounded loud and confident, so I felt sure we hadn't been discovered. Still, there were only so many places where we could hide.

I drew the stiletto, its new grip and cross guard making it feel solid and secure in my hand. The door slid open a crack and I peered outside.

Melting into the shadows, I lifted the stiletto and held my breath. The guard came into view, right in front of me, and strolled past. He didn't look at the door or even glance our way.

I stepped out behind him quietly, and with a practiced movement, hooked his neck and pulled him back and down. I very nearly struck with the stiletto, driving it into his chest, but something stilled my hand.

The impulse was to strike hard and kill him, but then

another impulse washed it away. The man was simply doing his job. Did he have a wife at home? Children?

Changing directions, I pulled the guard back into the room, tightening my choke hold. He only struggled for a moment, before going limp in my arms.

Ajax was next to me in an instant and grabbed his feet. We carried him to the far back corner, where the shadows were deepest. We tied his wrists and ankles, then gagged him.

"The old you would have slit that man's throat without a second thought," Ajax whispered.

I considered him in the darkness. Killing the man would have not just been rash, but it would have been infinitely harder to hide. Blood tended to get everywhere, and then you had to deal with the ramifications afterward.

"Perhaps losing my memories did me some good," I whispered back.

We searched the room together, only to come up empty-handed, then moved on to the next, and the next. They were mostly empty and even appeared to be in the middle of a renovation. Down the hall, we rounded a corner and came to a wide door. It was the duke's quarters.

Unfortunately, the door was locked, so Ajax made use of his ring of skeleton keys once again. One by one he went, trying, failing, and moving on. Eventually, after what felt like hours, the lock clicked and my large friend pushed the door open.

"Good job, uncle," I whispered, and pushed past. His head shot around and he glared at me.

"Arschloch."

"That sounds strangely similar to 'asshole'," I chuckled.

He growled and pulled the door closed behind us.

The duke's room was like a museum display, as the sheer quantity of treasures and finery made even the lobby pale in comparison. A large, marble fireplace sat centered on the widest wall and was surrounded by several beast pelts. A king-sized, four-poster bed sat on the opposite wall with a small sitting area in between. Next to the window sat a massive desk. It was second only to the bed in size, but its smoothly polish mahogany, with carvings to match. Tall bookcases lined the wall behind it, the leatherbound books all shining with rich gold and silver spine text.

"Lucky bastards actually live like this?" Ajax murmured. "Just look at it. There is more wealth in this one room than in the whole city of Vaduz."

"I know. If he weren't such a fat bastard, we could wear some of his clothes."

Even though we whispered, our voices sounded impossibly loud.

"He should have some good weapons, crystals, and other crap we can sell. Maybe he has another suit of that fantastic armor," I proposed.

Ajax's face soured.

"What?"

"Just remember. Only certain people have this kind of wealth, which means their treasures are likely known. If we steal the wrong things and try to sell them to the wrong people, we could put ourselves in a world of trouble."

"Noted."

We began rummaging through every cupboard and wardrobe. We worked the room quietly. And yet, over ten minutes later we had nothing to show for it other than some nightwear. Most of his valuables were simply too bulky to carry. Besides, nothing would be easier to track back to the source than sculptures and paintings.

"Where's the bastard hiding his real valuables?" I muttered and took the room in once more.

"You might have already found it if you used more than just your eyes! And you call yourself a wolf? Shameful!"

More than a little scorn poured forth from Ivory, but that was hardly a new thing. Still, he wouldn't have chimed in unless there was something important nearby. I tried to think about what Ivory meant and what I knew about wolves. They were quick, loyal, ferocious—and had a good sense of smell. Really? Did he expect me to go around and sniff everything?

I focused on the ether around me and inhaled through my nose. My senses narrowed until I'd pushed everything not scent-related aside. I sniffed and moved, then sniffed again, searching for anything out of order or unnatural. A few moments later I learned I had no idea what I was doing. Ivory was right. I was a horrible wolf.

Laughter echoed inside my mind as Ivory watched me struggle. Lucky for me he couldn't keep his nose out of other people's business.

"Start with something smaller. Try focusing on that image on the wall. There, to your right. Don't try to only smell but breathe deeply and try to taste the air as well. Try now and tell me if you feel anything out of order."

I wasn't sure whether Ivory was just screwing with me or not, but I did as he instructed, all the while moving closer to the painting. I closed my eyes before my lips parted, and I breathed in.

"What are you doing?" Ajax asked as he studied me.

I could hear the amusement in his voice, but I didn't grace him with a reply. Not right away. Instead, I focused on the painting and sniffed the air again.

I could actually taste something strange. It was...fresher than the other air in the room like I'd caught a lungful of fresh mountain breeze.

"There's something weird with this painting," I said and opened my eyes. I pointed at the oversized portrait of Duke Manfred.

The wolf chuckled in the back of my mind but didn't say anything else. I was sure that he found my attempt at claiming credit amusing, but it's not like Ajax could see or hear him.

"Thanks, Ivory. I promise I'll make it up to you if we find something good."

Ajax walked over to me and started sniffing at the painting, just like I had, but he obviously couldn't pick up on it.

Had Ivory's senses made the difference?

"Close your eyes and breathe through your nose and mouth. Try to taste the air, not just smell it," I instructed.

He looked at me, raised his right eyebrow, and smirked.

"You are fucking with me, yeah?"

"Huh? No. Why would I do that?"

"I'm not a dog, Tak. How do you—wait," and he sniffed long and hard, "There *is* something."

Well, that confirmed it for me. Ivory was right. Again.

Something was definitely odd about his painting, and it was up to us to figure out what. Just our luck that two brutes needed to solve such delicate issues.

"You'll have to learn to find answers for yourself, hairless ape. For now, you might want to move that painting and see what's behind it."

I felt around the edge of the frame, but it seemed to be securely fixed to the wall. I pulled gently, not wanting to rip or damage the canvas, but I couldn't pry it loose.

Ajax pushed me aside and stared at the image, then at the frame. He traced his fingers along the intricate carvings and stopped near an awkward groove.

"Gotcha," he whispered, tracing his finger back and forth.

"Got what?"

He pressed down on the groove and an audible click echoed in the silence, then it was followed by the sound of a whirring mechanism. The wall swung inward, revealing a small room beyond the painting. There wasn't much to it: a large table sat in the center with a stack of loose papers, several books, and what looked like a small ornamental wolf statue carved from bone. It was small enough to fit in my pocket, so I decided to grab it even if it likely didn't have much value. We were a wolfpack now, so why not add another member? Even if it was small, and not...real.

A jolt of power crawled up my arm as soon as I touched the small statue. I lifted it to my face, closed my eyes, and inhaled, using ether to enhance my senses. The taste and smell were unmistakable: fresh, mountain air.

"Takemi, start packing those notebooks and papers. I'll check if there's anything else we can plunder," Ajax said.

I slid the small wolf statue into my pocket and did as Ajax asked. My hands went to work, stacking and piling papers into my backpack. Since the books looked important, I wrapped them in cloth and stowed them carefully inside. This way they wouldn't jostle around and make noise if I had to move fast.

I sat down in the chair and checked the drawers next, but other than a small black address book there didn't appear to be anything of value.

"Even after the abomination, my weakest pack member, brought you the key to the puzzle, you still haven't figured out what you have? Sad."

Ivory's words set me back. He often referred to Omega as the abomination, but what had he given me? I tried to remember but...wait, other than dead animals. Okay, not true. He'd led me to the hidden bunker beneath the house, where I found my new armor and the submachine gun, but...beyond that, I drew a blank.

Takemi, you fool, I thought, as my hands jumped to my neck. I found the necklace, the small horn pulling free from inside my chest plate.

Slipping the chain over my head, I held it out in front of me and studied it for a moment. Although the chain was gold, the horn appeared to be made from the same kind of bone as the wolf statue. I lifted the wolf from my pocket and held it up to the light for a better look. It didn't take long to see that the wolf had a hole in its mouth. The horn fit perfectly.

I struggled through a moment of hesitation as the horn drew closer to the ornament, and for some reason, my heart started pounding in my chest. As quickly as the moment of panic set it, it was gone, and the horn slid inside and locked in place. Then nothing happened.

Ivory snorted as I cursed quietly to myself, but then a thought popped into my mind. I sensed two different kinds of ether signatures inside the statue. They too were waiting for something to happen. For someone to do something.

I pushed a strand of my ether inside and wrapped it around the two signatures, merging them into one. A loud click resounded in my mind, the sound startling me.

In the next moment, a strong wave of ether washed over me and almost knocked me over. I closed my eyes and knelt down, otherwise I might have fallen over. I sucked in a deep breath as the torrent of energy flowed inside me, but a heartbeat later, a glowing box appeared on the floor in front of me. Roughly five meters square, it resembled a metallic steamer trunk, with heavy banding and a curved lid.

It opened with a thought, revealing several weapons inside—swords, axes, a hammer, a bow, and even a spear. But none of them really caught my eye. I grabbed a one-handed sword embellished with gems and opened my eyes, only then realizing that the box had been in my mind. And yet, the sword was very real in my hand.

"Wha?" Ajax stammered. "Where did you find that? It looks very ceremonial."

"I don't...know exactly," I replied honestly. "I inserted this small horn into the wolf ornament, pushed some ether into it, and then closed my eyes. It opened up a sort of storage box...space?"

He stared at me for a moment, his expression changing from surprise to anger, and finally to excitement. I handed him the wolf, and he flinched, then closed his eyes.

"That is—scheisse! Look at all of these crystals, and axes, and. Wow, did you see these two white cores?"

"Yeah," I lied. Honestly, I'd been too distracted by all the shiny blades and other pretties.

"Here, give me that sword. I want to test something out."

I did as he asked, and a moment later when he opened his eyes, the sword vanished from his hand. Our eyes met and we grunted together.

"It is some sort of ether-fueled extra-dimensional storage space," Ajax exclaimed excitedly, and started stowing anything of potential value inside. In the end, we stashed three entire shelves of books, a chair, an antique magnifying glass, a large, hand-drawn map of the post-collapse world, and anything else we could find.

"How much space do we have left?" I asked.

"Enough for..." Ajax started, then winked, "a few pieces of art?"

"I'd rather not..." I started to say. As he'd said, they were expensive and relatively easy to track. Besides, no one would take them off our hands. At least not in Zurich.

"You're right. Don't get greedy. We have a small fortune stashed in this little wolf."

We nodded and adjusted our packs, making sure they wouldn't make any unnecessary noise, then quietly snuck out of the late Duke's hidden chamber.

I closed the painting and turned, only to not find the empty room as I'd expected but found a man comfortably lounging behind the desk. A broadsword rested on his shoulder, the flat of the blade catching the light.

"Hello, gentlemen," he said, throwing me a smug wink.

CHAPTER 11: EARLY PAYBACK

"Be careful," I said, turning to Ajax. "In our line of work, you only wink at someone if you're going to fuck or fight them, and I'm not really in the frolicking mood right now."

"You are crude," the man said.

"So I've been told," I shot back and scanned the room. "You're Alfred's dog! What is ole' Durheim up to these days? Well, when not imprisoning and torturing people, that is. Let me guess. Trapping and torturing small animals? Pulling the wings off of flies?"

"I am Alfred's dog? How would you know that?" he asked.

"Simple," Ajax said, "For starters, you stink of him. And second? I wouldn't expect that a stuffy prick like Alfred would risk his neck to come out here and confront us on his own. So, it only stands to reason that he would send someone like you. Close enough?"

The Seneschal smiled, confirming the truth.

"I work from the shadows in the city, yes. In fact, I particularly enjoyed watching the men rough you up. It was very...satisfying."

Four more faces appeared from the shadows, all guards

that had been treating us especially shitty during our stay in prison. And among them was the one I provoked on our last day, the door guard that smelled particularly strong of fear.

"So, we know who to thank for our shitty stay then," I said. "There was no survey available when we left, but let me tell you, I would not recommend your hospitality services to friends and family."

"You are all mouth!" he hissed and slapped both palms down onto the desk. "And for your information, I am no one's dog!"

Someone's a proud little guy, I thought, barely suppressing a smirk.

"I like dogs," I said, and Ajax nodded his agreement. "Which is why I feel qualified to say, that isn't how it looks I mean, you are here instead of Alfred, right? You are running his errands now?" I snickered.

"You have your tail so far between your legs you could have use it as a pipe cleaner for your pecker," Ajax added.

"I am the King's Seneschal. As you unwashed heathens probably don't know, I manage domestic affairs within the Kingdom. It would be well within my rights to draw and quarter, disembowel, and behead you two right here and now."

"Right here?" Ajax asked. "I see no horses. Were you planning on using your men for the drawing and quartering part? Because I doubt they are strong enough."

"Maybe...Chuck," I said, giving the man a name. He'd never offered it, so Chuck felt natural enough. "Maybe Chuck was speaking figuratively."

I watched his mouth twitch as he fought for composure, but I didn't push it any further. Hera had told us all we needed to know after we'd been set free. The Seneschal was one of the most powerful men outside of the king's bloodline.

"You might wonder why I'm here," he said and leaned back into the oversized chair. As opposed to the duke's large body, Chuck looked almost like a child in comparison.

"Wonderment? Not really," I replied tapping my katana's

grip.

"You are practically burning with curiosity," he said, turning nonchalantly to his men. In response, they walked into the room. "I can see it written plainly on your faces. But I should thank you. I have been waiting for you to finally bring me the key to that dimensional safe. Now be a good corpse and hand it over."

"Corpses?" I echoed, as my other hand moved for the wakizashi on my hip. Chuck pushed out of the chair.

"Before you get any ideas, just don't. You are a pair of two-star nobodies, and I unlocked my fourth vein last week. If you hand over the safe, I will consider letting you live. After all, you can't tell anyone I was here without first admitting that you murdered the King's cousin."

"We did what?" I asked, innocently. "We're corpses, though. Corpses can't hurt anyone."

I glanced over at Ajax as he carefully reached to slip the bag off his shoulders. Chuck's eyes lit up, greed clear on his face. He edged forward and held out his hand, prepared to receive the backpack.

"Just the ornament! I don't need or want your trash!"

I let my hand drift toward the stiletto's handle, where the weapon was discretely strapped inside my chest plate. Ajax nodded, and I followed suit. I read the big man's eyes, preparing to follow his lead.

We both knew Chuck wouldn't let us live. How could he? We would be witnesses, and the last thing he could afford was mercenaries running around with proof that he was scheming behind the King's back.

Ajax reached inside the bag and pulled out a small statue —a figurine of a wolf howling at the moon, and yet it wasn't the one I'd found in the hidden closet.

"Is this what you want?" Ajax asked, making to move toward Chuck until he stumbled over a chair. He fumbled with the small figurine and dropped it.

Chuck's eyes went wide, and in the span of a heartbeat,

dropped his sword and dove over the desk for the wolf figurine.

I darted in to 'help,' but he landed, rolled, and stood faster than I could contemplate his speed. His eyes flashed up at me then his hand snapped out, catching me with a punch in the chest.

The blow was hard. Okay, truthfully, it could pulverize a wooden beam, so I was lucky enough to be wearing armor. I hit the floor, rolled like a poorly felled tree, and lay there groaning. If that was just a normal blow, we were royally pegged.

"I might have let you live, peasants, if your mouths hadn't gotten the better of you. I guess I'll have some fun instead. I do have a few new skills to practice, after all."

I listened but didn't look up, as the simple act of breathing still hurt more than I cared to admit. A meaty 'thwack' echoed loudly next, followed by a grunt of pain.

"Fuck—you, dog!" Ajax coughed from the ground next to me.

"You two must have thought yourself so clever, yes? You thought that you got away with his murder, yes?" The man paused for a moment, but when we didn't speak, he yelled. "Didn't you? Admit it!"

Ajax's breathing steadied before he responded with a statement I agreed with wholeheartedly.

"Fuck you sideways!" the big man grunted. I could hear the pain in his voice, but in true fashion, Ajax was all spit and vinegar.

I finally managed to prop myself up on an elbow and found the man standing over Ajax. Chuck's foot sat squarely on my friend's chest, but as I rose, the movement drew his gaze. He frowned as if surprised that I could get up at all.

His foot snapped out and caught Ajax on the chin. My big friend's head snapped back and he collapsed. I could only hope that he was just unconscious.

"Big man, eh? Kicking others when they're down?" I asked, my anger building.

The Seneschal sauntered my way, his arrogance

practically oozing from his pores. The guards were still there, of course, and I'd need to take care of them if I wanted to help Ajax. I wasn't optimistic, however. A well-trained two-veined warrior against a newly-minted four-veiner? Yeah. The odds were stacked against me.

I regulated my breathing and slipped my hand into my armor, fumbling for the stiletto. My hand tightened around the grip, the metal cool and reassuring.

"Go on then," the Seneschal chuckled, "try and stick me with that! I could do with a good laugh! I've already unlocked more power than you will see in your lifetimes."

I grunted, cursed, and pushed myself up to my knees, then finally mustered enough strength to stand. Shit, his punch had laid me low. One f'ing punch. If I'd been weaker, he could have punched a hole clear through me.

"Are you...sure?" I asked, wobbling on my feet.

"Sure?" Of course I am. You poor fool, I am a noble! My word carries actual weight."

"Sir, are you sure?" one of the guards asked. "He is dangerous."

"Fool! What can he do to *someone* like me? My skin is tougher than steel and my bones the granite of tallest mountains."

I didn't wait for the guard to respond. Besides, I hated the way he said "someone." What a pompous turd.

<<**Burst of Speed**>>
<<**Enhanced Strength**>>

I activated both skills at the same time and a mass of ether flowed from my pool—at least a third of my total capacity. The strain of using them together almost made me vomit, but I just managed to hold it back.

I darted forward with as much speed and strength as my body would allow, thrusting the stiletto right at his chest. He lowered his arms and smiled wide as he prepared to bask in my tremendous failure.

The ice spider weapon hit his armor, the spike tip

cutting right through the metal and piercing his skin, muscle, and collar bone beneath it. He looked down, his smile pulling down into a confused frown.

"That was a nice try, but I..." he shuddered, just as the stiletto delivered its two-pronged attack.

He'd been so deep in his arrogance that he didn't feel the weapon pierce his flesh. It started to draw on his ether, filling me with indescribable strength, and proceeded to pump freezing venom into his blood.

"Surprise," I whispered, as icicles formed on the exposed skin of his neck.

My core swelled as the dagger drew on his power, then it abruptly stopped and the spikey blade glowed with streaks of red, yellow, and black.

I pushed the stiletto in a little deeper, breaking through and hoping to draw on his fire-ether. I reached down inside and pulled a little harder, as well. The energy didn't want to flow, but I was...persistent.

The Seneschal slumped to his knees, gasping in pain. I stopped the flow before his ether reserves overflowed my meager ability to hold and contain it. By the time I pulled the stiletto free, frost covered his neck, arms, and the lower half of his face.

"Wha...? What...?" he muttered through frozen lips.

His guards seemed to break from their stupor and moved in, forming up in a perfect line. Fools. Didn't they know rule one of sword fighting—don't make life easier for the other guy? Obviously not.

I dropped the stiletto to my off-hand, wrenched my katana free, turned, and cut in a wide arc. The razor-sharp blade hummed as it cut but met surprisingly little resistance. Following through with my turn, the guards fell as one, my blade having cleanly decapitated all but one of them. The blade hit the last in the chest, slicing deep into his ribs.

"W-W-What...how? You're just a two-veined...p-p-peasant!"

The ice from my stiletto kept the wound in the Seneschal's chest from closing, thus allowing his blood and ether to leak out. He collapsed forward to the ground, his frost-kissed arms barely holding his weight.

"I guess it just goes to show you, Chuck," I said, wiping my sword clean before sliding it back into its scabbard. "Perhaps you should have put your energy toward trusting people and not, you know, trying to kill them? In this world, being a dick will get you killed."

His mouth moved and his breathing became ragged, but he started to convulse and tipped sideways onto the ground. I realized then and there that although he'd been powerful in his own way, he wasn't someone who'd gotten there by his own merits, but rather by his sponsor, the King.

I stepped around him and knelt next to Ajax, first checking his eyes and then his neck for a pulse. A wave of relief washed over me as I felt the steady rhythm of Ajax's heartbeat through my fingertips. His ether was cycling, too, which was a good sign.

I nudged his leg several times until he finally shifted, and in true Ajax form, grunted. His eyes opened and he turned to me.

"You bastard! I'm not a dog, you're a dog," he grumbled and tried to sit up.

"What does that mean?" I asked.

"He was...I was..." Ajax continued, then closed his eyes, shook his head, and opened them again. "I'm just a little fuzzy-brained, I think."

"Get up," I said, and helped him sit. Then with a lot of cursing and straining on my part, he stood.

"What...did you do to...me?" the Seneschal wheezed.

Ajax looked to the partially frozen man, then to the dead guards, and their severed heads. He whistled low and scratched his beard.

I tossed the glowing stiletto into the air and caught it.

"I used this to siphon and absorb your strength. Here,

watch this." I turned to Ajax and flipped the short weapon over, offering the handle to my large, dazed friend.

He nodded groggily and grasped it.

The stiletto glowed to life with yellow light, as the ether flowed into Ajax. The big man staggered back, but recovered, the weapon fully refilling his pool. The groggy, almost drunk look lifted from his face, and he smiled.

The Seneschal's eyes glistened with greed and surprise, but he deflated, as he realized that the rare weapon wasn't, nor would it ever be, his.

"You must be feeling pretty stupid right now," Ajax said, handing me the stiletto back.

The dying man grimaced but did not respond.

"Do you think the guard upstairs is with them?" Ajax asked. "The man we tied up?"

I shook my head. He'd been wearing different clothes and armor. The Senschenal's men were dressed like mercenaries. Hey, it takes one to know one.

I rummaged through the dead guards' belongings. They were carrying a lot of money, but only had five crystals between them. It didn't matter, though, as we'd scored Manfred's stash. We would only use them on necessities when we decided to set out.

When I turned back to Ajax, I found him standing over the Seneschal, with his hammer poised to strike. The wounded man stared up at him with pleading eyes.

"I can give you anything you want. Anything!" he whispered.

Ajax shook his head but looked my way. Hell, it was a tempting offer, as men like him were actually in a position to make good on it, but the risk was too great.

"What could you possibly offer us that would outweigh the risks of keeping you alive?" Ajax asked and tapped his large hammer onto the man's shoulder.

"I know things! You killed the Duke, right? If you have his bank token, understand this. You can't use it! They have frozen his accounts and will arrest anyone who tries to use it! See? I know things. The kinds of things that could save your lives!"

He slumped and fell into a coughing fit, his breathing wet and ragged. I knew the truth of it. He simply couldn't survive, not if we wanted to live.

I walked over and grabbed the dead guard's body—the one with his head intact—and dragged it over to the Seneschal's feet. His eyes went wide as I pulled the dead man's jacket open and pulled forth a hidden dagger.

"Wait, what are you doing?" he wheezed.

"What does it look like?" I asked. When he didn't respond, I continued. "It appears that greed got the best of your men here. They tried to overpower you as you were looting the good duke's stash. You got three of them, but the fourth, wounded and dying, just managed to land a crippling blow."

"No!" he whispered.

"Unless you can give us a better reason not to kill you," I said, wrapping the dead guard's hand around his dagger.

"Wait! Just wait! I—yes! The bank storage. What about... what if I told you that you could get your hands on his accounts? I...could help you."

I walked over to the duke's table, took a pen and ripped off a piece of paper, and returned to his side.

"And?"

"The name is Heidi Lowitz. She works the vaults and lives across the street from the UBS Bank. You can't miss her. She is the tall blonde. Show her my insignia," he said, weakly pulling the medallion off his jacket. Ajax reached forth and plucked it from his shaking hand. "Give her Manfred's token. She'll give you the contents of his account, no questions asked."

"Okay. That is better, but still not enough. Goodbye—" Ajax said and hefted his hammer up high, preparing to bring it down on the man's head.

"You bastards! Wait! There is a stash filled with weapons,

tools, and riches! It belongs to Alfred and I will tell you where it is. Just...leave me here! Let me live. No one will find me for days so you will have plenty of time to loot and disappear! Please!"

I gripped the dead man's hand tighter, then playfully jabbed the dagger forward.

"Where?" I asked.

"Give me your word first. Your word as a man that you won't kill me!"

I shook my head.

"Sorry, I don't give my word unless I expect to keep it. I think that is what separates people like you and me. Your word means whatever you want it to at that moment, while mine defines me."

His face fell and he grew quiet.

"You were never going to let me leave here alive, were you?" he asked.

"Well, not once you tried to kill us."

"I suppose that is fair," he coughed and looked away. "Just give me your word that you will not hurt...her. Heidi. She is a good woman, loyal to Zurich."

I nodded, waved Ajax away, and moved forward with the dead man's dagger.

"Do you want to do it yourself?"

He shook his head, the movement weak. "No. Please. Just...make it as fast and painless as you can."

I plunged the dagger deep into the wound and twisted. He groaned and sagged, but I backed off. He looked up at me, his face wrinkling in confusion.

"We would make it quick," I said, looking to Ajax if you and your man Alfred hadn't mistreated our people so. I clearly remember one of your men torturing our female friend. They beat her. They cut her. And they tried to violate her, while you watched. This is for Hera."

He gasped and tried to talk, but I drove the dagger into him again and again. Then, as he lay bleeding, we put the bloody dagger into the dead guard's hand and hefted his body over the dying Seneschal.

We both knew that the instant their bodies were found all hell would break loose. Still, we'd have at least a day or two to prepare. That also meant we'd have to be quick and push our timetable.

"We can loot his body, right?" I asked.

"Why not? Who would ever know what the guy had on him?"

"Good point."

Ajax and I pillaged his corpse, taking his jewelry and valuables, but leaving any weapons behind. Those would be far too recognizable.

I felt upbeat as we backtracked through the mansion, wiping prints off door handles and anything else we might have touched. Not only had we located Manfred's stash, but we'd been able to exact a little revenge on one of the pricks who'd done wrong by Hera. We eliminated another enemy.

One thing did frighten me, however. I was getting a little too comfortable killing people, even if they were the bad guys. Still, I was operating off of something a wise man once told me. I didn't know what wiseman when he said it, or why, but the words were burned into my brain.

"Never give anyone the chance to hurt you twice."

With that in mind, we slid out of the manor and disappeared into the trees.

CHAPTER 12: SECRETS

It was a little over an hour by the time we made it back to our cabin. Ajax needed help to escape the manor, mostly to climb up the wall. I went so far as to use <<**Enhanced Strength**>> or I wouldn't have been able to help much. It was at that moment that I truly started to appreciate how big he truly was.

He stuttered and muttered after landing on the far side, something about a diet or exercise, but I waved him off. It didn't feel like the time to hassle him about something that wasn't the real problem. Besides, our fight earlier just confirmed what I had already been struggling with—we were far outclassed.

We could fight against someone with three veins, even if he had battle experience like the late Duke, but four veins? That was suicide because I couldn't count on all of them being as arrogant as the Seneschal. There was no way he could have known that I had the ice spike spider weapon, but if he had, I wouldn't have stood a chance.

In the end, it brought me full circle. We needed to gain strength and power so we wouldn't have to rely on luck.

I felt Ivory stir in the back of my mind, the spirit wolf

agreeing. Okay, that was problem two—I needed a way to visit my mind palace when *I* wanted to, not just in dreams.

"Should we take a look at our haul?" Ajax asked as he settled into a chair. He flashed me a weak smile, but I could tell he was still dealing with the aftereffects of that kick to the face.

He gingerly slipped the pack from around his shoulders and set it on the ground before him, wheezing as he straightened again. A bit of pink froth coated his lips. Damn, the big guy was in worse shape than I thought.

"We can check that out later. I am more worried about you. You need time to rest and heal," I said, grabbing the bag and pulling it away from him.

Ajax didn't fight me as I helped him over to his bed. He laid down, clutched a crystal in each hand, and closed his eyes.

I stood over my large friend for a long while after that, my worry increasing with every grunt, groan, and twitch. But a small undercurrent of ether formed around him after a while, and he fell into a more restful state.

"Do you need a doctor?" I asked a while later when his eyes fluttered open.

He shook his head. "It's going to take a lot more than that to kill me," he grunted and closed his eyes again. "Ether will help to suppress the pain. I'll be okay in a few hours."

More blood appeared on his lips as he spoke. If I didn't know any better, I'd think he was dying. Hell, maybe he was, but I liked to believe that he wouldn't do anything too foolish, even if his pride was on the line.

I pulled the wolf ornament from his pack, slid a chair to his bedside, and studied it quietly while he slept. I tried to access the internal storage at first, but nothing happened.

"*The key,*" Ivory hissed.

"I forgot about that thing," I whispered, the process coming back to me quickly. Without the key, it wasn't a storage device, but just a benign wolf statue.

With the key in place, the wolf opened, and I was finally able to look inside. Working as quietly as possible, I began unloading our haul.

I carefully stacked the wolf's contents into piles, inspecting the paper, books, and gear. Everything needed to be inspected and categorized, otherwise we might miss out on possible wealth or power.

Beyond the books and paper, there were seven weapons and a single set of body armor inside. Several swords, both of the one and two-handed varieties, a shield, a spear, a bow, and some daggers came out next. They looked well made, which didn't surprise me, considering Manfred's tastes. The body armor was a bit of an enigma, as it wasn't the archaic stuff the Duke and other nobles wore. And yet, it wasn't quite like the modern Kevlar and polymer stuff I'd found in the manor either. I set it aside for later, wanting to study it in greater detail once the sun rose.

A loud knock abruptly rattled the cabin door, startling me. I scooped our treasures back into the wolf statue, starting with the weapons and armor, but barely had time to hide those away and slide the statue under the sheets next to Ajax before the door rocked violently open. I turned, sliding my katana and wakizashi free at the same time. Hans Gruber stood in the open doorway.

"A little birdy chirped some interesting news my way," he said, striding into the cabin. "Specifically, that you...had some rather interesting papers. Would you care to share with me, freund?"

I didn't speak as he sauntered in but followed his eyes first to Ajax, and then to the stack of papers on the floor. *Shit,* I'd not had time to stash them away. Hans smiled, knelt over them, and placed his hand on top of the pile. They promptly disappeared, every single one of them.

"It's...good to see you?" I said, trying to sound polite.

"Oh, but I was never here, my good Takemi," he said with a wink.

"Would you like to sit?" I asked. "We haven't spoken for a while."

"Another time, perhaps," he said, nodding, and moving back toward the door. "Please, don't take me leaving as indifference or insult. Just understand that there are things moving behind the scenes here in Zurich, and I am needed elsewhere. Thank you for zhe...gift."

I stifled a grimace. It would have been nice to study the papers before he claimed them, but I knew we were on a short leash with the Protectorate. They undoubtedly had spies following us everywhere, regardless of whether we saw them or not.

"You had us followed? Do other people know?" I asked, voicing my concern.

He smiled, those blue eyes and perfect teeth gleaming in the light. Shit, he almost looked like a mannequin.

"No, they don't. And we will try and keep it that way. It does me good to know my best man was on the job. Sneaky, sneaky, Takemi. A job well done."

He nodded abruptly and swept outside. Just like that, a kicked-in door, some valuable papers were claimed, and he was gone again. Thus, life working in secret for the Protectorate.

"Shit," I muttered and closed the door.

Ajax was snoring, having slept through Hans' abrupt entrance and departure. I blew out half of the candles and focused on my surroundings. After several moments of intense concentration, I hadn't detected a single ether signature. Moving quietly, I moved outside and circled the cabin, expanding my radius several times. No one was in the woods either. Nothing.

I returned to our cabin, closed the door, and slid the deadbolt shut. I had to, as Hans had kicked it in and broken the latch. *Nice.* Then with a weary sigh, slid into a chair next to Ajax's bed. He grunted and opened his eyes.

"You just missed something...interesting."

He rolled over to better face me and I proceeded to tell him what had happened. In true Ajax fashion, he listened, took a moment to digest the news, then simply shrugged.

"We are running out of time. The Mêlée of Kings is quickly approaching."

I nodded, just the mention of it spiking my anxiety. To distract myself, I pulled the wolf statue out from under the sheets and reinserted the key. First, I pulled forth several small boxes and pouches. I opened the first under Ajax's scrutinizing gaze. Inside was a small, blueish orb.

"Scheiße, das ist eine wasserkugel! I mean, that's a water core!" he said, sliding effortlessly from German to English.

"Scheiße means 'shit,' right?"

He nodded and I chuckled. "You only seem to swear in German," I said, then held the orb up to the light. "It's so shiny!"

"What's in the next one?" he urged.

I lifted an eyebrow, then picked up the second box. Inside was another orb, this one glowing a dull red.

"Feuer."

"Fire?" I asked, and Ajax nodded.

"I almost feel sorry for Manfred," I said, studying the second orb.

"Almost," he nodded and pointed to two pouches waiting to be opened. "What's in there?"

I picked up the first one and looked inside. It was pitch black. "There's....oh, wait," I said, almost discarding it as empty.

A hint of ether emanated from inside, so I opened it again and probed into the depths, using my enhanced senses. It felt eerily similar to the wolf ornament, in that ether had been used to form a bubble of artificial space open inside. And yet, it felt different.

Instead of the wolf's two affinities, the bag had one. Fire. I pushed some more of my ether inside and felt it start to pull on my hand. It wasn't a forceful tug, but strong enough to notice. I let my hand slide inside and found the space cold, but also very much not empty. Something hard and sharp pushed against my fingers. Crystals! A whole lot of them, too.

"I think this is a storage pouch," I said, then pulled

my hand back out, clutching a handful of crystals. "Yep. It definitely is."

"Heard about them before," Ajax whispered, and shifted to get comfortable, "but never seen one. Hand me the other."

I handed him the second pouch and pulled the table closer, then started pulling the crystals out by the handfuls.

"This one is full of...oh, wait!" Ajax said excitedly as he scooted over, wincing from the movement. He was still in a lot of pain.

"What are those?" I asked as he pulled several massive crystals forth. They were at least twice the size of the others. They also glowed much brighter.

"These are the real deal. High-quality crystals from stronger monsters. Manfred must have been quite lucky, the bastard. Well, until he wasn't anymore."

I picked up the largest specimen and felt a much stronger ether signature inside—perhaps five or six times stronger than any I'd felt before. I also couldn't gauge how much ether was in it, like with an ordinary crystal. This one felt like a well, its magical supply running deep.

I placed the crystal back on the table, double-checked that my pouch was empty, and started counting. Seeing what I was doing, Ajax did the same, setting aside and counting the larger, more perfect crystals. Several minutes later, our count was complete. Adding in our current stash, we ended up with **813** ordinary crystals, and **34** perfect ones.

"Hera and Prom are going to flip their stuff," I laughed, after dumping the large pile back into the pouch. Even loaded with over eight hundred crystals, it barely weighed as much as an empty beer bottle.

"They'd better," he replied and leaned back in the bed.

Ajax's breathing was easier now, but I could still see he was in pain. More crystals wouldn't necessarily help him now, as he simply needed to process what he'd absorbed and allowed his body to heal. We moved on to the books. The first few titles looked strange, but that could have been because they were in

German. I scanned through the pages but didn't see anything important.

The last book was different, however as it appeared to be some sort of leather-bound journal. I handed it to Ajax so he could translate the Duke's writing.

"Let us see what our Duke friend wrote about," he said excitedly flipping through the first few pages.

He muttered and focused, his lips moving as he read. He suddenly held the journal out and shook it. A booklet slid free from the pages and landed on the bed. I scooped it up, my excitement immediately spiking.

"It appears to be an instruction manual," I said, recognizing the picture on the front. "Oh, baby!"

"For what?" he asked, his beard scrunching up.

I opened the leaflet but discovered that the interior pages were more or less a collection of loose pages and handwritten notes.

The first sheet was hard to read, as the ink was faded from age. A date was written on the top of the page: **7/03/2025**.

> *'The device appears to display data in the preferred language of whoever holds it. The level of technology involved in its creation must have been extraordinarily advanced. It can even respond to queries by the user and—'*

It went on in a long series of in-depth observations. Judging from the language, I guessed it was written by a researcher or scientist. Someone who had the time and resources to study one of the scanning devices. Only a select few would have access to the notes, and the rest would have to do with whatever information was handed down. So, it made sense that Duke Manfred had it in his possession.

"These scanning devices. When did the first ones appear?" I asked.

Ajax considered the question for a moment, his eyes drifting back as he fell into thoughtful consideration.

"Around twelve or thirteen years ago. Why?"

"Because reading this, I'm not sure that anyone developed these things at all. Do these look like notes of something that was created by...well, men? These are findings. Like they were studying relics."

Ajax accepted the sheet of paper and read for a moment. I sat and waited impatiently for him to finish, tapping my feet. My gaze drifted around the room, but when I turned back, I discovered that his eyes were closed.

"Hey? Are you dozing off?"

Ajax's eyelids flickered open and he grumbled, "No, I was just resting my eyes."

I could tell that he was struggling just to stay awake. In all actuality, he needed to rest and heal, not answer my questions.

"Where's the device we got from Duke Manfred?"

He tipped his head toward a small cabinet. I found the device wrapped in cloth and hidden between some towels. Smart.

Ajax was snoring when I turned around again. So, I laid a few traps outside the doors and windows. Some that would tell me if people were snooping, and a few rather painful old-fashioned bear traps. They wouldn't outright stop a powerful person, but they would sure as hell slow them down.

I boiled some water for coffee, cut myself a piece of bread, covered it with butter and fresh preserves, and prepared for some work. Settling into a chair by the table, I began my...scientific research.

First, I picked up the device and studied it thoroughly. It was rectangular, with an incredibly hard, clear screen. There was no technology in it that I could see, which seemed like the strangest part. Fingerprints looked to have been melted into the back of its body, where my hands naturally rested. Although it had belonged to Manfred, I couldn't help but feel like it was molded to fit me. *Strange.*

Holding the scanning device before me, I studied my reflection on its clear screen. It was something I hadn't really done since waking up in that triage tent, and especially since having the dreams connect and my flashback to the ether convergence. It just reminded me of everything I'd lost— a childhood and all of its memories, a family, the tradition woven into my mother and father's legacy, Nakamura dojo.

I was Kenji Nakamura, not Takemi, I'd loved a woman named Beth, and I had lost it all. That thought, most of all, sat uncomfortably in my gut, knowing that she, along with my family could still be out there somewhere.

Shaking those nagging thoughts away, I angled the screen away, so I couldn't see my reflection and pushed a bit of ether into the device. The previously lifeless screen reacted, displaying a colorful panel of words and numbers.

The first thing I noticed was the plus sign next to the S,

which I gathered meant that I was pushing the boundaries for two-veined cultivators. Now all I had to do was open up the third vein and start all over again. The thought made me tired, so I took a sizable drink of coffee.

Next, I checked my skills, just to see if anything had changed.

The only change that I could track was the completion rate of my battle skills. They'd both gone up, and I couldn't wait to see what was next. Would my blazing slash now engulf the target in flames? Or would the razor's edge allow me to simply cut right through the target and have the residual ether blow them up? It remained to be seen.

I cross-referenced the booklet and the researcher's notes on the device, then went through the basics. After a little reading, I discovered that I could ask it for a report on my current status. All I had to do was infuse it with ether and make a vocal request.

"Well, that sounds like fun," I whispered, finished my coffee, and picked the tablet back up.

I focused on the device again, pushed a spark of ether forth, and once the screen came alive, I stated my request.

"Report."

The display flashed and then went dark, lines of text appearing in quick succession.

START OF REPORT

Ether Gathering Realm: 2/12

Anomaly Detected:
Yang-Metal Affinity Channel is abnormal.
Connected from LEFT HAND to HEART instead of LARGE INTESTINE.

Suggested Action:
None.

Variant Trait Detected:
Dantean: Congratulations! Niwan(Mind) Palace is already Unlocked!

Note: This is incredibly rare before the Nascent Soul Realm, Only 1:744,153,677 cultivators have this Variant Trait on a universal scale.

Suggested Action:
Notify your Sect and request additional resources and training for Soul Power and associated combat skills.

Anomaly Detected:

Cultivation Method:
Not Found.

Suggested Action:
Contact Sect and request a suitable Method for efficiently absorbing and using Ether.

...

...

END—

"What in the flying f-sickles..." I hissed, cursing under my breath as I re-read the report.

I could read it plain as day but understanding what it said was another thing entirely. What did it mean, though? What was Yang? I understood what the Metal Affinity Channel was, for the most part, but not the part about the vein that ran from my thumb to my heart.

"But what does that have to do with Yang? Yin-Yang maybe?" I surmised out loud.

The screen went blank and new lines of text began to appear:

Yang is the positive, or masculine, form of energy and is often associated with the sun. Six of your channels (veins) are Yang and the other six are Yin, which is the negative, or feminine, form of energy that is associated with the moon.

Uncertainty Detected: Positive and Negative are references to forces, not ethical alignments.

"Okay! Ugh, thank you strange little device," I whispered, nodding."

I sat up a little straighter in the chair.

"What is it?" Ajax muttered, now looking over at me.

"This thing," I said, shaking the tablet in my left hand, "answered a question that I asked out loud. I mean, I wasn't really asking it, I just whispered something about yin and yang and it answered me. How weird is that?"

He looked at me for a moment, bleary-eyed and sleepy. Then he simply nodded. Okay, truthfully, it was probably one of those things a person had to see for themselves to appreciate.

"Just play with your little thing a bit quieter, okay?" he grumbled and rolled over.

"My little...what?" I asked playfully. "You have no context on that, buddy. Besides, Layla has never complained!"

The big guy waved me off and pulled the covers up to his chin. Returning my attention to the device, I asked my next query.

"What is the Nascent Soul Realm?"

The Nascent Soul is the Third Major Cultivation Realm. It consists of three stages: Preliminary, Intermediate, and Perfection. It revolves around forming the 2nd out of 3 Danteans and is instrumental in the mental and spiritual defense of the cultivator.

"How many realms are there?"

No limit is currently detected. A better query might be: "how far can I progress?" The limitations of this world are so basic at the moment, insignificant, so progressing past the 6th stage of the Ether Gathering Realm will cause a minor heavenly tribulation.

"Wait, what is a heavenly tribulation?"

A Heavenly tribulation occurs when a cultivator surpasses the limitations of either the world or its encompassing universe. The cultivator must then pass a tribulation successfully if he or she wants to survive.

"Alright, then what *is* a tribulation?"

A tribulation is a test of five elements. Each one will assess the worthiness of the cultivator, and in return, readdress the boundaries regulating them.

"Okay, reading that just gave me a headache," I groaned and rubbed my eyes. "How does this thing know all these things?"

I heard Ajax start to chuckle.

"I've never seen anyone as sane as you talk to themselves so much, Takemi. Then again, maybe you aren't sane."

"I did have a large portion of my skull caved in..." I

muttered.

He laughed and nodded.

"How are you feeling?"

"With the pain? It is getting better by the moment. Why?"

I pushed out of the chair.

"Because that guy kicked your head like a soccer ball. Honestly, I'm surprised it didn't fly right off your neck. Take it from someone that knows head injuries, the pain and disorientation can stick around for a while."

I walked over and placed the scanning device in his hands. His face wrinkled in confusion.

"I don't need to be graded again."

"Trust me, just push a little ether forth and ask it about your unlocked abilities."

He did as I said but didn't let me see the results.

"Why are you hiding it? What did it say?" I pressed, reaching over and trying to pull the scanner toward me. He grunted and pushed me away, successfully holding me off with one arm.

"That I have a skill called <<**Pain Suppression**>> and another called <<**Stone Skin**>>."

"Not bad," I said, and finally stopped wrestling for control. "I have <<**Burst of Speed**>> and <<**Enhanced Strength**>>."

"Really? Since when?"

I stared at him for a moment, trying to remember if it had ever come up, and if not, why.

"I thought the Duke told you...that I am a little different."

"Yeah, I think he said you were weird, but that's not exactly news."

"So, explain how you are even stranger than I believed," Ajax said, handing back the scanner.

I grinned. "Somehow, I unlocked something I shouldn't have. Something a full two realms early."

"Oh, so once I hit my fourth vein, I'll catch up with you?"

I sucked air in through my teeth, trying to find a nice way to break the news—that in reality, it would take a lot longer than that.

"Err, no. Two Realms, not two stages. The Machine will explain it, but you're basically at stage 2 out of 12 of the first realm right now, which is vein formation. There are fewer stages in the next realm, but that one is even harder to progress through. It is all more complicated than you can imagine, so right now probably isn't the best time to get into it."

His face paled.

"Confusing? That is no joke. I am struggling to just form sentences right now," he laughed and shook his head. "You are one lucky son of a bitch, Takemi. You take a blow to the head. One which should have killed you. It scrambles your brains, wipes your memories, makes you a nicer person, and unlocks special abilities? Please, take my hammer and bash my head in! Help a brother along."

I laughed. "I wish I could help you out. I do, but I think what I survived was one in a million. And judging from my fragmented dreams, it wasn't the head injury."

"Not the answer I wanted, Tak. Anyway, how do I use the abilities?"

I shrugged. "They all seem to be different for me. That would lead me to guess that yours are different still. Are you sure that you aren't already using pain suppression? Maybe it's a passive skill, one that's always active, unlike mine?"

"It's possible," he said and shifted to get comfortable. "The only way to test that would be to find a way to turn it off, and judging from my pain level, I don't think I'd like that. I will tell you this much, Takemi. We can't keep facing these high-level pricks in our current state. We're going to need more than luck and fancy ice spider weapons. We're going to need more strength."

I nodded in agreement. It was something I had planned on bringing up with him as soon as he was healed, but he'd brought it up first.

"Between the Duke and this Seneschal prick, we should have enough to push you into the third stage. You need to work on it now, Ajax. There will even be leftovers for the rest of us."

"Are you sure?" he asked. "You and your abilities seem to be what gets us out of these scrapes more times than not."

"But how long will that last? As you said, we're going to need more than luck moving forward. That means, getting you stronger. And when the others get back, helping them, too."

Ajax nodded and shifted again. "Yeah, you're right. I can't expect you to win all of our fights. What if someone brings a puppy with them? You'll start giggling and trying to pet it. Then we'll all die."

"See. This is why it needs to be you. So, as a group, we can overcome my natural weakness for soft and cuddly things."

"Okay, puppy boy, hand me some of those crystals so I can get started," he chuckled and held out his hand.

CHAPTER 13: RELEASE

After Ajax fell into his healing meditations, I paced for a long while, but after a time it became impossible to hold my eyes open. With thoughts of ether-scanning devices, Hans Gruber and the Protectorate, the deceased Duke Manfred, and everything else swirling around in my brain, I settled onto a chair, closed my eyes, and drifted off.

With almost no transition, I simply found myself on the stairs before the pagoda, right next to Ivory. The wolf spirit didn't even spare me a glance. He stared out into the swirling backdrop of my mind palace, his eyes unfocused.

"Thanks for earlier," I said, letting my hand come to rest on the barrier surrounding his pedestal. "Should we work on getting you out of there?"

His ears perked up and he finally turned his gaze my way. I knew he was instrumental in figuring out how the storage space worked, so he'd earned some respect.

"Yes. I believe that would be...appropriate."

"Any ideas?"

The massive spirit wolf opened his jaws and yawned wide, displaying his gleaming set of sharp teeth. Once done, he turned to me and shook his head. "Not a single one."

I started to circle, troubling over the issue at hand. No answers readily sprang to mind, but I wasn't known as someone who gave up easily, so I focused on the shimmering bubble. Omega had been able to nip at Ivory, even hitting the other wolf with a paw, yet my hands wouldn't pass through.

"Okay. Look at the problem. Formulate questions, and then test them," I said, setting my feet. "First, let's try ether."

I gathered two ether strands, one in each hand, then pushed them palms forward against the barrier. It pushed me away as if I were trying to force together opposing poles of a large magnet.

"Affinities," Ivory said and abruptly stood, then started to paw at the shimmering barrier. "You can't simply force your way in here. Nor can I force my way out."

"Alright," I mumbled, circling back in the opposite direction. Considering what he said, I changed my tactic. This time when I channeled, I pushed only a strand of metal affinity ether forth. When my hand contacted the barrier, nothing pushed it away. Nothing happened, beyond the lack of...repulsion. "What—happened? Did you feel anything?"

"I did," he replied, looking around. "I just don't know what."

I closed my eyes and felt for the barrier's ether, its flow, or its composition. I found it and discovered not one spiraling ether flow, but four.

"I feel it," I said, moving around the pedestal. "There's a multi-lock system in place, like four independent but overlapping bands of energy."

He pushed his snout against the dome, his nose smashing against the invisible barrier. His eyes burned like embers.

"Then it is simple, right? Match the energy and unlock the layers. What are you waiting for? Come along!"

"I'm just," I said, pausing. "I need to decide if this is a smart idea. What if I let you out of there and discover that you can physically harm me here? Maybe you can even take over my body."

Ivory snapped his teeth. "Are you going back on your promise?"

"I didn't say that. I'm just voicing a few doubts."

"If you back out of our agreement now, I will make you this promise. I will get out of this prison...somehow, and then you'd better watch your—"

"Oh, stop. You're just a soul, a passenger in my body. I am not going to leave you locked up in there forever. That sounds cruel. But I am definitely not going to go out of my way to set you free if you threaten me. Is that clear?"

Ivory watched me for a moment, then in a surprising move, he lowered his head.

"You hurt my feelings," the wolf spirit said suddenly. "It is so lonely in here. If you get me out of here, I'll do my best to help and not...eat your soul."

"As far as reassurances go, 'I'll do my best to not eat your soul' doesn't really fill me with the warm and fuzzies," I admitted.

"Fine," he snorted. "I will try extremely hard not to eat your soul. How about that?"

"It is a little better," I admitted.

Then, after a moment of pause, I focused on the remaining locks. They dissipated one by one, and when the final layer was released, the barrier disappeared with an audible *pop*.

Ivory got to his feet and tentatively leaned out, testing his new limits. When no barrier held him back, he leaned into my face, his snout inches away from my nose. I thought I'd have to slap him away and fight, but then he bowed his head and leaped off the pedestal.

"So, what now?" I asked, turning. The massive wolf stretched and yawned, then tipped onto his side and started to roll on the ground. After a moment of reveling in his newfound freedom, Ivory jumped to his feet and shook.

"We get to work," he said. "You are right. I'm just a

passenger here, and you are the vessel. However, I need to be honest. As long as you are alive, I will struggle with the urge to take over."

"Good. I mean, on the honesty part. But on the 'urge to take over' part let me respond with a warning. You are welcome here as long as you get along and don't hurt anyone. And don't even think of trying to hurt Omega. He's part of my pack. Just like you are unless you make me change my mind."

"Pack?" Ivory snorted. "That mutt?"

"A mutt is technically a mixed breed, so that term isn't accurate," I said, and for once, Ivory didn't have a rebuttal.

"Now, why don't you tell me how we can get stronger."

"For starters, force your third vein to accept the metal affinity. No combination comes close in rarity: one fire and two metal. Instant strength and toughness."

"I can live with that," I said, thoughtfully. "Can *you* always force a vein?"

"No, I can't. I think that I can only do it once since I only have one affinity myself. And that's still just a maybe, as I've never actually done it before."

"What about the locked and chained rooms inside the pagoda? Can you help me open those?"

He shook his head. "Maybe, but maybe not. There is something else I can teach you in the meantime."

"What's that?"

"Reinforce your skin using metal affinity. It will become even stronger when you've opened your next metal vein, but even with one, you should be able to shrug off ordinary attacks. Like that club the other day."

I nodded, as my interest was piqued. But chuckled.

"Why are you laughing?" he growled.

"It is just strange to be having a conversation with a wolf. One in which you know what a club is. And since we're on the subject. How are you so good with words in general?"

"I live in your mind, you hairless ape. Your mind interprets my intent and meaning."

"Oh, well that makes sense. And using the metal affinity to harden my skin?"

"Easy. There is no way to make it permanent, at least not at your level. All you need to do is focus on your ether and push it forth through your vein with the metal affinity. Let that ether leech out through your muscles and skin. It will imbue whatever it soaks and coats with that metal's hardness. But it will not be easy. First, you'll probably only be able to do a finger, then your arm...but with enough practice, you should be able to cover most of your body. Since you've already inherited two reinforcement-type skills and the know-how to use them, it will only be a matter of time and training."

Ivory walked away suddenly, evidently bored with the conversation. He lay down next to the koi pond and pawed at the surface.

"Please don't eat my fish."

"Ugh, he groaned and rolled over to sun his belly. "Out of all the creatures in the world, how is it I came to be stuck in your mind?"

"Did any of the doors open after I set you free?" I asked.

"Did you feel any open?"

"Good question," I said and turned to the pagoda and started climbing the stairs. It had been a long while since I explored inside.

I turned and considered the freed wolf spirit now lounging by the pond. Then a thought struck me. Could I populate the place with more beast spirits? Could they only be wolves?

"Just imagine," I whispered, turning and strolling into the pagoda. "Five Ivories living in my mind, driving me insane."

CHAPTER 14: GUARDIAN

I ran along with Pale Fox and Short Tooth, a peculiar sense of unease prickling the fur on my neck. We'd been traveling for some time, and while I missed Alpha, I almost missed Deer Eyes' burned meat more. As a whole, my new pack was starting to grow on me. Luckily, they didn't seem to fear me as much as before, and I liked that. For the first time, I belonged to a real pack—a stupid one, but a pack, nonetheless.

I'd given up on bringing them fresh kills after they ignored them. They preferred food from the strange skins they carried on their backs, Pale Fox especially. I thought them disgusting at first, based on nothing more than their smell. But Short Tooth, the she-wolf, gave me a bit and I was surprised by how tasty the food was. It wasn't burnt meat good, but it wasn't horrible either.

We ran for some time until my new pack got tired and had to sleep. I watched them eat, accepted some food from Short Tooth, and watched over them as they rested.

Once they were asleep, I slunk in quietly and took some food, then slipped out of their den. Two scents filled the air as I backtracked on our path from earlier. One smell was expected —our new pack member, Long Claws. As a bear, he was massive and powerful, but Pale Fox and Short Tooth refused to let him into their den, so I had him follow behind. Besides, he was slow and lazy, so we weren't forced to wait for him.

The other smell, however, was what prickled my fur —pale, furless wolves like Alpha, but not friendly. I could practically smell the aggression seeping off of them.

Wearily, I approached Long Claws and discovered the bear bedded down in a clearing. He smelled me, growled a challenge, and I responded.

Lumbering to his feet, Long Claws stood like a hill between trees, his breath fogging the air. He clawed at the ground before him, but I snarled, reminding him of who and what I was. Once he'd gone quiet and dropped his head, I placed the food I'd brought him on the ground and backed away.

Long Claws lumbered forward and ate the food, then, licking his chops, sat back on his haunches and considered me.

I growled and pawed at the ground. The bear turned his head, considering me. I growled again, and he grunted. Long Claws reared up and started to sniff the air, his large nostrils snorting loudly. When he crashed down to all fours again, the fur on his neck bristled, too. Good. He smelled the enemy wolves.

Leading Long Claws out into the darkness, we moved quietly together. We circled the ones following us—the pale, furless wolves evidently blind and stupid. We scouted their camp twice without them even realizing it. Long Claws crashed through a thicket and left massive prints in the soft mud, and yet the pale wolves didn't notice. Idiots. They were far weaker than my pack, especially Alpha and Deer Eyes. But still, I worried that they would hurt Pale Fox and Short Tooth.

Long Claws and I crept in quietly and listened, but unfortunately, I couldn't understand their annoying yippy bark noises. They were anxious and hungry, that much I knew. Their smell was all wrong. They meant harm to my pack, and I had to do something.

Long Claws and I returned to my pack's den and we

traveled through more bright and dark times. We came to the strange den in the rocky places, where Alpha mounted his mate often. Pale Fox and Short Tooth gathered Alpha's mate and the other female and we were off again, moving quickly through the forests.

By the time they stopped to rest during the dark time, the bad pack was closing in. Even though Pale Fox and Short Tooth couldn't smell them, I knew they were there. I tried to tell them, but they were stupid and did not listen.

When Alpha's mate closed her eyes to sleep, I decided to take matters into my own paws. I gathered Long Claws and together we set out to do their job.

When we spotted the enemy wolves, they were alert and watchful. And yet, they lumbered through the forest, stomping and making so much noise. These idiots were useless wolves.

I made up my mind to end them then and there. Long Claws rumbled next to me, quietly agreeing. I'd given my pack enough time to deal with them, but Pale Fox refused to listen.

I would take care of them, and then tell my alpha how weak and oblivious they were. Perhaps he would punish them.

It didn't take long for the enemy pack to send stalkers into the woods. The lights went out inside their cave, but they were not all sleeping. I knew they were stupid wolves, but completely horrible.

The stalkers scouted the area before returning quietly to their camp. I watched one of the five pale wolves sit up to guard the others, while another hid behind a tree near the fake cave's entrance. The last three others went to sleep. And boy did they sleep. I could hear their snores loud and clear through the trees.

These furless wolves were as bad at being predators as they were at being prey. At least prey would be alert and use their instincts and senses. These creatures were practically screaming for someone in the forest to come and eat them. Foolish pups. Stupid wolves.

Long Claws and I got low and crawled, then waited for their guard to move out into the trees. He did it regularly, stomping and crashing through the underbrush. We followed him, my fur changing to blend in with the trees and bushes.

With my camouflage helping me melt into the shadows, I circled a clump of trees and found the guard standing in the darkness. He smelled...alert. I detected aggression there, too. He meant to hurt something, and I guessed that was my pack.

I slipped forward, my paws silent against the ground, and yet he still did not notice me. I crept closer until it should have been impossible for him not to feel my breath against the back of his neck. I watched as goosebumps formed on his skin and his hand reached back to rub his flesh.

He froze as his poor wolf instincts finally kicked in. The guard suddenly turned right at me, his eyes large and full of a prey's fear. And yet he did not see me.

I snorted and he flinched, taking in a sharp breath. The bad wolf searched the darkness, his mouth moving, but forming no sound. Then I snorted again, only this time I let my camouflage slip away.

His eyes met mine and his annoyed, frightened expression on his face turned to one of pure horror. I snapped forward, sinking my teeth into his soft throat, and shook my head. His body flopped right off the ground, the force almost tearing his head clean off.

Long Claws lumbered forward as the guard bled out and died between us. These wolves were stupid creatures—slow and bad wolves, but they were still dangerous. I would show Pale Fox and Short Tooth that I could watch over them. They would tell Alpha when we got back, and he would praise me.

We stalked in on the enemy wolves' camp, the smell of their fire masking their smells. I urged Long Claws ahead, the bear excited by the smell of blood from my kill. He pushed up onto his hind legs, filling the fake cave's entrance, then lurched forward.

The bear hit the pale wolf, dropping his full weight onto

his chest. He picked him up in his jaws, shook him violently, and tossed the body out of the way.

I slunk in around Long Claws and found the others still sleeping. What horrible wolves. We'd just killed two of them and they slumbered like pups.

Creeping up to the closest prone figure, I stopped over top of him. Blood dripped off my snout and onto his face, the spatter immediately waking him up. His eyes shot open and he tried to roll away, but I was quicker. I jumped onto his back, locked my jaws on his neck, and twisted. It snapped loudly, and he went limp beneath my paws.

The other enemy wolves stirred then, alerted to our presence by the noise. Long Claws gave an impressive roar and charged in, swinging his massive paws. The claws hit the first, slashing them open from neck to belly. The bear fell on the last pale wolf and silenced their terrified scream. Then, with breath fogging the air, Long Claws turned to me.

I growled my approval, and the bear lumbered back outside. The enemy wolves' bodies scattered the ground around us. They were weak, fragile things, but somehow still dangerous. But not anymore. I'd kept my pack safe.

Snapping my teeth into the closest body, I lifted them easily off the ground and started to drag them outside. I couldn't wait to see my pack's faces when I brought them a trophy. When I showed them what Long Claws and I had done.

The next bright time was going to be a joyous occasion! They would yip and bark my praises, and if I was lucky, they would give me some burnt meat.

CHAPTER 15: REUNION

Ajax's loud grunting pulled me from sleep, and unfortunately, the pagoda at the same time. I'd not been ready to leave, and that simple fact along with my friend's inability to sleep quietly, left me in a bad temper.

I sat up in the chair and stretched, feeling a crick forming in my neck and upper back. Sleeping in chairs was no way to go.

The big guy rolled easily out of bed and sprang to his feet, and with a surprising spring in his step. I rubbed my eyes and yawned, fighting back a number of grumpy comments, then opened them again as his shadow fell over me. Ajax was different, that much I could tell, but it took me a moment to tell why.

"Well? What do you think? I am sexy, no?" he asked, turning and flexing.

"Total dad bod?" I grumbled and looked away.

And yet, I had to look again. Ajax looked a few years younger now. He had less gray in his beard, his muscles were more defined, and the insulation layer around his midsection —his words not mine—was almost gone. He looked practically fit and trim. Well, more fit and trim. "You opened your third vein?"

"Ja, das habe ich, Captain Fancy Pants," he beamed.

"Did you just call me 'Captain Fancy Pants'?"

"Jawohl."

"He opens his third vein and all of the sudden he forgets English," I grumbled and pushed out of the chair. My back popped in several places as I did so, but the crick remained in my neck.

"And I only used a little over forty crystals to do it," he said, looking me over. "Do not worry. We still have a shit ton left...plenty to open everyone's third vein. Once they arrive."

"Good," I said, trying to stretch.

"Takemi, you look like shit. Are you okay?"

"Let's just say, I slept in a chair and didn't get as much sleep as some people I know."

"Agreed!" I'll tell you what. We'll see our friends at the massage parlor. Miko can work on your back and I can see Bella —"

"You don't need to say it," I interrupted.

"It is just," he grinned and flexed. "I feel so full of life. And so strong. Bella is going to get all she can handle from me tonight!"

"Ugh, please. In your own room this time," I groaned and waved him off. "I'm gonna take a shower first."

After a cold and relatively invigorating shower, I dressed, grabbed a bite out of the small kitchenette, and joined Ajax on the front porch.

The sky was mostly overcast, but the pre-dawn sunrise was already making the horizon glow. Before too long the sun would rise and burn off the cloud cover.

We set out through the trees in silence, a thick early morning fog still pooling in the low spots. The cool damp clung to my skin, but I found it refreshing. I wasn't stuck inside a stuffy cabin for a change, so that right there was worth it.

Ajax started off at an easy pace, but gained speed, until I had to practically jog to keep up. I knew why, too. I'd had him use the scanner after I'd dressed. It showed that his newly minted vein possessed his highly coveted metal affinity.

"Calm down, dude. I know you are excited to get to Mike's forge, but my legs are nowhere near as long as yours! Are you more excited about the smithy, or seeing your masseuse friend again?"

"Working metal and humping women are two of my favorite things," Ajax said, throwing me a wink.

Despite the early hour, we walked in to find Zurich bustling with life. People carried packs, some pulled carts with wares, while others cleaned manure off the streets, or split firewood. It was a strange sight, considering how advanced the world had been. Now, people were forced to use eighteenth century techniques and technology to survive.

We turned down a side street and Mike's smithy appeared ahead, just as a commotion arose behind us. I turned, my hands reaching for the swords at my hip but a vice-like grip caught my right wrist before I could pull either blade free.

"Don't be rash," Ajax whispered.

I looked up to find the big man calm and collected, until his eyes flicked over my shoulder, and his bushy beard split in a wide smile. He kept me from turning the rest of the way, until someone leapt onto me from behind.

"I've missed you!" Layla gasped and squeezed me tight.

I tried to turn into her and return the embrace, but her grip was too strong. With Layla clamped firmly around me, I spun just as Hera punched Ajax in the chest.

"You big lug," she growled, punching him again, before trying to wrestle him back. "When did you break through? And wow, you've lost weight!"

Layla finally released her hold and I wrestled her around, pulling her into a deep kiss.

"Last night," Ajax explained, knocking her punch aside and throwing a jab back in response. "It could have been you, if you weren't busy taking a vacation in the mountains."

"Vacation?" she yelled and jumped at him.

He fought her off, but Hera proved to be the more persistent, and got under his guard. The two tumbled to the ground and wrestled for a moment, before my big friend simply threw his arms wide in surrender. Anyone walking by would have thought that they were trying to harm or even kill one another, but I knew better. Moreso than any others in our group, Hera and Ajax were like family.

"Did we miss much? Or just you becoming less fat around the middle?" Hera asked and pushed back up to her feet.

"Let me just say, yes. But we shouldn't talk about it in the open," Ajax replied and caught her off guard. He picked her up and swung her around. It was a strange sight. Even stranger that she let him.

"What about you?" I asked, after kissing Layla's cheek. "Did everything go all right?"

"More or less," Hera snorted. "Your furball found some people following us."

I tensed and looked around. "Who? Were they Protectorate?"

"We don't think so. But whoever they *were,* your pet wolf taught them a bloody lesson."

If Omega truly had found people following them, the bloody lesson wouldn't be harsh words or a spanking. That meant that someone was either looking to spy, kidnap one of our team, or rob us. All three possibilities worried me, especially considering we wouldn't know how they would respond to their people simply not coming home.

"It gets weirder than that," Hera said, moving toward me and lowering her voice. "It appears your wolf has taken in a new member to its pack. And...it is not a wolf."

"What do you mean?"

"While on the road, an animal raided our camp. With your wolf's help, we tracked it. It was a bear. Prometheus and I were in favor of leaving it be, but your wolf—"

"Omega," I interrupted.

"Yes, him. He would not back down. In fact, he actually overcame the bear. And it bowed to him. After that, they went everywhere together."

I chewed on that knowledge, but the idea that a bear followed them back from the cabin made me more than a little nervous. A wolf was one thing, but a bear felt like a completely different set of obstacles.

"How did you know where to find us?" Ajax asked and motioned to Mike's smithy with a thumb.

"Oh, little birdies chirp, and some of us know how to listen. Even all the way up in the mountains," Layla cut in, throwing me a wink.

I lifted her chin just enough so I could slide forward for a kiss. She stretched to her tiptoes and pulled more fully into my embrace. We kissed again before separating. I immediately detected something different about her—how she felt against me, smelled, and carried herself. It took me a moment to spot it.

"You've opened your first vein," I said, barely holding back my excitement.

She nodded, her mouth pulling up into a wide smile.

"Yes, but is that the...only thing you notice about me?" she whispered.

"No. Honestly, it took me a moment to notice because I didn't want to let you go," I said, letting my hands slide down to her hips.

"I do like this new you," she breathed, squeezing me again. "You really have changed...for the better."

"Let's chat inside," Ajax interrupted, pulling us both toward the smithy. We walked the rest of the way down the street, then up through the gate, and filed into the building. Once we were safely inside, Mike shut the door behind us.

The space, which had always felt so large and spacious before, was considerably more cramped now.

"Did you have to bring an army with you?" Mike asked. His expression softened once he looked around at the group, noticing Hera and the girls. "Ugh, hi... everyone. Willkommen! It is good to see you."

"Welkom to you, too, Mike," Hera said, playfully jabbing at his midsection. Then she came forward and wrapped the older man in a hug. The others waved or nodded in greeting.

"All right, big guy. Spill the beans," Hera said, turning back to Ajax. "Have you two been busy while we were gone? Busy doing the right things?"

"Busy? Oh, yes. You know Takemi. He is a trouble magnet, but a very profitable one."

The door opened and closed and I turned to find Prometheus moving toward us. He looked more than a little road weary.

"Did they tell you?" Prometheus asked.

"About Omega? Yes. But we didn't get into the details."

"It was the night we got to the cottage. Everything seemed fine, but when we woke up in the morning, I found five well-armed and armored men outside. Well, I found most of them outside. Your wolf lined them up for us, like he'd been out hunting rabbits and small game in the woods."

Our scout settled into a chair by the far wall, and Kate crawled into his lap. Layla pulled in tight to my side, her arms wrapped protectively around my midsection.

"How didn't you notice them following you?" I asked.

Hera and Prometheus both shrugged and shook their heads. They both appeared a bit embarrassed by the question, but I didn't blame them. Prometheus was as good a scout as could be found, and Hera had phenomenal instincts.

The people who tracked and followed the two without them knowing must have had three veins or more open and had probably been very dangerous. That just made me even more grateful that I'd sent Omega with them. Nothing got past him.

"Change your mind about Omega yet?" I asked.

"What part?" Hera asked. "I accepted your pet. Prometheus was the one scared of him."

Our scout shrugged.

"He's starting to grow on me. As long as he kills and eats our enemies and not me, I'm good."

"Oh, and before you hassle us, we made sure he didn't go hungry. So, you don't have to worry about that. The wolf made it clear he wanted our canned food," Hera added. "I don't think Prom or I will ever take him for granted again. Although, next time, he doesn't need to present us with their bodies. Those were not pleasant to bury."

"So they were pros? Any idea who sent them?" I asked, turning to Prometheus.

"No. They wore neutral colors, didn't have any insignias, and carried no identification or papers. But it is clear they were paid to come after us. Each man carried twenty-five crystals exactly, stashed away in identical pouches. I'm operating on the assumption that was half the payment, and they were expecting the rest after delivering proof we were dead."

"Someone is willing to spend two hundred and fifty crystals to kill you?" Layla asked.

"Sadly, yes."

"But who?" Ajax asked.

"Let's check the list," I said. "Nobles from Munich. Nobles from Zurich. Alfred and his cronies. The King and his bickering council. I'm guessing at least half of them want us dead. And while you guys were away, I might have pissed off yet another high-born ruffly-butt snob when we went to the fights."

"You know, Takemi. Before you woke up in that tent, that list was a lot smaller," Hera sighed.

"I know. This last guy, he promised a bunch of people two hundred crystals to kill Ajax and I. Mind you, that was after we took his money in a bet, but still. Sore losers, and all..."

"I'd kill you for much less," Hera laughed. "But speaking of crystals. How are we sitting? The girls used a considerable portion of our supply opening their first veins. I have less than eighty of what you gave us, and they are all small."

I did some quick mental math and scratched my chin.

"With that, we have somewhere in the neighborhood of eight to nine hundred."

Hera did a double take.

"What bank did you guys rob?" Layla asked.

"Manfred's stash, along with some well-timed bets on Takemi's unscheduled bout in the arena," Ajax replied for me.

"What!" Layla hissed. "Why were you fighting in the arena! Don't tell me they made you—?"

"No," I said, waving her off. And I knew where her mind went, especially after what happened to us during the tribunal. "We were in the crowd and watched an awesome girl fight some arrogant chump."

"And how did that lead to you fighting in the arena?"

"People kept calling her chocolate and booing her, even though she was obviously the better fighter. Then this Leo guy cheated. He threw something in her eyes to gain the upper hand and no one did anything. So...I stepped in," I explained.

"He stepped right into the ring and broke poor Leo's arms," Ajax laughed, slapping his thigh.

"Wait, what?" Prometheus demanded. "You fought Leo Lienhardt?"

I nodded.

"Oh, god, I would have paid to see that!" Hera laughed. "He is a dandy of the highest order!"

"Yeah, well, that little bout earned us enough crystals to get us all to the third vein in the long run. We just need to decide who goes first."

Their eyes lit up and I could tell they were already trying to jockey themselves to the top of the list. And to their credit, no one shouted or demanded to go first.

"On three?"

Hera's face practically shimmered with excitement as she turned to Ajax. The big man nodded. Hera turned back to our scout and together they lifted their hands, formed fists, and shook their hands three times. On the third shake, Prometheus opened two fingers and made a snipping motion while Hera's fist remained closed.

"Scissors!"

"Rock beats scissors! Hah, I win!"

I laughed as Prometheus promptly stomped his foot and cursed.

"Don't worry, Prom, you're up next anyway. Then me last."

"Oh? You're not pushing to blaze ahead?"

"Funny you bring that up. Ajax and I had a discussion last night, after we'd been forced to fight and kill someone with four veins—"

"What?" Hera yelled.

"Was this at the arena or a separate fight?" Prometheus asked.

"Shhh," I hissed. "We're alone here but there is no way for us to know if they have a way to listen in."

"Sorry," Hera whispered. "Tell us what happened."

"We broke into the Duke's manor and found his stash. Unfortunately, one of Alfred's cronies was waiting for us. Evidently, he'd been the one working behind the scenes during our interrogations. Perhaps even the one behind the attack on Hera. He was there to claim Manfred's hidden stash. I don't know how he knew about it, or that we would be there. It sounded like he was operating independently of both Alfred and the King, so he was very eager to make sure we were dead...quickly."

"A four vein cultivator? You fought him and survived?" Prometheus asked, his expression showing ample doubt.

"Well, it wasn't easy, let's put it that way. Ajax took the brunt of it, and I'm glad he is still with us—but with some luck, I took him out. That's my specialty, you know? Beating the odds."

"Not something to be proud of!" Layla said, "Because eventually you'll just lose."

"That's why it is important for us to advance," I said. "We can't get by on luck anymore. It needs to be strength. There's a lot we've been figuring out. For example, the scanning devices don't just show you your cultivation and body status, it can give you much more information. We just had to learn how to ask for it. I discovered that I have a variant trait that gives me access to something two realms earlier than normal people."

"Only two? That doesn't sound so bad. Just two extra veins?" Layla said.

I shook my head.

"Two realms, not two veins. I was struggling to explain the same thing to Ajax."

"Then…what are realms?" Hera asked and moved in.

"Let me put it this way, if certain people knew about my quirk, I doubt they would let us leave Zurich. The Ether Gathering Realm is split into twelve stages, one for each vein. Next comes the Core Formation Realm, which has six stages. My, ugh, quirk, or ability won't be available to you until you reach the third realm. And that's only if you're extremely lucky."

No one spoke for some time, until Prom muttered something under his breath.

"Speak up. You're not alone in the trees anymore," Hera said.

"Sorry. I was just wondering. How long do you think that will take, Tak?"

I shrugged. For all I knew, it could take decades or even a lifetime just to get to the second realm.

"I honestly don't know," I said. "Your guess is as good as mine, but at least we have some guidance now, so we know what to look for."

"Alright, and what about the device? You mentioned something about a proper way to use it?"

I showed them the strange, handwritten instructions and then demonstrated how it worked. Hera had a water and earth affinity, while Prometheus had fire and earth. Layla had opened up metal, and Kate, fire.

"So, judging from these instructions, people didn't build

the scanners?" Hera asked, after reading the last page. "What does that mean, exactly?"

"Well, from what I gathered, they got them from... someone or somewhere. It means that we still know relatively little about where they from, but more importantly, how ether changes our bodies."

"Seems you've been busy while we've been gone," Hera said, nodding at the device in Prometheus' hand. "Part of me expected to come back and find you two lazily drifting down the river in old, patched up innertubes or something."

"That was actually our plan for tomorrow," Ajax interjected with a laugh.

"Fine," Hera snorted, as I pulled a bag free, then started dumping crystals into my outstretched hand. "You boys laze about while I gain some strength. Prom, would you stand watch while I...do the work?"

"But Kate and I were going to..." he stammered and looked to us.

"Hold your horses," Kate whispered, silencing everyone. "Am I the only one struggling with this news? Takemi, you're saying that you are basically years, if not decades, ahead of us? I mean how is...?"

"Possible?" I finished for her and she nodded.

"Yes and no. I lucked out in one regard and essentially unlocked a third realm ability, what they call the Nascent Soul Realm. It allows me to own martial arts in a way, but it doesn't actually make me any stronger than you. It does grant me better control over ether, however."

"If you had to guess, Takemi," Prometheus cut in, "how long will it take us to catch up?"

I sighed and stretched my back. This wasn't an altogether unexpected response, especially considering Layla and Kate had finally started their cultivation, but I also didn't want to get too deep in hypotheticals. Especially considering how little we actually knew.

"According to the instructions and observations that

came with our scanner, Earth is still in what they consider an "embryonic state" in regard to ether. They believe the threshold to be the 6th stage of the first realm, but according to the Duke's journals, another increase is expected. When that happens, it could jump to the eighth or ninth veins beyond that."

"Fuck," Prometheus cursed.

The word fuck summed it up pretty well. Every time I felt like I gained a little better understanding of how it all worked, I just ended up with more questions.

"Let me just talk that out for a second," Kate said. "It has been roughly seven years since ether appeared. Now, mind you, mankind didn't know what it was doing for the first couple of years, but according to this instruction manual, and if the dates are to be trusted, someone knew about it right away. They were tracking ether and studying it. They've been experimenting with it this whole time and yet the limits in place right now have never even been achieved. What does that mean for us just starting out? That it'll take us fourteen, twenty, or maybe even thirty years to unlock what you already possess? Just to get to the third realm?"

"Maybe," I guess, then shrugged. "There is no way to be sure, at least not without practice and putting in some work."

"That just seems like a really long road, especially when you don't know where it will ultimately lead you!" Kate breathed.

"Agreed!" Hera said, then promptly grabbed the crystals out of my hand.

"Wait, where are you going?" Kate asked.

"Just because you don't know where the road goes, that doesn't mean I'm not going to go screaming down it as fast as I can...with my hair on fire. Besides, this instruction manual said something opening a passive or active skill with each new vein. That sounds like speed and strength enhancers to me, and I am all about it!"

"Like my tough skin. It can deflect minor blows," Ajax

agreed. We all watched Hera make for the door. Prometheus started to follow, but I waved him back.

"We'll help Hera. You need to get caught up with your lady," I offered.

CHAPTER 16: WEAPONS OF WAR

As soon as I spoke, everyone scattered.

Kate and Prometheus ran for the door and both Ajax and Mike disappeared into the smith's workshop. That left Layla, Hera, and I standing there, looking at one another.

"Okay, when I said we'll help, I wasn't...ugh, never mind," I groaned and we moved into Mike's sitting room.

Hera sprawled out on the sofa, while Layla and I took the loveseat, ironically. My feisty warrior heroine clutched crystal after crystal, her eyes closed in periods of intense concentration and what seemed like blissful serenity.

Layla snuggled into me, but it wasn't all affection. She was tired, made weary by the long hike from the cabin. Before too long she was fast asleep and I was, in a way, left by myself.

I leaned her over onto a pillow and stood, then quietly made my way back into Mike's workshop. I found Ajax at a far worktable, but he was so singularly focused, the big guy didn't even hear me walk in.

Mike looked up and smiled. Moving over, I leaned on his table and studied the drawing laid out before him. The drawing, made on yellow parchment, appeared to be segments of clothing. He turned it toward me, so I could better see.

"I have been working on an idea for some time," he explained. "And now that you and Ajax both have metal affinities, it appears to finally be possible. I am looking to use ether to strip down metal, and while it is in a soft and malleable state, imbed it into thread. We would then weave that thread into fabric and make clothes. With the right metal, processed in just the right way, I believe we could make ordinary looking clothes capable of stopping a blade."

I breathed. "That would be incredibly handy. It would be armor that isn't armor. Far less weight and it would make a person less assuming."

"To an extent, yes. But like Kevlar and other weaves, it would only be so strong. Anyways, I won't know the limits until I am able to produce some first. But enough about shirts and trousers, I see a question spiring in your mind."

I looked around and then pulled out one of Manfred's small bags. Reaching inside, I slowly pulled out the H&K UMP45, and set it on the table before Mike.

The smith's eyes went wide and he glanced toward the front door. He slid the firearm sideways, out of easy view if anyone were to walk in from outside.

"You should be careful of who you let see this," he whispered. "Truth be told, the King has a very strict policy on relic weapons. Guns in particular."

"I know," I said, turning it over so he could see the other side in the light. I'd only looked at it several times since recovering it from the shelter beneath the mansion, but here in the bright lamp glow, I could finally see its true condition.

The forty-five caliber sub-machine gun was covered in surface rust, but it was intact. Several small dents covered the top of the receiver, and the front sight appeared to be bent. Mike depressed the magazine release, and with several forceful tugs, managed to get it to slide free. It was still loaded with copper-jacketed, soft-tip hollow points.

"My thought was along those lines actually," I said. "Guns are rare. Functioning ones are even rarer. What do you think? Is it salvageable? I guess I should have asked already, do you know much about firearms?"

Mike straightened and smiled, then patted the H&K with a large hand.

"My father was a machinist for Sig Sauer before the collapse. Well, before his MS got bad and his hands started to shake."

To prove his point, Mike went to work. He pulled a beat-up old toolbox out from under the workbench, tipped it open, and immediately pulled forth and lined up a number of punches and tools.

Within moments, he'd knocked out pins and had pulled the upper receive and lower apart. He broke the bolt free and removed the gas piston. A few moments after that, and the trigger assembly lay in a neat line before us.

The internal parts weren't in horrible shape, but they were all covered in a light, reddish patina. Oil residue still covered the inside of the receiver, so that told me that someone had maintained it at some point.

"It is not horrible, but it is not great either," Mike said, knocking the pin out of the bolt and freeing the extractor. If it is scrubbed down and cleaned properly, I could re-blue most of these parts and reassemble it. If anything is damaged…"

"Then it gets more complicated," I finished for him.

"Jawohl," he breathed, examining the parts. "And I do not have everything I would need. I have steel wool but would need oil and a few other things. You would need to be very cautious about who you ask and buy from, but if I make you a list, and you can procure the items, I should be able to refurbish this beauty into a lean, mean fighting machine."

"Deal!" I said, holding out my hand.

Mike's hand enveloped mine and we shook.

"Leave it with me," he said, pulling a small pair of spectacles from his shirt and sliding them on. "I will continue to strip it down."

"Mike…" I started to say but paused. I'd had an idea

blossom in my head when I first found the gun in that bunker but was afraid to bring it up to Ajax or the others. They'd never seemed like the right audience.

"Hmm?" he grunted, half-turning my way.

"With everything we know about ether and affinities now. Do you think it is possible to somehow infuse ether into bullets?"

The smith turned fully to me then and lifted a hand to scratch his chin. "It isn't impossible. But to what end?"

"Fighting Alfred's man," I explained. "I was only able to beat him because I have this stiletto from the ice spider. That is a tool that allowed me to overcome his superior strength, but tools wear out and break. I need more weapons like that. Say, what if we were able to repair this submachine gun, and somehow infuse ether into the bullets. Or, maybe we cast bullets using crystal shards. However it works. That would be a projectile that wouldn't just penetrate armor, but likely penetrate ether-hardened skin, too. What would the ether do once a bullet mushrooms or fragments?"

Mike's eyes widened as he started to understand my direction. "The ether would release and violently so. If the bullet did not penetrate, it would be like a small, explosive charge. But if it did end up inside someone, that would be an incredibly effective, and potentially messy weapon."

"Precisely."

"Okay. I like it. Here, while you are out and about, find me these items," he said, and hastily scribbled a list onto a small, torn piece of parchment. I have lead, brass, and plenty of copper here as scrap, but I will need the other ingredients to continue.

- Sulfur
- Saltpeter
- Silicone lubricant or
- Potassium nitrate
- Sodium Hydroxide

I inspected the list for a moment. The top three items

felt easy enough, considering we could claim items made from those metals and smelt them down, but the bottom two left me confused.

"Where am I supposed to find potassium nitrate and sodium hyd—?"

"Sodium Hydroxide. Jawohl. And the silicone lubricant is important. But if you can only find potassium nitrate, that will work, too. Silicone lubricants bonds better to moving parts, especially under heat. The other two are to blue the metal, which will be very important now, considering that you want to ratchet up this gun's natural destructive ability. We can play around with ether along the way, to either harden the blued surface, or increase the lubrication's ability to reduce friction. Bring me those items, and this will be a piece of pie."

"Do you mean a piece of cake?"

"No. I like pie more."

"Deal!" I said and tucked the list safely into my armor and returned to the sitting room.

I helped Hera swap out her crystals several times, as a sheen of sweat had come to cover her forehead. She had just exhausted another set of crystals when Ajax stomped out of the workshop behind me.

Turning, I found him standing in the middle of the room, hoisting a massive battle hammer over his shoulder.

"Rejoice! For I have returned. And I bear the sweet fruits of my labors."

"Oh, is that what it was?" I joked. "From where I was standing, it looked like you were standing over a table and scowling at a pile of metal."

"Joke all you want, my little friend. But you cannot rush, push, or force perfection."

He held out the hammer and I accepted it, the heavy weapon sagging in my arms. I couldn't deny that it looked well-crafted, but geez, even with my significantly enhanced strength, it felt heavy.

"And you're planning on swinging this more than what?

Two times during any fight?"

"Ha!" he barked, his smaller belly jiggling just a little. "Many skulls will be flattened by this hammer in the battles to come. Mark my words!"

A faint smell of metallic ether radiated off the hammer, the signature vibrating through my hands and arms. My gaze lifted to the big man's hands, and it was only then that I noticed he was wearing tight-fitting gauntlets. It appeared that he'd used the rest of Ivory's bones for some hand protection. That was a smart move considering how long he left himself open between swings.

"It is very nice and shiny! What's with the gauntlets?"

"Like them?" he asked, wiggling his eyebrows. "I hit them with this hammer and it didn't even leave a dent."

"Impressive! Are there any bones left?"

He pulled one of the gauntlets off and tossed it to me. The armored glove wasn't as heavy as I'd expected and provided surprising flexibility. The gauntlet, like the axe, was practically ringing with metal affinity. I slid it on my right hand and felt it adjust to my smaller build.

"Yes, just like the capes," Ajax laughed. "And yes, we've got enough left to make more gauntlets like this, armor, or maybe some weapons. Perhaps a shield!"

"Or a few arrows," I interjected. "Prometheus would definitely benefit from some armor piercing arrowheads."

"Agreed." Ajax mimicked pulling a bow back and releasing. "We'll see what we can come up with."

"And Hera?" I asked.

"Mike and I can look at forging a new spear. But that'll take more metal than arrowheads. We'll also need to source the right kind of wood for a handle."

"I think I am going to find this Heidi Lowitz and see what she has to say," Ajax said, after storing his hammer away. "I need a bit of a walk and some fresh air. Takemi, I'm not taking you. You make simple conversations complicated."

I flipped him a playful bird as he laughed and

disappeared out the door.

The big man left me with a groggy Layla, Hera still absorbing her crystals, and Mike working intently in the workshop. I pulled out the list of ingredients I'd need to get the H&K fixed and operational and added an item.

- Wood for Hera's spear.

Layla rolled over on the loveseat, yawned, and sat up.

"What are you looking at?" she asked.

"Oh, just a list of things I'll need to procure...somehow," I said, folded the list up, and put it away.

"I need some new clothes and supplies, considering Kate and I had to leave almost everything at the cabin. Care to do a little shopping?"

"We probably shouldn't leave Hera..." I started to say, but Mike cleared his throat in the other room.

"I'll lock up behind you and watch her. Go ahead."

CHAPTER 17: YOU NEED WHAT?

Layla and I made our way into Zurich, the city now alive with activity. I felt a little guilty leaving Hera under just Mike's supervision, but we heard him lock the door when we left, and that was a hefty deadbolt sliding shut.

We walked down the street and made several turns in silence. Layla picked up on this right away and actually trailed behind me for a while, so it wouldn't necessarily look like we were traveling together. Smart girl.

Once approaching the market, I pointed ahead and cut down a side street. Then, after weaving my way through a complicated series of side streets and alleys, I tracked Layla down again, but only after making sure no one was following me.

Zurich's central market was huge, spanning dozens of streets on either side of the river. Stalls and wagons covered the bridges, too, as produce growers, bakers, and craftsmen alike shouted to get people's attention.

"Okay, that was dramatic!"

I sighed and slumped against the side of a building, then pulled her into a tight hug. She didn't fight me but melted into me. When we pulled apart again, the questions were still there, waiting to be answered.

"It's been interesting, to say the least," I started. "Beginning with the fact that literally every group with designs for power in this city are watching us. And if they aren't watching us, they are trying to use us against the others."

Layla snorted. "Is that all? You made it sound like something serious."

"Right? Well, try this on for size. Half of the King's council wants us dead. I'm pretty sure the King does, too, but he needs us to represent Zurich in this Melee of Kings, where he hopes to bid on ether-rich zones. The Protectorate lobbied in our favor, but as with everyone, I'm not completely sure what their motivations are. The city is essentially sealed off right now, but Gruber has been allowing us to leave...sporadically. Now I find out that someone followed Hera and Prometheus to the cabin, and they meant you all harm. Oh, and we were running a little errand for our protectorate friends the other night, and one of Alfred Durheim's lieutenants—he never did tell us his name—corners us in the late Duke's mansion. He wanted us dead, too."

Layla started to shake her head but waited until I was done to speak. Part of me knew what she'd say even before she started.

"Screw this place and screw them. We don't need this. Let's just go. There are whole cities out there left uninhabited. We could find a little place of our own. Maybe we could just live at the cabin."

"You have no idea how good that sounds," I said and kissed her cheek. "But these are not the kind of people we can afford to anger. Alfred said that if we tried to skip down, he would send men to Vaduz and not just burn the whole city down but track down anyone that ever knew us and have them publicly executed."

Layla's eyes went wide. "And you believe him?"

I nodded. "I think he would kill everyone...no, anyone

that got in his way. The whole lot of them are crazy."

She went quiet for a few moments, as if troubling over our predicament.

"So, you can't leave but you can't really stay, either."

"That is more or less our dilemma. Hang around in a city full of people that either want us dead, or hate us, but need our help. It doesn't fill me with the warm and fuzzies."

"So, Takemi—" she started to say, but I stopped her, then leaned in, and whispered in her ear.

"Kenji. Or, you can call me Ken."

Layla eyed me for a moment. "Hera told me! How much can you remember? Do you remember us?"

I nodded but switched directions and shook my head. "Some memories came back, but not much. It was strange. I kept having the same dream, but it was...broken? Missing details? We'd left Zurich and found a mansion in the hills. We stopped there for the night and poof," I said, emphasizing the noise with a popping gesture. "The dream came together and I suddenly knew my name and where I was from and who I'd been..." I trailed off, deciding that telling Layla about a woman I'd once been in a relationship with, perhaps even engaged to, was not a good idea.

She waited to see if I would continue.

"Well, that seems like a good start, at least. Maybe more will come back later."

Layla squeezed my arm and we started walking together again. I could tell she was happy, but worried, too. If more of my memories resurfaced, would that change who I had become? Would I revert back to the old me? The one that seemed content to use and cast her aside? Part of me had the exact same concern. I was less concerned with reclaiming my old self anymore. Survival had become my number one goal.

We walked through the market stalls, marveling at the wide array of cultivated crops. For a mountain city with limited farm land, the people seemed to be doing well. But judging from the size of one summer squash—almost seven and a half feet long—I guessed that ether was at play.

Layla and I left the outdoor market behind and walked down the streets next, looking in through the large, front windows.

"What will you do?" she whispered, as we stopped before a small leatherworker's store. "If you go and fight their melee, and win? What would stop them from just killing you?"

"Sadly," I exhaled, "nothing. Although I would like to think gratitude would go a long way. I found a weapon in the bunker beneath that mansion I told you about. If I can get Mike the right materials, he said he can get it working for me. My hope is that it will provide enough of a deterrent if someone were to turn on us."

"Another sword?"

I shook my head and refused to explain further.

"Well, let's find me some clothes and then see if we can't locate what we need," Layla smiled, and pulled me into the leather shop.

I swallowed my pride and helped her shop for clothes for what felt like days. In reality, it was a few hours. But together, we were able to get her and Kate well outfitted with some durable, travel-friendly outfits.

We'd barely walked back out of the last shop before Layla grabbed my arm and pointed across the street. My gaze locked onto a man standing by a lamp post, the oil flame already flickering.

"No, not him. Look at the shop. It is an alchemist's shop. I'd imagine that is as good a place as any to start looking, right?"

I crossed the street at Layla's urging, my gaze still locked on the guy with a staring problem. When I got closer, I realized he was blind and begging for spare change. Boy, did I feel like an ass. I'd also never told her what kind of weapon Mike and I were working on, so I started to wonder how an alchemist would be able to help.

A small bell jingled above the door as we walked in, and

I was assaulted with an invisible cloud of complicated smells and aromas. Not all were pleasant, although my eyes and nose didn't immediately start to burn, so that was a good sign.

The shop was small, with neatly stacked barrels against the wall to our left, and floor to ceiling shelves occupying the walls ahead and to the right. A long, high workbench sat at the back of the space, where a tall and rather spindly man worked with a set of scales.

"Willkommen," the thin shop owner said, without looking up from his work.

I returned the greeting and moved to the right and started inspecting the items on the shelves. Assorted glass containers covered the racks, each full of a different ingredient or concoction. Labels had been painstakingly handwritten and stuck in place, although I could not read the writing.

The tall shop owner continued to mix compounds as we worked our way around to his workbench. Up close he looked even taller, with a rounded back, shoulders, and bent neck. He had a long, narrow jaw, thin lips, hooked nose, and relatively small, dark eyes. In more than one way, he looked like a crane, just minus the wings and wearing spectacles.

"Was kann ich für Dich tun?" he said, inclining his head toward me.

"English?" I asked hopefully.

The shopkeeper sighed dramatically, took off his reading glasses, and nodded.

"Yah. A little."

"Perfect," I said and pulled the list out of my pocket. "I am looking for..." I paused before reading the first item and decided that it might be better to just have him read the list instead.

Sliding his spectacles back down his nose, the alchemist accepted the note and started to read. His eyebrows rose as his eyes tracked downward, and by the time he finished and lowered the list, they had disappeared into his hairline.

"I have sulfur and can mix together some of these

others, but…" the alchemist abruptly stopped and removed his glasses. He looked over my shoulder and shuffled around to the door, dropped a locking bar into place, and hurried back.

"Okay. I know who you are. We all do. You wear zhe wolf cloaks to identify yourself as some sort of pack. All of the shop owners have been warned about you, told to stay clear. They said you are trouble and will only bring down trouble and despair onto our heads. I shouldn't have even let you into my shop."

"Stay clear? Wait, hold on a minute," Layla said, shaking her head.

"No, I am sorry. My business is struggling enough as it is. If they find out that I helped you, it will be the death of this shop…"

"Please," I said, fighting his attempt to shoo us toward the door. "Do you have these ingredients? I can pay. We can be in and out. No one will see."

"I am not a fool. I know what you are making here," he said, holding up the list. "Sulfur, saltpeter, and potassium nitrate. You are making explosives. Do you know what they would do to me if they found out I provided you with those ingredients, and zhen you…say, blew up some building here in zhe city? They would string me up and let everyone bludgeon me with stones. And if that didn't kill me. Then the birds would pick me apart afterwards. Nein! Nein!"

"Wait! Please!" I said, set my feet in the ground, and pushed back. The spindly man simply bounced off of me, his effort to shove me back to no avail. When it became clear that he couldn't push us out, he spread his arms, and changed tactics.

"Bitte. I have a wife and children. They will suffer. We will all suffer."

"Listen to me. I don't want to blow anything up," I said. "Yes, I need these ingredients to make gunpowder, but it is for out there." I pointed to a vague direction beyond the city. "My team and I are venturing into the zoo very soon, and we are doing it *for* Zurich. They can tell you whatever they like, but the truth is, we are representing this city and everyone in it. If you help me, then you give us not just a better chance to survive but succeed. For Zurich."

I gave him my best sales pitch, and although not all of it was completely accurate, it also wasn't a lie. We were representing Zurich, and thus, him. The gunpowder, if Mike could get the H&K working properly in time, was also one extra tool to help keep us alive.

"You said your shop is struggling," Layla said and moved in, laying a hand on the alchemist's arm. "How can we help?"

"I..." he stammered for a moment. I watched the battle rage in his mind, as he fought for reasons to kick us out. But Layla had a calming effect, and if his shop was indeed struggling, then he was likely weighing the odds. After a painful few moments of deliberation, the alchemist exhaled dramatically and nodded, then patted Layla's hand.

"It would probably be easier to just show you. Come with me," he said, and gestured to a door behind his workbench.

We followed him through the door and into a storeroom. This space was almost larger than his shop. Beams and posts supported large crates and barrels, but I saw burlap sacks of dry ingredients as well. The space smelled like leather and aged wood.

The alchemist produced a key from his apron, unlocked a door, and pushed it open. We all filed out into a small yard, the exterior perimeter surrounded by a stone wall.

A smell hit me almost instantly—manure.

The alchemist, stretching to his full height in the open air, walked over to a weathered, wood trough where an antique wheelbarrow and shovel sat. Flies buzzed around the trough where the last vestiges of manure sat in a dry pile.

"If you walked here through the market, then you know how important farming is to Zurich. If you understand this, then you also know that fertilizer is of the utmost importance. The majority of my business, or, at least what used to be my business, is in that. And yet, a few months ago, a wealthy man in town took over."

"Took over? What are they using for fertilizer?" Layla asked, but her eyes dropped to the empty manure trough before the alchemist could respond. "Oh. Yes. Got it. Manure. But...how does someone take over the manure trade?"

The alchemist slumped. "The King and his bureaucrats control every element of trade in the city. Only those granted with permits can raise livestock. It used to be that manure had to be collected and properly disposed of. But now that the livestock farmers know how valuable it is, they sell it off to the highest bidder."

"And this man stepped forward and simply offered the farmers more money than you?" Layla asked.

The alchemist nodded. "Noah Weber. He claims to be a distant cousin to the Duke of Saxony. If such a person even exists."

"How can we help?" Layla asked, stepping in to take over the conversation. I had zero qualms with her doing so, as she'd always shined while helping solve disputes in the tavern in Vaduz.

"It's not even like his product is good," the alchemist said with a shrug. "He doesn't process or refine it, just packages up raw manure and ships it out in wagons. My fertilizer was prime, safe, and stable."

"So, your only real problem is supply, right? Does the King have any say in who the farmer's buy their fertilizer from?"

"No. And my customers know that my product is better, but they have no choice right now."

I listened to Layla and the alchemist go back and forth on the issue. A dozen ideas popped up in my head, but to my shame they were all related to violence or the threat of violence. I almost chuckled when I realized that I'd been considering threatening cattle farmers with violence unless they sold their animal's excrement to someone else.

Looking up, I realized that Layla and the alchemist had gone quiet and were both looking at me.

"Hypothetically speaking," I started, putting on a straight face. "Does it matter *where* the manure comes from? And how much would you need to get your fertilizer business back up and running?"

"The source is actually quite important. Droppings from wild animals is usually composed of more variety. Those animals are also more likely to absorb naturally occurring ether, as well. So, all the better. With my chemical processes, I could quite easily produce two to two hundred and fifty kilograms of fertilizer using only thirty-five to forty kilos of manure. That would get me back in business, although I would have to secure a new, regular supply."

"Takemi, why are you asking? You wouldn't know where to find...oh!" Layla said and seemed to finally understand why I had asked.

"It feels weird talking about animal poo like this," I said, chuckling. "But if I can get you forty kilos of...the dirty stuff, will you provide the items on my list?"

The alchemist thought for a moment, his expression changing several times, then he turned to me and promptly held out his hand.

"Jawohl. I would honor zat deal."

I grasped his hand and gave it a sturdy shake.

"Kenji Nakamura," I said, "but you can call me Ken."

"Very well, Mr. Nakamura. I am Heinrich Bachman. If you can deliver me what you claim, I will have your goods ready. I only ask that you do not share from whom you acquired them. The Protectorate would not be pleased if they discovered I was making such ingredients for someone."

"Fair enough," I said, nodding. "I'd better let you get back to work, so you can complete my order. Besides, I have some wood and...other things to collect."

CHAPTER 18: WE'RE RUNNING OUT OF TIME?

The smithy was surprisingly empty when Layla and I returned. Mike was sitting in a shadowy corner with a cold drink in hand. The H&K was nowhere to be see, so I started to wonder about where he'd put it and how much work he'd gotten done. I'd learned one thing about Mike and Ajax since being introduced to their shop. When those guys started a project, they didn't stop until it was done.

Layla handed me the long piece of ash we'd procured while in the city, but as I set it on the workbench, I noticed a finished spear laying out in the open.

"Don't apologize," Mike said, finishing his drink. "You weren't out too long. I got to the point where I couldn't do anything else on your...special project, and was bored, so I made Hera a spear."

I nodded, sizing up the new weapon.

The spear was easily seven feet long, with a stout, multibladed tip. The forged blades on the front were nearly thirty centimeters long, with the central, stabbing edge twisted like a drill bit. The two secondary blades were shorter and slanted at what appeared to be a forty-degree angle. Small cutting edges had been soldered into place behind that, meaning that if Hera missed a thrust, she could inflict almost as much damage with the return pull. The spear shaft was dark, oiled wood, wrapped in braided leather. A shiny metal shoe sat on the rear of the shaft, serving as an additional weapon and counter weight.

"It looks like a deadly weapon, especially in Hera's hands," I said.

"Thanks," he said, opening an antique fridge next to him. The smith pulled two bottles of cold beer out and handed them to us. "Compliments of our local brewer. All I had to do was find a way to embed ether crystals into the coolant. As it turns out, ether and old-world refrigerant work very well together, and it doesn't need electricity. I developed an efficient way to keep food cold and earned free beer for life all in one lucky stroke!"

"Genius!" Layla said, before tipping the bottle back and taking a drink.

We shared a drink in silence, before Mike cleared his throat.

"How was your search?"

"I found a man, an alchemist who can get me what I need, but I need to do something for him. Let's just say I have to do a little gathering."

"Okay. Well, if you are going to want your...special thing done before you all have to leave the city, you'd better get a move on. Ajax said your departure is fast approaching, and I am not a genie."

"You made a refrigerator that runs on crystals," Layla said, "That sounds awfully magical to me."

"But still. Try and give me as much time as possible, because although I might look like a wizard, I am only a craftsman."

"A really, really talented and good looking one!" Layla added.

The smith waved her off, as crimson spread to his cheeks. We finished our beers, checked in on Hera, who was still sprawled out on the sofa, an empty pile of crystals covering the ground beneath her, and promptly left again.

"A really, really talented and good looking one?" I asked Layla as we moved toward the south gate.

She shrugged and threw me a mischievous smile.

"Men work faster and harder when they feel appreciated! I am just trying to help out and do my part."

"I have zero complaints with that," I laughed.

We strategized on the move, considering all we really had with us were four hands, no gloves, and a couple storage bags. The idea of carrying animal poop back into the city with my bare hands didn't really excite me, so we cut west and over the bridge on our way south.

We only had to zigzag our way down two streets before I found a general goods store called Führmann's Trockenware. A little, old couple ran it. The woman was tiny, with a stooped back, and short curly hair. Her husband, Gunter, was nearly my height, with a short nose, and fantastic head of pure, silver hair.

They greeted us as we walked in and then escorted us around, pointing to all the products they made right there in house. The problem wasn't finding something that would work for our...dirty job. It was picking the *best* thing. They had burlap sacks, woven baskets, pine crates, wheel barrows, metal bins, feed troughs, chicken wire, and so much more.

In the end, I went with burlap sacks, as it felt like it would be less suspicious carrying sacks back into the city, than pushing a wheel barrow full of animal crap past the guards. Then again, it might be fun having them summon Captain Gruber, just so we could watch them try to search the contents of our cart.

Layla led me into the hills outside the city, and despite my suggestion that she walk behind me once we drew closer to Omega's camp, she refused.

"Just wait and see," she said.

The wolf, it turned out, established residence in the old mansion outside the city. And who could blame him? It came complete with a partially collapsed in-ground pool, a carriage house full of critters, and a bunker for every wolf's nuclear fallout needs.

We circled around the right side of the massive structure, after crawling through the hole in the wall. It seemed empty and abandoned, until something rustled in a bush on the far side, and a moment later, an enormous dark shape bounded right for us.

I feinted left but went right. Layla stood her ground, held out a hand, and yelled, "sit!" To my amazement, Omega skidded to a halt in the grass, going from a full sprint to sitting in a blink of an eye.

"He's actually very well behaved when handled properly," she said, with a proud smile.

"I'd say," I said and approached.

The wolf had grown since I saw him last, but it went beyond his height, width, and girth. His gleaming fur was thicker, his ears larger and taller, and the metallic spines growing out from around his shoulders were more pronounced. There was a strength and confidence radiating from his eyes that was absent before. Omega wasn't just growing into his potential, but he was becoming a hunter.

"Hello, boy," I said, and approached.

Omega growled and snorted, eyeing me for a moment, before lowering his head and nuzzling my hand with his nose. I smoothed back the fur between his ears, quietly admiring how much larger he felt. In a strange moment, the wolf vibrated. He closed his eyes and leaned into me, the spark between us flooding me with recognition and familiarity. It was in that moment that I realized how much I'd missed the wolf.

"Okay, now what?" Layla asked, looking apprehensively around the courtyard.

"Now we look for...poop," I said, throwing on my best

fake smile.

"Oh, yay! Hey, Kate, what did you do this afternoon?" she asked, then turned, as if talking to someone else. "Oh, Prom took me to this nice little restaurant down on the river and we had a delicious candle-lit dinner. Then we went for a walk and made love under the moonlight. What about you, Layla?"

I snorted, knowing exactly where this was going, but didn't want to interrupt. The show was too entertaining to miss, besides, she'd insisted on coming.

"Well, first Ken took me on a nice little shopping trip into the city and we bought a stick." She turned again.

"A stick?"

"Yes. A stick for Hera's spear. Then we bought bags and went for a hike up the mountain. He took me to this beautiful, crumbling mansion in the forest and then picked up poop together." She put her hands on her hips and tipped her head to the side.

"You picked up poop?"

"Yes. Forty kilograms of it—"

"And you're going to help me carry all eighty pounds of it back to the city, too! If we can get it all into two bags, maybe we can hold hands on the way?"

"Ahhh. You're sweet!" she said.

"I know how to show a girl a good time."

We laughed good and hard after that, then went to work, searching the mansion's grounds. Omega had just returned from his trip with Prometheus and Hera, but evidently the man hadn't been unoccupied while he was gone. We quickly found several...sizable deposits.

The wolf watched me gingerly scoop the excrement off the ground and into a bag. But his excitement turned to curiosity as we continued to work. By the time we rounded the last corner and approached the front again, Omega was leading from spot to spot, his nose down and tail wagging.

We cleared the yard and had what felt like five to ten kilograms total. A weird thought, for sure, being disappointed that we weren't able to lug around more poo. But we had a wolf with an ultra-sensitive nose.

Omega led us out through the wall and into the woods, his massive, dark form bounding bunny-like through the underbrush ahead. We'd only tracked for ten, maybe fifteen minutes into the woods before a herd of enormous elk broke from their hiding. I jumped back and drew my katana to protect Layla as they first appeared, but my wolf counterpart effectively drove them off to the north.

Evidently, these elk were three to four times the size of any deer I'd ever seen before. Their hoof prints were three times as wide as my foot and twice as long. Good grief. But what is large, needs to eat a lot, and that also means...

"Shit. Holy shit. Unholy shit. This is ridiculous," Layla cursed dramatically a short while later. The elk didn't just fulfil our quota of forty kilograms but surpassed it many times over. I fought the urge to gather everything we could find, and instead decided we didn't want to set an unrealistic expectation with our new alchemist friend.

We tromped back toward the mansion just a short while later, hefting heavy, triple-bagged burdens of pure fertilizer potential with us. Oh, the things I was willing to do to secure a safe future for myself and our group.

Omega escorted us to the wall of the mansion and I moved to give him some goodbye scratches, only to pause as my gaze caught on something massive and brown laying in the middle of the trail ahead. The wolf's hackles raised, the hair on my arms standing on end at the same time.

"Is that—?" I started to ask.

"Yup," Layla nodded, showing a bit of apprehension. "I think we all developed a different name for him by the time we got here. I call him Lazy Bones."

Omega led me toward the hillock of brown fur, then loped ahead, growled loudly, and snapped his teeth into the bear's backside. It groaned. That was all.

After not receiving a response, Omega jumped forward

and hit the bear with his front paws again and again. Grunting, the large animal proceeded to roll over and scratch its belly. Then, apparently untroubled, the bear Layla called Lazy Bones turned its massive head our way and considered us...upside down.

I slid my katana back into its scabbard and moved forward. The bear watched me, its nose moving as it sniffed the air. I dropped the bags of animal droppings as the massive brown shape rolled over and pushed off the ground.

Omega snarled and circled, but my instincts told me not to move. And it went beyond the simple fact that backing away was prey response. I'd accepted Omega into my pack but done so establishing myself as the stronger wolf. If he brought this bear into our little animal family, then that would mean I would have to hold myself as someone unafraid. A leader, tall and strong.

Lazy Bones groaned and snorted, his terrifyingly long claws rending the dirt as he moved. On all fours his head hung above mine, but when the bear pushed back onto his hind legs, he stood like a wall of muscle, fur, and teeth.

He didn't roar or growl, bare his teeth, or swipe those deadly claws, but just stood there. I pulled both my katana and wakizashi free from their scabbards and stepped forward. The blades hung loose at my sides, but I made sure he could see them.

Omega snarled and Lazy Bones finally roared. The noise was impressive. A rib-shaking bellow that actually changed the raging drum solo of my heart. And I stepped forward, not back.

Lazy Bones shook his head and roared again, this time pulling his lips back to expose some of the largest teeth I'd ever seen.

Alpha's don't back down from anything, I thought, trusting in my strength. I stepped forward again, pulled my lips back, and snarled right back at the bear.

He dropped to all fours before me, the impact shaking

the ground. It also brought his face to within inches of mine. He breathed and snorted, tasting the air. Was he testing my scent? Smelling for fear?

I raised my arms, lifting both blades above my head, and pushed ether forth into my muscles. Then I screamed, pushing my voice forth with more force than I ever had before. Sucking in my air, I continued until my voice became hoarse and my throat became raw. And in a moment that satisfied me beyond words, Lazy Bones pawed at the ground, shook his enormous head, and sagged back onto his haunches.

The bear snorted, rumbled quietly, and bowed his head.

"Holy shit," I breathed. "I think I just accepted a bear into the family."

CHAPTER 19: WE ALREADY HAVE PLANS

After his authority show, Lazy Bones relaxed and started to mill around the mansion's courtyard. It was surreal, watching the mammoth creature lumber to and fro, like a hill of fur and muscle. But as lethargic as he appeared, I knew that if something angered or challenged him, he would change, and few animals could match a bear's fury.

If he was truly safe to keep around, Lazy Bones would make our group stronger. That is, if we could find a place to call home...away from the scheming lords and factions.

I romped with Omega for a short while. The wolf clearly missed me and it just made our departure again even more difficult. As much as I enjoyed Zurich's amenities and perceived safety, I longed for something quieter and less populated.

Hans Gruber's men flagged us down as we approached the south gate.

"You know the drill, sell sword. Nothing enters the city without our say so," the lead guard said, the ornamental plume on his helmet blowing in the wind.

I studied him for a moment but suppressed a smirk. The feathers made them look like birds. Or men pretending to be them, anyways.

At my direction, Layla dropped her heavy bag onto the ground next to the two I was carrying. I pulled all three open and stepped back, thoroughly prepared for the show.

The guards came forward and stooped down over the bags. One man actually moved to reach inside, but flinched and stepped back, waving his hands before his face.

"Was ist diese scheiße?" one guard cursed and turned away.

"Um, that is...animal feces," I said, crossing my arms over my chest. "You know? Scat, poop, kaka, excrement?"

"We know what zos things are," the lead guard growled and wrinkled his nose. "But why are you carrying around shit in bags?"

I stifled several dozen witty and sarcastic remarks, realizing that the more I played around, the more I increased the chances of getting myself, or others, into trouble.

"I thought it was a strange request, too," I sighed, "but we have a mutual acquaintance that is running some agricultural experiments and was in need. It's not my usually kind of job, but you know. When a friend is in need, you help out."

"It smell so bad," one of the guards complained and spat onto the ground.

"You stop smelling it after a while," Layla said and shrugged.

"The King has declared the city sealed, but Captain Gruber has afforded you certain liberties. No one said that people cannot carry poo into the city, so I guess you can go. Just be quick about it. And for God's sake, wash your hands," the lead guard said.

I mock saluted and we closed the bags, hefted them to our shoulders, and with smiles larger than the circumstance warranted, trekked back into the city.

Layla and I quickly became somewhat of an oddity, not that two people carrying bags of poop down the street shouldn't. But people caught whiff of us coming, moved out of the way, and then made their opinions about our smell publicly known.

"Nothing to smell here, people," Layla said, lifting her eyebrows at an older couple. We both laughed hard at that one, despite the crowd's disapproval.

The sun was setting by the time we arrived at Heinrich's shop, so we cut around the side, and let ourselves through the small gate in the fence. I dropped my heavy sacks into the alchemist's empty manure trough and then took Layla's burden off her shoulder.

We'd barely had time to turn around when Heinrich appeared through the back door, his face wrinkling up in confusion.

"You are back already? I didn't expect you for...well, I figure such an errand would take a day, perhaps more."

He joined us at the trough and leaned over the bags, inspecting our delivery from a safe distance.

"It looks and smells rich," he said.

I nodded, although I didn't know exactly how to respond. Was "rich" a good thing, when describing an animal's droppings? If it was like food—Ahhh, why did I go and do that, gross—that usually meant the richer, the better, right?

"This is sehr gut!" Heinrich nodded and then turned to me. "I didn't expect you back until at least tomorrow, but I have been working on your order, and have something I would like to show you. Come."

Layla and I followed the alchemist back into his shop, the tall man locking the door, and pulling the shade down over the window behind us. We walked into his shop, only to find the space alight from candles and several oil lamps. The space looked cozy, even with the Bunsen burner and other equipment bubbling away on the workbench.

He waved us over to the workspace and I spotted a number of stoppered glass bottles, as well as several bowls holding powdery substances. The air smelled funny—the odors were sharp and biting, the kind that made my nose and eyes burn a little.

"Some of your needs are easy," Heinrich started to explain and lifted a bottle of yellow powder off the workbench. "Sulfur. This I keep in stock to make certain medicines. Oil mixed with silicone, a simple process."

He picked up a bottle of cloudy liquid and set it next to the yellow powder, then continued,

"The potassium nitrate is not easy. But knowing it is used to make gun powder, let me first say this. The sulfur is worthless without it, and potassium nitrate, which is also known as saltpeter, is not something I can quickly make."

My hopes fell as he spoke, as I realized the weapon I'd hoped to use as a negotiation aid, wouldn't be available.

"But..." Heinrich said and reached under his workbench. After rummaging around for a moment, he straightened and set a black bottle in front of me. "I just happen to have a humble amount of ready to use gunpowder here. It belonged to my brother. He loaded his own cartridges."

The bottle featured a simple white label, and although most of the ink had faded, I could just make out "RUAG Ammotec" with a chart of much smaller letters.

"I have been meaning to throw the whole lot away— scale, press, and all the other tools, but it is all yours if you want it. We will consider the debt settled for the shipment you brought me, but you must mustn't tell anyone that it came from me."

I felt a smile spread to my face as he started to pull tools, scales, and other supplies out from under the workbench. I saw a bag of empty brass casings, dies, and so much more.

"And the other compounds I need will be included?" I asked, hopefully.

"I imagine you wanted the sodium hydroxide to make a gun bluing compound. You would need the saltpeter for that, too, but I have something that will work in its place," he said and walked to a nearby shelf. Holding up a candle for light, Heinrich studied labels for a long while before pulling one small bottle free and returning.

He set it down before us, the liquid inside almost shimmering in the light.

"This is mixture of mercury and chloride...bichloride, to be specific. Mix that with the sodium hydroxide under heat and it should provide the same effect. But be cautious. Mercury should not be allowed to touch the skin."

"I'll take it all, but are you sure that you don't want more in return?" I asked.

Heinrich vehemently shook his head.

"You are doing me a favor by taking this off my hands. These items are all verboten. So, you should pack them away and hide them well."

Pulling a spare bag free, Layla and I packaged up our new treasures. We made for the back door to leave, but Heinrich blocked our way before we could step outside. When he spoke, his voice was so low I could barely hear him.

"I do not know who you are planning to fight, but that is not my concern. As long as you do not harm the good people, the commoners here in my city, I will consider you a friend. The powder I have given you will only go so far, but if you pledge to continue bringing me manure for fertilizer, I will cultivate as much saltpeter as you need. Jawohl? We have a deal?"

Heinrich held out his hand and I shook it, studying the alchemist's eyes. There was no malice or trickery there, just the tired gaze of a man trying to survive.

"You have a deal, Heinrich."

We stuffed the bag of reloading supplies into one of the bags we'd used to carry back the droppings, providing a little insurance in case someone got overly curious. But with nighttime descending, the streets were filled with far less traffic.

Layla and I arrived back at Mike's smithy to a rather full sitting room and boisterous conversation. Hera stood in the middle, a massive pile of spent crystals laid out at her feet. Ajax was just inside the door, with Kate and Prometheus bracketing Mike.

"Where in the furthest depths of hell on Earth have you two been?" Ajax asked, spinning around on us.

"Whoa. It is good to see you, too, my good...freund," I said, using one of the few words in German I'd been able to learn.

"Did you see my new spear?" Hera asked, interrupting.

"I did," I responded, and tossed the burlap sack into Mike's hands. He lifted it to his face, sniffed, and almost dropped it. "Look inside."

Mike hesitantly peeled the burlap open and peered inside. Then he cursed.

"This is...perfect. Where did you...? Never mind, I don't need to know," he said, looked up and flashed an excited smile, and ran back into his workshop.

"Back to your spear," I said, turning to Hera.

"Want to spar? I want to see if I can get past the legendary guard of Takemi Two Blades."

"Is that really such a good idea right now?" Layla asked.

"Just a little sparring session can't hurt," Hera argued. "Unless I skewer him, that is! Ahahahaha."

"If anyone is gonna skewer him, it'll be me," Layla argued and stepped forward.

Hera's eyes went wide, Ajax chuckled crudely, and Kate's mouth fell open.

"You shady lady," Kate laughed. "I didn't know you were the take charge type, sis!"

"Okay, I am suddenly not in the mood to spar anymore," Hera sighed.

"Is everyone done with all the chit chat?" Ajax yelled, his tone decidedly less jovial than everyone else. I stiffened as everyone nodded and waited for him to continue.

"Word has come down. We depart for the Melee of Kings in the morning. So, take care of whatever business you might have tonight. Come dawn we are on the road."

That news crashed down over me like a bucket of ice water. We'd been preparing for the melee and lost track of how much time was passing.

Ajax opened a wine cabinet on the far wall, rifled around inside, and reemerged with a dark red bottle.

"The woman. The banker...Heidi?" I asked.

"It wasn't the, ugh, how would you Americans put it? The financial win fall we were hoping for?"

"I think you mean a financial windfall," Kate corrected.

"Ahh. Whatever. You know what I mean," Ajax spat, and for one of the first times, he looked upset and frustrated.

"They...meaning the nobles, know something is off. I went to see Heidi, and wouldn't you know it, there were no less than eight people watching the building. I stumbled onto one of them purely by accident. Luckily, he didn't spot me and I was able to just saunter on by. But once I looked, I spotted them easily enough. They know something happened to this Seneschal guy and they are protecting their money."

"What does that mean?" Layla asked.

"We're running low on funds," I explained.

"We could double our crystal stash easily enough," Prometheus chimed in. "If what Hera told me about this underground Arena is true."

"Wait. You want to fight? In the arena?" Layla said.

"If they let us, it is not a bad option," Ajax said, working to remove the wine bottle's cork.

"We bought two new travel bags. Leather and high quality," Kate explained. "We are going to fill them with clothes, basic hygiene, and water. But what we really need for the road is food. We are representing Zurich, but they refuse to provide anything to help with the travel. In fact, judging from Prom's interaction with a few food vendors earlier, I think they are being forced to charge us double, maybe even triple."

"We risk our lives and fight for them, so they can lobby new treaties and gain access to ether rich zones, and they price gouge us?" I asked, the thought making my blood boil.

"They hold all the cards," Ajax responded.

"I've got a bad feeling about this whole mess," Prometheus whispered.

"Me, too," Hera spat, "but what do we do? They're holding Vaduz over our heads. That creep, Alfred, promised to firebomb the whole town unless we tow his line. What is stopping them from just—"

"Surrounding and killing us once this Melee of Kings is over?" I interjected. "Nothing. And that is exactly what I expect them to do."

The group went quiet for several long moments. I heard Mike moving and banging around in his shop and could only hope that he was listening and making progress on my secret weapon.

"I think I need a close-range weapon for when I'm out of arrows. And more arrows," Prometheus whispered.

"We can do something about that," I responded.

"They'll just gouge us on price. And what will that leave us with for everything else?" he shot back.

I looked to Ajax who nodded. "We'll get you set up, but only once we are out of the city," the big guy said. "Speaking of which, we retrieved these from our treacherous little friend the other night."

He dropped eleven rings into my palm. I recognized several as belonging to the Seneschal. Ether started to pool in my hand and I felt Ivory's presence shift.

We identified two of the eleven pieces of jewelry that were ordinary and spent the next twenty minutes embedding them with ether, and then expanding it to form storage rings. They were small, each about half the space of my wolf statue, but would do in a pinch.

"Hera, one for you, and the other goes to Kate and Prom for now," I said, handing out the two rings.

"We know they need us," Ajax said, took a swig of wine straight from the bottle, and passed it to Kate. "But they don't need all of us. That means from this moment forth, we don't go anywhere alone. We watch each other's backs, and we don't take chances."

"So, you're saying I shouldn't pick fights with them once we're on the road?" I asked.

"More or less, yes," he said, as Kate handed me the bottle.

I tipped it to my lips and took a drink. "Well then, who's up for one last night in the town?"

CHAPTER 20: SWINDLING SWINDLERS

Layla threw me a nervous glance as we settled into our seats in the underground arena. We scooched up to the crescent-shaped table as I surveyed the crowd.

The typical haze hung over the space, but it was quieter than the last time we'd gone. It was early, and half of the seats were still empty, but a quick glance up confirmed that most of the premium boxes above were full. From what I could tell of the shadowy spaces, that is.

"With everything going on, I still don't think this is a good idea. We should have stayed in, packed, and prepared to get out of town quietly," she whispered and leaned into me.

"I don't disagree," I responded, as my gaze caught on another group of people entering. It was no one I recognized, but in a city like Zurich, that didn't mean much. How many people did Alfred have in his employ? How many people did the King have following us? And of those groups, how many wanted us dead?

Too many questions, I thought and shook myself free. *Stay in the present. Distracted people die.*

"But Ajax is right. We don't know what we'll find on the road. And we know even less about what awaits us in this 'zoo'.

We need to be prepared for anything. Meaning, potentially buying our way out of some bad situations. A big stash of crystals and other valuables is a must," I added, then leaned in and kissed her cheek.

She nodded but didn't relax. How could she? She'd just arrived in the big city, heard nothing but stories about danger, and the first place she went was a seedy, underground fighting pit.

"If I have to fight, I'll be safe," I whispered and squeezed her arm. She draped a hand over mine and squeezed back. "I'm stronger than anyone I've seen fight down here."

"Than anyone you've *seen*," she whispered, correcting me. "What I'm worried about are the ones you have *not* seen! Don't get yourself hurt, because then I would have to start kicking some ass."

The mock-angry expression filled my mind with images of her sprouting horns and going wild, killing everyone in the arena.

The arena filled around us and the fights began. Layla, Hera, Prometheus, and I watched the bouts for almost half an hour before Ajax arrived. A well-dressed, middle-aged woman accompanied him, her heels thumping loudly against the stairs.

I twisted in my seat to greet them and found my attention drawn to her outfit. She wore an expensive-looking blue dress, the shape and cut revealing more leg, stomach, and cleavage than Layla would prefer. Although, I took no issue with it.

She had long black hair, wore bright red lipstick, and accentuated her eyes with green eyeshadow and black eyeliner. She looked like a million bucks, or crystals, in our case, which just caused the butterflies in my stomach to take flight.

"Hello, Ajax's people," she said, waving to our table. Her eyes didn't linger on any one of us that long, which gave her a rather dismissive air. Her nose wasn't elevated, so she had that much going for her.

"We've got a really full card tonight, so you're being granted a single match to see if the crowd likes you," she continued, her eyes sweeping out over the crowd. "I can and will offer you more mat time depending on how the crowd reacts. Like I said if they like you."

"That sounds reasonable," I replied and squeezed Layla's hand. "How soon?"

"Soon," she replied simply. "Your chosen fighter can follow me."

I looked at the group, and they all nodded. Layla squeezed back as I moved to stand. We'd talked about it, and all came to a consensus, but that didn't mean she loved the idea. It was up to me to prove her fears wrong. Or, if I couldn't, at least handle whatever came my way.

"I will take you to one of the staging rooms so you can prepare for the match," the woman said and directed me to follow.

"Try not to kill or hurt your opponent too badly," Ajax said while settling into my seat. "At least not too quickly! Work the odds."

"That is good advice. Our fans enjoy a good fight, not a slaughter. Good, heated matches bring in more money for the house. When the house earns, so do you."

"That makes sense. I will do everything I can..." I said, drifting off in the hope she would offer her name.

She offered me a sly smile, but turned and continued, her name still a mystery. I followed, sticking to the plan. Ajax and I knew we wouldn't be allowed many fights. The arena needed to keep things fresh, and moving, so, it just made sense. But we needed to make as much money as possible. Thus, I'd given the big guy ample room to bargain with the odds makers. This woman, it appeared, was one of them.

I followed the mystery woman past tables and yelling spectators, then down and around the arena floor. She led me to a small room, where she paused, knocked on the door, and pushed it open.

"Wait here," she said, pursing those glossy lips. "Remember what I said. We want a show, not a massacre."

I nodded and stepped inside, while she closed the door behind me. I found a spartanly-furnished space. Clothes racks covered the far wall, while a small table and a chair sat to my right. A paper bag lay on the table, its top pulled partially open. I approached and leaned over to look inside. Inside were a pair of khaki shorts. I held them up and figured they would reach my knees.

I was actually a little surprised they'd left them there for me. Fighting in my everyday clothes was fine, but this would make it a little easier to move around and help me blend in with the other fighters.

Holding the shorts up, Leo came to mind. How was the little bastard doing? Had he recovered from his beating? Or, learned anything?

I snorted, knowing full well that spoiled snots like Leo didn't learn.

Next, I changed. It felt strange putting on the shorts and not wearing a top, as I had become so used to wearing my armor and gear. Time seemed to drag as I waited in the room, my body cooling. I moved around and shadow boxed, stretched my limbs, and did some push-ups.

The door opened abruptly a short time later and a young woman in a tight black top and a pleated miniskirt appeared. She looked like a ring girl from head to toe, with blonde hair pulled into a tight ponytail, rosy-red cheeks, and dark red lips.

She eyed me for a moment before lingering on the myriad of scars that ran along my body. Her cheeks flushed when she met my eyes but relaxed a bit when I winked at her.

"It's your turn, sir," she said.

"Thank you. Maybe you could cheer me on?"

The blonde chuckled and led me out, her hips swaying enticingly before me. It didn't help that her mini-skirt barely covered her ass and naturally drew my eyes. But that was her whole point, drawing looks.

I walked ringside as the announcer spoke, his voice magnified by a large, metal cone.

"Ladies and gentlemen! Welcome back a second-time fighter to our arena. Last time he defeated Leo the Lionheart in a bout that shook the heavens! We are proud to bring you the *Wolf Slayer!*"

My retinue erupted into cheers and applause, but the rest of the crowd's response was lackluster. I tried not to care too much as it was unlikely that they'd seen me fight. Now, if I was an asshole like Leo, I probably would have taken their lack of enthusiasm as a personal insult. Luckily, I was only moonlighting as a brawler, and besides, having lots of people bet on me would have made it far harder for us to make money.

I nodded towards Ajax's table before grabbing hold of the ropes and swinging up and over the top with ease. I deliberately stumbled on landing, but just a little, which drew some mocking jeers and laughter. If times were different, I might have made a fine actor.

"And fighting against our wolf-slaying sheep, we bring you Finn the Finisher!" the announcer yelled!

The crowd erupted in loud cheers, which stung as much as being called a sheep. I bit my tongue and smiled, understanding the tactic. It was either to goad me or manipulate the odds.

Finn the Finisher? Honestly? What sort of reject came up with that? I thought as my opponent made his way toward the ring.

He was confident, that much was clear. Finn walked with his shaved and well-oiled head held high, like Caesar reborn. He wore a pair of red and white shorts, eerily similar to what Leo wore, and I wondered if they were related or fought on the same team.

Great. A revenge bout? Is that why he called me a sheep?

As physiques went, Finn was well-toned and muscular, but in the "showy" way. He lacked the tone and scars of a real warrior—one that had been tempered by the struggle of life and death situations, not a show-sport like this.

His eyes were full of disdain, and when he flipped over the rope, landing heavily on both feet, he flexed and growled. I didn't flinch.

Finn only grew angrier at my lack of response. Good. Rile him up. Get him angry. It'll just make the fight even easier.

I moved to take in the crowd but saw Finn move out of the corner of my eye. He tried to slap my face, but I neatly dodged the strike. That sneaky bastard hadn't even waited for the announcer to count down. That settled it in my mind. If he was going to act like Leo, then I was going to treat him like that useless prick. Just like a punching bag.

I bounced gently on the balls of my feet, my knees bending as my legs coiled beneath me. I needed to draw the fight out, but Finn looked prepared to lose quickly. That meant I might have to take a little more damage than was otherwise necessary.

For the good of the group, I thought and exhaled forcefully.

Finn closed in on me, his foot snapping out in a kick aimed at my right hip. I drew on my ether to increase the strength of my strike. My chest warmed as my right hand snapped down, deflecting his foot. I followed up with a sneaky left hand, but the backhand was ten times more potent than the blow.

An angry red welt formed on his face, stretching from his chin down to split his bottom lip. The next part was going to suck as I needed to give them a good show. To do that, I needed to give him an opening.

Finn guarded himself quite well, proving to be a quality defender. We danced around each other for a few moments, sending some jabs and kicks, but nothing landed after my first hit. It felt as if he was finally starting to see me as an opponent rather than a victim.

I snapped a kick out at his thigh, guarding my face with

my hands but I left my torso open for a counter.

The idiot didn't take the bait. Instead, he kicked out and pounced at me. His head hit my wrists as he threw his arms around my neck. When his legs dug into the back of my knees, I knew instantly what he was trying to do. I threw myself sideways, dropping all of my weight on his left knee.

I heard him suck in a breath as pain shot through my ribs. I thanked him for the discomfort with an elbow to the nose. Cartilage and bone crunched under the impact, but I didn't follow up. Instead, I gave him the chance to reclaim control of the situation.

Thankfully, he didn't let me down. Blood dripped onto my chest as he wrestled me around and gained leverage, before raining blows into my ribs. I halfheartedly blocked the first few, until he connected and the pain in my side doubled. My breath caught and my diaphragm seized up.

Okay, that sucked, I thought and tightened up my defenses. But sensing blood, Finn continued his attacks.

It took me several precious seconds to figure out his timing before I caught his arms and wrenched him down into a headbutt. His already bleeding nose was broken completely and he rocked back from the blow.

I tried to push him free but buckled as he recovered and jabbed at my neck. His fists worked in at my chest, neck, and face, blows landing like working pistons. He pushed off and dropped a knee for my face, but I compressed my abs and brought both knees straight up.

With one leg off the ground, my move—as painful as it was to my wounded ribs—successfully tipped him sideways and to the mat. I carried through with the movement and channeled more than a little ether, driving a kick right into the other man's leg.

Finn let out an anguished cry as the blow rolled him over, then tried to stand and howled in outrage, trying to make up for the girlish scream.

"I'll kill you, you bastard!" he wheezed, clutching his leg.

"You're so fucking dead!"

Finn hobbled to his feet as I stood, and to his credit, he came right at me. I hit him with an efficient leg sweep. Feet knocked wide, he tipped sideways onto his right elbow, hitting like a solid chunk of meat. I moved overtop him but jumped back and dodged an awkward kick. I was struggling to draw this match out as long as possible.

Finn's nose was badly broken and oozing blood down over his mouth and chin, but his lips were puffy, and even one of his eyes was swelling shut. When had I hit him in the eye?

I circled and watched him as he tried to get to his feet. He was struggling just to stand, which told me that he was likely done. But damn sakes, the show was everything.

I wanted them to think that I didn't realize how badly he was injured. So far, everything I'd done would look accidental, maybe by luck, and that was okay. As long as the crowd didn't leave knowing that I was considerably more powerful.

Finn grunted and pushed himself up onto one leg, but the spot on his thigh where my kick landed was red and swollen. I'd given him a decent contusion, maybe even a hairline break in the bone. Whoops. As soon as his weight came down on that leg, he collapsed.

I circled again and continued to bounce, but then looked at the announcer, waiting patiently. He seemed to finally break from his stupor and lifted the metal cone to his lips.

"Well, ugh...what an unexpected fight! It appears that Finn the Finisher has been finished!"

His deep, resonant voice echoed through the concrete underground. Then as one, the crowd erupted in cheers and jeers. Some, it seemed, hated my guts, while others had apparently wagered on me to win.

"Call the fight!" I hissed. "He can't continue like that."

"Ugh, yes! Sorry. Sorry, I was just taken aback by your performance," the announcer said, chuckling and bowing. The cone went back to his lips. "Without further ado, I declare the Wolf Slayer the winner, via technical knockout!"

I jumped out of the ring and was halfway to my ready room when the woman in blue slipped out from behind a column ahead. She wagged a finger my way and blocked the path.

"Like I said, only one bout...unless you prove popular."

"Okay, as memory serves that wasn't exactly what you said," I argued.

"Close enough," she said, waving me off. "Ajax was right. You are technical. I'm giving you the next slot. See if you can't work the crowd up a little more. The longer you stay out there, the more money they'll wager! The crowd does love a good show of endurance."

Two bouncers appeared behind the woman then— massive men that would make even Ajax look small.

"Oh, come along. Don't act as if you don't like to fight. Besides, I know why you are here. You need the money. Trust me. The more time you spend out there, the more you will make."

I clenched my jaw and turned, moving back toward the ring. The crowd erupted in response, the hazy layer of smoke twice as thick as before. A man stood in the ring on the far side, waiting for me. He was a big bastard, and not just taller than me, but wider, too.

He stood like a solid wall of flesh and muscle. From his face, I guessed he was somewhere in his late thirties, but judging what I knew about ether, that didn't mean much. He could be younger or older, so that fact alone didn't mean much.

My new opponent sized me up quietly as I jumped over the rope and into the ring. Well, that wasn't good. I was used to pompous bastards who were busy strutting like peacocks around the ring. This guy was an entirely different beast.

"Guess they found me a real fighter this time," I whispered, trying to stay calm. And yet, the more I watched him, and his alarmingly cool outward appearance, the more I started to doubt.

The big man wore his white hair short to the scalp. He

had a broad forehead, deep-set eyes, and a nose that looked like it had been broken more than once. He was muscular, but not in the showy way, like Finn or Leo. This guy looked realistically strong. The kind of strength cultivated from a life of struggle and trials. A red rampant lion tattoo adorned his left pec. The image stirred something in my mind, telling me he was either royalty, somehow related to royalty, or heavily favored by them.

I stretched my arms and shoulders, working it out in my mind. Was this some kind of set-up by the Seneschal before he'd died? Was Alfred involved? Or was this Leo's attempt at payback?

"Too many questions," I growled and slapped my head, then dropped into a balanced fighting stance.

The bell rang, but my opponent did not move. He'd been watching me talk to myself. Mind you, I probably looked more than a little crazy.

Then, without warning, the big guy charged like a bull. I changed stances, preparing to stay light on my feet. It was the appropriate technique against a bull-rusher, after all. And yet he stopped once he was in range, and struck like a viper, his fist moving faster than I could track.

I just ducked the blow, sidestepped, and snapped out with a straight kick towards his stomach. He twisted and dodged my foot but stumbled in the act. I kicked again, taking advantage of his lack of strong base, then spun and threw an elbow into his shoulder for good measure. It felt like I hit a concrete wall wrapped in leather.

Turning and dancing away for space, I ducked a punch, but couldn't avoid the kick that followed. His heel found my knee just as I turned, the devastating force behind the strike knocking me clean off my feet.

I rolled and rolled, then pushed off the ground in time to see the same foot flashing towards my face. I squatted and backflipped, the awkward angle making me land on my knees. He was there again, as I tumbled sideways, and then forward in a desperate flight to escape.

The bastard wasn't just quick, but he was faster than me and larger and stronger! I swept into a cartwheel, spun a heel strike right at his face, and finally managed to win some space.

Someone called in a ringer, I realized, but the more important question was, who? This man was well-beyond me, in both strength and speed.

I circled and watched him for a moment, but he gave nothing away—no tell or flinch to give me advanced warning of what he was going to do. Was this what it felt like for the others to fight me?

Wading forward, I switched styles, moving into a Muay Thai kickboxing stance. It would provide me a more upright base with more power in the kicks.

Swinging with my right leg, I went right at his left thigh. The kick connected, and I pushed in, my aching ribs arguing as I brought in a flurry of knees and elbows.

The big guy grunted and staggered back, but straightened, and in a moment that made my blood go cold, smiled. Was this guy a robot?

He switched his stance to match mine and jumped forward, matching my kicks and elbows precisely. I felt each one hit, battering my legs, sides, and arms. Bruises formed almost instantly, as even my flow of ether struggled to supplement his strength.

This man, whoever he was, had hit his third vein already, that much was clear. There was no way a body could produce that much power unless it was tempered. Even worse, most of his attacks left him wide open but judging by how he shrugged off my best kicks and elbows, it made me wonder if I could actually harm him. And if he could absorb that kind of beating, I did not want to know what would happen if he got his hands on me.

I grimaced as I lifted my left arm to deflect his kick. I both heard and felt the bone snap in my wrist. Biting through the pain, I ducked, and spun, slamming the heel of my right foot into the side of his knee. The big man grunted and fell sideways. No one ever expected that one, especially after absorbing such a blow. *Enjoy your broken knee, asshole.*

Clutching my broken wrist to my body, I greedily pulled on my available ether. The power surged through me as I launched forward, bringing my leg up into a compact and violent Muay Thai knee strike. The blow hit him square in the jaw, the bone shattering instantly.

I landed, winced, and jumped back. Even a solid hit on his face made my whole leg ring like a bell. Hell, it felt more like I had kneed a solid bronze statue.

The big guy seemed to float there for a second. And I prepared another even more desperate strike, before he slumped sideways, unconscious.

I swayed for a moment and then slumped to the mat, breathing deep to keep my head from spinning. The pain in my broken wrist throbbed in time with my heart, but I struggled not to show it.

Ether flowed up my arm, forcing the bones back into alignment. My mind flashed back to when I woke up in the tent. I could have easily gone a lifetime without feeling that pain again, as the grind of bone on bone was a sensation someone doesn't forget easily.

I turned and found Ajax in the crowd, the announcer's voice now lost to the roar of the crowd. Our eyes met and I nodded to my healthy hand, which I used to tap out "T-R-A-P" in morse code. He frowned but nodded, and then repeated it several times, making sure I saw it. When I confirmed, he unobtrusively slid my sword belt off the chair next to him.

"Fighter, are you alright?" the announcer asked, snapping his fingers in front of my face. Honestly, I hadn't even noticed him approach "Are you prepared to continue?"

"Assuming my next opponent only has two veins opened, sure. I'm not really interested in fighting two cheaters in one night."

He flinched but recovered, stifling a cough. But it was

too late. He knew I'd figured it out. He turned and looked up to where several shadow figures stood in a private box. Then ever-so-slightly, he nodded. Time seemed to grind to a halt as silence fell over the arena.

"*You are almost incapably primitive,*" Ivory groaned in my mind. "*I still don't understand how you hairless apes managed to kill me, with your shocking lack of strength and instincts!*"

Ivory's words grated on my already inflamed nerves, but I did my best to not lash out.

"*Do you have any suggestions? Or are you just looking for an opportunity to be a prick? Maybe you want to spend some more time on the pedestal of shame?*"

"*Naturally,*" the spirit wolf replied. "*I have better ways, but I'm not in the habit of defying the laws of the wild. The strong survive, and the weak are prey.*"

Ivory was definitely still raw about his time on the pedestal, I knew that much. But this went beyond simple retaliation. He had to know that if I died and my floating, magical dream pagoda ceased to be, then he would fade away, as well.

"*I'm sorry. It does mean a lot to me. I'm just in pain. I wasn't serious about putting you back on the pedestal—*"

He snorted and I had to really restrain myself from losing my shit.

"*Fine! Besides, I know you aren't weak, so I will aid you! You must simply acknowledge that I am a King amongst beasts. A reasonable one at that.*"

"*Thank you, oh great king,*" I said, swallowing my pride. Yes, I wanted to say something else entirely, but I kept that to myself.

"*You are a variant, so you have a metal vein in your left index finger. You don't know this, but normally that variation would allow the individual to mend their own bones. You cannot do that yet, but there should be some benefits you can tap into. Use your metal affinity.*"

"*How?*" I asked.

He groaned and snarled something I couldn't hear. If he were there in front of me, and perhaps a person, I guessed that he might be face-palming.

"Urgh, I know you aren't stupid, so don't pretend to be. Let me rephrase, you aren't 'that' stupid, but your sheer lack of foundation is almost a disability! You have ether in your core, don't you? I can see it, so I know for a fact that you haven't burned through it all."

I thought about it for a moment as I scanned the crowd and finally asked my question.

"Why do you want me to use the metal affinity?"

"Simple: to repair your bone. Even if you can't mend the break yet, you can force the ether inside the tissue to bolster and strengthen the bone. Yes, regular ether will work...as you have already done. But it is nowhere near as efficient or strong. Try the right way for a change."

"Are you the next contender?" the announcer asked behind me. "How many open veins do you possess?"

"Two, just as requested," a cold, strong voice replied.

I turned and studied the newcomer for a moment. He wore black fatigue pants and an equally black tank top. The look practically screamed mercenary. I would know. He returned my gaze, his expression frustratingly neutral. But it went beyond that. His eyes were practically devoid of any emotions.

My sense of unease grew. Was this new fighter confident because he knew I was already injured? Or did he know something I didn't?

"I smell metal on him, and it has been oiled recently. Trust your senses. Let your instincts take over," Ivory said sharply.

And I swore that I could almost feel the oil's sharp odor burning at my nostrils.

I looked to Ajax, but there was no way for me to communicate my fears. Not with the crowd's noise and the distance between us. At that moment, I wished for a better way to communicate. Ivory sighed.

"You can communicate silently, but you need to develop your spiritual sense more. If you ever progress that far, then I might humble myself enough to train you. In the meantime, I feel the need to remind you that you four can feel each other's emotions. Ugh, you are such a pup."

The new fighter stretched, his eyes never leaving me. He looked as if he didn't have a care in the world. I glanced to Ajax, my eyes sweeping the crowd. They seemed to get louder by the moment, the noise a constant *thrum-thrum-thrum* in my ears.

I looked to the announcer, and flinched back to the fighter, just as his arm went back. A black combat knife was in his hand, but before his arm could snap forward to hurl it at me, something sailed over my right shoulder and slammed into his chest. The impact knocked him back into the ropes, and he nearly tumbled over.

My wakizashi rolled toward me—the projectile that had knocked him back, and I scooped it up. I fumbled to break the blade free but couldn't hold the scabbard tight enough with my wounded arm.

"Son of a bitch!" I cursed as the merc came at me, his large combat knife swiping wildly through the air. I brought the wakizashi up, but the blade was still trapped in the scabbard.

I blocked the cut and kicked out, my foot connecting solidly with his groin. He groaned and staggered away, giving me just enough time for a second try at pulling the blade free.

I stabbed towards his face, but this was the wakizashi, not my katana, and the shorter blade lacked any real reach. The merc jerked back and flinched, holding his blade up defensively.

Without thought, I activated <<**Burst of Speed**>> and <<**Enhanced Strength**>>, draining some of my ether reserves. He stepped back as I lunged forward again and our blades crashed together.

When I withdrew my blade, the merc fell back, the fingers on his left-hand tumbling to the mat in a spray of blood. I kept my advantage and pressed forward, swinging the short blade in an arc. The first strike knocked his combat knife down, but the second buried my weapon in his neck.

The merc's eyes locked open in a look of complete and utter shock and horror.

"I guess I wasn't the easy kill you were hoping for," I hissed, and ripped my blade free.

He hovered there for a moment, his mouth open and moving, red blood pumping down his black tank top. But then he fell over.

I spun on the spot, flicking my blade out before me and sending his blood splattering in a wide arc. The crowd erupted into manic cheers, as some rose to their feet and screamed, while others fell to violence.

Were they that happy seeing a man lose his life?

I looked to my group as Ajax laid a man low with a single punch, and then lifted a large pouch off the table before them. Prometheus ushered the girls out and into the aisle, while Hera jabbed her spear at a salty-looking group of men.

Desperate to join them, I hurled myself over the ropes and sprinted for my waiting room. I kicked the door off its hinges, scooped up my belongings in my injured arm, and ran.

I bowled two men out of the way as Ajax appeared at the bottom of the stairs. He pushed past me and lunged for the shadows. When he reappeared, the woman in blue was struggling to free herself from his grasp.

Ajax leaned in and they shared a brief but heated exchange, then she nodded and pointed ahead. Ajax pushed her in that direction, his sizable index finger held tight against her back. She led us through a row of columns and back under a dark canopy of concrete, down a shadowy hallway, and to a sturdy-looking door. Even with my enhanced senses I could barely see but watched as she pulled out a key, twisted it in the lock, and pushed the door open. We hurried through with Ajax bringing up the rear.

The big man pulled the door closed and they bolted it

shut. We moved forward again in silence, as the lady in blue led us deeper into the underground maze. The further we went, the thicker the air became with fear.

Passing through a narrow corridor lit by flickering candles, we continued for another minute before walking into a lavishly furnished room. I dropped my gear onto a table and turned, expecting some answers.

"I'm sorry, please!" she started as Ajax loomed over her, his hands balled up into white-knuckle fists. "I didn't accept money. B-B-But they threatened my family!"

"Oh, well then it is okay," I said, wiping my wakizashi clean on the khaki shorts. I laid the weapon on the dark wood table and started to change. "I don't mind if someone orchestrates my death, but only if someone's family was threatened."

The lady in blue watched me for a moment, evidently trying to figure out if I was being serious. But it became clear from the simmering murder in Ajax and Hera's eyes that I was not.

"I think you owe us something," Prometheus said, his voice icy-calm. He was the levelheaded one of the group, after all.

"I—"

"Yes. Owe is right," I interrupted her as I pulled my katana free. Her eyes grew wide as they tracked down the long, gently curving blade.

"I didn't know they were going to try to…kill you. Please. They said they wanted to teach you a lesson."

"That could be interpreted a lot of different ways," Ajax grumbled. "We want our winnings and then some."

"Okay," she said, nodding eagerly, "here." She walked over to a large wooden bookshelf covering the far wall and pulled on an iron candleholder.

A section of the bookcase slid aside, revealing a dark corridor behind it. Torches lined the wall, and in the distance, I could see the river. A heavy thud echoed behind me, and I turned to find that the woman had deposited a sizable chest on the table next to my gear.

"Here, take what you need."

Neatly organized piles of crystals sat inside, seemingly every size, clarity, and color. I nodded to Ajax, who promptly reached inside and started claiming our share.

"Please. You must believe me when I say that I didn't want anyone to get seriously hurt—"

I moved in to claim the rest of my gear and cut her off.

"Who approached you? Who set this up?"

She shook her head, that previously meticulous mask of makeup and carefully sculpted hair now a mess of flyaway and running mascara.

"I didn't know them and they never did say who they spoke for. But they knew where I live, the names of each of my family members, what they look like, and exactly where they sleep..."

I growled. "This fucking city. Talk about a den of snakes."

"For what it is worth, I hope they don't hurt you or your family," Ajax said, after shutting the chest. "But if you'd like my advice, you should gather up your loved ones and get out of the city as quietly as you can."

She sniffled as we pushed past her and into the tunnel. A rowboat was waiting for us at the small dock, providing just enough room for us to sit.

I cradled my aching wrist to my chest as Ajax grabbed the oars and started rowing. We slid out onto the dark water as the woman in blue watched us from the tunnel, her tear-filled eyes glittering in the moonlight.

I genuinely hoped that she and her family didn't come to harm, but I'd come to understand that Zurich was an unforgiving place, full of greedy schemers.

Luckily, we'd made our preparations. We had food, clothes, and most importantly, crystals. All that remained was to absorb enough power to get to the next rank.

CHAPTER 21: THE BAD PACK

The dark time came, and the breeze picked up. With it came the scents of two-legged wolves. I didn't recognize their smells, and the fur on my neck bristled. Their odor was...aggressive. At the same time, I could feel Alpha, Deer Eyes, and the others. They were on the move, and yet, they weren't moving toward me.

Where were they going?

I roused from my nest inside the crumbling two-legged wolf cave and slunk outside. Long Claws lumbered up behind me, his large nose working over the air. He smelled them, too.

We slipped out into the open air, and I immediately lowered my body to the ground. The bad wolves smell was all around us, circling on the wind. That was only possible if they'd surrounded our den. How had they done that without me hearing them?

I slipped quietly to the wall and found the gap Alpha always entered through. Something moved on the other side, the plants telling me everything I needed to know.

I snapped my teeth at Long Claws, telling him to back up. He turned and lumbered down the wall just as the tip of a bright claw appeared through the gap next to me. The two-legged wolf crawled through next, his body reeking of angry, violent smells.

Waiting until his head and shoulders appeared, I snapped down hard, catching his neck between my jaws. He stiffened as I squeezed, my teeth punching through his soft flesh and breaking the delicate bones beneath. Then, ever so quietly, I pulled him through the gap and set his body in the tall plants.

A quiet whistle sounded outside the wall, and another echoed it somewhere behind me. The two-legged wolves were talking, communicating in their bird-talk. A shadowy form appeared on top of the wall behind me and dropped to the ground, right in front of Long Claws.

My large companion launched himself out of the shadows, falling on the two-legged wolf with tremendous fury. He was loud. The enemy wolf's screams were louder.

I jumped out of my hiding spot as Long Claws' jaws tore into the wolf, his bones crunching loudly. Their whistles and calls were instantly replaced by loud, panicked voices, and my ears perked. The smell of anger and violence increased.

I felt a surge of power course through me as the wolf's screaming abruptly stopped, and with a primal snarl, I leaped forward into a run. My hunting vision swept in, cutting through the shadows and revealing more bad, two-legged wolves. Some tried to crawl through holes in our den's outer wall, while a few climbed over the top. Those wolves seemed apprehensive about the high drop to the ground below.

The closest enemy stood just as I leaped. His eyes went wide as my teeth sank into his shoulder. I picked him up off the ground and shook him as hard as I could, then tossed his body to the ground.

I twisted as the wolf screamed from the ground. So, he hadn't died. Impressive. I stepped in closer, growling right into his face. I enjoyed the horror in his eyes, but then he soiled himself. Why would he want to mark the ground beneath him? Was it fear? Such weak wolves!

I leaned in and bit down on the wounded wolf's throat, finishing him off as two other wolves stalked toward me, their bright claws held high. I growled a challenge and squared off, snarling so they would know I was serious.

They fanned out and tried to push me into the corner. I lunged and snapped my teeth, but their bright claws flashed at my face. I sank back into the shadows and willed myself to vanish. My fur bristled as my camouflage hid me from sight. The two enemy wolves chattered to one another, then the one on the right lunged and stabbed into the darkness. But I was already gone, circling to get behind them.

I savored their confusion as they fell into the darkness with abandon, chopping, and hacking at the shadows with their bright claws. Stupid wolves.

Snapping my teeth, I caught the closest wolf by the leg and dragged him back into the darkness. I gave him a violent shake and his body hit the wall next to us, the impact spattering his dark blood on the stone.

Long Claws resolved out of the darkness and fell on the other wolf, the bear crushing him beneath his considerable weight. I pitched my head back and howled to the night—to let the moon know about our hunt, and so Alpha would hear me.

Long Claws and I stalked through the den until we found the last of the enemy wolves. I growled low as we spotted him, the air filling with the bitter smell of urine. He turned and tried to run, but I was faster.

Jumping on him from behind, I knocked the wolf to the ground, the impact slamming his head into the stone. I clamped my jaws around his slender neck and twisted, savoring the loud crack of breaking bones. I had become strong since my new pack took me in. Sure, I had to work for it, but it was thanks to Alpha.

With the last of the enemy wolves killed, I howled again. Somewhere in the distance, another wolf answered. Not a member of my pack, but definitely another hunter. Long Claws growled next to me, and I responded. He was right. It was time for us to find our pack.

We charged out into the darkness, the forest accepting us like old pack mates. I could feel the fear and anxiety from my pack as Long Claws and I moved in. They were in trouble, that much was clear. Was it the enemy wolves? Were they hurt? Fighting? There was an underlying smell of pain, but it was fading away, leaving a metallic aftertaste in my mouth.

As we closed in on Alpha and the others, Long Claws and I realized why our pack was afraid. They were fleeing from something. Then we got closer and realized that another large pack of enemy wolves was closing in on them.

Another group had gotten close enough to be a threat. I could feel them and their anxiety just as easily as their bloodlust. This was getting tiresome, but I had to help. Maybe it was time for me to leave a message—one the other enemy packs would fear. I'd make sure it was something they'd never forget.

My pack was close, but I felt their tension. Long Claws and I drew close enough to smell them, and I noticed a strange trail on the ground. It was made up of cut trees and had two large metal bars resting on top of them. It smelled heavily of oil and smoke. My pack seemed to be moving along this trail.

We veered off and circled, finally coming to a stop beside a thorny bush. We spotted the first enemy wolf after a few moments. He was very well hidden, but my senses were sharp.

I crept up within range, and when the timing was right, I pounced. My weight knocked the wolf out of the bush and onto the muddy ground. He growled and yipped in his strange language, but unfortunately, he was going to be an example.

With speed he couldn't match, I darted in and snapped my teeth on the soft mass of flesh between his legs, jerked once, and then stepped away to let him scream in agony. And oh, did he wail.

Long Claws and I backed away as his companions closed in on his voice. We lurked in the bushes, listening, and smelling them until they'd converged over their wounded wolf. We attacked.

All in all, Long Claws and I massacred another five enemy wolves, all reeking of anger and violence. They all held bright claws, too. At least one of their number fled into the night, but that was okay. They could yip and bark a warning to their packmates. They could help spread my warning. Come near my pack and lose their mating parts.

After the quiet resumed, Long Claws and I tracked our pack up the iron path. They'd run as soon as we attacked. That was good. Alpha was a smart wolf.

He stepped out before the others as I loped onto the trail, revealing myself, his bright claws catching the moonlight. But he relaxed as he recognized me.

"Omega," he yipped and held open his arms to accept me.

CHAPTER 22: THE ROAD TO MUNICH

The events at the arena, although not completely predictable, forced us to accelerate our timetable. Luckily, Ajax is a bit of a nervous-Nelly and insisted that we pack up and stage our personal belongings ahead of time. So, when the arena matron let us slip out through her escape passage to the river, all we had to do was locate the train tracks and follow them out of the city.

What we hadn't expected was our reunion with Omega once we left. The wolf had not only been alerted to our imminent escape, but he'd also stumbled upon a would-be ambush.

Layla and Kate weren't the same for some time. Evidently, hearing a giant wolf and bear tear men apart in the woods around you can upset some people's nerves. It wasn't just the girls. It rattled me, too.

Only two train stations were still in operation. The beating heart of the old Swiss rail service was the Hardbrücke station in downtown Zurich. Luckily, we weren't restricted to that as our only option. I could just imagine trying to sneak back into the big city with a wolf and bear in tow. Beyond the fact that Zurich was sealed, every single bridge was likely locked down with double or even triple the normal guard. We only succeeded in getting out because the river took us beyond the wall and past their patrols.

It was possible they saw us on the river, despite the darkness. That explained the ambush. Or, they might have let us leave, so they could follow. There were simply too many variables and possibilities to be sure. And for a guy already struggling with memory loss and occasional crippling headaches, I had to let the mystery go before my grey matter imploded.

"Can you scout ahead?" I asked Omega.

Omega growled and looked into my eyes. He couldn't speak, per se, since he was a wolf, after all, but we communicated through emotions. He agreed and gave off a feeling that made me think of urgency, then darted off into the woods.

Our destination wasn't south, despite our travel in that direction. Hell, our actual destination was the old Flughafen airport rail terminal north of the city, but we had to gain enough distance from Zurich in order to skirt around to the east and approach safely.

"What did he say?" Prometheus asked, after coming up from behind.

"Can't you feel it?" I asked, throwing him a wink. "He'll scout ahead, but considering how far south we went, I'm guessing our route east and then north should be clear. If we're lucky, the people pursuing us will think we continued south."

"Okay," Prometheus said with a nod, but I could tell the situation made him uneasy. He was used to being our scout, our advanced eyes and ears. Change was a hard thing for some people to accept.

"I still can't believe we didn't manage to get our hands on all the crystals. Bastards shouldn't have bet against me if they didn't want to lose," I muttered to Ajax.

"Are you salty about them trying to kill you? Or that we only walked away with a thousand crystals?"

"Both?" I chuckled. "That whole thing could have gone sideways really fast."

"Could have gone sideways?" he scoffed. "Don't you mean 'more sideways'?"

I nodded, conceding the point, just as Hera pushed between us.

"I know we're in the wilderness, but how about you two either chat quieter or wait until we're safely on the train and away from Zurich? I feel exposed, even this far from the city," Hera muttered.

"That is fair," I replied and gave the forest a wide scan. The terrain was beautiful, but I was beyond ready to get further away from civilization. "I don't like this calm before the storm."

"*You* are the storm," Hera whispered.

We hiked the better part of the morning, stopped for a break and some food, and then used the afternoon to make the passage north. We could have gone faster, but by taking our time we allowed things in the city to cool down a bit.

Omega reappeared as the sun started to set, signaling that we were approaching the airport. I smelled coal, as well, which told me the train was in. Holding the animals back, Prometheus and I scouted the train station.

The King had gone to great lengths to convert the space since the collapse, as what had originally been a small city-wide transit line had been modified with its own protective wall and battlements. The rail itself was different, too, as more track had been installed to tie the line into the main spur coming out of the city.

We snuck up to the wall and listened as a group of guards converged.

"...not going outside after dark ever again!"

The panic in the man's voice took me off guard. And although I couldn't see his face, I could clearly sense his fear. Had something else happened? Or...were they talking about us?

"I'm not, either! They found four men's bodies. Their privates were torn clean off by some...wild animal! They say it was a pack of wild dogs, but I don't buy it. Could be a wolf, or something bigger. Maybe a cat."

I shuddered at the thought, my hands involuntarily flinching towards my own privates.

"They found over twenty dead!" another man chimed in. "Every one of them was a two or three-veined mercenary! My brother thinks it was the devil, come to finally repay his debt on humanity."

"The devil?" a third man scoffed. "I heard it was a gigantic demon wolf!"

I barely contained a snort. That many men losing their lives wasn't a laughing matter, but the number did surprise me. If twenty had been killed, how many more escaped? It appeared that someone had gone to great pains to either capture or kill us the night before.

Prometheus and I moved silently down the wall and scouted the rest of the station. Luckily, the train was too long to all fit within the station's protective wall, so large doors had been opened to accommodate for its length. I counted one steam engine, a coal car, eight passenger cars, a mail car, four box cars, and no less than a dozen cargo cars on the end.

We returned to the others and reported in.

"Over twenty men?" Kate hissed. "That is a lot."

"More than that, actually," I replied.

"What are you on about?" Hera asked, after rejoining the group.

"Omega castrated four mercenaries last night. The enemy apparently staged raids on the mansion in the hills and surrounded us as we left the city. Our animal protectors killed over twenty. All two and three-veined cultivators," Layla explained.

"Shit. We were lucky his pack kept him hungry, or we might have had a fight on our hands," Hera chuckled.

"And here I was thinking that he'd killed just a few in

the woods around us," Ajax breathed. "My nethers tingle just thinking about that big beast's crotch ripping exploits."

"Don't be crude," Kate spat.

"Not crude," the big man laughed, "Just feeling very lucky at the moment." He patted his groin and whispered under his breath.

"Back to business. What is our play here?" Kate asked.

"We have to consider that they know what Ajax, Hera, Prom, and I look like," I said, forming a plan in my head. "And since we don't exactly know who wants us dead, I think we should send Kate and Layla in to buy tickets and the rest of us will hop on right before the train leaves. There are a number of cargo cars at the end of the train. I think we might be able to sneak Omega and his new friend in there for the ride."

"If someone opens that car once we arrive, they are going to be in for a big surprise," Ajax laughed.

"Then we'll just have to be prepared."

"A train, huh?" Layla said, quietly. "In a world where everything simply stopped working, how did they manage that?"

"Coal," I explained. "They took these old steam engines out of museums and put them back to work. There is nothing electrical on them, so they are relatively ether-proof."

It was a strange thought, that a world running on sophisticated technology networks and high-speed data transfers would revert back to steamboats, trains, and air balloons. But it was our new reality. Hell, as a world, we'd reverted in more ways than that. Feudal states, kingdoms, rival aristocracies, duels, and more.

Layla and Kate purchased tickets and returned, while the rest of the group changed into the least conspicuous clothes we could find. We moved into the station as two groups then, with Kate, Ajax, and Prometheus posing as a family, and Layla, Hera, and I following a short distance behind.

We'd stashed Omega and Lazy Bones in the second

to last box car, after discovering the door was broken and awaiting repair. Nothing was inside, save for some dusty boxes, and loose straw on the ground.

I strolled lazily toward the depot with Layla on one side and Hera on the other. They were cousins, traveling to see an aunt, while I was Hera's on-again, off-again boyfriend. And boy did she play that part well. Everyone involved, including the man at the ticket booth, to the luggage attendants, and the security guards heard all about how we'd only been dating a short time and she wasn't sure if it was going to work out. Layla played along, although a little too convincingly for my taste.

"Is this how we're getting to the Zoo?" Layla asked once we'd checked in with our tickets.

"Not the whole way. We're going to Ulm to get you and Kate situated first. Once you're settled, we'll head out on foot to the Federsee from there. It's a wildlife reserve, mostly birds, but it has changed over the last decade. That's the largest Zoo now and the location all European powers hold for their Melee of Kings."

"I see," she said, her eyes studying the long train. The engine was hissing and gurgling, a gentle stream of smoke rising out of its stack. "And your wolf?"

Our disguises—if we could really call them that—made the boarding process incredibly easy. It helped that Kate and Hera played the parts of overbearing and loud girlfriends, and as history has shown, most people in service tried to avoid people like that.

The train loaded and before long we were underway, the antique steam engine chugging and pulling us through the countryside. The ride was surprisingly comfortable, and yet, while everyone else lounged and relaxed, I struggled. It was already hard enough to sit calmly, all the while knowing a pair of massive animals were inhabiting a train car somewhere behind me. To make matters worse, I had Ivory in my head, and the spirit wolf pulled no punches.

I sat upright in my seat with a crystal in my left hand, diligently absorbing its ether. But the flow was slow. The vein hadn't been fully developed and still needed some work. It was like trying to build a road out of gravel, with a bucket. And the more of the road I finished, that just meant I had that much further to walk back for more gravel. In a word, tedious.

It made me realize how little I'd known about ether and cultivation up to that point. Now I knew my vein wasn't working optimally.

"Do you think that it builds character to work so hard on something that should be easy, or are you just a masochist?" Ivory jabbed.

He made a series of chuffing and barking noises in my mind, which I took for his version of laughter. I glared at the crystal in my hand and wished it was the spirit wolf instead. I very much wanted to slap the shit out of him.

"If you have a better suggestion, then say so, flea bag!"

"I have no fleas!" Ivory growled. *"I don't have a body anymore!"*

Damn sakes, I'd walked right into that one.

"...but as much as I like to see you suffer, it will cost my soul if you die. That's the only reason I'm going to help you."

"Noted. But is it really the only reason?"

"Yes," he growled, *"Now find your center!"*

I stifled a sarcastic comment because I knew it would only make him angrier.

"What do you mean by center?"

"It's something different for everyone. Relax. Your mind and soul should naturally gravitate towards an almost hypnotic state. It shouldn't be hard for you, considering how little you have going on inside your head."

"That sounds like meditation?"

"Sure. If that is what you want to call it. Just find that peace and then focus on the ether in your body. Once you feel it rotating, you should also be able to visualize it. When you see the twelve spokes of the wheel then you will know you've succeeded,

two should be bright. One white and one red, they represent the two veins you have formed."

I shook away the shock. Ivory seldom spoke this much, let alone helped me too readily. I shifted in the seat, struggling to put myself into a posture conducive to meditation. Layla watched me with a confused look on her face. I smiled and gestured for her to do the same, after dumping a handful of crystals into her lap. I gave her a recap of what Ivory told me and she nodded excitedly.

It took me a while before I could bring everything into alignment. The problem was blocking out the noise and movement of the train, the people talking, and my own frustrated, swirling thoughts. But once I did, a blurry wheel of rotating ether appeared in my mind's eye. It clarified with focus, revealing ten translucent spokes. Two were vivid, while the other ten looked like ghostly outlines.

Ether spun along the spokes and regenerated with every full rotation. Then on the next cycle, compressed, and started over again.

"You control how fast the ether cycles. The rate of the spin is your indicator. Focus and make it go faster now. You're barely using a fraction of your capabilities."

I did as he said and concentrated. The wheel started to spin faster, and as it did, drew in more ether as it went. The energy compressed inside the wheel, becoming a darker, denser mass of potential. And when the cycle was complete it settled towards the middle, where it displaced the lighter variation. It was only then that I realized I was drawing ether in from the air around me. The flow was slow but steady.

"Okay, good. Now, take a deep breath followed by three short ones. Breathe in through your mouth and out through your nose while focusing on each revolution of your core. Try to time them together, a short breath should be a single rotation and a long one should be three."

I put his words into action and the flow of ether from the air around me increased dramatically. And yet, it didn't flow into me through my veins, but seeped in through my skin, muscle, and bones, only to be greedily absorbed by the rotating core.

"Good, keep on doing it like that. Now absorb as much as you can from that bag of crystals in your lap. Once you feel like you're full and cannot absorb any more, that is how you'll know you have started building your third foundation. Only then should you start pushing that darker, more condensed energy outwards. It will burn, but that condensed ether will be four times as effective in forming your veins!"

And just like that, I understood what he meant. The way we'd been cultivating wasn't just primitive and inefficient, but it was downright wrong. The thought brought me back to Ivory. What *was* he really? And how did he know how to process ether like that? Surely, he was no ordinary wolf. Hell, he was more than just an exceptional one. Sure, beasts could naturally draw in and store ether, but to create a complicated and efficient means of processing and utilizing it?

Well, that pushed into advanced, sentient being territory. Perhaps I had grossly underestimated him. I suddenly realized that there had been more to Duke Manfred wanting to find the wolves than simply unlocking a metal affinity. Had the answers been in those papers stored in his private stash?

I exhaled and opened my eyes, feeling the fool for letting Hans claim the paperwork before studying it in detail. Layla was glaring at me.

"Are you done making a fool of me?"

"Making a fool of you? What do you—?" I drifted off, only then noticing the crystals in the bag before me. They glowed brightly, the air above them fogged with a dull blue and yellow cloud of ether. The fog was floating right into me.

"I can't focus if you keep making the crystals ring like that," she said, nodding toward the bag.

"Ring?"

"Yep. Ever wet your finger and trace the lip of a wine

glass? The vibration makes the glass ring. When you focused, the crystals came alive. I've never heard of someone drawing off a whole bag at the same time before."

I turned left to find the others watching us intently. Hera and Prometheus were most curious. Taking a deep breath, I explained everything. Naturally, it wasn't as eloquent as I'd hoped, but I got the core concepts across.

They all went to work, trying to replicate what I'd done, allowing me to return to my focus. I closed my eyes and found my core. Sure enough, the bag of crystals came alive, the ether trapped inside them singing a delightful song of future power.

Was this how nobles cultivated? I'd always wondered why so few people had hit the second or third veins. And yet, men like Alfred or Manfred regularly displayed more power. Perhaps this was one of the answers.

I steadied my breathing and started to cycle ether once again. This time, knowing I wasn't just pulling it in from the ambient air, but also the bag of crystals, I got greedy and tried to pull it in fast.

My core flashed bright and spun a single fast revolution before a violent burst of ether escaped and flooded my body. The pain was intense. Only when most of the escaped ether was gone, did the core stabilize and pain recede.

"Foolish pup! Greedy feeders are rarely rewarded. You cannot draw it in too fast! It could have torn you apart. Or at the very least, crippled you. Foolish, hairless ape!"

"Sorry," I replied, feeling the fool. *"I won't do it again."*

"What's done is done. Now, use that condensed ether to start forming the third vein. It is your second metal one. Once formed, you'll be able to develop the vein itself in no time. Perhaps an hour, at most."

"Thank you, I mean it."

Ivory didn't reply, he just retreated to the back of my mind, evidently content with my thanks. Sure, if he weren't a dick most of the time, I wouldn't be arguing with him. This was a good start, I hoped. Still, I could feel his presence around my core.

I closed my eyes and immediately noticed a difference as the second metal affinity lit up ever so slightly. And not just that, the highly compressed ether had changed places with whatever else had been in my core before. I was sure that my capacity had risen and would continue to do so with every passing moment.

"Why is he grinning like that?" Prometheus asked just as I opened my eyes. I threw him a wink.

"My unwanted tenant just taught me how to absorb and compress ether much faster."

"Oh? How? Why? Can we do it, too?" Hera asked.

Ajax pushed out of his seat and plopped down next to me. His meaty hand dropped on my shoulder.

"Explain it to me, Master Kenji," the big man said. "And make sure you use language even I can understand."

CHAPTER 23: DANGEROUS TIMES

Our train took on water and coal at the Swiss-German border, stopping at an ancient-looking station in Schaffhausen, a city on the Rhine River. Ajax and I took this break as an opportunity to stretch our legs.

"They're good people. That's all that matters," Ajax said after I'd asked him about Layla and Kate's destination. I didn't feel great about offloading them in some other location, with people I didn't know, especially after they'd just come from the cabin.

Ajax didn't blame me for my concerns, after all, none of us were really all that trusting anymore. Especially me. I could only imagine what my fractured skull looked like in an X-ray. I didn't want to leave the girls with just anyone, so I had to make sure.

"Ulm has probably seen better days," I muttered. "And how far is it from the Federsee?"

Ajax sighed and gave me one of those looks that exhausted parents gave their kids.

"Fifty-five or sixty kilometers southwest of Ulm. It is roughly a day's travel if we push it. And before you ask again, I will tell you why we are taking the girls to Ulm. My friends there are academics. I studied with them at university. I took them under my wing during their first year in school—showed them around, guided them to the best professors, and helped them avoid the dodgy parts of town. They talked regularly about their family in Ulm and said they would settle there. They are good people, Kenji. I have no doubts that they'll repay the favor."

After reboarding, the train chugged north for another five or six hours, before finally arriving in Ulm. Sadly, the city was what I'd expected. Once a cozy, mid-sized city, Ulm had truly reverted to its medieval roots.

Without the resources to build with stone, the residents instead erected a stout, timber wall around a portion of the city. Those buildings not inside the wall had weathered. While some looked inhabited, the vast majority were crumbling and damaged.

The girls filed off the train behind us, and although they didn't speak, I could sense their fear and apprehension. Thanks to the end of the train being so far away from the town, I was able to let Omega and Lazy Bones out of the car. My wolf companion led the bear out into the woods and away from people. But before I'd even made it halfway back to Layla and Kate, I sensed the wolf watching and following me. I scanned the tree line, as well as the long grass, but saw nothing.

"Your camouflage is getting good, my furry friend," I whispered.

We moved as a group through Ulm's gate and stepped back in time two thousand years. The roads were cobblestone and dirt, and while some of the thoroughfares had been covered with straw, long stretches looked like mud. Wagons and horses lined up on one side, while men and women carrying baskets walked on the other.

The buildings were showing age. The paint was fading and flaking away, while at least half the structures I could see from the main road were missing windows or doors.

"This place looks like a medieval ruin," Layla breathed,

as a man led a mule-pulled dung cart past us. "This is where you want us to stay? I think I would have rather stayed at the cabin."

"Me, too," Kate agreed.

"Come along," I said, hooking my arm through hers. "It can't be that bad. Let's check in with Ajax's friends and get a better lay of the land."

We walked up the roadway a bit, the Ulm commoners giving us a wide birth. It did feel a bit strange. No one waved or greeted us, and those few merchants we did see made no attempt to draw our attention or sell us anything. That was really strange.

"Talk about a full one-eighty from Zurich," I whispered, leaning into Prometheus. "Everyone there was busy getting in our faces. Here, they can't get far enough away."

"That is no joke," the scout whispered back. "It feels like I might get a knife in the back before a handshake around here."

We turned off the main street and into the alleys and Ulm grew darker and more decrepit. Full rubbish bins filled the crowded spaces, while rats scurried away as we approached. Ajax led us past a massive church, with the tallest steeple I'd ever seen.

"Did you know that Albert Einstein was born here?" the big man asked. But before any of us could respond, he froze, his eyes locked on a particularly dilapidated house ahead and to the right.

I knew why right away. If the building's appearance wasn't enough, it was practically surrounded by hoodlums. There was no other way to describe them.

Two men in brown trousers sat on the crumbling front porch. One drank from a brown earthen ware pitcher, while the man next to him slapped a short club against his thigh. One leaned against the left side of the house, but his body was hidden in shadow, while a fourth walked a noticeable patrol around the perimeter. They were all armed.

"Stay with the girls," Ajax said, stopping me.

"Wait up!" I called and turned to Layla. "Stay with Prom and Hera. If anything happens, get back to the train right away. Don't walk. Run. Got it?"

Both girls nodded, their eyes still locked on Ajax's retreating form. I knew what they were thinking, but I couldn't let Ajax go alone.

"Kenji," Layla said, stepping forward. "Be careful!"

I grabbed her hand and kissed it.

"I will. Besides, I've got a guardian angel looking after me."

Her face screwed up for a moment, but then I turned to jog away. She couldn't feel Omega like I could. The wolf was somewhere nearby, and he'd been quietly feeding off my emotions. In simple terms, the wolf's blood was up.

"Are you sure that this is the right place?" I asked as I caught up with Ajax. The hoodlums had already noticed us.

"Ich bin mir sicher," Ajax grumbled and pulled the hammer from his back.

"Are we in trouble?"

"That depends on what happened to my friends, and how these cretins respond," he explained.

I nodded and I broke the Nodachi loose from its scabbard on my back. I hadn't used it in a while, seeing as most of our fights recently had been in close quarters.

The house spoke to me as we approached. The front door had been kicked in, while the windows on the first floor were broken. And not shattered, as if from a storm, but broken in from a rock or club. A large scorch mark covered the right side of the porch, where some of the wood had been blackened by fire.

This house saw a fight, that was sure. But when? And how had it gone down?

"Hallo du!" Ajax bellowed. "Was machst du hier? Das ist nicht dein Haus."

"So much for doing this quietly," I muttered.

"Who are you?" one of the hoodlums from the porch

shouted back. He pushed his way to his feet and then smacked his club against the post.

"Where are the Fischers? A family lived in this house. Where are they?" Ajax asked.

"Don't know," the hoodlum replied. "They are probably in the same place as all the families that lived in these houses... somewhere else. That is if they are still alive. We own this neighborhood now. It is ours. Got it?"

I followed his gesture down the street and realized that all the houses in the line looked the same—kicked-in doors, and broken windows with obvious signs of fire or violence. Shit. Had Ajax's friends fallen victim to some kind of turf war?

"I'm only going to ask once more," Ajax said, settling at the bottom of the porch stairs. "Where are the Fischers? And what did you do to them?"

"Don't know. Don't care," the man said, then bent over to spit at Ajax's feet. "But I will say this. Probably the same thing that is about to happen to you. Fools that wander onto our turf get cracked skulls. If they survived our clubs, then they might still be alive."

The thug laughed as his mates came up behind him, with more filing out of the house.

I watched the man, previously hiding in the shadow on the left side of the house, approach. He held a similar club in his right hand, and a long tactical knife in his left. My big friend couldn't see him.

Ajax smiled and laughed in time with the thug, then abruptly brought his head forward hard, slamming the crown of his skull into the hoodlum's midsection.

"Shit," I cursed as the others reacted.

I pulled the nodachi free just as the man hiding to Ajax's left sprinted forward, his knife poised to strike. I focused on the ether inside me and activated my enhanced speed and strength. Swelling with power, I streaked forward, hitting the thug in the chest and shoving him backward. I didn't stop moving until my big blade pinned him to the house next door.

He looked at me, his eyes wide in shock, and then after gargling for a moment, went limp.

"Sorry, dead guy," I said and pulled the sword free, "but you shouldn't have tried to hurt my friend."

I ran back around the corner, only to find Ajax standing over the two men from the porch. Judging from their mangled faces and the blood dripping from his hammer, I'd say they got a taste of their own medicine. Good.

Ajax spun toward me, a slightly manic gleam in his eyes.

"Easy, big guy. It's just me," I said, holding up a hand. Ajax looked back down at the dead men and seemed to snap to his senses.

"What happened to—? Did I do that?" he asked, pointing his hammer at their bodies.

I recognized the signs of battle lust—the jarring drive to violence that momentarily transformed my large and jovial friend into a hammer-swinging monster.

"The couple that lived in this house. They are gone. And we should get out of here before more of these thugs show up," I said. In response to my suggestion, the front door of the house opened.

"Shit!" one man gasped, his gaze locking onto the two dead thugs.

Ajax and I backed away.

"You two did this?" he said, as voices echoed from behind him.

"They attacked us," I tried to explain. "We were just asking about the people that used to live in this house. We didn't want any trouble."

"Well, it sure as shit looks like you found some irregardless," the thug said as men piled out of the house behind him.

Ajax bristled. "It is regardless. Irregardless isn't a...oh, never mind."

We backed away as the porch filled with men, all armed.

"Looks like you boys need to learn a lesson. I think we'll

have to beat it into your skulls. You'll be lucky if you die, too. You wouldn't want to know what Hertzberg would do to you!" the thug spat, jerking his head threateningly at Ajax.

He laughed and turned to look at his compatriots, but he turned back just as my counterpart's hammer thumped into his chest.

The blow slammed him back into the others, and they all fell, tumbling like bowling pins.

Ajax backed up next to me as the thugs recovered and leaped off the porch. All except for the man that Ajax hit in the chest. He was still down and clutching his ribs.

"Do we fight or run?" I asked.

"I'm not going down with some fool's knife stuck in my back. If these bastards are dumb enough to kick good people out of their homes, then they can answer for it."

"Fair enough," I said and readied my nodachi. "Least kills pays for dinner."

Ajax lifted his hammer and laughed as the men swarmed in.

I sidestepped for room and lunged in. My nodachi sang a deadly tune, cutting through a hand swinging a club, then a long dirty kitchen knife, and even a shield as I tapped into my super human strength.

Those three men fell, and yet they were not killing blows. I'd hoped that the others would see them as examples and flee. Only, I had no such luck. More thugs spilled out of the Fischer's house, but also from the house next to it, and the alley between them. Shit, they flowed forth like cockroaches.

Ajax bludgeoned one man to death, hitting him square in the head and caving it in. And even with that gory spectacle, the thugs pressed in.

I cut ahead, stabbed hard, and slashed left, working to avoid my big friend on the right. I ended another man with a nasty slash down from his shoulder, clean through to his belly, decapitated another, and deflected several violent club swings.

My arms tired as the nodachi was no light weight, and

despite the strength skill, which ate away at my ether reserves. We'd killed half a dozen men, and yet more were streaming in, not just replacing the fallen, but doubling their numbers.

"That was a nice warm-up!" I whispered and swung my sword before me, trying to get the crowd of thugs to stay back. "We could cut these bastards in half all day, and I think more of them would still come. Any ideas?"

"Kill…all of…them," Ajax grunted and swung his hammer into the closest man. Instead of stopping with grace, his hammer flew from his hands and toppled ungainly through the air, landing in the dirt a dozen paces away.

"The…hell?" Ajax cursed. "The damn thing swung out of control!"

"Maybe you need to work on that grip," I teased, "work more forearm exercises into your fitness regimen?"

"Ahh! Shut up, little man! Or I'll pick you up and swing you as a weapon," Ajax growled, as he unhooked his hand axe from a belt loop.

"You're dead…"

"Worm food…"

"Dog meat," the thugs yelled, jabbing and swinging their clubs as their growing numbers surrounded us. I couldn't get an accurate count, but I had to guess there were a dozen of them, maybe more.

"Where do you pricks come from? Is there a storage box full of generic assholes sitting in a house somewhere with a sign on it that reads 'open for added stupidity'?"

Ajax laughed and swept his axe at waist level, pushing three men back. A tingle shot up my spine and a tremendous swell of anger filled my guts. My senses brightened and my nose filled with the musky smell of dirty, unwashed bodies. I knew what it was immediately, grabbed Ajax by the collar of his armor, and wrenched him back.

Omega, almost perfectly camouflaged, bolted from the darkness between houses and hit the group of thugs like a wrecking ball. He knocked three men aside, grabbed the fourth in his jaws, and threw him aside like a rag doll.

Ajax and I took advantage of the chaos. We waded forth, cutting, chopping, and stabbing. To the thugs' credit, they rallied and fought back. Until they realized what they were fighting.

"It's a goddamned monster! A monster!" one hoodlum screamed, right before Omega leaped onto him and pulled off his head.

The remaining crowd of thugs scattered. Those that could run, at least.

The last man still fighting swung his club at my face, but I deflected the blow wide. Then I reversed my grip, and instead of skewering him through the chest, I rammed the pommel of my heavy blade right into his head. The thug went down like a sack of potatoes.

Ajax snapped his axe back onto his belt and retrieved his hammer, while Omega prowled around me.

"You'd better vanish," I whispered. And although the wolf could not comprehend the words, he understood my meaning. A ripple coursed over his fur and Omega started to fade, until he blended perfectly into the dirt road.

"I mean to find out what happened here," Ajax howled.

"Ask that one when he wakes up," I said, pointing to the man I'd knocked unconscious.

Without a word, Ajax grabbed him by the shirt and started pulling him back towards Prometheus and the others. Omega loped along behind me, then cut through the alley, where his camouflage rendered him completely invisible.

Prometheus and Hera snapped to when we appeared down their street but followed without question as Ajax dragged the unconscious man behind an abandoned house.

He tossed the thug up against the wall, then grabbed him by his long hair and lifted his face. His eyes fluttered open a few moments later and he cried out.

Ajax's interrogation was short but effective. It turned out his friends, the Fischers, had simply been in the wrong place at the wrong time. The thugs moved into town from Stuttgart, after being displaced from their territory by a rival gang. They'd killed the local Sheriff first, then took over the town block by block. The Fischers refused to give up their home, and like so many other families in Ulm, paid the ultimate price.

The thug told us that they'd taken over Ulm because of its proximity to the bunker of an abandoned air force base. The thugs hadn't meant to kill so many inhabitants of the city, but once people started to resist, it snowballed out of control. The gang recruited a large portion of the town, thanks to fear, but their leader lived in the bunker now.

Ajax was set on his course before we'd finished our interrogation. Prometheus and I tried to talk him out of it, but the big man was on a warpath.

"Stay here if you like. They pay...blood for blood. The town will finish what we started. They are like a virus, and the good people will rise up and purge them."

Hera stayed with Layla and Kate. Although she volunteered to do so, we could tell that she wasn't happy about it. The rest of our pack was going to war.

From what our captive had told us, their group hadn't started out as a simple gang of thugs. The men at their core were disbanded mercenaries. Perhaps not unlike us. That gave us a powerful advantage as they were operating individually, without the backing of a kingdom or sovereign. We also possessed the element of surprise, as long as we got there before any of the escaped thugs.

They wouldn't be expecting an attack either, much less a team of three-veined veterans accompanied by an invisible wolf. Well, one at three veins, and two nearly there.

I sent Omega out ahead to scout the path. He could also run down any runaways that were trying to hurry back to their leader. Prometheus led us down the old freeway, through bushes growing up and out of the cracked pavement, and along lines of long abandoned vehicles.

The air force base was in a shambles, as several large helicopters had either crashed on arrival or while trying to take off. As a result, the traffic control tower was rubble, along with two of the hangars. Several helicopters had been left in varying states of preparedness, although those had been stripped and vandalized.

It was dusk by the time we arrived at the bunker. It sat on the western periphery of the base. The thugs had gone to great length to hide the entrance with dirt and bushes, but they'd not bothered themselves to remove any of the signage.

"You'd think if someone didn't want to be found, they would have taken those down," I whispered to Ajax, and he nodded.

A thug walked a patrol above and behind the bunker, but we watched as a barely noticeable blur crept up on him from behind, and then the man simply disappeared. A few swaying branches were the only indicator he was ever there in the first place.

"Your wolf is getting a little too good at that," Ajax muttered. "What happens if he decides we're not his pack anymore?"

"We'll just have to make sure that he feels nice and welcome," I said as Prometheus led us right up to the door. The scout slipped inside, and we followed, having to step over the body of a dead man. You could say a lot of things about Prometheus, but he was quiet and deadly.

Ajax and I moved far slower down the winding concrete steps, knowing full well that if we rushed, we'd make enough noise to alert everyone below. Maybe it had something to do with his cultivation, or maybe he'd just worn his really sneaky boots. Who knew?

I felt fur brush against my arm as Omega moved up next to me. I hadn't even heard the wolf enter—not his breathing, or the click-click of his claws on the concrete. Hell, maybe it was the wolf's presence driving Prometheus to be better. If the two were competing to be the best and stealthiest killers in the pack, we'd all benefit.

I stopped at the bottom to catch my breath and looked around.

There wasn't much to the place, as the passage at the bottom of the stairs branched off in three directions, and there were three of us. Glowing crystals had been duct taped into place on the walls, their radiant light dispelling most of the gloom.

"Are you ready?" Prometheus whispered from the shadows, nodding to the left.

I cycled some ether and waited for my heart to stop racing. Ajax sagged against the wall, panting for air. Neither of us liked stairs that much, going up, or down, especially after running for several hours to get there.

Omega huffed quietly and snorted, letting us all know that he was tired of waiting. I patted him on the head and quietly slid my nodachi back into its scabbard, then drew my katana and wakizashi. I pointed toward the center corridor and moved.

"Hey! Who's that?" a man asked as he unexpectedly appeared in the doorway ahead. The tip of my blade slid easily into his throat, silencing him forever.

"It's me," I whispered, letting his body quietly slide to the ground.

I moved into the next room and quietly dispatched a thug sleeping in his cot. Another man woke as I straightened, but before he could muster a single shout, a furry mass of teeth and claws descended on him. He died, gargling in his own blood.

Thanks to our informant, we knew the bunker was laid out in a grid. We also knew roughly where the barracks were, the mess, showers, fitness area, and where their leader slept.

I headed for the barracks, while Prometheus took a passage to the right, intending to cut the head off the snake. I knew it was my scout friend's attempt to test himself, and I was all for it. Omega moved with me, sliding quietly into rooms before me, and only going for the kill once I'd entered. He was efficient and didn't mutilate anyone. It was like he'd been watching me and was trying to mimic my style.

Fifteen minutes. That was all it took for us to sweep through the bunker and kill everyone we found. Omega slipped away after we thought we were done. In the end, he found a few that were hiding. If this was what compressed ether could do for us, then I couldn't wait to get the team to their third and fourth veins.

We met in the mess hall afterward, to sort through everything we'd seen, what we knew, and to decide on our plan moving forward. Prometheus voiced his frustration, as the thug leader hadn't been in his quarters. Ajax stumbled upon him in a corridor and bashed his head against the wall. We found a cold box of drinks, practically drooling as we pulled forth three ice-cold beers.

Omega appeared again from a side passage, his jaws clamped onto a thrashing man. Still very much alive, the man screamed and yelped once the wolf let go.

I fought the urge to put the man out of his misery, but in the end, bound his wound to stop the bleeding. We propped him up on a bench and began the download.

"Answer our questions and you live," Ajax said, taking the lead. "How many of you are left? And how many are topside?"

The wounded man clutched at his leg and shuddered. It was another few moments before he found his voice.

"I...don't think there's anyone left. Although we have a second...group in town."

"What second group? What town?" Prometheus asked, feigning ignorance.

"We've got over thirty in Ulm now. They've taken over at least two streets. Maybe more."

We drilled him for a while longer, although most of the intel he shared wasn't particularly useful. He passed out after that. Ajax voted to kill him, while surprisingly, Prometheus wanted to keep him alive. In the end, I sided with our scout, as living people were better bargaining chips than dead ones.

"So, what now?" I asked as Omega jumped on the table and lay next to me. It sagged and groaned under his weight.

"I just don't know," Ajax replied as he let out a deep sigh. "I haven't had a chance to mourn my friends, Kenji. I thought we would meet up here, have a few drinks, and catch up. Then the girls could stay here, safe and sound, while we continued onward. My whole plan is just...shit now."

"The best we can hope for is what? Settling them somewhere safe?" Prometheus asked. "Or do we take them with us?"

Ajax shook that idea away. "They will become leverage for every scumbag and treacherous noble out there."

"So, what about Munich?" Prometheus proposed.

"But isn't that where that...noble's son, ugh..." I stammered struggling with the twit's name. "Bauer. The Bauers are from Munich, right?"

Ajax nodded. "But Munich is a big city, with strong walls. If we could get into the city anonymously, then the girls would be completely safe.

"It couldn't be us," I said. "They saw our faces at the arena. Prom, it would have to be you and Hera."

"The girls are gonna be so pissed," Prometheus added.

"Sure are," I said. "We should head back. And Prom, you can take lead, so you can tell the girls."

CHAPTER 24: DOORS

Prometheus and I made the long trek back to Ulm, while Ajax stayed behind at the bunker to clean up from our kills. We arrived in town, only to find another, much smaller train sitting outside town. Pulled by a small and nondescript steam engine, the train was only three cars long. They'd been up-armored, too, with heavy metal plating reinforcing the car doors and access panels.

We gawked and almost moved right by until a familiar face appeared in the rear car's open door. Hans Gruber waved us over, his blue eyes twinkling in the sunlight.

"Greetings, Hallo Freunde," the Protectorate captain said.

Prometheus raised a hand and waved before he realized what he was doing.

"Takemi, my friend. You do not look surprised to see me."

"The only thing I expect out of you, Hans, is the unexpected. Honestly, that is the only way I can get by anymore," I admitted.

"We have much to discuss. Please come in. Your Freunde are already here," Hans said, gesturing us towards the train.

"We really need to gather our gir—" Prometheus started to say, but Hans cut him off.

"Your ladies are already here, and they are safe and sound. Now come in. I just had my attendant heat some water for tea."

Reluctantly, we stepped up into the car and followed Hans inside. We stepped into a clean, yet utilitarian space. Leather upholstered benches sat to the left and right, while the middle of the car featured a round meeting table, surrounded by simple, wood chairs. Four out of the eight chairs were filled with Hera, Layla, Kate, and to all of my surprise, Mike.

Prometheus moved forward to check on Kate, but I locked eyes with Layla, and then Mike. Ajax's smith friend looked frazzled, to say the least.

Layla threw her arms around me and kissed my cheek when I joined them at the table, then at Hans' insistence, we sat, and his attendant served us tea.

"Your first question is undoubtedly why am I here," Hans said after dropping a cube of sugar into his tea. "The second is likely, why is he here," he said, pointing at Mike, "and why are your ladies in my train car."

"I think that covers the first wave of questions pretty good," I admitted.

"Sehr gut," Hans said with that disarming smile of his. "Firstly, as you have already surmised, Zurich is in turmoil. Some of the factions have diverged."

"Meaning…?" Prometheus pushed.

"They went against the King's implicit instructions to leave you be. The Protectorate intercepted no less than eight kill squads the night you fled the city. I am regretful that we were not able to locate the ones waiting for you outside the city, but from what I have been told, you scattered their pieces far and wide."

"Where is Kruger?" I asked, leaning in.

"He already left Zurich, but will meet with you at the Melee," Hans said. "You still have the full support of the

Protectorate, and to a slightly lesser degree, the King. I knew you would need proof, so that is why I recovered and provided your man here with safe passage."

Hans pointed to Mike, who gave me a rigid nod. He supported what looked like a guitar case in his lap, his hands gripping it so tight his knuckles were white.

"What happened?"

"Not long after you all left, a kill squad tried to kick down my door. When they couldn't batter their way past my reinforced doors, they resorted to throwing Molotov cocktails through the windows. The animals burned down my smithy, and half the block with it," Mike explained.

Now that he said it, I noticed what looked like soot darkening his beard, nostrils, and the skin around his eyes.

"My men dispatched that squad and pulled your man out," Hans explained.

"But surely you didn't have to bring him all this way?" I concluded. "And how did you know that we would be here?"

"I have my sources," the captain said, flashing me a smile. "Besides, I wanted to reassure you that the Protectorate was and is still behind you. That we mean to honor our end of all deals."

"It is nice to hear that some people can still be taken at their word," I said.

"Exakt!" Hands nodded. "But we also wanted you to know about the fracture in Zurich. We do not know how far some of these groups will go to harm you. They may have sent couriers out to foreign-speaking mercenary groups. Once a hit is issued, it can go far and wide."

Hans had cookies and crackers brought in and we ate and talked for a while longer. It was strange how forthcoming he was, as like before, I was struck with the compulsion to believe him. Hell, I wanted to really like him. But everything he told us jibed perfectly with what we'd seen and heard, so far.

"What will you do next?" I asked him as we offloaded from his train.

"I have weasels to root out in Zurich. I must oversee the pacification of the city before heading to the Melee myself. Trust in your instincts, watch your back, and be careful who you let into your circle."

We watched as his locomotive turned around in the turntable, then chugged south and towards Zurich once again.

"Honestly, when he showed up, I thought we were dead for sure," Hera breathed once the train was out of sight.

"He scared you more than the thugs hiding in Ulm?" I asked.

She nodded.

"But you missed that part. The residents rooted them all out. They hung every single one of them from trees outside of town. They got scary about it, actually. Said that if anyone came to town with dark or bad thoughts, they only needed to look to those trees for a change of heart."

"They seem like good people," Kate cut in. "Just good people pushed too far."

I filled them in on what happened at the bunker, and of course, Hera was annoyed. She'd been looking for an opportunity to test out her new spear, and we'd left her without targets to practice on.

"You'll have plenty of chances soon enough," I told her.

It was almost daybreak the following day by the time we all made it back to the bunker. Mike walked that whole way in silence, clutching that large, hard case to his side. We were greeted by an excited Ajax and a surprisingly clean space. Omega bounded up to me and almost bowled me over.

I wasn't sure what the wolf had been doing, as he left big, bloody pawprints all over me.

"Don't worry about the blood. It's pretty easy to break it down using ether," Ivory chimed in as I slapped Omega's paws away.

"You don't say…and when did you plan on telling me about it?"

"Never. Or, if I felt bad for you. Or, something."

I snorted.

Hera ran ahead of us, and Omega turned to her instead, playfully running after the woman. In some ways, he could pass for a dog, but then I thought better of it. He was twice the height of the largest dog breed in existence.

"There's nothing but empty land out here," Kate said as she scanned the old air base.

"That's probably why this merc outfit lasted so long. Just think that they could have survived out here if they hadn't gotten greedy," I said, letting my gaze sweep out over the ruined tarmac. Dry grass crunched beneath my feet as I moved, prompting me to look down.

It wasn't just the grass, though. I hadn't really noticed it before, but the land around the base was dead and barren. Perhaps that was what drove them into Ulm. If they'd been unable to grow their own food, then they would have either gathered what they needed, or in their case, pushed into a more fertile area.

Hera disappeared back into the bunker, and Omega followed with Kate, Layla, and I heading down a few minutes later. Ajax stayed outside, talking quietly to Mike. It made me feel better seeing him finally talking to someone.

"He's kind of cute. Like a puppy," Layla chuckled when we reached the bottom of the long stairs. "But then you watch him maul a group of thugs to death, and well, it kind of kills that thought. Doesn't it?"

"It really does," I agreed.

I meandered around the bunker for a while, helping the others tidy up and clean. But I returned to the surface not long after, to check on our other animal companion. Lazy Bones followed us from Ulm, but the bear wanted no part of the bunker. Instead, he bedded down in the ruins of a nearby hangar.

I checked on him, only to discover him curled up in the far corner, snoring loudly.

"Were they truly bad...guys?" Layla asked after I'd

returned to the bunker, securing the outside hatch behind me.

I considered the question for a moment before answering.

"I think at one time they were probably a lot like us, but they started using their power to not just protect themselves but take things from other people. They killed Ajax's friends and God knows how many others in Ulm. They tried to kill us. So now they are dead."

"Were they weak, like us? Kate and me?"

"Yeah, just like you," I joked.

Layla jabbed me in the ribs for that one. We explored for a while after that and discovered that the bunker was actually much larger than we thought. Its previous merc tenants had never ventured beyond a pressure door located in the back of the mess. Once Ajax muscled it open, we realized that it extended back and down, into a deeper and even more secure portion of the complex.

Behind twenty-foot-thick walls of concrete and steel, we discovered a massive generator. To our astonishment, it turned over and started. Overhead lights flickered on and off for the brief twenty to thirty seconds while it ran. But then it sputtered and died.

"How is that possible?" Kate asked. "I thought ether suppressed everything electrical."

"Maybe this is far enough in the ground that it hasn't been affected by it?" Prometheus proposed.

We stood around, scratching our chins and contemplating that dilemma for a while. As it stood, the generator wouldn't run as it was and none of us, save for Mike, knew enough about diesel engines to fix it, so we sealed the room back up. I'd ask Ajax's friend about it, but I decided to wait until he'd had a chance to digest recent events first.

After further exploration, we discovered an entire freezer room. We didn't know why or how it remained so cold, but it was *cold* even without the generator running.

"We could store a lot of food in here," Hera breathed,

watching her breath fog the air.

We found an armory, a radio room, a map room, and a chemical detoxification chamber next. Unfortunately, someone had emptied the armory long ago. Perhaps when everything collapsed and the soldiers abandoned the base.

"What did you find down there?" Prometheus asked as he joined the others in the barracks above. The scout straightened after shoving a footlocker against the wall and cursed. Something popped in his back. "You would think that after hitting the third vein back pain would be a thing of the past."

"Or you're just a faker," Hera laughed. "You must still be in your second."

"They're both wrong," Ivory offered. *"Your bodies will only be remolded once you hit the second realm."*

"I have it on good authority that you will never have back pain again once you hit the second realm," I said, turning to a door in the back of the room. "Are those the showers? I think we all need to get cleaned up, have a bite to eat, then grab some rest. Then we set out again?"

"Yes. Through that door, turn left, and go straight past the shitters," Ajax said. Mike grumbled something behind him, but I couldn't tell what it was.

I turned and slapped my thigh. Omega came running, but when he tried to stop, slipped, skidded, and sprawled to the ground. While next to me, the wolf rolled and growled, practically begging to have his belly scratched. I obliged.

"I think he's broken," Hera laughed. "Just look at him."

"He's not broken, that mutant is just happy to be by your side again. And he's bothering me to tell you!"

"Thank you, Ivory. I'll relay the message."

"Do you girls want first crack at the showers?" I asked as I put my arm over Layla's shoulder.

"Maybe. Why? Is there a…oh, wait. I almost asked if they had hot water, but without the generator running, how would that work? Never mind. Ignore me."

"You go first," Kate offered, then winked at Layla. "You leave Omega with me in the kitchen…and we'll prepare some food."

Layla looked up at me, her cheeks catching fire.

"I think I like this plan," I said and took her hand.

Layla and I made for the showers just as Omega whined and turned on the spot. I looked down at the wolf, and in response, he sniffed the air, then bolted from the room and into the hall. Disturbed by his strange behavior, we followed.

"What in the hell has gotten into you?" I asked as we caught up with him, and yet, he sniffed the air, circled, and took off at a run again. At the next intersection, he stopped. He turned left and started scratching at a blank stretch of wall. When he backed away, I noticed that he was clawing at a small vent located just above the floor.

"There is something behind the wall," Ivory whispered. *"Do you remember what I taught you? Use your senses."*

I nodded and focused in. He was right. When I really concentrated, I could feel a faint trickle of ether coming from the wall. I placed both palms against it and pushed a gentle stream of ether forth through my metal affinity vein. The wall instantly started to vibrate. A moment after it started to vibrate, the metal grew soft beneath my palm. And yet, the wall constituted far more mass than I'd ever tried to manipulate before.

A far cry from molding wolf bones, the wall resisted my intrusion. Sweat broke out on my brow and the back of my neck, but I pushed harder. A trickle of warmth ran down my top lip from my nose.

I wiped it away, only then realizing that it was blood. Redoubling my efforts, I pushed even more ether into the bulkhead, fighting to peel open the metal. It fought me, and so I fought back.

Finally, after my arm started to shake, my hand slipped inside, and I used the momentum to pull the softer area apart. But it hardened almost instantly, the jagged metal cutting my palm and fingers.

I winced and pulled my hands back, blood trickling down and onto the ground. The wounds weren't particularly deep, but I didn't even have a chance to wipe the blood away before Omega leaned in and started to clean the area.

"Thanks, Bud," I whispered, and patted the fur between his ears. "Let's see what you found here."

I peeked into the hole, but it was too dark.

"Here, take this," Kate said, handing me a flare from her pack.

I couldn't remember ever using one, but with my history of fractured skulls and memory loss, that didn't mean much. I studied its design for a moment. The cap on top had a striking pad. When I pulled it free, I noticed an exposed tip, not unlike a match, on the flare itself. Angling it away, I rubbed the two together and was rewarded with a flash of bright light and heat. Thick smoke surrounded me as the flare burned.

"Shit, this thing smells like a fart," I cursed and then pushed it into the hole in the wall. I peeked inside, squinting through the smoke and bright light.

"What is it?" Layla asked. "What do you see?"

"Not much but I think it's safe to drop the flare." I threw the flare straight ahead and watched as it landed on the ground. The space beyond the bulkhead was a room with shiny metal tables, and what looked like lockers to my left.

"Well, what is it? What do you see?" Ajax pressed.

"It is a whole room," I grunted, working to widen the hole.

Prometheus and Kate ran around me, turning down both sides of the next passage, but we could find no doors, hidden or otherwise, that would lead us into the space. They returned and waited, as I slowly but surely molded and widened my hole. Once it was large enough, I leaned my head through and took a look.

The space beyond looked just like the armory we'd found below, only this one wasn't empty. Far from it. We'd discovered a hidden cache. But of what? I'd need to get inside for a better look.

"Look inside," I said and pulled away from the hole in the wall.

Ajax moved in and poked his head through, just as the flare died. Mike hovered behind him, his curiosity growing.

"I don't see anything," he groused. "Just darkness."

"Well, you're going to have to trust me then," I said, patting him gently on the rear.

"Hey, hands off!"

"Surely there is another way in there," Prometheus proposed. "That is, without having to destroy the whole wall."

I moved in once Ajax cleared out, sticking my arm all the way in. I felt around the hole, toward the ceiling, and then the floor, but couldn't find anything. I pulled back and knelt down in front of Omega.

"Boy, can you feel anything else? Something that resonates from the room?"

Omega whined again, nudging my hand with his snout, and then turned back to the room. He sniffed the air and growled softly, then moved to the left. I followed him down the passage, past the barracks, and then moved right. We'd moved only a dozen paces down that hall before he stopped in front of a large poster hanging on the wall to our right.

He pawed at the poster, his claws tearing clear through the soft paper.

"What is it?" Layla asked.

"The question at hand," I said, looking to Prometheus and Kate. "Why would you go to such trouble to hide a door? Just one door?"

Kate and our scout shared a look. It might have been that they both scoured that very hallway and had completely overlooked the poster, or, more realistically, that they knew I was asking rhetorically.

Layla stepped back and grabbed ahold of Kate.

"Hey, stop it!" Kate whispered.

"Protect me. Especially if a monster jumps out to eat us?" Layla said, but she threw me a subtle wink.

I snorted, lifted my hand to the top of the poster, and tore it off the wall. A peculiar-looking pressure door sat behind it. Barely four feet high and two feet wide, the portal was controlled by a small panel next to it on the wall. My index finger slid onto the open button, although I wasn't surprised when nothing happened. The generator wasn't running, so nothing had power.

Luckily, without power, the lock seemed to have been programmed to fail open. I found a strong grip, set my feet, and slid the right-side door open. And yet, the portal was so small, that Ajax and Mike would have no chance of slipping through unless both doors were fully opened.

I tried to push the left-hand side of the door open, but it was stuck fast. After several unsuccessful attempts, I straightened, cursed at the door, and waved the others back.

"Take a few steps back. Just in case something explodes," I said. Ether rushed from my core and out through my arms, covering me in a dull, white glow.

"Time to use some **<<Enhanced Strength>>**," I said, feeling the power course through my body.

I channeled all of my strength forward, my arms, back, and legs coiling beneath me. The door groaned and creaked but resisted, so I pushed harder, and harder.

"Be careful..." Layla started to say. I half turned to give her a smile, just as I funneled all of my available strength into the door. I leaned in, grunting, just as something cracked loudly inside the wall, and I pitched forward.

I saw the door disappear into the wall, just as my face collided hard with the wall. Stars exploded before my vision and a wave of darkness rolled in right after.

The pagoda formed before me, resolving out of the mist. I heard Ivory's voice calling to me, beckoning me toward the koi pond, but my legs and feet never solidified.

I tried to move forward as excitement filled me. Surely,

new floors and abilities had been unlocked since my last visit, and I was desperate to explore. And yet, I could still feel my physical body, my face lying against the cold, metal floor. I could hear the others chattering around me, too, their worried voices breaking through the fog.

"…good show, you bloody idiot," Hera said, her voice louder than the others.

My body rocked from one side to the other, and the pagoda simply melted away. My eyes popped open, and I found Hera standing over top of me.

"There he is! Captain battering ram is back from sleepy time," she hissed, beaming. The others crowded in, their faces all tight masks of worry.

"…not smart," Prometheus chastised.

"I would have thought having your head caved-in once would be enough," Ajax added, and with Hera's help, they pulled me to my feet.

I wobbled for a moment before my legs grew steady.

"Yeah, that was kind of…dumb," I said, cradling my head. Talk about plan backfire. I'd been attempting to show off my power and, despite managing to open the door, I also gave myself a concussion in the process.

"That was highly amusing," Ivory growled. *"Can you do it again? I don't think watching you bash your head against the wall will ever get old."*

"You first," I replied.

"Are you sure you are okay?" Layla asked, holding my hands.

I nodded. My head ached, but the shame would stick with me for a bit. The experience also taught me an important lesson. I'd been able to travel to my pagoda occasionally through meditation, but also sometimes through dreams. If I were to take my quest for strength seriously, I would need to find a reliable method of traveling there.

The hidden chamber was pitch black, so we retrieved some of the glowing crystals from the passageways above.

Once we'd returned and started setting them, I realized why someone had gone to such lengths to hide the room.

What had originally looked like an armory, in actuality, was so much more. Stainless steel worktables lined the outside wall, while several stout workbenches filled the middle of the space. The back wall was covered in heavy-duty cabinets, and two closets yielded more racks of equipment, components, and several large boxes.

The room was a lab and judging from what we found scattered on the workbenches, an important one. Several simple milling machines sat to the right of the door, with several boxes laid out next to them. They were filled with what looked like gun components.

"If they were just making guns down here, why go to so much trouble to hide it?" Hera asked.

I picked up a pile of loose papers, then a clipboard, revealing a scanning device beneath it. Mike shuffled by behind me, his eyes alight with curiosity and excitement.

Several bowls of crystals sat to my right, a pile of crystal powder, and a core. A latticework of metal and wires had been built around the core, from which no less than two dozen transparent wires extended.

My gaze followed the wires to an interesting module. It looked roughly similar to the scanning devices but had been riveted into the upper receiver of a battle rifle.

"They weren't just making guns down here," I said, shuffling through papers. Unfortunately, the writing was all in German. "It looks like they were trying to make firearms that used ether."

"That would change things," Mike grunted, moving in next to me. "Such a weapon would be devastating in the right hands. Like the first warriors to use bows and arrows, or siege weapons."

"Maybe they didn't leave it on purpose," Prometheus proposed. "I remember what the initial collapse was like. People got frantic and violent. Perhaps they never got their experiments to work? Or, maybe those mercs showed up and killed or ran them off before they could finish?"

"It could be any number of a dozen possibilities, and truth be told, it doesn't matter 'why'. All that matters is that we are here now. And that leads me to my next question. What do we do with it?"

As if on cue, we all looked to Mike. He took a half-step back and looked around, then nodded.

You are right," he said, scanning the space yet again. "The room isn't just important because of the work they'd been doing in it, but the possibilities it represents."

"Could we stay here?" Layla asked.

Hera immediately started to shake her head, but Ajax cut her off.

"Why not?" he asked. "It is secure, below-ground, and has space enough for many people. And if Mike can get the generator running, the promise of power. Fuel could be an issue, but it is not without promise. There is food stashed here, large water tanks, and a filtration system. This place is more defensible than anything we've discovered yet."

I started to nod even before Ajax was finished. The others started to talk, negotiating the pros and cons of keeping a presence inside the bunker. Mike abruptly walked to the back and set the hard case on a table. He pulled open one locker, then another, and all down the line.

Drifting in behind him, I watched our smith friend rummage through the closet, before pulling out the sturdy metal boxes I'd spotted before. He unclasped the first, looked inside, and then pulled out another.

"Aha!" he growled, turning the case toward me.

Inside, stacked neatly and filling the whole space, were white boxes with red writing. Even in German, I could recognize the word 'Munition'. Mike scooped out four boxes, set them on the table next to the hard case, and tore open the first. Shiny, copper-clad ammunition sat inside, perfectly preserved.

"Those bastards set fire to my shop before I could

complete my work," Mike said, unlocking the long, hard-shell case. Then he lifted the top and stepped back, revealing the H&K UMP 45.

"I thought you said they interrupted your work?" I asked.

"They did. But luckily, I finished this first. I was working on ammunition when they showed up. I was only able to make ten ether crystal rounds. Now that problem is a...well, non-issue."

He lifted the submachine gun out of the case, removed the magazine, and pulled the charging handle back. The bolt slid back smoothly, then snapped forward again. It looked, smelled, and sounded nothing like the gun I'd found beneath that mansion. Hell, now it looked practically brand new.

"Okay. What now?" I asked.

"We have ourselves a little test fire," he said, turning for the door. "Bring that box of ammunition and the loose bullets in the case. If my predictions are right, this thing will really knock your socks off."

I scooped the box off the table and excitedly followed. Today was a good day.

CHAPTER 25: BANG-BANGS FOR LESS

Mike led me up and out of the bunker. A rather weak sun hung overhead while we trekked out into the air base but clouds were building on the horizon, the dark kind that threatened rain and storms.

We skipped over four different spots until we found an old training ground complete with an outdoor firing range. Bonus. Sandbags and tires had been piled up on both sides of a tall berm, forming a tidy, little training area.

"And look at that, we don't have to build something we need for a change," I yelled, as I lined up old cans and bottles atop a pile of sandbags.

"I would prefer this to be indoors," Mike grumbled. "There is no way of telling how far the sound will travel. The last thing we need is to let the world know that we're developing new weapons."

"Don't worry," I said, returning to him on the firing line. "Omega and I did a wide sweep around this place and there is nothing, and I mean *nothing* anywhere close. And Ulm is far enough away for them to hear. I think we're safe."

"Okay. Fine," the smith growled and pulled the UMP out of the case. He'd cut away the foam on the inside, creating a storage space for the submachine gun, the two magazines I'd found with it, and a paltry pile of ammunition.

"Have you shot anything like this before?"

I shook my head. "The closest I came was shooting pop cans off a log with my uncle's old revolver," I admitted.

"Close enough. This is a gas piston operated submachine gun. This stick magazine holds the bullets. Once it is loaded, you insert it into the lower receiver here," he said, demonstrating the action. "Once a loaded magazine is seated, either slap this paddle-style bolt release, or reach up, grab the charging handle, and pull it down. The action should force the bolt forward, strip a round off the top of the magazine, and load it into the chamber. With me so far?"

I nodded, watching him intently. It looked simple enough, but I knew that once adrenaline started flowing, the simple could quickly become cumbersome or downright impossible.

"This circular lever down here is the fire selector. It is on safe now, but if you click it to the next position, that will put it into semi-automatic mode. That means one trigger pull will give you one round. Remember the old adage," he explained, pointing at the single red bullet indicator next to that mode, "red is dead. Click it to the next one for fully automatic. Once you pull the trigger, the gun will continue to fire until the magazine is empty. Make sense?"

I nodded as Mike set the UMP down. Next, he picked up the empty magazine along with one shiny bullet from the small pile. There were maybe a dozen rounds in total, perhaps a few more. He held it up so I could see the tip, which appeared to have been filled with a waxy substance.

"These bullets are hollow point rounds. I filled that small cavity with a mixture of charged crystal shards and bee wax. Most people don't know it, but ether crystals are very stable, even when broken. And yet, if you act upon its delicate structure with enough energy, the ether will release. I have never tested the theory, but the small bit of ether could detonate on impact."

I watched as the smith loaded a single round into the magazine, tapped it against his head, and then inserted it into the UMP. He flashed me a quick smile, silently gestured to his ears, and hefted the firearm to his shoulder.

Stuffing my index fingers into my ears, I stepped back and watched. Mike released the bolt with a practiced slap, brought it to his shoulder, and took aim.

The UMP barked once, although the bang was quieter than I'd planned for. What I had not planned for was the detonation down range.

The bullet hit the empty tin can in a flash of expanding green and blue light. I felt the heat on my face, even standing some twenty yards away.

After making the gun safe, Mike and I progressed forward, only to find that every bottle and can had been knocked off the ledge. But what surprised me most, was what happened to our target.

The bullet passed through one side of the tin car, but the ether detonated as it hit the opposite side. The resulting release of energy didn't just tear the can in half but left the metal glowing hot.

Mike whistled low as he kicked the glowing metal with his boot. And when he lifted his gaze to mine, his mouth split in a wide, almost childish grin.

"Again?" he asked.

"We have to make sure the results are repeatable," I replied and smiled, too.

We went through almost half a dozen of the rounds in order to find two that worked. Mike explained that it was the primers, as those rounds—the ones that had been in the gun when I found it—had been subjected to too much moisture while in the mansion's bunker.

The third working round hit a glass bottle and didn't just shatter it, but broke it, and then promptly refused it into a bizarre shape. It looked strangely like a blooming flower.

We returned to the bunker after a successful test firing, but I didn't manage to utter a single word. Mike talked the whole walk, his excitement growing with every step forward.

The others surrounded us at the bottom of the stairs. Evidently, it was time for a round table meeting.

"We need to decide how to move forward," Ajax said after we'd all found seats around a table in the mess.

We talked for an hour and still hadn't come up with anything beyond the two most obvious solutions. We could take the girls with us to the Melee of Kings, but the mere thought of doing so made me queasy. Or, we could leave them holed up in the base. Mike was vocal about the second option, as in his words: he was setting up shop in the bunker and continuing the former inhabitant's research on ether-based weaponry.

It was damning that we were the reason the smith lost his shop and home, and in a way, we owed him a replacement.

"There is no way in hell I would stay without him," Layla admitted when finally granted the ability to speak.

"I'd be more comfortable staying if both Mike and Hera stayed behind with us," Kate added. At that, Hera's cheeks turned scarlet.

"I am not getting left behind again," she growled and slammed a fist down on the table. "I need to punch, elbow, or stab someone."

"Noted," Ajax breathed, his eyebrows rising dramatically.

"Let's take another run through the whole bunker with Omega, just to be safe. Maybe we can move Lazy Bones closer to the bunker entrance. Anyone that would stumble on this place would likely turn tail and run if they saw him," I suggested.

"That is if he'll stay," Mike cut in.

"Good point," I conceded.

"And the wounded guy tied to the chair downstairs?" Layla asked.

"I almost completely forgot about him," Prometheus

said. "I don't like the idea of him being here when I'm not. Why don't we take him into…"

"Leave him here. I will put him to work," Mike said and crossed his thick arms over his chest.

"Are you sure?" I asked.

"I would not have suggested it if I weren't," he said.

"I'm not comfortable with him here," Kate said.

"Can't you take him back to Ulm? Maybe the locals will have a way to deal with him?" Layla added.

"They'll hang him from a tree with the others," I said.

"Maybe we should give him some say?" Prometheus proposed. "It could be that he isn't really a bad guy and threw in with this lot out of desperation."

No one argued that point and a few moments later, Ajax returned with our wounded captive. Layla and Kate both pushed their chairs further away when he entered. I didn't understand why, as he wasn't an overly intimidating fellow.

"You have two choices," Ajax said. "First, we can take you to Ulm, where the townsfolk will probably hang you from a tree."

At that, the wounded thug's eyes went wide.

"Please. I don't want to die. You have to understand, I was starving when they found me. They gave me food and water. Without them…" he said, his legs shaking.

"Or, you can stay here and help repair this place. Do you have any skills or trades?" Ajax asked, cutting him off.

"I mean, I'm not a fighter like you lot. I was a farm worker before the collapse. You know? Tending crops, fixing fence rows, and every once in a while, fixing grandpa's old tractor."

I watched Mike's eyebrows disappear into his hairline.

"You have experience with diesel motors?" he asked.

The thug nodded animatedly. "Was my trade for a time. Tractors, combines, and trucks. There wasn't much I couldn't fix…of course, now that skill isn't exactly of benefit to anyone, with what ether did and all."

"Leave him here with me," Mike said.

"Now wait just a second," Kate argued.

"Not in a million years," Layla chimed in.

Mike set his feet, cleared his throat, and sighed.

"I could use an extra set of hands. And if this young man knows how to work with diesel motors, then he might be able to help get the generator running. If that were to happen, we could have heat and light."

"We have crystals and blankets," Kate argued.

"And hot water," Mike countered.

"I change my mind," Layla said, distancing herself from her sister. "If he can help with that, I'm okay with him staying."

"Layla," Kate whispered.

"What? Mike is twice his size. And besides, if he tries anything, we can just feed him to the bear."

"The bear?" the wounded thug gasped.

"Yes. We have a thousand-pound, hungry, and completely loyal bear as a pet. To him, we are pack. To him, you are just food," I said.

Ajax chuckled knowingly.

"Please. Give me a chance to prove myself. I'll fix anything you want. I won't make trouble. You'll see."

"Your name?" I asked.

"Benjamin Weber. But you can call me Benji. Everyone always does."

"All right, Benji. Prove your worth, and you'll have a place here. But betray us..." I left the threat unspoken, as I knew the imagination was oftentimes far more effective at stoking fear than the explicit.

"How long before you need to leave for this...Melee?" Mike asked.

Ajax scratched his beard. "Our time's running out. I figure we need to head that way tomorrow, to give us enough time to travel. I don't feel like running the whole way like we had to do with Zurich."

"Definitely not," I agreed.

"I'll take my new...apprentice with me to the lab. We'll see how many of those ether-filled rounds I can crank out before then. You'll be stuck with cold showers, unfortunately."

"What lab?" Benji asked as Mike pushed him into the hall.

"The lab you idiots didn't even know was here," the smith replied as the two moved out of sight.

We cleaned and organized as much of the bunker as possible after that. And with all of us working together, we managed to get a lot accomplished. Kate and Layla swept and mopped, while Prometheus, Ajax, and I toted garbage to the surface, removed some broken furniture, and organized all of the food in the pantries. Most of it was freeze-dried veggies and military meals ready to eat, but it was better than nothing.

Time ran on and we started to run out of things to do, so Layla and I retreated to the showers. I'd become accustomed to cold showers at the barracks in Vaduz, and it's not like bathing in the wild was any better.

Layla and I took quick, efficient showers, and had just started to fool around when Omega pushed his way into the barracks and almost jumped us. The wolf's fur was caked with blood and dirt, which did nothing for his already pungent smell.

"He's gonna make me puke," Layla gasped, trying to push him away.

"Yeah. He is ripe," I agreed. We looked at each other at almost the same time. Then glanced at the door.

"Close the door," she whispered, and I slunk from the bed. Omega watched me curiously as I tiptoed across the room, then shut and latched the door.

"Grab the shampoo and a brush," I said and threw myself on the wolf.

It took both of us to wrestle Omega into the shower. He thought we were playing at first until the water started to flow. Then it turned into a no holds barred, man vs wolf throwdown, and the prize? Our sense of smell returned.

Layla lathered Omega up as I held him clenched between my knees and my hands on his shoulders. Once he was fully soaked and shampooed, he flopped to the ground and started rolling around, growling, and yipping.

"He is a freak, I tell you," Ivory said. *"But he is...strong. Not nearly as strong as me, mind you, but he's got good instincts."*

"Whoa," I replied, sarcastically. *"Are you sick or dying?"*

"Ha, ha, and ha. No and no. I'm already dead, you poo-flinging primate."

"In truth, I've never had to fling my own poo. Now other people's...?"

"You are such a barbarian. And you call me a beast."

"Thank you. I mean it, Ivory. I really do. Your help lately has made all the difference. For what it is worth, I am sorry for sucking up your soul or something."

"Or something, he says. Where I come from, we ate animals like you for breakfast!"

I stopped for a moment, suddenly remembering I'd never even so much as asked him where he was from. He knew more about ether than any human I'd met. Even more than the pompous nobles, but how?

"Where are you from...exactly?"

"Well, that's quite simple. I am from...

His voice trailed off and he went quiet. I didn't press him on the matter and busied myself rinsing the shampoo out of Omega's fur. By the time we were done, Layla and I were both ready for another rinse.

"I don't know," Ivory said when we'd started toweling off. *"My memories are foggy. But I can remember running through the woods with my pack, and happening upon a...well, I suppose it was a rift. It was dark and swirling, like a tear in space and time. Being the curious creatures we were, we walked through it. When I came to, I was back in the forest. Only my body was growing rapidly. My mind changed, but so did my appetites. I started hunting ether-rich animals, which helped me grow even stronger. Then I fought and*

beat my old alpha. Although, we didn't kill him. Instead, we let him starve. He followed us for years, slowly wasting away. I can see now how cruel it was."

"Wait. Was Omega your old alpha?"

"Yes. Why else would I hate him so much?"

"Alright, I guess that makes sense, but how do you know about ether? How to use and cultivate it?"

"Because it is second nature to me. I...didn't know that until the ether changed my mind. It opened my eyes to what I already knew but helped me understand the 'hows' and the 'whys'. You could say that I was granted rational thought and a voice."

"Interesting. Go on," I replied as Layla and I raided the lockers for towels and clothes.

"I remember going back to that forest years later. I searched for the ether source that changed me. When I found the rift again, it was like the darkness beyond was calling out to me. I approached just as something emerged from the other side. I lost consciousness as it drew near. When I woke up hours later, I was in a completely different part of the forest and filled with feral rage."

I thought for a second and paused as I toweled off Layla's back. She looked over her shoulder but I leaned in and kissed her cheek. Omega looked up at me and whined as if understanding what we were talking about.

"I'm not quite sure I follow. Something came out of the rift?"

"Yes. Animals from this world can absorb and be changed by ether. But other...things pass through the rift from other worlds? I do not know what it was, only that it radiated so much ether that I could not stand to be too near it."

"I think I..." I stammered, trying to force my thoughts back to that fractured dream. Yes. I'd been there at the start. I'd seen a rift form while lying there, bleeding from an accidental stab wound.

"You're scaring me, Tak. What is it?" Layla hissed. "Talk to me!" She was facing me now. I'd become so lost in my own thoughts that I had almost completely checked out.

"Sorry. I was just trying to...remember something."

"*You are a wolf. But the forest you were running in, was it here? Or did you pass into our world?*"

Ivory yawned.

"*Finally, he asks the right questions. Yes, I passed into your world from another. One that is actually quite similar. But I was changed as soon as I came here. So much so that when I came into contact with a beast from my own world, I could not get too close. My body was pure metal affinity before I arrived, but the longer I was here, the more I changed and evolved. The more I became like the ordinary wolves in my pack.*"

Ivory faded into the back of my mind then. Now I knew there were two types of beasts, those that absorbed a mass of ether and were changed by it, and those that actually traveled to our world from another.

"Kenji?" Layla whispered and got my attention.

"I'm sorry," I apologized and pulled on my shirt. "There are some things I just discovered. Let's get dressed and talk in the mess hall."

We arrived in the mess hall several minutes later, only to discover that Mike had brought some of the experimental equipment from the lab and spread it out onto the tables.

He watched me walk in, then explained before I could even comment.

"It's too dark in there. I'll move it back into the lab once I figure out lighting."

"Fair enough."

"I wish this puppy was finished. It looks like a real street sweeper," Hera yelled excitedly, and lifted a weapon assembly off the table.

It was big, with a motorized housing connected to multiple barrels. The word *mini gun* popped to mind.

"We need to talk," I said, and everyone turned to me.

"Well, that sounds ominous," Kate whispered.

"Who died?" Prometheus asked.

"No one has died. At least not yet. I mean, something did die," I said. It was disappointing how much his question had flustered me. "Give me a minute to explain, and I promise it'll make sense. Maybe, more sense."

"We are, as they say, all ears," Ajax said.

"Remember the mind palace thing that I unlocked?"

"The place you visit in your dreams?" Kate asked.

"Yes. That."

"Why must you constantly rub our noses in it, Tak?" Hera grumbled. She was playing with her spear, or more accurately, trying to push the bladed tip through a spoon.

"Ivory, can you show yourself to them? Is that possible? Because it would make explaining you way more time efficient."

"I am sleeping," Ivory replied.

"No, you're not. You just replied."

"Shit. I did, didn't I?"

I remained silent for a moment, waiting for him to respond.

"See, he's doing it again. He just spaces out...it's like the lights are on but no one's home," Layla said.

"Your mate is smart but perhaps not smart enough. You need to tell her you are simply ignoring her because she's annoying."

"Stop wasting time and show them!" I snapped, not caring who heard. Silence fell over the room, as everyone started looking around.

"Show who what?" Hera asked Ajax.

"Is he talking to a giant, invisible rabbit?" Prometheus whispered. "I saw that movie as a kid and it freaked me out."

"See what you did now?" Ivory chuckled. *"Now all of your friends are wondering if you're crazy or not. All I have to do is say and do nothing. They'll wrap you up in rope and cast you out. Like a...lunatic."*

"That would not be helpful!"

"Fine. Where do you want me? In what pose? Something carnal? Doggy style? Maybe a runway strut? I know...upside down, walking on my ears!"

"Can you just...show them!"

"Alright, alright! Sheesh."

Ivory whined as I felt a massive surge rise from the center of my core, before spreading outward in all directions. The glowing ether flowed over the table and coalesced into the form of a wolf. It was white as snow with fiery, red eyes.

"Meet Ivory. The shit-talking, asshole wolf that lives inside my mind."

"Hello, hairless cretins. Blunt-toothed, poo-flinging primates! What is…up?"

"Wha…lives in your head?" Ajax asked.

"Up until recently, in a cage sitting outside my mind palace. But he's earned a bit of trust and can now roam the grounds, so to speak," I explained.

We embarked on a long journey of chit-chat and stunned silence. I told them everything we knew, talking for over two hours. We discussed theories and had Ivory help them with their cultivation, breathing, and absorption methods. I was far ahead of them in that regard, so it felt good to give them some one-on-one time with a…master.

Ivory was snarky as ever—annoying, sarcastic, flippant, and at the same time, hilarious, and kind of endearing. Good. I was glad that he could inflict himself on someone other than me for a change.

When he was done, Ivory went back to my mind and set the expectation that he'd be sleeping and was not to be disturbed. Even better. I'd have some peace for a change.

We ate, rested, and the others went to shower. All except for Mike, who hadn't really left his tinkering projects…even during our talk. Layla, Omega, and I remained behind to clean the table and put away the plates and cutlery. The food was nothing special, just some reconstituted stew and crackers, but it was hot, and that made it taste ten times better. Omega whined, but only because Ajax wasn't cooking for him. The wolf had gotten spoiled.

We did a final run through the compound, going from room to room, opening every door, storage compartment, and service space. We didn't find anyone. When it came time to do a sweep outside, I took Benjamin, intentionally leading the limping young man past Lazy Bones' new den. When he spotted the bear, I think a little pee came out of him.

"See," I whispered. "We have a bear. A hungry...angry bear."

Benji nodded, his large eyes never leaving the sleeping bear's dark outline. Per Mike's instructions, we explored the base, searching for a few key items our smith needed. Behind one of the few intact hangers, I found several large, above-ground tanks. After simple translations, I discovered that one was diesel and the other jet fuel.

We filled four large jugs and returned to the bunker. Then, with Mike's help, we drained the old fuel out of the generator's tank, removed, and cleaned the glow plugs, and emptied the water-separating fuel filter. After adding new, filtered fuel, and pre-warming the glow plugs, we turned the generator over. It cranked for almost two minutes before sputtering to life.

This time, it didn't die. Lights started to glow to life around us, the illumination hurting our eyes at first.

"Hah! Isn't this great?" Layla laughed as she danced ahead of me. "Now I can actually see where I'm going! In the morning, I'm making coffee!"

"That sounds downright magical," I said, as we joined the others above.

The mess hall was buzzing with activity, as Ajax and Hera were scooping up Mike's experiments and carrying them back to the lab. I followed, only to discover the secret room practically buzzing with energy.

Meters and machines whirred, as monitors glowed blue against the far wall. Mike was standing at one of the workbenches, the surface before him illuminated by no less than four bright lights.

"We keep this place, Takemi," the smith said, without even looking up. "Whatever it takes. We need to keep this place."

"How cozy do you reckon we can make it? How secure?" I asked.

"As cozy and secure as we need," Mike said, looking up from a bowl of melting bee wax.

CHAPTER 26: TIME TO GO

The night went by far too quickly, as it marked our departure from Layla and Kate once again. She stirred next to me as I tried to rise, her arms clamping like a vice around my chest.

"Don't go," she whispered.

"I don't like the idea any more than you," I admitted. "Or leaving you behind, but it makes me feel a little better knowing that we have a secure bunker and that Mike will be here with you."

"Don't worry, I'm not going to throw a fit like last time," Layla whispered. "That was immature. I should have known better. We'll stay busy while you're gone. I'll clean this place up, do the laundry, and dishes, and paint the walls if I have to. You just make sure you come home."

I leaned in and kissed her, letting my lips brush against hers for a long moment before pulling away.

"I'll bring you a souvenir," I whispered. "Maybe a dragon tooth."

"You already brought a wolf and a bear into the family, so why not a dragon as well?" she asked, playfully slapping my chest. A smile replaced the sadness I'd seen only moments before. She had changed since I met her in Vaduz after losing my memories, and sometimes change was a good thing. I'd left her behind in a fit of anger last time. It wasn't something I wanted to repeat.

"Here. Kate and I made these in the mess yesterday. These are for you," she said, handing me a small plastic container. "I made you cookies."

A smile formed on my face as I accepted the container. That small token, and the thought behind it, meant more to me at that moment than all the "I love yous" in the world.

"Cookies?" Hera said, sliding out of her cot. "Where are mine?"

"We just baked enough for the boys," Layla said.

"That's blatant favoritism!"

"Sleep with me next time before you leave and I'll make you your very own box of cookies," Layla said, blowing Hera a kiss.

"Challenge accepted, pretty girl," Hera said, walking towards our cot. I grabbed Layla and held her protectively.

"You'd better be careful, Tak, or I'll steal her away from you," Hera laughed as Ajax pulled her out of the room. Prometheus was busy saying his goodbyes to Kate, so I gave them a minute.

After Layla changed, we moved from the barracks into the mess hall, where Omega lay at Ajax's feet. And no wonder, he was slipping the wolf one bite of his food for each one he ate himself. Layla and I ate together, enjoying a hot cup of coffee. Now, that was a luxury I had missed.

We'd barely finished when Mike ambled into the mess hall. He had the UMP45 slung across his chest. I also noticed a thick, nylon belt around his midsection, holding what looked like several thick magazine pouches. The smith looked exhausted and I feared that he'd stayed up all night working on our new weapon.

He dropped heavily into a chair next to us, unslung the submachine gun, and set it down before me. Then he unclipped the belt and added it to the pile.

"Did you sleep at all?" I asked.

He shook his head and yawned. "Too much to do. Too much to explore," he said, and although he looked tired, an undeniable fire burned in his eyes.

"Here. Eat something," Layla offered and scooped some reconstituted eggs and bacon onto her plate and slid it before him. Without argument or hesitation, Mike tucked into the food.

I took that moment to examine the fruits of his labors.

"The ammo we found in the lab is solid," he explained between bites. "I treated them the same as the others. All in all, I had enough bee's wax on me to finish fifty-nine rounds. Each stick magazine holds twenty-five, so you have two fully loaded magazines and nine spare rounds in this pouch."

"Couldn't quite get that round number of sixty, heh?" I asked, chuckling.

"Almost," he agreed. "The idea of ending on an odd number like that almost drove me mad."

I geared up right there in the mess, and after adjusting the duty belt down to my size, I clipped it into place. Needless to say, it went very well with my matte black, poly-weave tactical armor.

The UMP45 was another matter, as my first instinct was to hide it away in a storage bag. But the more I thought about it, the more I realized that I both needed to keep it a secret and also make sure it was available. In the end, I decided to sling the submachine gun, but slide it around to my back, so it was hidden by my cloak.

It was almost sunrise by the time Prometheus ushered the sisters back into the bunker. They secured the door with a satisfying *clank* and we moved off to leave. We were on our way to a place full of unknowns. Enemies? Certainly. But who? And more importantly, what, awaited us?

No one spoke for almost half an hour, as we each sorted through our complicated thoughts. Omega bounced around us happily, having drug our lethargic hill of grumpy bear out of his napping spot.

Omega ran back and forth, sprinting ahead, his now clean fur shining in the early morning light. He jumped up onto broken vehicles, slunk through dilapidated buildings, and reappeared through crumbling walls. It filled me with a level of security I'd not known in the wilds before. With the wolf running an almost silent circuit around us, he was far more likely to identify or unearth threats long before they ever saw us. And with Lazy Bones, grumpy and hungry behind us, it meant that enemies couldn't simply sneak up on our trail. Not without dealing with him first, at least.

Ajax was the first to break the heavy silence as we finally reached the open road and left the dust, dirt, and dead soil behind. I didn't realize how much I missed the green, live plants until we'd left the deadlands behind. That thought made me wonder if the ether weapons they'd been creating and experimenting on had something to do with the barren state of the vegetation.

"It is a distinct possibility," Ivory agreed after I proposed the question.

"I'll be brief," Ajax said, abruptly. "Bern, Zurich, and Basel represent Switzerland. Munich, Nuremberg, Salzburg, and Augsburg represent southeast Germany. Stuttgart, Frankfurt, Karlsruhe, and Mannheim represent southwestern Germany, and the only other city-state that has a small claim is Strasbourg."

"But why the hell way out here?" Prometheus asked. "I mean, besides Ulm, which isn't much of a city anymore, there is nothing around."

"Precisely," Ajax said, nodding. "But if you look on the map, Federsee lies within the triangle of power of Zurich, Stuttgart, and Munich. That should tell you all you need to know, right there."

We walked another twenty minutes before Omega spotted something unexpected on the road ahead. A horse-drawn carriage was rolling slowly down the road and moving straight for us. My hand immediately shifted to the hilt of my katana and the hairs on the back of my neck prickled. I'd learned to trust my instincts, so I whistled, calling Omega to my side.

The wolf bowled through the underbrush to the right and circled, before sitting at my right side. He sniffed the air, and I watched as his hackles raised. The wolf could sense the ether radiating off the carriage, too.

A carriage driver pulled on the reins once they were close and stopped the horses. He appeared to be in his forties, wearing a black top hat and matching tailored suit. He sported a thick handlebar mustache and I couldn't help but appreciate how well-maintained it was.

"Guten tag," he said in fluent German. He looked us over, one by one before his eyes settled on the wolf. "Sind sie hier fur den kampf des konigs?"

"Guten tag, freund," Ajax replied, with a friendly wave. "Ja. Wir sind für den Wettbewerb hier."

"Ahh, aussenseiter...umm, pardon. Outsiders. Very well," he replied with a thick German accent. "I was on my way home, but I guess I could do one last round."

"Round?" I asked. "What do you mean, sir?"

He looked at me and inclined his head.

"I ferry dignitaries from the train station in Ulm to the meeting grounds in Federsee. They house everyone in Castle Klinik Bad Buchau before the melee begins. If you would like, I can turn my wagon around, so that you all might rest on the way there. It would only be fair that you arrive in pristine condition."

"Is the castle where they host the fights?" Prometheus asked.

"Oh, no," the carriage driver said, shaking his head. "They started building a sporting stadium at Eintracht before the collapse. Evidently, it was to attract some large event called...the Olympics. I think that was it. Ja. The sporting complex is where the fights are held."

My hand landed on Omega's nose and I patted his head.

"There are five of us," I said, nodding at the wolf. "Is there room for everyone?"

"Your wolf can run along the carriage if you want. As long as he doesn't attack my horses."

I looked down as Omega whined, nudging my leg with his nose.

"Don't complain. We'll just be inside the carriage. Please stay away from the horses, all right?"

"Ja! Good, good. The name is Holger Schmidt, freunde. What city are you fighting for?"

"Zurich," Ajax said, offering him his hand. "We're… paying off a debt."

"Hah, a debt, you say? Yes, the Swiss cities are renowned for this. Now hop in. We don't want to be late."

We approached the carriage, while Prometheus scanned the road behind us. He whispered "bear" but I waved him off. The less the carriage driver knew, the better. Some might accept a wolf companion. But I guessed that he'd likely not accept our larger pack member.

Prometheus, Hera, and I loaded into the carriage, only to have Ajax close the door behind us.

"What are you doing?" Hera asked.

"I'll ride up top with our host. You three rest."

The carriage rocked as the big man climbed up onto the bench to sit next to Holger, and a moment later, we felt the carriage rumble forward. After turning around, I focused on Omega. I could feel him somewhere to our right, but he was in the forest now and keeping a good distance. *Good boy.*

Prometheus tapped at his wrist and raised three fingers.

I groaned, knowing what he meant.

"Will do. You go sleep."

"Me, too," Hera muttered. "We'll need all the rest we can get. Once the shit hits the fan, that is. With God knows how many pompous leaders present, this thing can only be a freaking mess. Who knows when we'll get to rest again."

I removed the wolf ornament and opened it with some ether, then stowed the UMP inside. Next, I removed a small pouch of crystals. We were still well-stocked, but for a reason. They symbolized our wealth. And judging from what I knew about nobles, I wanted every bit of strength and leverage I could find.

Pulling forth two ether-filled crystals, I started to draw on their power. In response, the windmill deep inside me started to spin. I settled into a steady rhythm of drawing, condensing, and drawing more ether. Once one crystal was empty, I stashed it into a spare pouch and pulled out another.

Ivory's presence grew stronger in my mind, as the spirit wolf seemed to circle my ether activities. I was at the very peak of what a two-veined cultivator could become, and it felt great, but I needed to break through and open my third vein.

"*Keep pulling the ether in,*" Ivory finally said. "*We're about halfway there.*"

"*How many do I need?*" I asked, wanting some way to track my progress. It had already been a few hours since I started, but it felt like mere moments. The carriage rumbled down the desolate highway, but the trees and plants were thicker now, obscuring the remnants of the old world.

"*Perhaps a hundred more. The mind palace is needy. It is easily claiming half of every crystal you absorb.*"

"*The mind palace, or you?*" I asked, playfully.

"*Wh—what? You dare accuse me of theft?*"

"*No. But you are taking some, correct? What changes once you've absorbed enough ether?*"

Ivory didn't respond for some time.

"*I should be able to manifest my spiritual form for longer periods.*"

"*But won't that drain my ether?*"

"*No, I won't. There is a lot of residue that sticks as you cultivate and absorb ether. I am slowly building a core so I can absorb whatever your core doesn't. You will never even feel it.*"

"That makes sense," I said.

Our conversation died away and I simply enjoyed the flow of ether through my body. It was both warm and cold at the same time, a mildly pleasant and addictive sensation. Strangely, the feeling I had before I started the process was being replaced by something else entirely. One moment I felt I was at the top of the world, and the next my body became heavy and sluggish. It felt exhausting to simply hold myself up on the bench.

"You're almost there. Keep going," Ivory said, his voice bright with excitement. *"Once you've absorbed enough, we'll force the next metal vein open."*

If what I knew was true, opening that second metal vein was going to improve my body more than anything I'd done up to that point. But not just that, I would be able to work metals in ways I hadn't before. An image popped into my mind. I was fighting someone, but instead of parrying their sword, I grabbed it with my bare hand and melted the blade with a mere touch.

My feet started tingling and a burning ache settled into my toes, before creeping along my soles, up my heels, and into my calves. It was a mind-numbing pain that served as more of a distraction than anything else. I pulled off my shoes and clenched my jaw, not wanting to wake the others. My socks were next to go. They were drenched with very dark, almost black blood. Several small holes had formed just above my toes, as well as a bigger one on my heel.

Blood and other bodily excretions were seeping out and I immediately wondered if the ether was purifying me or melting down my soul and pushing it out through my feet.

"Don't worry, everything's fine. It is just impurities. The third vein is particularly hard because of your second metal affinity. That usually never happens."

I focused but pushed some ether forth, using the power to burn the gathering muck away. I didn't want to thank our host for the ride by leaving his carriage a gross, sticky mess.

"Focus! You're about to burn through your third vein! Focus on that, not a mess on the floor."

I steadied my breathing and narrowed my concentration to the task at hand. More holes opened up, but now in my hands and my arms and...*fuck!*

I pushed the door open and stumbled outside, working to undress as I fell. The last thing I remembered was Ajax yelling, the horses whinnying, and distantly, Omega barking.

I awoke sometime later, the sun setting overhead. Everyone was standing above me, their faces tight masks of worry.

"You picked a rosy time to break through," Ajax grunted and heaved me to my feet.

I covered my privates, suddenly realizing that I had succeeded in stripping myself bare. We had stopped near a river to water the horses, and I took that opportunity to wash and inspect the changes. I was caked in dried muck and blood, but my muscles were...noticeably more defined, especially in my arms, chest, and stomach.

Scrubbing quickly, I dried off and dressed, then joined the others at the carriage once again.

Hera shook her head. "You do make everything more dramatic, don't you, Tak. Mumbling, stripping naked, and falling out of the carriage. And here I was worried that this whole trip would go by and I wouldn't see anything entertaining."

"Um...you're welcome," I said.

I rifled around in my bag and found the scanning device, then walked away from the others. Stopping by the water's edge, I took a breath and moved to activate the device. Only, someone spoke next to me.

"What is he... really?" Holger, the carriage driver, asked as he pointed to our left. I spotted Omega between two trees, a sense of relief flooding me as a result. Some of it was mine, but some also came from the wolf.

I wasn't entirely sure how to answer, and it wasn't

because I didn't know. But more so, I didn't know who he truly was. We were approaching "be careful who you trust" territory, and I wanted to safeguard as many of our secrets as possible.

"Will you tell me who you are if I tell you, Mr. Schmidt?" I asked.

"That is a perfectly reasonable request," he said, twisting the ends of his mustache. "I am a veteran of many wars, against both beast and men. I, like so many like me, still serve my sovereign. Thanks to our relative peace, and in many ways because of the Melee of Kings, I have not had to fight for some time now. I own this carriage and the horses pulling it. When not needed as a soldier, I fill my time ferrying people around. I find it very...fulfilling."

"I see," I replied and thought about what that meant. He was a warrior like me. Although, unlike me, he'd been fighting for much longer. I could respect the position, especially the Zen-like calm he found in the simple task of driving a carriage. "He is a wolf. We adopted him a while back after fighting his pack. But like so many creatures, ether has changed him. In a way, I don't think we know what he will eventually become."

"Oh? How curious," he said simply but did not comment further.

Holger returned to the horses then, affording me a rare moment of privacy. I did not waste it, as I pulled the reader out of my armor and pushed ether into it. I was more than a little curious to see what opening my third vein had done to my stats.

I was a bit disappointed at first. My muscle and bone were the worst out of the five status points. But how? I'd put on considerable muscle mass and definition. Still, the moment I saw the three stars, I forgot everything, even the big letter C to their left. The next change was to my bonus stats, and just as with two veins, they'd risen by ten percent. My stamina, strength, and perception were all at thirty percent. So...it was clear to me why people could become so much stronger after going up a single vein. They didn't just earn new bonus stats, but every new vein netted them a ten percent bump.

I asked the device but received a reply I'd expected. Every new vein added to the body's potential. That's why the stats only increased by ten percent every time a new vein opened. Once I hit the next realm, new stats would open up. If I survived that long, that is. As things stood, I would worry about it then and not a moment sooner.

I checked my skills next and found something new—Ether Blade. Quite fitting I guessed.

SKILLS

VEIN ACTIVES
- ○ BURST OF SPEED
- ○ ENHANCED STRENGTH
- ○ CAUTERISE WOUND
- ○ PAIN SUPPRESSION
- ○ ELEMENTAL SHIELD
- ○ MEND BONES
- ○ ????????
- ○ RELIEVE FATIGUE
- ○ FLEETFOOT
- ○ ????????
- ○ ????????
- ○ STONE SKIN

VEIN PASSIVES
- ○ STAMINA   10%
- ○ STRENGTH   10%
- ○ PERCEPTION   10%
- ○ PERCEPTION   10%
- ○ SKIN TOUGHNESS 10%
- ○ BONE TOUGHNESS 10%
- ○ POISON IMMUNITY 50%
- ○ STAMINA   10%
- ○ AGILITY   10%
- ○ ????   10%
- ○ AGILITY   10%
- ○ BONE TOUGHNESS 10%

BATTLE SKILLS
- R2 BLAZING SLASH   67%
- R2 RAZOR'S EDGE   52%
- R1 ETHER BLADE   23%

Cauterize wound was one of my new vein skills. I had an idea what it would do but wasn't quite sure how it translated to actual combat. I hated the idea of testing new abilities during life-and-death combat but wasn't sure I would get many opportunities before it all really mattered.

Maybe I could challenge Hera to a sparring session, so she could test out her new spear. If I let her hit me, just a little, then I could test out the vein skill, too.

"Congratulations on opening your third vein, young sir," Holger said. I turned to find him standing just behind me. He'd returned from tending the horses and I'd never heard him. "It appears you are well-versed with the newest tech. I am surprised and impressed."

I stashed the scanner into my armor, not wanting him to read any of the stats or skills. Sure, he might have already, but one couldn't be too careful. Yes, he'd told me a little about himself, but in reality, I still didn't know who he worked for. And the suspicious part of me doubted that he simply just ran into us on the road. Dead warriors rely on luck. The ones that survived also didn't believe in coincidence. I'd learned enough from my time in Zurich to not take everything at face value.

"Thank you, Holger. I can't help but notice you're quite strong yourself."

He nodded, the faintest hint of a smiling pulling at his mustache.

"I am on the lower end of my fourth vein. We carriage drivers need to be able to protect our charges. What kind of chauffeur would I be, if I allowed those in my keeping to be harmed? Come along, young wolf. We still have a few hours on the road until we arrive at our destination."

I nodded and followed. But it was not lost on me that he'd called me "young wolf."

CHAPTER 27: ARRIVAL

Approaching from the north, I spotted the nature preserve well before we arrived. It helped that the road took us up and over an elevated ridge that skirted the whole area.

The place truly looked wild. An enormous grassland constituted the northernmost tip of the preserve. Hera and I hung out the carriage window for a better look and spotted several large herds of elk. Smaller animals moved through the grass, but I couldn't tell what they were.

Further east I could see buildings clustered together, what were evidently the remains of residential neighborhoods. Nature had claimed them now, as trees and grass had overgrown the streets and buildings.

We didn't spot signs of life for another fifteen to twenty minutes, as bonfires appeared in the twilight. They covered the grasslands surrounding Federsee lake and wetlands—dozens of large, raging fires. The smoke drifted high into the air, drifting like fog with the lack of wind.

We arrived in what had formerly been called Bad Buchau. The former city was just as dilapidated and overgrown as the rural communities to the north, except here they seemed to at least manage and clear the roadways.

I spotted the sprawling mass of the Olympic village we'd heard about, the partially constructed stadium and support buildings now just crumbling relics. The place was swarming with people carrying torches. More bonfires had been built around the stadium, shrouding the large, round structure in a halo of smoke.

Federsee lived up to the label of a zoo. That is, until we approached our destination, Castle Klinik. The white fortress rose from the wilderness, its tall, steepled roofs standing out in stark contrast. It, unlike everything around it, had been painstakingly maintained. But beyond that, a sea of medieval huts, homes, and markets had been erected around the castle. Lanterns hung from poles in the streets and candles glowed in the castle's many windows.

"I'd always heard that zoos were where people went to die," Hera said, pointing at the castle's glowing windows. "But this place looks downright cozy. And do you smell that? Someone is roasting something!"

We offloaded from the carriage not far from the castle and stepped right into a market.

"Do you see that large, oval tent set up next to the castle? That is where you need to go. If you have people here waiting for you, they will be there," Holger explained.

"Thank you for carting us all the way down here," I said, shaking the man's hand. "I hope we didn't change your schedule too much."

The carriage driver waved me off. "Don't think about it. I will simply stay here tonight and head back tomorrow. The food here is far better than anything I would find in Ulm or Memmingen. Can I leave you with some parting advice?"

"As a rule, I never turn down good advice," I said.

"Smart. The people here are friendly and hospitable but watch your backs during the melee. All the groups represented agree to a pact of no aggression while congregated, but you know how some view agreements. And keep even keener eyes on your coin purse. Pickpockets thrive here."

"We will. Thank you, freund," Ajax said, slapping the carriage driver on the back.

I left the others at the carriage and walked west, needing only to travel three blocks before the forest grew thicker and the buildings more dilapidated. Whistling low, I crouched down and waited. Nothing happened for several long moments, but then a twig snapped and a bush shook a hundred paces and to my right.

Omega was halfway to me before his camouflage melted away. I cried out and actually fell over but had no time to recover before the wolf's weight was on me. It was all death breath and wolf kisses after that.

My wolf companion growled and pulled away as I slipped a lead over his neck, but a moment of scratches calmed his nerves. He would have to play the part of a wolf-dog, while we were there, or miss all of the action and stay hidden in the outskirts. I knew it was a gamble, but with the sheer number of uncertainties stacked against us, I wanted every possible weapon at our disposal.

I met up with the others and we set off into the beating heart of the melee. Hera pulled us through the market, where we perused stalls, smelled food, and listened to a few dozen criers tell the world at large what products we could not live without. Ajax tested a handful of those proclamations and discovered that their boasts were somewhat inflated. Except for the woman selling hand pies. They were stuffed with meat and vegetables, with a flaky, pastry outer crust.

"My god, I could eat these things until I explode," I mumbled, chewing through my third already.

After a short walk through the market, we decided to check out the large tent. Armed guards patrolled the perimeter of the castle grounds, but no one moved to prevent our entry. They gave Omega second glances, however, and cut a wider swath around us as a group.

Open braziers sat barely twenty paces apart here, filling the air with the smell of wood smoke. Banners flapped from long poles set all the way around the massive tent, giving me a strange sense of nostalgia.

I couldn't immediately tell why, but it was obviously connected to some memory still locked away in the damaged, out-of-order portion of my mind. Then a few men pushed out of the tent and it all connected.

They wore plate armor over shiny mail, the fine silks of their outer garments covered in matching standards. They wore swords, too, although that wasn't anything strange in this world.

"This place is like a renaissance festival," Hera breathed. "I freaking love it!"

Then it all connected. A joust. Sometime in my childhood, I'd gone to a similar festival and watched armored men on horseback joust.

"Will they joust?" I asked, excitedly.

"Don't be silly," Ajax said. "I mean, maybe. I really don't know. People always told me that melees were bloody free-for-alls where almost no one survived. This seems practically civilized."

I studied the banners as we approached the tent. They were from every powerful family, kingdom, or stronghold in the region, although I didn't know enough about them to recognize any one banner.

We made our way around, studying each of the banners. I saw a coat of arms with lions holding scepters, eagles with wings spread, atop a nest of arrows, badgers, gilded shields, and even what looked like a serpent-shaped dragon. One standard caught my eye, as it featured what looked like a weasel, holding a fig branch, while dancing on the edge of a sword. I wanted to know who that group was, just to tell them how much I appreciated their standard.

When we reached the far side of the tent, the terraced gardens sprawled out south of the castle. Beyond lay a large field, filled with glowing, square tents. The banners flew there, too, identifying the individual camps for each of the represented delegations.

"Does anyone else feel weird that we're representing Zurich and have no idea what their crest looks like?" I asked.

Hera shook her head.

"...be representing ourselves," Prometheus mumbled.

Ajax stepped forward, squinted, and pointed toward the far right. "It's that one. Do you see it? The shield with the blue and white on it?"

I spotted a cluster of tents midway through the field. One large round tent was surrounded by six smaller ones. It looked even more like a medieval proving ground now, as I spotted a wandering musician, strumming on a lute, no less.

We made our way through the sea of tents and approached Zurich's designated area. Everything looked pristine from the grass around the tents to the two tall wooden poles holding the entrance aloft. I don't know why, but I'd expected a muddy field, filled with stinky, shirtless men trying to kill one another. This was a very pleasant surprise.

Zurich's standard flapped in the breeze above—a shield with a diagonal line that ran from the upper left corner and stopped at the lower right. The line separated the blue on the bottom and the white on top.

"Are you all ready?" Ajax asked, his hand hovering right before the tent flap. "Once we walk in there, we have to ride this thing out until the end. Regardless of the outcome. So, we put on our game faces and act like professionals. Right?" He looked at me.

"Me?" I asked jabbing a thumb into my chest.

"Strictly speaking, your mouth has gotten us into more trouble than anyone else's," Hera said.

I screwed up my face, wanting nothing more than to throw a strong rebuttal back at her, but I knew she was right. So, not wanting to sound petulant, I simply nodded my understanding.

A particularly small, bald man hurried toward us from the left, and before Ajax could open the tent, he called out.

"You there. Stop there," he called, as his seven companions fanned out to either side. I instantly remembered the small crest embroidered on his jacket: a black stallion on a yellow shield. They were from Stuttgart.

My hand tightened on Omega's lead as the wolf bared his teeth. The small, bald man flinched but kept coming.

Ajax dropped a reassuring hand on my shoulder and stepped past me, blocking their path. Several others joined him, but they didn't look so intimidating. More like the 'elites' from Zurich that died with a single attack.

"I think you are confused, ja? Perhaps looking for a different tent, freunde?" Ajax said, his large thumb pointing back over his shoulder. He had the unique ability to sound both warm and threatening at the same time.

The Stutt was either too stupid or ignorant for his own good, as he stepped right up to my big friend, and actually went up onto his tiptoes.

They had no idea who we were or how strong we were, yet they waltzed right up and into our faces. A crowd was starting to form, as men and women pushed out of their tents to see what was happening. *Great*, even when we weren't looking for trouble, it found us.

"You wear no standard or sash identifying your allegiance. That is explicitly forbidden while on the melee grounds. The Charter of Kingdoms is extremely specific."

"I'm sorry, but who are you?" I asked, fighting hard to keep my snarky side in check. "We literally just got here—"

"We are those that demand the rules of the melee be enforced!" the short man snapped, cutting me off.

"Okay, first, interrupting someone is rude. And second, you are yelling. We *were* trying to explain that we just arrived…like, just now!" I retorted, and although my voice was loud, I managed to plaster a smile on my face and keep my temper in check. Damn, it was so hard! The bald shit had an infinitely punchable face.

"No! Unacceptable. Throw down your weapons and get

on the ground! Those without allegiance are forbidden from this place!"

"Forbidden?" Prometheus echoed and looked around.

"What is going on?" Hera asked.

"Hold on a second, freund," Ajax said and stepped forward. My big friend held his hands up, in the almost universal "I'm not being threatening, so just calm the fuck down" gesture. Except, our bald Stutt flinched hard. I could see the violence born in his eyes even before he reached for his blade.

"On zhe ground!" he snarled and ripped the blade free, then leveled it right at Ajax's chest. His men pulled their blades forth, just as their diminutive leader advanced on Ajax.

"Omega, blade!" I snapped, as the Stutt neared my friend. I could practically smell the violence on him, and knew that if I didn't act, it would be too late.

The wolf coiled and sprang forth, catching the bald Stutt's weapon hand in his mouth. He growled, bit down, and wrenched him away from Ajax.

"Ahhh! Scheisse! My hand."

I pulled Ajax behind me and wrenched my katana free from its scabbard, then squared off against the other men.

"How about this. You lower your fucking swords, or I have my dog here chew his hand off and swallow it!" I hissed. "Enough, boy!" I yelled and slapped my thigh. "Come here."

The warriors edged toward me, their knuckles white around their weapons. But Omega snarled again and twisted his head. The bald Stutt cried out and finally dropped his sword, then waved the others away frantically.

"Do as he says. Lower them!"

"Omega, release!" I snapped, and the wolf opened his jaws and slunk back.

I moved forward and kicked the small man's weapon away, just in case he or one of his cohorts decided to pick it up again. A horn blared suddenly as several men on horseback appeared. The gathered crowd parted, allowing the riders through. Some, I noticed, bowed or dropped to a knee.

"What is this?" the man on the lead horse demanded. His German accent was almost as thick as his salt and pepper beard, which blended seamlessly with his long, white hair.

He gestured to the crowd and flashed a set of almost perfectly-maintained teeth. He wore an outfit similar to the Stutts, but not identical, which set my gears grinding. Then my gaze swept behind him, to the man on the next horse, and I audibly cursed.

Hans Gruber leaned forward, inspected the wounded man, his mangled hand now clutched against his body, and smiled.

"Captain," Ajax said with a small bow. "These…men stopped us when we were trying to get to our commanding officer to report. They deemed us unworthy of this place, it seems. Then that guy," he said, pointing at the man with the mangled hand, "drew his weapon and tried to attack me."

The crowd went quiet, all except the wounded man, who started whimpering quietly.

"Follow me," the bearded man on horseback said, then promptly turned his mount and trotted away. The Stutts followed after him, not one of them turning to sneer or snap at us.

"Takemi, you and your team follow me," Hans said.

The ghost of a smirk broke through his usually placid façade. He'd never admit it out loud, at least not in front of the other factions, but we had gained favor. We showed that Zurich wouldn't back down from a fight, even if the opponent was the mighty Stuttgart.

Several of the onlookers patted us on the backs as we passed by, and I started to feel at home. Perhaps I had worked myself up about the Melee of Kings for nothing?

"Remind me to never pull a knife on you when your wolf is around," Hera whispered as she leaned in. "I'm surprised he didn't chew that guy's hand off and swallow it in front of him."

"I think he would have, if I'd told him to," I said.

"It's good that you didn't. They might have demanded that he be removed," Ajax grumbled.

Omega whined and rubbed against Ajax's leg, so the big guy rubbed the wolf's head affectionately.

Captain Hans Gruber rode his horse around to the backside of Zurich's tents, dismounted his horse, and tied it to a post. When he turned back to us, he wore a wide smile.

"I am glad that you all are good to your word," he said, allowing his German accent to thicken. "Gut. That means we do not need to hire hunters to track you down and kill you."

"My money is on us," Hera muttered. Gruber looked at her with that irritating twinkle in his eye. God, how charismatic could one guy be? Here he was talking about having bounty hunters track us down and kill us, and I'm worried about saying the wrong thing and offending him.

"I think you know that we gained an appropriate amount of strength for this very occasion," Ajax said.

"Oh, yes. Of that, I have no doubts. But do not fool yourself. Those men do not comprise the best of Stuttgart. You got into a scrape with some of their rabbles, but do not let it go to your heads."

"Cubs grow to be lions, not sheep," I said, holding out my hand.

"Or, in your case, wolves," Hans said, accepting my handshake.

"It's good to see you, freund," Ajax greeted him next. "We're here, so why don't you tell us what we need to do?"

He nodded toward the tent, and we followed. Ajax went in first, Prometheus second, Hera third, and…not me. Hans stopped me at the tent flap and pointed at Omega.

"He will have to stay out here. Kruger is allergic to most…animals," Gruber said. "So either leave him there or don't come in."

Omega nudged me forward and then sat, waiting expectantly.

"You stay out of trouble, boy," I said.

He nodded as if understanding. Hell, he was a mutant wolf altered by ether. I had the disembodied spirit of another wolf-like creature living in my head. I was fairly sure he did understand me. Then, as I watched, his fur started to shimmer and he melted into the darkening night.

I pulled the flap aside and ducked into the tent. The old me would have been shocked by the interior's opulence, but the post-brain damage me, knew how these people operated. Zurich had spared no expense furnishing the space.

Rich, wooden furniture filled the tent, and along with the fabric, dividers helped partition the space into immediately identifiable areas—a living room, kitchen, and a war room.

None other than King Otto Von Obermeister sat on a large, dark wood throne. Every polished surface on the large chair was covered in gems and crystals, the gaudy seat radiating enough ether to light up a house. He wore a rich, blue silk shirt, white trousers, and a gold embroidered cape over it all. Alfred Durheim, the snake, stood just behind him. I immediately wanted to see how much pressure it would take to pop his head off his neck.

"The rabble has arrived," Alfred drawled, nodding lazily toward us. The King chuckled quietly as if the two enjoyed some private joke.

"Keep laughing, shithead," I mumbled under my breath, and silently envisioned unloading an entire magazine of ether-charged .45 caliber rounds into the two. The mental image cheered me up.

"This lot looks practically," Otto started to say, but paused to pick at his nail, "ready for a fight. And what's that he's wearing, Alfred? I have never seen armor like that."

Alfred perked up and scanned me with his pale eyes. "Where did you get that? Is there more?"

"No," I said, simply, and bowed my head. I wasn't going to give them anything.

The two men came together and whispered for a few

moments.

"What a shame," Otto said, once again picking at his fingers. "They were wasted on commoners. Are you quite sure that you wouldn't like to give them to your king? Your sovereign?"

I smiled and shook my head, thoroughly enjoying the petulant look growing on his face. Ajax shuffled nervously between feet, just as someone else entered the tent. I turned just as Kruger stood to his full height and looked right at us.

"Ah, gut. Wir haben dich gefunden," he said, moving forward and slapping Ajax on the shoulder. "Hello, freunde. We'll be brief, as I know you have been on the road all day."

Alfred coughed, either to interject or to remind Kruger that he was there, but to our Protectorate patron's credit, he didn't flinch. Kruger shook Prometheus' hand, kissed Hera's cheek, and settled on a chair to the King's left. Alfred shifted uncomfortably behind the throne as Kruger filled a wine glass and took a sip but didn't seem comfortable openly jousting with him. That was a first.

"This is gut. Now that everyone is here, we can move up our timetable a little. We start tomorrow morning, so get a good night's sleep."

"Yes, rest your manners, because if you offend anyone here or embarrass Zurich, it will not end well for you," Alfred cut in, evidently finally finding the nerve. Or, the balls.

"We won't," Ajax said matter-of-factly. "We're here to fight for Zurich, not you, Durheim. We serve the Protectorate, herrn Kruger."

"Gut, gut!" Alfred said, slapping his thigh. Then with his arrogant aire returned, the King's right hand stepped out from behind the throne. "But we are happy...to see you all healthy. It will be a tough week, I can assure you."

He grabbed an empty glass, took the pitcher Kruger had used and filled his to the top. He downed half of it in one drink, cleared his throat, and topped the glass off again.

"The first part of the Mêlée of Kings will be held in what

they call the zoo, the wild lands north of the wetlands."

"We saw it," Prometheus said, "Will it be in the stadium? Or the wilderness surrounding it?"

"Yes and...yes," Alfred said, waving the questions off. "You must understand, the competitions are kept secret from all participating kingdoms and nations. You will not actually know what you are to do until right before it starts. It is the only way to ensure a level and fair playing field."

"What do we do? Is it a free-for-all?" I asked.

"As I said, the format and specifics will be revealed. We do know there are a dozen legitimate parties here competing for negotiation rights. Four will move on to the next round, while the mêlée only recognizes a single winner. Yes, the rest can still fight for crumbs, so whatever you do, at least get to the second round."

"We will," the four of us said in unison, having already practiced our group responses. It was stupid, for sure, but we knew our place. We would be obedient as long as their goals coincided with ours.

"Where do we rest and sleep?" Ajax asked. "Until it starts?"

"Hans will show you," Kruger said. "Use this time tonight to make any last-minute preparations. The village has everything you'll need, from seamstresses to smiths, and more. Buy gear, fix broken stuff, or pay for time with women. Or men," he added, noticing Hera.

"Women are okay with me," she said, lifting one eyebrow.

"When should we be ready tomorrow?" Prometheus asked, looking to Alfred and Otto. The king simply glanced away, but Alfred's eyeballs almost popped out of his skull.

"Eight in the morning," he said, stretching his neck. "Now begone. We have profoundly important matters to attend to. You have Kruger and Gruber. They can keep you up to date."

"My King," Ajax said. Then we all bowed and turned to

leave, following Hans out of the tent.

"We made sure to procure you the best tent possible, mein freunde," Hans said cheerily. "Follow me, if you will."

He strode off and we fell in line behind him. I felt Omega's fur brush against my leg and smiled. We moved right to one of the smaller tents, and Hans lifted the tent flap, before waving us in. I entered last, with the wolf's camouflage melting away as soon as we were inside.

The inside of our tent was spartan compared to the Zurich command tent. Two bunk beds sat on opposite sides, with a small round table set between them. Four chairs surrounded the table. What looked like a large treasure chest sat off to my left. It was closed, but I could feel a considerable amount of energy radiating off it.

"That is a cold chest. It is stocked with cold drinks, a platter of cheese, meat, and some fruit. Eat, drink, and rest. After tonight, you won't have a bed available to you for a few days."

"Herrn Gruber," I said, grasping his hand and shaking it. "Alfred mentioned the first challenge, but what do you know of beyond that?"

He shrugged, squeezing my hand. "In all honesty, I'm not quite sure. I could tell you what they did for the last melee, but they're never quite the same. They intentionally corral the largest, most dangerous beasts and monsters into the zoo for this event. The teams that survive and come back with the biggest cores and rarest trophies will go to the second round. But you shouldn't look at it as something that straightforward. It isn't just the beasts you will be facing in there, but in all likelihood, the other contestants, too."

"We never get anything straightforward," Hera muttered. "I'd rather we just fight and kill people. Beasts don't usually screw one another over based on treaties and land rights."

"I do not disagree, fraulein Hera. The rules are the rules and this event is designed to be cut-throat. If someone attacks you, kill them, but that does not mean you have to go on the offensive and murder the other teams. In the end, diplomacy is the goal, so keep that in mind."

"Understood, Herrn Captain," Ajax said.

Hans patted the big man on the shoulder, bid us all good night, and left.

"You heard him, Kenji," Prometheus said, elbowing me as he walked by. "We need to try and be diplomatic. That means no murder sprees."

"I hate it when you try and put me in a box, Prom," I said, as I started to slough off my armor.

CHAPTER 28: START THE HUNT

We tucked in and fell asleep. Morning came quickly, which always seemed to be the case when a fight was imminent. I kicked my feet out of bed and sat up, noticing Omega curled up at the entrance. I rubbed my face just as a horn sounded somewhere in the camp.

Hera's legs dangled down the side before she dropped off her bed and stumbled, then sat right next to me. She flashed me a smile and nudged my shoulder.

"You all survived, good," Ajax said, rolling out of bed.

"Did you expect an attack last night?" Hera asked, after covering a yawn.

"No, but you fart like a beast," Prom jabbed.

"I only do it because I know you like it so much," Hera replied.

They started laughing and stopped when Omega growled. Within the tent's confined space, the sound was low, loud, and unsettling.

"Uh oh, you two are making the wolf mad," Ajax said.

"No," I corrected, "He's hungry. That is his 'feed me or become breakfast' warning."

"We can feed Tak to the wolf," Hera offered.

"He likes me most of all," I yawned. "How long do you think you lot would last if I were gone? I think you would end up bear poop after just a day or two, Hera."

Hera rolled out of bed and before I could guard myself, she tackled me onto my bed.

"Bear poop?" she hissed, and clamped her legs down, then with surprising force, wrestled my arms above my head, and pinned me down.

"I'll tell Layla you tried to have your way with me last night," she said, as I fought to break free.

"She wouldn't believe you," I countered. "We all know you've had your eye on her anyways."

"I am an opportunist," she said, struggling. Despite my newly opened third vein, I couldn't just throw her free. Hera's grappling technique was sound. She abruptly smashed herself flat against me and ground her pelvis against mine.

"You're lucky. Or...maybe not," she breathed in my ear. "When Kruger brought up men or women to satisfy us last night, it got me all worked up. I almost broke down and crawled into bed with you last night. You would have been so sore this morning!"

I flinched but managed to wrench one hand loose, then grabbed her side, where I knew she was ticklish. Hera twitched and fought to cover up, so I used the opportunity to roll her right off the bed.

"What are you two whispering about?" Prometheus asked, watching us.

"You don't want to know," I laughed and pushed myself up.

The horn sounded again, just as Hans walked into the tent.

"Good morning, freunde! I hope you slept well. Oh, gut, she is exercising," he said, pointing to Hera on the ground.

Hera smiled, looked at me, and winked. Then she mouthed, "you know you want it," and sprang nimbly off the ground.

Great, I thought. The last thing I needed was complications in my love life. And that wasn't to say Hera wasn't attractive. Far from it, but I'd always thought she leaned towards others. Then again, it had been quite a while since she'd had anything resembling affection.

"Get dressed and meet me outside in ten minutes. The hunt is about to start." Hans moved to leave but noticed Omega. He pointed at the wolf and looked at me. "I like your wolf, Takemi, but if you take him, you'll be putting your whole team at a disadvantage. The others complained about your beast and are demanding that they be allowed to use their reserve warriors to compensate. A wolf is worth a cultivator, they say."

"Hah!" I snorted. "If only they knew. Omega is worth a whole team on his own. If they are only demanding one, then we will clearly have the advantage."

"You are sure? We cannot take chances on this, Takemi. There is much at stake. Remember, the Protectorate's protection can only go so far. If you overleverage your hand, Alfred and the King will move against you."

"Trust me," I said, strapping on my armor. "That leverage is about all we've been thinking about for the last few weeks. We've got this."

"Gut," he said, with a crisp nod, then walked out.

Just under ten minutes later, we gathered in front of Zurich's main tent. We joined several other groups of cultivators, all sporting armor adorned with Zurich's standard. Either we weren't the only squad representing the city, or they hadn't told us everything.

"What's with these clowns?" I whispered, leaning into Ajax. As I did one of the men turned and looked our way. There was no smile, head nod, or warmth in his eyes. Nothing to indicate he viewed us as teammates. If anything, he regarded us as competitors.

Prometheus and Hera leaned in, finally noticing who and what we were staring at.

"They are Prime," Hera whispered, "Probably friends of those assholes that hassled Layla back in Vaduz. We should watch our backs around those guys."

Prometheus gave me a look. He was the only one that actually knew what happened to those guys, after all.

Kruger noticed us and motioned for us to join him. We walked past Zurich's Primes and settled on his other side. Some of the "elite" squad seemed powerful if you only took into consideration their open veins, but after my time in the arena, I knew there was more to strength than just potential. They felt almost clone-like in their powers, which didn't really fill me with hope, especially if we were supposed to rely on them. A squad needed variety, individuals with specialized strengths and abilities. If it were just a bunch of vanilla copycats, they would quickly find themselves in a situation they had no answers for.

We joined Alfred and the king inside the tent. The two looked our way but didn't say anything as Kruger unfolded a map.

"We have no idea what will await you inside, but we can give you some ideas. This is the lay of the land," he said, tracing around a section of the map.

I leaned in, spotting the castle and wetlands to the south, but Kruger's attention was further north. The stadium and old Olympic village appeared to be the epicenter of the zoo, with several small communities scattered around it. What I hadn't seen from the carriage was the large wall they had erected around the whole area.

"You will enter here at what they call the 'dark gates'," he said, pointing to a gap in the wall.

"But what is inside? Your map has almost no detail," Ajax said, his brow wrinkling.

Hans chuckled and moved in next to Kruger. "Oh, there is plenty on the map. And knowing you lot, you saw this area on your way south. The stadium is the center of the area, and it should be your primary focus, as the largest specimens usually congregate there."

"He is right," Kruger agreed. "We know the villages around that are likely full of lower-tiered creatures. There is an old windmill and the ruins of a castle here." He pointed to a spot some three to four inches to the right of the stadium. That will be a safe bet for stronger creatures as well. The further you can get into the ground, the stronger they will become. The old stadium has some four to five layers below ground."

"What are those?" Prometheus asked, gesturing to three small dots well north of the Olympic village.

Kruger pulled another sheaf of paper out of the stack and put it on top. The first drawing resembled a cave entrance just east of the castle, another a farm to the north of the windmill, and the last was a small lake that separated all three and the stadium.

"They are strategic points...ugh, areas where our seers have been able to pinpoint strong ether signatures. We obviously cannot tell what is there, or how powerful they are, so, be cautious. These beasts are carefully selected and hunted just for this competition, so do not take them lightly. You lot have become stronger, but some of these are truly monsters."

"Yes, they can tear you apart. Danger, fear, death, screaming, and all that...blah-blah-blah. Just don't come home empty-handed. Zurich cannot afford to leave another melee with anything to show for its efforts. We need the crystal veins that—" Alfred started to say, but the King shut him down.

"Enough, Alfred! They don't need to know anything beyond their task at hand," King Otto snapped.

Ajax and I shared a surprised look and focused on the map.

"Where will the other teams go?" I asked.

"You don't need to know that," Alfred hissed, evidently stung by the King's reprimand. "All you need to do is not embarrass Zurich!"

We shared a knowing look, as everything had become clear and murky all at the same time. Hell, I was fully onboard with simply getting out alive and disappearing to some quiet part of the world where they could never find us.

"You emphasized diplomacy," I said, looking to Kruger, "But how much crap should we take before we defend ourselves?"

"Kill them if they are a threat, no matter who they are. Even if they are from Zurich. I'll take care of the rest. Mind you, if you come out of there wearing trophies from Stuttgart champions, expect to incur plenty of wrath. So, be smart."

"With that said," Hans interjected as the King's eyes started to bulge. "I don't think anyone will purposefully mess with you. They might have opened more veins or have solidified their gains, but you lot have cultivated a healthy reputation of savagery, bloodlust, and mayhem. Anyone disciplined will likely give you a wide berth."

"As they should," I muttered.

"Solid. No one fucks with us, and we won't fuck with them," Ajax said, a funny little vein bulging on his forehead. "We're professionals...here to do a job for you, so let us get to it."

"You are in the presence of our benevolent king, you violent monkeys," Alfred hissed. "You *are* here to serve him. You *are* here to serve Zurich. Before setting out on this quest, you should prostrate yourself before him and kiss his feet!"

"Our skill is the reason why we are still alive," I said, correcting him. "And I kiss no man's feet—"

"Don't," Prometheus hissed, pulling me back.

Alfred stepped forward, his face turning an uncharacteristic shade of red. I don't think I'd ever seen him mad before, and the result was impressive.

The third horn echoed outside and Hans put his hand up to stop anyone from speaking. "We will have to postpone the foot kissing until later."

"Please, freunde. All of you, outside. It's about to begin and we have a walk ahead of us."

Hans promptly left the tent and we followed, not

acknowledging the King and Alfred as we went. I found Omega sitting like a statue just outside, his ears perked.

"Come, boy. Let's go," I said and ruffled the fur between his ears. He growled affectionately and followed.

I hadn't realized how early it was before, but the sky was still dark. The eastern horizon was a bit brighter, but my guess was it was still almost an hour from dawn. Hera yawned behind me, as Prometheus moved next to me. His eyes were weary, but not all from a lack of sleep.

"You look tired," I said and he nodded silently. The past month plus had been a whirlwind and not the good kind. We'd been bouncing from one misadventure to another, fighting to bring things under some semblance of control. At some point, we would need a break from that cycle.

Omega whined and joined me, brushing up against my leg as we joined a steadily growing column of people. Torches illuminated the path north, winding like a glowing serpent through the misty darkness.

We walked through the castle grounds and out through a gate in the wall, then up through the wetlands. The path was lined by soldiers on either side—an impressive array of warriors wearing every standard and color. Were they an honor guard, making safe the passage to the zoo? A show of collective force to dissuade any up-and-coming power from thoughts of assassination or war? Or all of the above?

Ajax pulled food from his bag and we ate on the way, chewing through some rather tough jerky. It was one thing while out in the wilderness, but here, with the village surrounding the castle so close, I longed for the delicious hand pies we'd had just the night before. There were so many other food carts and stalls, and we'd barely started exploring the place. I longed for the chance to settle down someplace secure, where we had the power and control, then start exploring this world of ours.

We passed around the wetlands, the foggy area filled with tall reeds and buzzing, chirping frogs. The sky was a pleasant shade of orange by the time we arrived at the wall, and I understood why we hadn't seen it from the road above. Built out of large chunks of stone and iron banding, the wall surrounding the zoo had been almost completely covered with creeping plants. It blended in with the surrounding forest so well that if a person wasn't paying close attention, they might walk smack-dab into it.

A large set of doors was set in the middle of the wall, the stout portal held shut by a massive, tree-sized locking bar. Soldiers patrolled above that, their torches throwing off wisps of smoke. So, those had been the torches we saw from above.

A man stood on a platform built against the wall, his dark blue cloak and curly, white wig making him look a bit like an old-world judge. He watched us congregate below, his double chin wobbling as he moved. Once the stream of people stopped, he nodded to someone behind us, and promptly slammed a gavel down on a pillar of solid stone.

"Willkommen, Krieger. Willkommen, Teilnehmer," the man said, his voice deep and resonant.

"He says, 'welcome warriors. Welcome contestants'," Ajax said, leaning in to translate.

"Euer Tod, euer Blut ehrt diesen heiligen Ort."

"Well, that is morbid. He says, 'our deaths and blood will honor this sacred place'."

"I'm not sure I like the sound of that," I whispered back.

"Wir sind hier für den Kampf der Könige!" he said and continued in a long and impressive-sounding speech. Ajax stayed on my shoulder, translating as he went.

"You are here for the tournament of kings. You all have been assigned a most important duty: to represent your kings and queens!"

The man spoke dramatically, his voice rising and falling in pitch. I listened to Ajax but studied the groups gathered around us. Quite a few of them looked strong.

A particularly tall and broad-shouldered man caught my eye. He was easily a head taller than Ajax, who already towered over most of us, and stood there with his arms crossed. He was eyeing Omega, but so were many others.

The standard on his armor drew my attention, as the patch seemed to radiate ether. It was a red shield featuring an eagle. The body and feathers were all white, but it had a golden beak and claws, with a crown perched atop its head.

"Frankfurt," Ajax said, noticing my attention. "They're a mean group, from what I hear. Their city is well-protected by geography, and they have access to several zoos. They're practically swimming in resources."

"So, he is as strong as he looks," I whispered, "Great."

"I don't think I could take him. At least not in a fair battle."

The judge continued to talk, outlining the rules and expectations. As it turned out, the zoo wasn't just massive, but its wall enclosed some forty-five square miles of ancient, dilapidated, and ether-plagued landscape. Oh, yeah, and it was filled with ether rifts. If we entered one, there was no telling where it would take us. Or for that matter, what we would find on the other side. But that was the risk.

It all came down to who hunted down the biggest game and brought back the biggest cores. Those left standing at the end of seven days would have their bounties weighed and valued, then the winner would move on to the next round.

"Seven days, and here I was thinking we'd be stuck in there for a few hours. And it is a requirement that we're alive at the end?" I breathed.

"Yes, alive, funny guy. And I am starting to understand why so few teams come out of this thing alive at the end," Ajax grunted.

I muttered, and Omega whined again, licking my wrist.

"Don't die. I am starting to like my new existence," Ivory said.

"That is less than helpful. Do you want to know what would be helpful? Tell me how to access my mind palace at will. Can you do that, please?"

"Ugh…no. You're far too weak to come and go at will. It should ordinarily be opened in the third realm, so, I think you should count yourself lucky to go there occasionally…on accident. But…I might have a way."

Ajax was watching my face but pointed over my shoulder.

"Tell me."

"There is a chance I could pull you in by force, but my core would have to be full."

"And is it?"

"No, of course not. But once we get into this zoo place, I think it could fill up quickly. That is if you lot manage to kill and absorb enough raw ether. I feel some truly powerful presences inside."

I filed that away for later and looked over to where Ajax was pointing. I couldn't see anything because of the crowd, but when I stood on my toes, I could barely see something just off to the side of the camp that I hadn't before. It was an almost imperceptible swirl that ran clockwise. It just floated there in mid-air, minding its own business.

I nodded in its direction and cocked my head questioningly, but he just shrugged as well.

"Wir haben ein problem hier, wie manche leute wissen. Ein team hat einen wölf."

Ajax tapped Omega's head and nodded to the judge.

"He's talking about our little friend here."

"What's he saying?"

The big guy pressed an index to his lips and listened as the judge spoke.

"The melee council has declared that we can choose to either leave the wolf behind or they will impose a penalty of twenty percent. It will apply to both the maximum size and the number of cores we bring back," he explained.

"What say you, Zurich?" the judge said, switching to English.

We came together and whispered, working out the pros and cons of both options. In the end, Hera articulated the point perfectly. We were all warriors, yes, but Omega was a born hunter. We were going to face unknown creatures, there was no telling how they would react to us, but there was also no way of knowing how they would react to him. Having the wolf at our side was a boon we could not give up.

"Herr Richter, wir nehmen den Wolf mit. Er ist ein Teil der Familie," Ajax said, squaring his shoulders.

I didn't know what that meant, but he sure sounded good saying it.

Ajax leaned in after the judge nodded.

"We're receiving a twenty percent penalty for him, but we all know it's worth it."

Omega, as if understanding what was going on, snorted and licked his chops. I grinned, knowing that even with a penalty, taking him with us would undoubtedly stir up more trouble.

"Don't disappoint, wolfy," Hera said. "Now is your chance to show us just how strong you've become. Size should matter after all."

With the judge done speaking, the groups of cultivators clustered together, gathering with their superiors. Gruber joined us.

"They wanted to kill your wolf, but we told them that he is a harmless pet, meine freunde."

"He's more like family now," I said, offering Hans a wolfish grin of my own.

He shrugged, his blue eyes sparkling. "Blut ist dicker als Wasser, ja?"

"Is that, 'blood is thicker than water'?" I asked, picking up on a few of the words.

"Gut! Jawohl. Seeing you all dressed up in your tactical armor and those expensive wolf cloaks…I wouldn't want to fight you either. So, watch your backs while you are in there. I will try and get the other Zurich groups to leave you alone, but I'm not completely sure if they will listen. Some have likely been paid to kill you. That is not our doing. I hope you understand."

"As Kruger said," Ajax replied. "If they attack, we'll defend ourselves."

Hera and Prometheus remained suspiciously quiet, but I didn't mind. They were on edge and nervous. Good, that meant that they cared. Our shared goal was to all get out alive.

I thought back on Layla and her smile. Her scent and our time together. She was my goal, my destination.

The horn blared for the fourth time, and Gruber turned toward the waiting doors.

"Good luck, freunde. Godspeed. Now go. And make sure you target one of the three landmarks I showed you on the map. If and when you push into one of the rifts, give yourselves plenty of time to get back."

I offered him my hand, and he shook it excitedly, then greeted the others one by one as we made our way toward the portal. If I had to be honest, I was more excited than ever. From what we heard, the zoos were strange places full of ether and treasure. Some said time passed differently inside, as well. Maybe we could even get our hands on some elemental cores so we could use them and open the fourth vein once we'd consolidated our gains in the third.

It was one of those things I couldn't hurry. First, I had to build up my body until I broke through to the next vein, learn what I had unlocked, and then dedicate myself to gaining the next progression.

We stood in line behind the Frankfurt team, which sent a chill down my spine. The big guy looked even bigger up close, and all I could do was imagine him squashing me like a ripe melon. He was in his fourth vein, I could tell that much. The amount of ether radiating off of him made the hair on my arms stand on end.

The judge pointed to the door, and a crew lowered a counterweight, lifting the locking bar. It creaked open, revealing a surprisingly dark and overgrown space beyond. The first teams entered, including our Frankfurt friends.

The big man turned and looked right at me, and said, "Endlich hat Zürich einen kompetenten team gefunden. Viel glück wünsche ich dir." Then, with a nod, he turned and followed his team into the darkness.

"What was that about?" I asked Ajax. His tone hadn't sounded threatening, on the contrary, he sounded downright friendly. Had he just nicely offered to pluck my head from my shoulders?

"He wished us good luck and said that Zurich has finally found a formidable team. Or something like that," Ajax said as he dropped a big paw-like hand on my shoulder. "Don't fuck this up, Kenji."

"I won't, Rupert," I replied. It meant something that he'd used my real name, and his smile confirmed it.

The doors closed again, as the judge waited for the next horn.

"This whole thing gives me the chills," Hera muttered as we filed forward. "I've only been thinking about fighting and killing stuff since getting my new spear, but I...I'm...terrified."

"We're in this together," I said, pulling her into a hug. Her behavior earlier suddenly made sense, when she'd admitted that she almost crawled into bed with me. She was frightened. Perhaps more so than ever before. When faced with that kind of fear, people had a tendency to gravitate towards activities that made them feel alive. Sex was one of those things.

"If we get separated, meet up at the castle ruins," Ajax said. "Avoid the landmarks Hans highlighted, and for the love of God, don't get yourselves pulled into any rifts."

"You heard the man," I said, slapping Prometheus on the arm. I tightened my grip on Omega's lead and gestured the other forward, right up to the large, moss-covered doors.

A strange weightlessness washed over me as we got close, but I knew it wasn't fear or excitement. Whatever was beyond that door was powerful and otherworldly. The source of ether? And if so, what had it done to this little patch of our planet?

The horn blared ahead, the noise making Hera jump. Prometheus' tightened his grip on his bow, and Ajax his hammer. I reached down and unhooked Omega from his lead just as the locking bar started to lift free. Then the doors creaked open and my stomach dropped to my feet.

"Let's go kill some stuff," I said, my hands shaking as I stuffed the lead into my pack.

CHAPTER 29: INTO THE ZOO

Omega led us through the massive doors and into the darkness beyond. It might as well have been a portal, for how different the world looked inside that wall. A thick mist seeped up and out of the ground, but it was the vegetation that most surprised me.

Thick, shooting ferns rose on our right side, the waving fronds looming twelve to fifteen feet in the air. They weren't just large, but they were surreal. Everything was from the grass, flowers, trees, and leg-sized ropey vines.

We'd only moved forward eighty to a hundred paces but already couldn't see the door from which we'd entered. The idea of another team moving in behind us kept us going, as I wasn't crazy about having potential enemies sneak up in the mist.

The forest closed in around us until we had to pick our way through a tunnel of leaves and branches. Then, we just walked out into the open.

My senses came alive as a strong and spicy scent filled my nostrils. I heard chirping birds and the deafening bellow of some distant beast. It took me a moment, but I shook my head, struggling through a woozy, almost drunk feeling. A strong breeze blew in from the west and broke the blanket of mist apart, revealing a wide, sprawling landscape before me. The fuzzy sensation in my brain almost instantly cleared and my legs solidified.

I turned and found the others behind me. Hera was bent over, with her head between her legs, while Prometheus looked how I felt—drunk or hungover. Perhaps both.

"What in the Hölle was that?" Ajax grumbled and spat onto the ground. "That mist...it...it tastes like onions."

"Why are you tasting it?" Hera asked, then straightened.

"Because I have a beard, woman. It clung to my beard."

Omega whined and moved up next to me. He didn't just appear to not be fazed by the ether mist, but rather, he seemed to be growing in it. Was that possible? We'd just walked into the zoo and the wolf already looked a tad thicker on the shoulders. Perhaps I was seeing things.

"I think I blacked out," Prometheus said.

"Seriously?" Hera asked.

"Maybe. I don't know. But just for a moment. I honestly have no idea."

"Then why are you talking about it? Geez," she breathed and pushed him away. Prometheus fell over like a felled tree.

"Knock it off, you two," Ajax hissed. "This is precisely the kind of behavior Alfred and his poopy-butt King will use against us later."

I loped forward a dozen paces and skidded to a halt. With the mist gone, I realized that the ground dropped away before my feet. No, not just drop away, but we were perched onto a cliff. The stadium and the rest of the zoo lay far below in a valley, with entire portions of the green landscape shrouded by dense mist.

"Well, there it is. No wonder Hans said to save plenty of time to get back out of the zoo. Just look at that climb!" Hera gasped.

I looked around and spotted a trail cut conspicuously into the rockface, forming a rather severe switchback. Omega followed my gaze, growled, and took off in that direction.

"Did you see that?" I asked the others. "The wolf thinks we should keep moving."

"You are an asshole," Ajax grunted as I ran after him.

It took us the better part of an hour to navigate our way down the trail. Ajax slipped and almost fell at least half a dozen times. I reminded him that he was lucky to be alive. For some reason, he didn't like that. He reminded me that I was an asshole as soon as we stopped to rest at the bottom.

We set off toward the center of the large space, as the stadium seemed to be the most logical place to start. It also helped that it was the closest recognizable structure. I'd barely made it four steps forward before a large bush ahead and to our right started to shake.

I narrowed my eyes and dropped a hand to my katana and wakizashi. Something large moved behind the leaves, bending a thick branch with an audible *crack*.

"Please tell me that is your wolf," Hera cursed, leveling her spear. Then turned and realized that Omega was sitting to my left, watching the bush. "Shit!"

"Fan out," I said, "We shouldn't give anything in here free shots at all of us together."

Ajax hefted his hammer and moved left, Prometheus nocked an arrow and moved right, while Hera, Omega, and I took the middle of the clearing.

The beast erupted from the bush in a shower of twigs and leaves. All I noticed were its deep-set, red eyes, and massive front teeth. The rest was just a mass of brown as the adrenaline spiked and my instincts took over.

Omega leaped forward and circled to the right, channeling the beast right toward Hera and me. It snapped its teeth, squealed, and charged. Even in my tunneled vision, I could see that it was at least three feet tall and roughly rat shaped, with a long, lashing tail tipped with a nasty, barbed spike.

I held my shorter blade up in defense and the katana

over my shoulder, preparing for a killing strike. The massive rat landed on its front legs, twisted about, and snapped its teeth. Ajax roared and brought his hammer down, aiming for its head, but the thing contorted its body, twisting away. The big guy pitched forward, having missed completely.

Omega jumped in and snapped at the large, rat creature's hindquarters, but again it jumped and spun. Hell, it almost looked like it was dancing.

"What is this thing, a fucking ballerina?" Hera snarled, jabbing her spear at its side. Prometheus pulled and loosed an arrow, but the projectile passed clear under it.

I identified the problem right away. They were all aiming their attacks at the creature when it was on the ground. Then it would simply jump and contort its body enough to make them miss. It was a simple but effective strategy.

"Come at it from both sides at the same time," I yelled to Hera and Ajax.

They moved away from me, bracketing the creature. It watched them, hissing, and snapping its large, yellow teeth. Omega slunk around behind it, effectively boxing the beast in.

"Now!" I said.

Ajax and Hera attacked at almost the same moment, hammer and spear flashing in. Predictably, the massive rat leaped straight up into the air, pinwheeling its body around. I lunged in after a two-beat pause, allowing the creature to reveal the extent of its movement. I channeled my strength into a single, devastating cut.

My katana came down hard, slicing right through the creature from nose to its nether regions. Its body fell open like a gooey rat sandwich, landing in identical halves on the ground.

"A damned rat," Prometheus cursed and nudged the closest half with his boot toe.

I approached and stood over the halved beast, a strong ether signature pulsing from somewhere inside. I poked at a few spots with the tip of my sword before finding it: a small, almost fist-sized core. My sharp blade made quick work of the tissue around the core before I pulled it free and set it on the ground. It was round and roughly gem-like, with a faint bluish light pulsing from inside. I was lucky, as judging from the location of my cut, I'd come incredibly close to cutting it in half, too.

Omega walked up and sniffed the core, then sat on his haunches and yawned.

"One down," I said, scanning the trees.

"Six days and a bunch of hours left," Hera finished for me.

"We're going to have to find much more dangerous beasts than this if we're going to have any chance of winning this thing," Ajax breathed while picking the mud off his hammer.

"Well, that is a terrifying thought," Prometheus laughed.

"Anything else out there, boy?" I asked Omega. He stood, turned to the jungle, and sniffed for a moment. With one ear lying flat, the wolf turned back to me, growled, and snapped his teeth. "I guess that's a yes," I muttered just as Ajax turned and looked at Hera. It was only then that she was frozen in place, staring at the giant rat's remains.

"It is just a rat, Hera," the big man said.

"I-I-I think it stopped being a rat once it grew to be over ten inches tall, Ajax. I h-h-hate r-r-rats."

Prometheus snorted. "So, you're telling me you'll square off against a dozen armed men, fight a giant, man-eating bear, get surrounded by and almost eaten by a pack of monster wolves, but you're scared of rats?"

"I hate...rats!"

"And considering rats represent probably one of the smaller examples of vermin, I'd say the next few days will be full of surprises! Let's just make sure we don't get eaten by one," Ajax said, and we all agreed.

Omega led us forward, through the trees, and onto a

trail. We walked for barely five minutes before the wolf's hackles raised and he started to growl.

I held my blades out before me and proceeded forward cautiously. The trees thinned out barely fifty paces ahead, revealing a body on the ground. Whoever they were, the beasties had picked their bones clean in short order and left their armor scattered.

Omega growled quietly as we stepped around it and I spotted another body twenty paces further down the trail. Three rats were busy snacking on this person, as they clawed and pulled on the dead man's armor.

I looked around me, motioning outward to the others. The signs were all there, the bent and broken branches, the matted grass, and blood-smeared leaves. The rats had been hiding in the dense trees and sprang their ambush with deadly effect.

"Prom," I whispered and gestured forward.

Our scout nodded, stepped forward, and released an arrow in one, fluid motion. The compound bow snapped quietly, but the projectile itself made no noise.

The closest rat jerked and lifted its head as the arrow hit, passing clean through the base of its skull and into the forest behind it. The beast slumped, dead before it knew what happened. As it died, I caught motion ahead and watched as a swarm of rats materialized. Two of the beasts pulled something bloody and mangled between them, but it was too chewed up to identify. That was how they hunted, overwhelming even much stronger beings with sheer numbers.

I stopped counting at twenty but nodded to Hera and Ajax. My katana and wakizashi slid back into their scabbards and I pulled the heavy nodachi off my back.

"I'll take the middle. Hera and Ajax, stay behind me. Prometheus, use your arrows to bunch them up," I said and ran forward.

<<Enhanced Strength>>

<<Burst of Speed>>

Omega tackled a rat that burst out of the forest to our left, the previously hidden rodent tumbling in a ball of fur and snapping teeth. The wolf got the better of that encounter, as his jaws latched onto its neck, and with a savage snarl, shook his head.

The rat's head and body flew in two different directions as my skills kicked in, pulling a noticeable swell of ether from my core in the process.

I hefted the nodachi over my shoulder, prepared to swing, and after a moment of hesitation, activated **<<Blazing Slash>>**. More ether rushed forth as the big blade cut hard through the air.

The nodachi chopped through four rats in a single strike, a trail of fire setting the severed pieces on fire and hitting a few more in the process. I turned the blade over and brought it up hard, catching another creature under the chin and splitting its face open.

Maintaining the momentum, I swung it wide, hitting two more. It truly was a crowd control weapon.

Ajax's hammer came down hard, crushing a rat's skull, while Hera danced like a scared girl behind us, jabbing her spear out at full length. She hit one beast, and then another, the sharp wolf-bone blade punching clean holes each time.

Prometheus hung behind us, working with Omega to group the rats together. Arrows streaked in, one after another, hitting jumping rats in their faces and necks, killing them almost instantly. When the dust had settled, barely two minutes had passed. Or, so we guessed.

Several of the rats continued to burn, so we liberated the dead beasts of their cores and added them to the fire. Omega stopped right next to me, with a glowing blue core in his mouth.

"Who's a good boy! Hand it over," I said holding out my hand, only Omega didn't drop it in my palm but swallowed the thing whole.

"Hey!" I said, in surprise, only to watch the wolf pounce on our pile of salvaged cores, grab another in his jaws, and swallow that too!

I dove at him as he snapped at a third, but he growled and jumped away.

"He's going to bite you," Ajax laughed. "Find him something he'd like to eat even more and he'll stop."

"He seems to like your cooking the best, why don't you give him something..." I started to say, just as a mass of ether blossomed in the wolf's belly.

Omega laid down, rolled over onto his side, and simply stopped moving. A significant rumble echoed out of his stomach and I backed away. Would he explode? Fart noxious gas that killed us all? Or...?

Before any of us could react, the wolf groaned, gagged, and then proceeded to spectacularly vomit onto the ground. I circled and cringed, noticing the black muck he'd thrown up. It looked suspiciously like the crud we'd excreted when opening new veins.

Omega tried to stand but whined and fell again.

"My God, what is happening?" Hera gasped. Ajax was halfway to the wolf before he froze in his tracks.

Body shaking, fur shimmering escaping ether, Omega abruptly started to grow. His legs grew longer, his shoulders wider, and his head larger. Not just that, his fur darkened, and peculiar spines broke through from underneath. He gnashed his teeth and pawed at the ground, both his claws and teeth growing considerably. He went quiet and still then, as we all shared shocked and alarmed looks. Then, Omega promptly shook, licked his lips, and pushed to his feet.

When he stood, the wolf was easily ten inches taller than before. Instead of coming to my waist, now his shoulder rose to my chest, and when he turned and looked at me, we were practically eye to eye.

"So, what just...happened?" Hera asked.

"Ingesting those cores helped him open his third vein. He'd

been so close for a long time," Ivory said, his tone a bit too condescending. "The mongrel will be weak for a while until his body has adjusted. Although I will say, he looks intimidating, so that will help."

"He has veins, too?" I asked.

"Who…are you talking to?" Prometheus asked, and then caught himself. "Is this that Ivory…wolf…thing?"

I nodded.

"Yeah, he just told me Omega opened up his third vein. Little bastard scared me shitless. I thought he was dying."

Omega jumped and bolted off into the trees. He looked a little cumbersome as he moved, but watched as he collided with a tree, and knocked it over. On a bright note, I could more clearly sense his emotions now, so that would help.

We gathered up all of our rat cores and stowed them away, then prepared to move on.

Omega broke back through the tree line a short while later, his fur now dripping wet. Evidently, he'd found some creek, river, or stream to jump into. Normally, I would have been pleased, only now he smelled like a blood wolf mixed with stinking creek water. Hera gagged when he ran by her.

"You need to teach him how to use ether to expunge the muck and stench," I said.

"Why would I do that? Serves you right for adopting the mutant."

We set out again, moving in the stadium's general direction. So far, we'd descended a massive cliff, found a team of warriors picked clean by giant rats, and Omega had opened a vein. Our time in the zoo would not boring, that was clear.

I touched the trunk of a tree as we moved through and didn't just feel a spark of ether, but a veritable stream of the stuff. It wasn't a deluge, mind you, but more than I'd experienced from any one source in nature. When taken on its own, the tree wasn't unique, but considering that we were surrounded by tens of thousands of trees and plants, then it was clear this place was overflowing with power.

Ajax pulled out a compass and found true north. We didn't know where we were on the map exactly, but from what I remembered, the stadium was centrally located in the southern portion of the zoo. If we used that as our target, we could continue and eventually come to both the castle and the ruins.

We talked it over for a moment.

"They said the castle attracts stronger monsters and beasts, which is kind of what we were searching for," I said.

"Sure, but that is also what everyone else is searching for, too," Ajax replied. "We might get our asses handed to us by a super beast or take an arrow to the back while we are trying to kill one. I trust people less than animals. My vote is the road less traveled."

"Here, here," Hera said, throwing in her support.

"You always go with what Ajax proposes," Prometheus said.

"Not always. Just...when it makes sense.

"And it always makes sense," Ajax laughed.

"Do we wander around or?" I asked, bringing up the most important question of the day.

"I vote for the windmill," Prom said. "I think most will aim for the stadium or the castle first, so that means we should set our sights on something a little more out of the way."

"I agree with that one," I said.

"It appears we are at an impasse," Ajax said.

"Hera?" Ajax asked. "What if we scout the stadium and the ruins on the way to the windmill?"

"Fine, but if the castle looks quiet, my vote is we hit that first."

"I can live with that," I added. "And if not, we switch to the ruins, then the windmill and everyone gets what they want."

Ajax nodded, his beard splitting in a satisfied grin.

"Very good. The stadium, the castle, ruins, and then off to the windmill. Worst case scenario, the wolf can distract our enemies while we escape and move on."

Omega growled strangely as if he were trying to talk. Then he licked Ajax's hand.

"I think he likes the idea," I said and ruffled the wet fur on his head.

"He seems to like you even more now," Ajax muttered. "I'm kind of jealous."

"Don't be. He just wiped his snot on your hand."

"Gross," he said, wiping it on a nearby tree. "Wolves bond for life. Maybe he sees you as his wife or something. Make sure he doesn't do stuff to you when you're asleep."

Hera and Prometheus laughed at that, and I didn't have a rebuttal. Quieting, we spread out and started making our way toward the stadium.

I picked through everything we'd seen and what potentially lay ahead of us—castles were definitely my thing, and then there was the promise of loot, big monsters, and valuable cores. I understood Prometheus' apprehension. After all, if the rats here were seven feet tall and capable of swarming and eating strong warriors, then what would an apex predator be like? What would Lazy Bones be like if left in a place like that for long?

Reminded of the bear, I almost asked the others if we should summon him. Bears were resilient creatures and fantastic climbers. If we could put out a strong enough signal, I was willing to put money on him finding us. But then I heard Prom's voice fill my head. The argument the simulated Prometheus made was spot on. If the other kingdoms and strongholds argued against us taking Omega into the zoo, what would they say if we came out with the wolf and a bear?

After half an hour we finally broke through the dense trees and walked out into a grassy area. The stadium loomed large above us but was still a fair distance off. With no enemies in sight, I pulled out one of the cores and studied it. The ether inside had a...watery feel to it if that made any sense. I offered it to Hera.

"What?" she asked, accepting the core. "Do you want me to eat it like the dog did?"

"First, he's not a dog, and second, no. Feel for the ether inside and try to absorb it. I think it matches your affinity."

Hera did as I asked, a blue light quickly enveloping her hand. It pulsed like that for a moment, before creeping up her arm. She gasped and dropped the core. It rolled for a moment, before settling against a rock. Its color and ether had been drained away.

"Wow. It emptied that fast?" Prometheus asked. "Do you feel anything?"

Hera nodded and held her hand out to me.

"You want more?"

"No, I want the scanning device first. Then, maybe I will take another one."

I did as she asked and handed her the small scanning device. She pushed some ether forth into the device, nodded to herself, and with a smile on her face held her hand out again.

"I'll take it she likes the results," I said, dropping another in her waiting palm. That core went almost as fast as the first, and her eyes widened as the scanner updated.

"Do share," Prometheus prompted.

"All of my stats went up by a single point after absorbing the second core," Hera said, and I moved behind her to better see the screen.

I took the scanner next, pushed a little ether forth, and proposed the first question.

"Can you analyze our surroundings?" Bold letters appeared on the screen.

You are in an ether-rich zone. Designation—zoo. Ether fluctuations near you range between 71% and 1,500% of normal atmospheric ether saturation, with a scanning accuracy of +/- 5%.

"What does that mean?" I asked, unsure of what the device was telling us.

Ether ranges in its atmospheric density around you. Earth norm range is "Low" (+.05% to 29%) to "High" (+71%) except for unstable areas where ether spikes can exceed current reading limits. [Warning] Ether pockets of extremely high density can support rifts. Some designate these areas as pocket dimensions. Rifts are unstable and incredibly dangerous.

"So, what are rifts?"

Rifts are tears in space-time and can exist beyond what is called a pocket dimension. They are normally self-contained but can be connected to an exterior world.

The pocket dimensions do not necessarily accumulate more ether, and in recorded events, have shown to actually have lower ambient ether than the Earth-bound space around the rifts. [Warning] In some recorded instances, when the pocket dimension is connected to another world, ambient ether levels can spike to beyond readable limits. In these cases, organisms found in that space can be significantly larger, stronger, faster, and more aggressive. They develop cores within the first fifteen days and absorb more ether with every passing day. The older the core, the more ether you can absorb.

"That's handy," Ajax said, nodding at the scanner. "Think it can tell us more about the cores?"

I nodded. "What can you tell us about beast cores in general?"

A monster core is a solidified mass of ether, infused with an elemental affinity, depending on the host. Normally, every core found inside a pocket dimension is associated with a single element, meaning that you would need to have an open vein in order to absorb that core's ether. A human body can absorb up to five low-ranking, two medium-ranking, or a single higher-ranking core. A full ether pool needs up to [12] hours of processing to stabilize the gains.

"What about our opened veins?" I asked. "Do we just need to open a vein with the appropriate element?"

Incorrect. In your case, you can only absorb metal-affinity cores due to your two opened metal veins. Metal affinity is very rare, and unless you open up another fire vein, you will be limited to only metal-affinity ether.

"Fucking Ivory," I grunted. "You could have told me sooner!"

"You never asked," he replied. *"Besides, you should be grateful. If you ever find some metal elemental cores, you'll be able to draw twice as much from a single core due to your double veins."*

"Bastard."

Ether swirled around us as Ivory materialized in his spiritual form. He circled me, snapping his teeth at me.

"You are an ungrateful cretin!"

"And you're a leech! At least earn your keep!"

"Ask and you shall receive."

"Wait, hold on," Ajax said, regarding the glowing wolf. "I don't understand. Why were we hunting you when Manfred could have just as easily acquired cores from a rift and done it that way?"

Ivory regarded the big guy and snorted.

"Because these cores start to lose their power the moment they are removed from their pocket dimensions. Nobles are not willing to take the risk. And before you ask, yes, some cores can be stabilized for a short time after their collection. For example, purple, red, and orange cores can be preserved, but only for a short time. As soon as they are pulled through a rift, this world starts sucking them dry."

"Shit, this is a lot of information to process," I grunted.

"Join the club, pretty boy," Hera added.

Prometheus watched us, his bow held loosely at his side. "What does that all mean?" he finally asked.

"For starters," Hera said, leaning on her spear, "That

rifts are dangerous. If we pass through one with a high enough ether concentration, it immediately starts breaking down our bodies. Forget about absorbing it, we'd probably melt into puddles on the ground. And say we do happen into a juicy pocket dimension full of beasts of the right affinity. We would need to take precautions while in there, otherwise, our treasures would slowly bleed dry once we came back."

"Shit," our scout breathed. "And they know that? They send us in here to hunt beasts, to try and survive, all the while knowing that anything we'd find in here, if we don't use it, will be relatively useless?"

Ajax nodded. "I think that is kind of the point. It's the sport. The big game hunt of it all. Whoever's team survives until the end, showcasing the most strength and the best trophies, wins. And glory to their kingdom."

"It is a surprise any of them survive," I said, starting to walk forward. "But with that logic, you would think we would see some nations start to accumulate truly powerful warriors."

"It makes you wonder," Ajax said, moving up next to me. "Maybe that is why we see so many wars and foolish competitions. Perhaps it is all the different kings and queens working to make sure their competitors don't get too strong."

CHAPTER 30: MY WORTH

I watched my pack finish yipping and growling. They'd done a lot of it since killing the squeaking beasts. They really were a strange lot—so noisy and unaware. Was I the only one that smelled the threats on the wind? This place was practically stinking with danger.

I approached them and growled. Alpha looked at me, then turned and snarled at the rest of the pack. They finally went quiet, and after a moment, we continued.

I ran out ahead of the others and through the thick brush. Even though I couldn't understand their yips and barks, I could feel where they wanted to go, so I explored the route and made sure it was safe. I could also feel my alpha, which made me feel stronger inside.

The forest ahead was lush and made my skin tingle...more than any other forest I'd ever been in. It was the power, the energy that made me grow stronger. There was more of it in the dirt, plants, and trees around me than I'd ever felt before.

The beasts were almost as plentiful as the energy, but they were infinitely more dangerous than any I'd seen before. Even the small creatures, the prey animals, moved around as if unafraid. I wished Long Claws was with me, as he was slow, but also strong.

A smell filled my nose and I slowed, just as the forest thinned ahead. An enormous fake cave rose above as I scanned the area. Fires burned from the upper levels, but the plants had spread out over its shiny surface. So much so that I could almost forget that the two-legged wolves built it.

I smelled blood and guts ahead, and although I could not see the source, part of me knew that it was more of the two-legged wolves. Stupid wolves. They had probably stumbled into another pack of hungry beasts and realized that they were not scared of their bright claws.

What made them so confident? Yes, they could be strong, but they were small. And frail. And smelled funny.

Beasts came into view from the left They were similar to the brown, four-legged beasts we'd killed before. The ones that tasted really good. *Deer.* I think that was what Alpha called them.

These were much larger and more dangerous, however. Several appeared to be female, but the largest in their pack had a massive, head-full of antlers. They reminded me of the long stick Short Tooth used. These deer-like creatures also had tough hides and long, strong legs. I licked my lips but knew these creatures would not be an easy meal. Although...

My stomach rumbled as several smaller creatures came into view behind the others. They were younger and I knew that would mean their meat was more tender. Salivating, I slunk sideways, watching the beasts move.

Something screamed from inside the large, round two-legged wolf structure. It could have been a beast, but I couldn't be sure. The long horns heard the cry and perked up, their ears twitching. Half their numbers moved off, trekking away from the structure. The others followed after a moment. The small one, I noticed, lingered toward the back of the herd.

I focused, activating my camouflage, and followed. My mouth watered as I moved, the creature's scent covering the ground. Stopping to watch, I licked the ground.

Baring my teeth, I became translucent, merging with my surroundings. But my scent remained. I wasn't sure if they would run, or if they would remain and fight. Then my stomach rumbled, and I knew what I needed to do. The mutated deer needed to die for my sake.

Alpha's emotions washed over me then and I knew that he wanted me to show myself. To return to the pack, but my stomach rumbled deeper and harder than it ever had before. I needed food and in a bad way.

Something spooked the long horns and they moved left and then right. I felt a strange tremor in the ground, although I couldn't tell if it was their hooves or something else.

I circled through a dense copse of trees and moved as fast as possible while keeping my paws quiet and my body hidden. The distance to the small longhorn closed and its smell filled my nose. Then I realized why it had caught my attention. It was wounded, its blood tinging the ground around its hoof prints. It staggered as it walked, favoring one leg.

My stomach growled again. Somewhere in the trees, Alpha called my name. I would take down the longhorn and drag its body back to the pack. That would make him happy, and Deer Eyes could burn some of its meat for me. They would bark and yip my deeds to the sky, so all the other wolves could hear.

I closed in until barely two bounds separated me from the wounded longhorn. It looked my way, then once it felt safe again, started to eat the grass. This was it. My chance.

The ground shook as I jumped from cover and the wounded long horn jumped right off the ground. I lunged and snapped my jaws, but just missed its rear leg. It bolted into the trees, bleating a loud and scared warning.

The herd all started to run, just as the ground jumped to my right. I leaped clear, chasing my prey as something large and green exploded from the dirt. Before the dust could fade, I spotted a large, bulbous worm, crashing through the trees as it went after my prey.

Giving chase I tried to jump onto the worm's back but bounced off of its round body. One moment I was in the air, and the other I hit a tree. The blow ached deep inside me, but I snarled and went right back at the worm. My claws and teeth hit its green body, but it was covered in hard, gleaming scales.

It slithered between the trees, ignoring me as it pursued the wounded longhorn. Trees groaned and broke under the long beast's weight, its body ripping some trees clean out of the ground.

I wasn't about to relinquish my prey, so I ducked low and ran as fast as I could, and finally outpaced the creature. The green monstrosity finally seemed to notice me. It turned its wide head, a long, forked tongue flickering out of its wide mouth. Massive, venom-dripping fans extended, sending a cold, jolt of fear through my body.

I yipped and tried to retreat, but the serpent lashed out, hitting the tree next to me and rending it to splinters. Running and jumping as fast as I could, I outpaced the wounded longhorn. The rest of the herd was above and next to me now, their hooves thundering against the ground.

Then the forest simply came to an end. I skidded to a halt, my claws tearing at the ground. The rest of the herd raged ahead, having missed the large outcropping of rock. The wounded long horn tried to escape to the right, but the serpent's head lashed in, blocking that path. I tried to escape to the left, but the creature's long body curled around, blocking that retreat.

My lips curled up, revealing my teeth as the big green creature moved in on the longhorn. I snarled, snapped my teeth, and lunged at the serpent's face. It hissed and recoiled, then darted forward so fast I almost couldn't see the movement.

I ducked and turned, narrowly missing the enormous fangs, and lunged in biting the serpent not twice, but three times. My teeth stuck in the creature's tough scales and it pulled me violently off the ground.

It wrenched me in one direction and then back in the other. I scrabbled against its thick body, my claws scoring its hard scales and knocking one loose. With a pop, my teeth came free and I dropped. I hit the ground hard but absorbed the landing, the green serpent's blood in my mouth. I had wounded it.

I will show Alpha how strong I've become, I thought, dug my claws into the ground, and charged.

I hit the serpent's head, pushing forth every bit of savagery possible. I bit and clawed but somehow unlocked the strange power inside. It burst out from my chest and flooded the rest of my body, pushing out through my muscles, and into my claws and teeth.

Finding purchase, my claws and teeth cut right through the beast's tough scales, my newfound power melting the tough skin beneath. Armored plates broke loose and fell to the ground, a healthy splatter of green blood coating me and the ground next.

I sank my teeth into the serpent's soft flesh and shook my head, only to have it rear back, and in the next moment, I flew free. The ground reached up and grabbed me, the impact knocking away my breath. Struggling to roll over, I fought to my feet and moved to charge again, just as something flashed in from the side.

The serpent's tail hit me in the side and sent me flying. I struck a large rock and rolled to the ground, coming to rest next to the wounded longhorn. It had been trying to push back into the shadow, to hide.

I fought to stand again, but a painful twinge bit into my back. My hind legs wouldn't work. I snarled angrily and rolled as the monstrous serpent slithered right at me, its eyes gleaming with hunger.

So, this was how I was going to die? Eaten by a wretched serpent? I looked over at the wounded long horn, its dark eyes full of fear. I didn't even want to eat it anymore. In the end, I'd protected it more than safeguard my next meal.

Goodbye, Alpha, I thought as the hungry mouth descended.

A shadow passed over us all then, as something landed next to the serpent. Light glinted and shadows danced, but I didn't see it properly until the massive rack of sharp antlers hit the serpent, scraping loose scales and gouging reptilian flesh.

The serpent hissed and reared up as the enormous long horn jumped before us, its antlers held high, like an army of bright blades. Then the enormous stag lowered its head and charged.

CHAPTER 31: MIGHTY STAG

"Where did he run off to...?" Hera hissed.

"Why did he...?" Prometheus chimed in.

"You're going to get us killed," Ajax bellowed.

But I ignored their questions as I sprinted off in Omega's general direction. Ivory was screaming in my mind. Most of it was frantic, scared nonsense, but the one line I did understand was:

You need TO HURRY!

I used **<<BURST OF SPEED>>** but still didn't feel like I was moving fast enough. I could feel his distress. His pain. But scariest of all, his fear. Since meeting the wolf, even when malnourished and weak, I'd never known him to be fearful. But now? My heart was racing, my chest compressing down around it, and my throat was closing.

"Shit! Fuck! Damn!" I cursed, feeling as if death's jaws were closing down around *my* throat. "Hold on, buddy!"

I burst out of the trees and into a clearing. Even in my haste, I could see the mess of deep prints marring the ground. A number of trees had been damaged or knocked over ahead, the undergrowth smashed flat in a wide swath next to it.

Chopping my katana down and back up, I forged my

own path through the scratchy branches. Angry screams and snorts echoed ahead, followed by the *boom-boom* of something heavy hitting the ground. *Holy shit,* I thought, as the sounds of conflict grew closer and louder.

I renewed both of my skills, the ether in my core dropping again. My strength and speed doubled, but so did my anger, and unfortunately, my fear. A tree cracked loudly and fell over just ahead, the branches narrowly missing me.

I dove right and rolled, as a massive, green snake came into view. The word massive didn't do it justice, as its body was easily as high and wide as I was tall. Easily sixty feet long, the serpent had a rattle tail and narrow, diamond-shaped head. It hissed, snapped forward, and withdrew, squaring off against...I did a double take. An equally large stag shook its magnificently equipped head at the snake, its hooves churning the soft dirt.

Behind the stag lay Omega. The wolf growled and snapped his jaws, dragging his body toward the snake, but he couldn't seem to move his hind legs. The stag was protecting him from the snake? Whaaa?

Finally breaking free from my stupor, I shoved all the ether I could spare into my legs and pushed off. The snake loomed high in the air and snapped, again and again, large globs of noxious venom spattering from its sword-length fangs. The stag drove its head into the serpent's body, driving the whole beast back into a tree. Wood splintered and cracked and the snake shrieked.

Its tail lashed around from the side, breaking more trees off at the ground, then knocked the stag right off its feet. The noble beast had weapons, but it couldn't hold off a monster like that forever.

I heard the others reach the clearing behind me—their confused, scared voices lost to the beast battle. The snake coiled around the stag, then opened its mouth, either to deliver the killing bite or swallow it whole. My response was automatic—right arm cocking back and snapping forward with all of my available strength. The katana tumbled through the air, before hitting the scaly beast in the side of the head.

With very little mass, the thrown sword bounced off the snake's scales, but it did manage to get its attention. With venom flying, the serpent turned my way and hissed. I screamed, pulling the nodachi off my back. An arrow streaked in as the snake moved toward me, the sharp, bladed tip punching clean through the armored scales.

Providing just enough distraction for me to get close, I prepared <<**ETHER BLADE**>>. Part of me knew it wasn't the best choice, as the snake wasn't made of metal, but I hoped the skill and my power would help to break through its tough scales.

Another arrow hit the snake in the neck, causing its head to jerk to the side, just as I brought the nodachi down. The big blade left a trail of blue ether in its wake as steel met scales. The sword bit and cut cleanly, as I allowed the movement to carry it through to the other side.

Shit, I thought, knowing my gamble hadn't paid off. The scales were simply too tough.

Too close to retreat, I wound up for another attack, but paused, noticing that the scales I'd hit were glowing and throbbing with a bright, blue light. A heartbeat later, they detonated in a violent flash of light and smoke. The blast knocked the snake over and blew me back. Luckily, I still had all of my appendages and could still think straight.

"Help Omega," I yelled to Ajax as he picked his way toward me.

The snake hissed and thrashed as Hera loomed over me, but the distraction had allowed the stag to regain its feet as well. It hissed and tried to coil itself up, but it was obviously wounded now. My ether attack, despite not working as intended, had stung it.

The serpent spun about suddenly, and I spotted a large patch of missing scales where my sword hit. Its light green flesh was covered in dark blood. The stag rammed its massive rack into the snake and pinned its body against a tree yet again. I used that moment to push my attack.

"Hera, I need a step!" I yelled.

"So, find a ladder," she shouted back but rammed her spear straight into the snake's scales. The tip of her spear, specially forged to pierce armor, punched clean through the scales.

I ran, jumped up onto a fallen tree, and then used her spear as a step to get onto the snake's body.

"You're welcome!" she yelled, pulled the spear free, and attacked again.

I scrabbled against the snake's slick body, but just managed to set my feet, then lifted the nodachi high, and activated <<ETHER BLADE>> once more, effectively draining most of my ether reserves.

Time seemed to grind to a halt as the nodachi swung, the blade glowing an angry blue, and then it hit the snake's unprotected flesh, bit deep, and then promptly lodged in place.

"Shit," I cursed as an arrow whistled in from the left, hitting the snake in the face. The projectile lodged itself between two scales, but I barely had time to process that before the gathered ether of my attack was released. The explosion blew me free, the world pinwheeling crazily around me. Somehow, I landed on my feet, although the momentum carried me over and into a crazy, tumbling, stumbling, roll.

It was painful, but honestly, more embarrassing than anything else. I stood as the stag pulled back, releasing the snake from the tree.

My ether blade had blown a gooey hole in the creature's side, as its blood freely spattered the ground. But it wasn't quite dead yet.

"Ajax. Do you remember that one time you pounded in the stakes for our tent too hard?" Hera yelled.

"Of course, you never let me forget that one," he yelled back.

"Let's show this snake what that's all about," she said and

ran in under its head.

With its body weakened by my attacks, the snake's head drooped toward the ground. It snapped weakly at Hera, but she rammed the spear up and into its mouth, the blade biting into the soft, top pallet.

Ajax launched himself forward and up, showcasing a surprising amount of ups for a big guy. He brought the hammer down hard on top of the beast's skull. The impact knocked its head down, skewering it fully onto Hera's spear. The bladed tip broke through the top in a geyser of blood and brain matter.

The snake's tail crashed to the ground, flattening a small tree in the process. Hera pulled her spear free, the blade covered with more than a little pulpy brain.

"Who wants to go first on what happened?" she asked, stabbing the spear into the snake again for good measure. But the snake was clearly dead. "And what is with the stag?" Hera yelled as she pulled her spear free.

I scooped my katana off the ground as Prometheus nocked another arrow and turned his bow toward the stag. It stood over Omega as if now protecting the wolf from us. It lowered its head, snorted, and pawed at the ground.

"Don't hurt it! It was protecting Omega!"

"But why would a beast do that? Maybe you shouldn't let it leave," Ajax said.

"Leave?" I asked, watching the large, horned deer. Point in fact, it wasn't trying to go anywhere. Nor did it appear to be scared of us. It watched me for a moment, before dropping its head and looking at Omega. It nudged the wolf with its nose, a look of genuine sadness showing in its large, dark eyes.

"*That stag is special,*" Ivory said. "*It's like me, a being from another world. You should kill, eat, and absorb it. Perhaps you could trap its essence in your mind palace like you did with me.*"

"Um...morbid," I said. "Don't tell me you're getting lonely up there."

"*Of course not! I like the quiet.*"

"Oh, good."

I watched as the stag nuzzled Omega again with its nose, this time transferring a mass of ether to the wolf.

"It wants to talk to you," Ivory said as the stag looked up at me. *"He said there is a pond deeper into the forest. Beyond the place where the two-legs go. That means your kind in case you didn't catch it. He says to take Omega there and lay him in the water."*

"Okay," I said, raising my hand to the stag. It was an instinctual movement, but the stag tensed. "Where is the pond?"

"Feel for him," Ivory said. *"Make contact with him and feel for his ether. If you form the connection, then you will be able to push and receive emotions. It will guide you. Once you latch onto the thick concentration, you will find it."*

"Did Takemi lose it?" Hera muttered. "He's talking to a stag."

"Maybe," Prom whispered. "But we live with a wolf and now we've got a bear. Considering that, it feels less weird."

My hand came to rest on the stag's nose and a ripple passed through the large creature. I could see it move down its side, back, and legs, the muscles twitching. Then I was filled with a confusing mixture of emotions. It was like with Omega, but stronger and more concise. I felt fear, uncertainty, worry, and joy, all in order. Then in my mind's eye, I saw Omega. The stag wanted to help the wolf. He wanted to help us.

Breaking contact, the stag stepped back and watched me, as if waiting.

"The stag wants to help us. Ivory showed me how to communicate with it," I said. "Evidently, there is a pond or a body of water deeper into the zoo. A place where people don't go. If we lay Omega into the water, it will heal his body."

I knelt down next to Omega and smoothed the fur on his head. He whined and tried to get up, but again the rear half of his body refused to move. He'd broken his back or his legs. Either way, we didn't have time to wait for him to heal naturally.

"Ivory, does he have any internal injuries?"

"Do I look like a nurse? Ugh. No. No internal bleeding."

"Good."

"We've been here for half a day and we almost get eaten by giant rats, have our wolf run off and almost get eaten by a house-sized snake, and now we need to follow a magical stag into the wilderness for a mythical lake with healing powers? Am I recounting all that correct?" Prometheus asked. "And if that isn't all weird enough, how are we supposed to get our...rather large wolf there? If you haven't noticed, he's gotten big."

"We could make an improvised stretcher," Ajax said, leaning on his hammer. "Tak and I can drag him, Prom will scout ahead, and Hera will cover our rear."

We looked around for thick branches, and thanks to the snake's deforestation, had plenty to work with. We gathered supplies, cut them to length and laid them out, then tied them together with a paracord. Lastly, we covered the top with a layer of leaves and worked together to slide Omega into place.

Hera used her wickedly-sharp spear to cut the snake open and found the core. She handed the soccer ball-sized orb to me, its surface covered with green glowing, etched patterns. The ether inside was so strong it made the hair on my arm stand on end.

I looked back at the snake and shook my head. I wanted to carry the whole animal back with us, but it was far too big.

"Shouldn't we collect some of the snake's valuable parts?" Prometheus asked.

"No," Ajax replied matter-of-factly. "We'll do that once Omega is safe. If the opportunity arises."

"He looks so frail," I whispered. "I don't wait to lose him."

"And you won't," Hera said, putting a hand on my shoulder. "He's part of the family, whether Prom likes it or not."

Ajax nodded and grabbed his half of the stretcher. I

followed suit, lifting the other side. I fought the impulse to activate my enhanced strength skill, as I didn't want to exhaust my depleted ether stores. If something popped up, I wanted it available.

We moved through the forest for close to half an hour but didn't make any real progress. The steep and rocky terrain didn't help, but luckily, we didn't encounter any beasts. I spotted numerous indicators of snake movement, so we guessed that was why the area was clear.

Prom scouted ahead and backtracked several times, checking on us. I struggled with Omega's burden but used the chance to narrow my focus on our surroundings—the smell, sound, and strands of ether radiating out of the dirt, rocks, and plants. Some ether sources were thicker and purer than others and worked to fool my senses. It felt like listening for a sound while someone played loud and aggressive music in the next room.

"*This place is so confusing,*" I said.

"*Everything here is saturated, so naturally it will distract. You need to learn to ignore the dense sources and focus on only the ether you can draw toward you,*" Ivory responded.

I pulled the stretcher but let my vision go fuzzy, trying to do as he suggested. It took a long while, but I was finally successful at blocking some of the ether sources out. Once that was accomplished, I started to pick up on so many more.

We followed the stag through the forest, but we'd been moving for some time before I realized that all of the ether signatures around me seemed to be originating from the same source. Whatever it was, it seemed to be ahead. After an arduous hike, and with daylight fading, we finally came within view of a clearing.

"I feel a lot of ether radiating from there," I whispered to Ajax.

"Then this must be it," he said.

I could just see through the trees and spotted a narrow valley, and beyond that, what looked like an expanse of water.

To the left, where the water met land, something large moved. My eyes struggled to focus in the failing light, and by the time I could move forward for a better look, it was gone.

"Did you see that?" I asked Prometheus.

"Not properly," he said, shaking his head. "But it was big."

"We need to know what we're dealing with before we go stumbling in there with that stretcher," Hera offered.

"I've got your back," Ajax whispered and moved up next to me. Prometheus nodded, readying his bow, while Hera stayed with Omega.

I crept toward the forest's edge and knelt, my big friend and the scout moving behind and on either side of me. I narrowed my eyes, then rubbed them, but couldn't seem to see the area ahead clearly. It was obviously a lake, surrounded by rocky bluffs and forest, but beyond that, it was like standing too close to an impressionistic painting. If I had to guess, and I hated doing that, it was the ether. If this was a source, then maybe I was dealing with a rift.

I drew my wakizashi and inched forward, finally stepping into the clear. Nothing happened. I kept moving and approached the water's edge. A strange, electric sensation passed over me, and like stepping through an invisible barrier, I could suddenly see.

The lake was not large but its water did appear to be deep, and directly in the center, floating just over the surface, hung a slowly revolved swirl of glowing power.

"Ivory, is that what I think it is?" I asked, my memories spinning back to the day my life changed. What scared me most was that I could feel the rift in my stomach, right behind the scar of that fateful wound.

"It surely is. And judging from how calm you feel on the inside, this isn't the first rift you've seen. Do tell?"

"That is a long story, but I have a feeling that you might be better equipped than most to understand," I said and opened myself up to him.

CHAPTER 32: OLD LOVES

I knelt at the water's edge and placed my palms flat against the ground. The ether wasn't just plentiful here. It was staggeringly pure. It hit my hands like a wave of biting fire ants, the enervating sensation forcing its way into my hands, up my wrists, and into my arms.

Pulling away, I staggered back. My heart raced and my insides spun. Hell, it was several moments before I knew who and where I was again. It felt like I'd been on a rollercoaster, but not in it. Perhaps strapped to the front while it barreled out of control.

I pitched forward and shook my head. It was only then that I saw what was beneath the water's surface. I'd been so distracted by the swirling rift and the reflection of the clouds that I didn't notice them before. Now I saw them clearly—crystals, hundreds, no, thousands of them. Some looked to be taller and wider than me. I looked over to my right and waved for Ajax to join me.

"Look," I said and pointed.

"Merlin's beard," he whispered and leaned forward. His hands brushed the water and he jumped back, shaking out his fingers.

"It stings, doesn't it?" I asked.

"Like liquid fire crawling up my fingers. Is that...?"

"My guess? It is about the purest ether a person can find in this world."

"I can't imagine what it would feel like...inside me," he breathed and scanned the pool. I knew what he was thinking, as it was probably one of the same seventeen things I had going through my mind, at that moment, too. What did we see by the waterside when we'd first approached? And if it wasn't just a trick of the eyes, why hadn't it attacked us? Was it like the stag or Lazy Bones?

That of course opened up a whole new subset of questions. Because the stag not only didn't attack us, but it saved Omega from the snake. And if this place was full of powerful, intelligent, and sentient beings, did that mean we'd been murdering things since the collapse?

I shook the questions aside and pushed to my feet, then backtracked to my injured wolf friend.

"What is it? What did you see?" Prometheus asked.

"I don't know yet. Come on, let's get him to the water. This place is buzzing with ether," I explained.

"Are those...crystals?" Prometheus muttered, as we gently placed Omega's body on the sand.

"They are," I said, rubbing Omega's head. "The more important questions are: are they growing like that because of the rift? Or are they the source *of* the rift?"

I untied and kicked off my boots, then my socks and pants. The others watched me, but it was Ajax, who'd touched the power, that spoke up.

"Maybe it would be safer to just push him into the water with sticks, eh? We don't know what ether that strong could do to a person."

"I'm not leaving him alone," I said and handed Prometheus my sword belt. "I've encountered a rift like this before and it did something to me. Perhaps it is why I was able to unlock the palace in my mind so early. Perhaps it is why creatures like Omega, the bear, and the stag are drawn to me. I'm not sure. But I do know that I can feel it, deep inside me. Maybe it kills me. Or, maybe it helps unlock more of my memories. At the very least it should heal him, but there is only one way to find out."

Before they could protest, I pushed Omega out into the water and stepped in. It felt like a combination of fire and lightning marching up my legs as the water lapped further up my legs. My muscles jerked and spasmed as my skin became a boiling point of both fire and ice. And that was the truth of it. It felt both hot and cold and the same time, but I could not tell if it was healing my wounds and purging weakness or breaking me down.

I supported Omega in my arms as we pushed deeper in, the water rising to my chest. He sank until only his head extended above the water. He whined and looked right at me, his dark brown eyes full of confusion and fear. Then he licked my cheek and I nearly lost it.

It was my fault, after all. He was intelligent and desperate to please us, and we'd brought him to a place overflowing with danger, temptation, and unknowns. I struggled to hold back my tears as he whined again.

"It's going to be alright, buddy," I whispered and pressed my forehead against his. "It's not your fault."

Yes, the fault was mine, as I'd taken his trustworthiness and reliability to heart. He was a wild animal, after all, and I'd treated him like a well-trained, domesticated dog. Of course he'd run off, chasing enticing scents and food. I should have known better.

We pushed further out into the water, half-step by half-step, the potent ether swirling around me like hot currents. I felt the knot in my belly, that old scar where my father's sword cut clean through me. Something was pulling on it as if I'd been hooked by a fisherman and they were reeling me in. I turned my head, only to confirm that it was the swirling rift in the center of the small lake, but what was beyond it? And why could I feel its pull?

Omega whined, his body shaking against me. He licked my cheek as if to reassure me. That made me chuckle, as I was the one there to support him. He started to tremble violently and I could see the pain in his eyes.

"You're going to be okay, buddy," I whispered, moving out as deep into the water as I dared. The water was cold and tugged on us both, so I clutched him tight. He'd sink without me and without the use of his hind legs, there was no way he'd keep his head above the surface.

"What was that?" Prometheus whispered.

"What was what?" Hera hissed back.

"I heard something move behind us. Beyond the barrier."

"Quick, fan out," Ajax growled and lifted his hammer.

I turned awkwardly in the water, my feet sliding on the slippery rocks, but watched helplessly as my team prepared.

"*Ivory, can you feel them? Who is approaching?*"

"*...five of them. Human, like you, but that is all I can tell from this distance. The ether from the rift is too strong. It is interfering with my senses.*"

"Five humans," I hissed at Ajax, and the big man nodded without looking back.

"*Three are coming in from straight on, and I believe two are flanking the lake. They are either very wary of what is here, or they are looking for you. Judging from our time together, my guess is the second one.*"

"*I don't have a rebuttal for that,*" I responded.

We saw the figures moving beyond the veil, but they were just dark and blurry outlines.

"Come on, be friendly," I whispered and watched the barrier.

The lead figure moved through the veil, the tip of their long sword appearing well before the warrior wielding it. My hopes surged and then plummeted as their armor and standard appeared next.

"Ah, gut. We have found our freunde. Look, guys, our

brave mercenary teammates!" the man in the lead said. The others on either side of him chuckled but didn't smile. If anything, their eyes gave away their true ambitions—violence.

"Just out for a random stroll to an ether-rich lake deep into the zoo, eh, freunde?" Ajax asked, tightening his grip on his hammer.

"A random stroll, that is a good one," the leader laughed. "You know they said you lot were funny, but I wrote it off. As it turns out, you are adorable."

I tried to sink a little deeper into the water, to hide the fact that I was there, but I had to keep Omega's snout above the surface or he would drown.

"To your right and left," Ivory prompted.

I turned and noticed figures well to the sides of the others. Both held stout crossbows and they were pointed right at me.

"Shit," I mumbled, blowing a bubble in the water.

"We don't have to do this," Ajax said, as Prometheus noticed the men with crossbows. He turned his body subtly, giving him a more favorable shot at the man on the left.

"We paid good money to find out what happened to our brothers. It wasn't a mere coincidence that two of our commandos went missing in that little mud hole of a town you call Vaduz, and then you lot show up in Zurich not long after. Prime has long memories, *freunde*."

"I honestly have no idea of whom you are talking about, but I can assure you we did nothing to your commandos—"

"Who said they were commandos?" the man asked, cutting him off. "I never said that. Did you?" he asked, pointing to the man next to him.

"Nein."

"Your women worked in that pub, yes? The little one with the cobblestone walkway next to it?"

Ajax didn't respond, nor did I, although a horrible feeling was building in my gut.

"We drank there for like two or three days. It took us that

long to beat the truth out of the owner. To his credit, he only squealed after we'd removed the fingers from his right hand. But fear not, we slit his throat before we burned the pub to the ground. He was loyal, even under duress, so that has to mean something to you, right?"

I watched the bow start to shake in Prometheus' hands, all the while Hera's face tightened into an angry mask of rage. I was insulated from that horrific news because of my memory loss, but Kate and Layla both worked at the pub and they had all become friends.

"What's a little bit of murder for Zurich's finest?" Ajax growled.

"It is not murder when it is retribution. You have no idea how hard it has been to wait for this day. All the money and favors that had to exchange hands to ensure you lot were forced into this melee. And now you are finally here!"

"You all went to that much trouble, just because you thought we hurt your friends?" Hera asked, leveling the spear at the prime leader.

"I would have gone to that much trouble just because you filthy sell swords put hands on our friends. Prime is the leading power here. People need to respect us, and if we let an offense like that go unpunished, we would lose..."

"Are you finished blabbering on?" Ajax asked, cutting him off. "Honestly, I don't even know your name. I've never seen you before we arrived here, and I don't even harbor any ill-will towards you. But you are so pompous and self-important. If we're to die, can it be from blades and not boredom?"

"You dare," their leader hissed back.

"What is your name?" Ajax interrupted again. "That way if I die, when I make it to the pearly gates and shun heaven, I will know whom I'm supposed to haunt."

"Richter Von Limehouse, Captain of the first Prime Dragoons—"

"Right," Ajax said, cutting him off for the third time. "Richard lemon shack. Got it. And you lot? Do you have names?"

"Garold..." the man next to Richter said before his captain cut him off.

"You don't need to know them."

"Actually I do. You see, we are here in the service of the Protectorate. And if we don't die, I want to know your names, so that I can give them to Kruger. I imagine he will want to pay a visit to your families.

"The Protectorate will have no power in Zurich by the time we get back. That change was already being set into motion before we left to come here. Kill the swine in the water first. Shoot him and his precious dog."

"He is a wolf!" Hera snarled as Prometheus pulled his bowstring back to his ear. And yet another voice echoed out from behind the Prime commandos and stilled our scout's hand.

"It looks like a party by the water and we were not invited," a woman said.

Richter spun around, leveling his sword at the newcomers who wore chainmail and plate armor, adorned with colorful sashes. I didn't recognize the colors or the crest but counted six in their party.

"Do you speak English? Hello?" she asked when no one responded.

"Yes, we speak English. Which is perfect, so I can tell you to shove off. This is none of your business."

"I'm afraid that everything that happens inside the melee is everyone's business. The charter is written that way, specifically to help avoid...unnecessary violence between kingdoms."

Richter gave her a curt nod, his jaw visibly clenched.

"What is to say my people and I weren't just minding our business, filling our water skins, and you simply walked in and attacked us? We were just...defending ourselves."

"Well, that would be tragic," she said, her accent finally clear to me. It was French?

"We wouldn't fight you," Hera said, moving her spear between Richter and the man next to him. "These scumbags were looking to use the melee's chaos to kill us and hide the bodies. Then he would probably just blame it on beasts when they left. If they move against you, consider us your allies."

"Interesting," the French leader said, still eyeing Richter. "So, the wolves from Zurich are divided."

"Zurich is stronger than ever!" Richter yelled.

"Is it?" Ajax asked, patting his war hammer. "After what you just told us, is it?"

Omega whined and licked my face and then the wolf did a peculiar thing. He kicked with his hind legs. I felt his muscles bunch and coil as he fought to propel himself through the water. After a moment of indecision, I released my hold and watched as he swam deeper into the lake, moving in a straight line right at the massive, underwater crystals.

"It looks like your pet is leaving you," one of Richter's men laughed. He was standing to my left, his crossbow tracking the swimming wolf. I knew better, however. Omega was simply stretching his muscles and testing the limits of his body. He was also soaking up every last ounce of ether he could.

"Prometheus, if that idiot's finger slips off the trigger and he shoots my wolf, I want you to put an arrow through his throat. Can you do that?" I asked.

Prom smiled and swung around, his compound bow now aimed at the offending commando. I stepped out of the water, the ambient air somehow feeling even colder. My muscles spasmed and shook, but I had, for the most part, gone numb.

Once free, I bent down at my pile of clothes, ripped the nodachi free from its scabbard, and moved up next to Ajax. Only wearing a soggy pair of boxers, I knew that I was quite the sight, but the time for appearances was far behind us.

"Okay, Richter. I am ready," I said. My gaze crawled to the French team's leader, who threw me the subtlest of winks.

I prepared a mass of ether as the power swirled inside my body, readying both my speed and strength skills. Without armor, I would be an easy target, but I could easily cut one, and maybe two of them in half before they caused too much damage.

A loud splashing, paddling noise rose behind me as Omega finally emerged from the lake. I heard and felt him shake, the cold water splattering my back and legs. But when he stepped up next to me, I realized that his body was changing.

His fur was bleaching white, while red streaks appeared on his shoulders, back, and haunches. He was even bigger and stronger than before, with the tips of his ears now above me. I could also feel his thoughts more keenly. He was angry, but also ashamed of running off and getting himself into trouble.

Omega growled as he approached Richter, the sound reverberating deep in his chest. The Prime commando took an involuntary step back. Evidently having a horse-sized wolf walk up and stare you in the eyes was an unsettling thing, even for a chumped-up blow hard.

I rubbed his head and patted his broad shoulders, then nodded and spoke.

"Okay. It appears we're ready to die. Go ahead, Richard, give us the ole express lift to the other side," I said.

Richter shifted his weight between his feet and his teammates looked at him uncertainly. Omega growled again and licked his lips, revealing his impressively sharp and long teeth.

"Go on then. Show us your mean faces," Hera said, jabbing her spear forward.

The French warriors closed in from behind, reminding Richter and his men that they were not just being watched, but surrounded, and outmatched. After several moments, in which a throbbing vein appeared on Richter's forehead, the Prime commando flicked his hand over his shoulder.

As quickly as they had appeared, our treacherous Zurich

counterparts retreated beyond the barrier and disappeared.

"Thank you," I said, addressing the French troop.

"Bien rencontré," their leader said and dipped into a shallow bow. "We heard rumors that there was turmoil in Zurich and tracked you once you entered the zoo. The Prime marched right by us, unaware, so we eavesdropped. It is amazing what you can learn simply by listening."

"Still, you didn't have to risk your lives to help us. That is a rare act these days," Ajax said.

"Well, truthfully, it was for a reason. We heard a tale of a rogue mercenary unit out of Vaduz was marching all over the Swiss countryside in the company of a massive wolf. Naturally, our interest was piqued."

"Fantastic," the French woman breathed. "But where are my manners? I am Joan, and this is my team, Claude, Marie, Jon, Gabriel, and François."

I introduced our team, leaving myself and Omega for last. The French team seemed most interested in the wolf, even congregating around him.

"We are a bit of an oddity," Hera chuckled. "We also have a bear now, and if the walk up here was an indication, a stag has been added to the family." As if summoned, the stag appeared barely fifty paces up the lakeshore to our right. It materialized out of the woods like a ghost.

"Magnifique," Joan breathed, then half-turned to the woods behind us. "Anita, did you hear that? They have a bear and a stag with them? And they are friendly."

"Who are you talking—" Ajax started to ask, just as someone pushed out of the bushes not five paces away.

"This is Anita. She is the real reason we intervened on your behalf," Joan explained.

"Hello," Anita said, although she sounded and looked more Italian than French. "I am a free researcher. I met Joan and her team on the way to Federsee and convinced them to sneak me into the zoo."

"Where are you from?" I asked, directing the question at

the group in general. Joan addressed me directly. She had long black hair tied in a ponytail, a short nose, freckled cheeks, and striking purple, blue eyes.

"Strasbourg," she said, pointing to the crest on her armor, "Although the city died in the collapse. We hail from the Château de Spesbourg, a renovated castle south of the city. We have no king or queen, just a small merchant council, a village of dedicated residents, and a respectable fighting force. We are allowed to exist and given representation in the melee because we safeguard the border roads to Paris."

"That makes sense, logistically speaking," Ajax said.

"I know this sounds forward," Anita said, leaning toward us, "but if what she said is true, and you actually have a wolf, a bear, and a stag with you, I would very much like to study them."

"Study them?" I asked.

"Yes." Anita nodded vigorously, the movement dislodging her light brown hair from its messy bun. She had dark eyes—brown that were a shade closer to black than gold.

"I won't answer for my teammates here, but you should know. Allying with us comes with significant risks. There are plenty of people, mostly from Zurich, that want us dead."

"That isn't new," she breathed. "But there is a chance we could help each other."

Hera and Prometheus looked at one another and then at me.

"Oh?" I asked, and we all went quiet, waiting for her to explain.

Anita looked at us, then to the rift floating over the lake, and finally at Joan and her people. The French leader nodded, and our new researcher friend cleared her throat.

"The truth of the melee is that it is more a distraction than anything else..." she trailed off.

"Explain," Ajax said, crossing his arms over his chest. Hera leaned on her spear like a walking stick, and Prometheus twirled an arrow between his fingers.

"You have to look at it like this. You win simply by walking out of here at the end. What you gather, what you do in here, none of it really adds up to anything. Leaders gamble on which teams will die when they fall, and how, but mostly, for the time you are in here, they are negotiating and squabbling over alliances, vassal states, supply chain rights, and ether rich zones."

"You're saying this challenge is just a masquerade?" I asked.

"An elaborate one, but yes. And in their eyes, a necessary one. Some look at it as a way to temper and strengthen elite military units. Others aren't willing to risk their own, so they choose to be represented by contract mercenaries. Others see this as an opportunity to have some...disposed of," Anita explained.

I looked to Ajax.

"Those swine," he hissed, shaking his head.

"What a waste of time," Hera said. "Why have it at all?"

Joan inched forward. "It's not all for nothing. Surviving the zoo brings prestige and honor to your kingdom or sovereign and a team's placement does hold weight for that ruler in the next melee. But it is more for those the sovereigns view as peasants than anything else. It keeps them complacent and happy. It gives them a spectacle and lets them believe their ruler is fighting to better their circumstances."

"Those teams back there," Hera said, pointing over her shoulder with a thumb. "The ones eaten by the rat creatures and the other one with the snake. They died for nothing? They died for the...puppet theater?"

"It depends on how you look at it," Joan admitted. "Less alive means it decreases our chances of being cornered and killed by the others. And the fewer teams alive at the end...well, that changes how they view the survivors as well."

"Ugh. I feel sick," Hera groaned. "We fought that whole time to survive the factions that wanted us dead, and all the while, the ones protecting us were just doing it so we could die in here?"

"That isn't necessarily the case," Ajax said. "I believe Hans Gruber. He didn't have to tell us about the power battle going on in Zurich. The city is split down the middle and I think he wants us on their side."

"So, what do we do?" Prometheus asked.

"It looks straightforward from where I'm standing," I said, and everyone turned to look my way. "We take the opportunity to learn everything we can—about this place, ether, the rifts, and the creatures...both from our world and beyond it. We poke our noses in some rifts. We fight back if beasts are hostile, and we gather every ounce of material possible. But we do it for us, not them. We make good on our obligation to Zurich and when we get out of here, we use what we claim in here to find a place of our own."

"I don't know what it will look like or where it is going to be, but I do like the sound of that," Prometheus nodded.

"Where do we start?" Ajax asked. We turned as a group to Anita, who seemed to shrink under our collective gazes. Then she confidently raised a hand and pointed right at the swirling rift.

"The ether pouring out of the rift is forming crystals at an exponential rate. We should harvest those and then see what the space beyond the rift can tell us."

I slid the nodachi back into its scabbard and handed it to Ajax, before turning back toward the water.

"I'm already cold and wet, so I'll go. But, Joan, your team is going next...if we run into any more lakes or ponds," I said and waded back out into the cold, ether-rich water.

CHAPTER 33: NOT EVERYONE IS BAD

It was almost two hours later by the time I had harvested all the usable crystals. The large ones, I noticed, were part of the rift and gently phased in and out of visibility under the water. The closer to them I got, the stronger the pull beyond my belly.

I wasn't really in the mood to be pulled into another dimension without my friends or weapons, so I stayed clear. At least for the time being. That was fine with me, as I wasn't about to start hauling seven-foot tall crystals out of the water, although I did quietly fantasize about how much ether they could hold.

We decided to camp by the lake for the night, as we were quickly losing light and we'd already had one run-in with hostile forces. It wasn't openly stated, but we'd joined forces with Joan and her crew. It did make me feel a little better, knowing we'd doubled our numbers, which would make watches that much easier. We'd give it the night but if the French group from Spesbourg proved honest and trustworthy, we would discuss our mutual paths moving forward.

While the others set up camp, Anita made her rounds, using a bizarre little device to scan what I pulled out of the lake. It didn't look like the scanning device we'd gotten from Manfred but was cylindrical and seemed to glow when she passed it over things. The color it glowed seemed to change, considering the item scanned. Crystals, water, and rocks from the lake shore all returned a cool blue response.

Judging by her expression, that wasn't anything out of the ordinary, but when she scanned Omega, the device glowed red and her eyebrows rose dramatically.

"Interesting," she mumbled to herself.

"What does that mean?" Ajax whispered, leaning in close.

"I really have no idea," she admitted, although just a few moments later, she moved over to me and started passing the scanner over my body. I watched the device but tried to play my interest off as indifference. Across my right arm, it glowed blue-green, my left arm, red, and near my abdomen, it flashed a whole kaleidoscope of colors.

When she finally looked up at me, I found that I couldn't keep my curiosity back any longer.

"What does that all mean?"

"It means we need to talk," she said and pulled me away from the others.

"I'm going to walk the lake," I said to Ajax as we passed, "and make sure our friends from Zurich haven't come back."

"You want me to go with you?" he asked, reaching for his hammer. I waved him off.

"No, you stay and rest."

Prometheus prowled through the edge of the tree line when we passed, our scout ready and willing to shish kabob anyone that slipped through the ether veil. He gave me an efficient nod before turning his attention outwards again.

"Okay, first, what did all the colors mean? And how does that thing work?" I asked, nodding at the device in her hand.

"It's surprisingly uncomplicated, actually," she replied, holding it up. "We have determined that ether is simply energy...in its purest form. Yet, it bonds very easily to different molecules from our world. Say, for example, iron. Some would call this a metal affinity. Although it is true, it is overly simplistic and misleading. Certain people can bond ether to minerals stored inside their body. It really only takes trace amounts in actuality, but it fundamentally changes the structure of the ether. You probably already know this, but people can open veins inside their body, and channel certain types of ether. In reality, the person is changing their body more than the energy they are absorbing. The process realigns their molecular structure, alters their chemical composition, and as a result, their very biology. Your arm glowed red, which indicates an iron or similar heavy metal affinity. If we were to cut you open, we would find that your ether vein, your flesh, and blood, are embedded with the pure metal element."

"Okay, that sounds a little scary," I chuckled. "Will it eventually turn my entire body to metal?"

Anita shook her head. "No, there is extraordinarily little bleed to the surrounding tissue. Although as you draw that modified energy through your vein, it can be redistributed to other areas, and if done properly, translate the metal's properties: hardness, malleability, electric conductivity, etc."

"Wow, you know more about this than anyone I've talked to before," I said, "But you should know. A while back I took a hammer to the skull and only recently got a small fraction of my memories back. So, a lot of things are new to me...again."

"I heard," she said and promptly looked away.

"You have?"

She nodded and it was several moments before she looked back at me. "We heard stories about a rogue mercenary crew out of Switzerland challenging the established authority. Obviously, that garnered quite a bit of attention. Some stories were believable, while others were not. Mind you, that was before I saw you and realized that you are in fact traveling with a real-life wolf."

"Yeah, I didn't want to let him die. Then he followed us

for a while, and before I knew it, he started growing on us. Now, I can't imagine going anywhere without him."

"I can't tell you how good that is to hear. And that is why I am happy I found you," she said, staring at the revolving rift flowing over the lake.

"So, I take it our meeting wasn't just happenstance?"

Anita shook her head. "No. And let me tell you why. Part of the reason why we know so little about the space beyond the rifts is here," she explained, pointing at the ground beneath our feet. "And I don't mean this lake specifically, but the melee. The kings and queens of this new world understand the power of knowledge and that is why they collect, empower, horde, and kill researchers. Many wars have been waged over the pursuit of knowledge, libraries and strongholds burned, and worse. Ether-rich zones aren't just a breeding ground for strength, but they are the means to answer certain questions. And as many rulers hope, a source of power that they might tap into and exploit. I have been trying to get into this zoo for years but as a free researcher struggle with certain deficiencies. Naturally, the first is my inability to protect myself. It was only recently that I discovered Joan and her troop. They are the first to help me gain access to this place."

"You mean to travel through the rifts to learn their secrets, but you need fighters to get you in and out?" I surmised.

Anita nodded. "With the hope that I can learn as much as possible. If I can, then I might be able to answer the most important questions. Namely, what caused the ether convergence that collapsed the old world. What will ether do to our bodies long term, and what will happen to the Earth if this convergence is allowed to continue? Will it be torn apart? Will it be slowly consumed and turned into something unrecognizable?"

"That is a lot of questions. And I assume you would like our help gaining access to these rifts? Maybe…keep you alive?"

"Honestly, the staying alive part sounds like the best

part," she chuckled. "Where are my manners? Let's back up a moment. I have heard so much about you—your name and exploits, but we haven't formerly been introduced. You are Takemi, right?" she asked and offered her hand.

I accepted her handshake. "Not anymore. That person died on the battlefield when I took that blow to the head. My name is Kenji Nakamura."

"Kenji, all right," she said with a smile. "If you help me for the next six days, provide me with security, and access to as many rifts as we can find, I will repay you with the greatest power of all."

"The greatest power of all, eh?" I asked. "That is quite the pitch. How can a guy say no to that?"

"My hope is that he can't. But seriously. The power I can offer you is knowledge, Kenji. Free and unadulterated knowledge. If the rulers of Stuttgart, Zurich, Munich, or Paris knew I was here, I would not last long."

It abruptly dawned on me that I was standing before one of the single greatest resources available. Yes, crystals could fill me with power and help me grow stronger, but Anita was poised to answer all of the questions holding us back. My mind spun as I considered the possibility of taking someone like her back to our hidden bunker and teaming her with Mike. But she also presented an opportunity for me to begin learning a bit more about myself.

How had ether changed my body when that first rift formed above me? And why were these beasts and ether-changed animals drawn to me?

Realizing that I couldn't afford to say no, I stuck out my hand and shook hers again.

"You have a deal, Anita..."

"Van de Berg. Anita Van de Berg," she said, filling in the rest.

"As it stands, our group has become a haven for displaced or disenfranchised souls in need of family and safety. I think you will fit in nicely."

"Fantastic," she beamed. "For years I thought the hard part would be getting in. Then I finally found someone to get me in. Then the hard part would be getting someone like you to hear me out and accept me."

"And now?" I asked.

"I think it is going to be getting back out again in one piece," she admitted.

"We can help you with that. But I think your first step is going to be...blending in," I said, stepping back and taking her in.

She wore what looked like hiking gear, with rugged boots, a moisture-wicking, long sleeve top, and a wide-brimmed hat. It was probably a great outfit for her job, but unfortunately, it would make her stick out like a sore thumb.

"Do you have any other clothes?"

"I have a sweater," she said with a smile.

The stag appeared then, exuding almost as much curiosity as Anita. It circled, watched us, and moved a little closer until its gradually shrinking circular path brought it right up to us.

"Wow. I've never been so close to a...wild one before," Anita said, holding her hand out for the large animal. It leaned down and sniffed it, then allowed her to pet its dark nose.

Standing next to our new researcher friend, the stag looked absolutely monstrous, especially considering the bits of reptilian skin and scales still skewered to its rack.

Anita pulled out her scanner and tried to scan the stag but the lights spooked it, and before she could try to calm it, the noble beast leaped off into the woods.

"Don't take it personally," I said, pulling her back towards our camp. "We only met him yesterday."

"But still...never seen one come up to people so readily. He is so tame. So much..." Anita went on and on, starting a new question or observation before finishing the last.

We bedded down and slept, although Joan woke me up some hours later for my turn at watch. I rose without complaint, although my eyes burned. Hera and I patrolled around the camp together but my gaze kept drifting back to the rift floating above the lake.

I could feel the gentle pull at my core, even then, as if a fractured and lost portion of myself was trapped somewhere beyond the floating tear. And although I didn't necessarily want my missing memories back, I felt a burning need to understand the connection. Okay, I would be lying if I said I wasn't curious about Beth. She was more than lost love, but a question I couldn't answer. Was she still alive somewhere? Was she tormented by the thought that she'd accidentally killed me? I knew that doubt would likely drive me insane, given enough time.

I banished those thoughts and finished my rounds. Sunrise came quickly, as the sky changed from black to navy blue, periwinkle, and then finally a beautiful starburst orange. We roused the others, had Ajax prepare breakfast and addressed what I viewed as the most pressing need.

"Anita needs to look like one of us. She needs to look like a warrior, even if she doesn't fight," I said.

"But this…is all I have," the researcher said, unslinging her pack and pulling it open. She rifled through the contents, stacking everything into neat piles at her feet. I saw notebooks, a bundle of pencils wrapped in a rubber band, her scanner, a pair of binoculars, tweezers, empty vials, and a pack of assorted field gear.

"I have some clothes that would probably fit her," Hera offered, rifling through her stuff.

"Try on these bracers," Joan chimed in and then the group fell into one of the most spectacular sessions of "clothing swap" I'd ever seen.

By the time we were done Anita was almost unrecognizable in a cotton tunic and pants, outfitted with mismatched mail and leather armor. One of the French fighters gave her a sword belt and strapped on a dirk but judging by how the researcher eyed the hanging weapon, she'd never used one and unless in dire straits, never would.

Once camp was packed up and put away, we congregated around the water's edge. Omega sat next to me, panting heavily, his gaze locked on the water. I couldn't tell if he was nervous about going in again, or excited.

"What should we expect on the other side of that rift?" Ajax asked Anita.

"Once you get close enough, it will draw you to it. Don't fight it, just let it pull you in. There will be some disorientation, maybe some spinning, and you might get sick, but that will pass. Every rift is different though, depending on where it leads. The important thing is to go in quiet but to be prepared."

"Omega, Prometheus, and I will go first. Give us a few minutes and then follow us through," I said and Prom gave me a nod. Hera stared me down.

"Oh, and one last thing," Anita said, hooking me by the arm and preventing me from stepping into the water. "Transitioning between worlds through rifts is a tricky business. You might not look like you do here. Your voice might sound different, as well. Be prepared for the shift."

"The shift?" I asked.

Anita nodded. "Completely unpredictable. Just keep an open mind and try not to freak out."

"Oh, lady, Kenji 'Takemi' Nakamura freaking out," Prometheus said, laughing, "never!"

"What can I say? It comes naturally to me. But today, I will try and suppress that superpower," I said and pushed into the cold water.

Prom waded in next to me, but I was waist-deep before I turned and realized Omega was still standing on the bank. He whined, looked down at the water, and then back up to me.

"Come on, boy! The worst that can happen is your fur might turn purple."

He whined again, pawed at the water, and finally crept forward.

"Purple would be a fitting color. For you both," Ivory said,

chuckling in my mind.

"Oh, we would totally rock it."

"My god, this water is...painfully...cold and...hot at the...same time," Prometheus sputtered, his teeth chattering together between words.

"I'd love to tell you that it gets better, but it doesn't," I replied, fighting with all my strength to sound calm. The ether was burning its way into my skin and muscles, forcing its way up my veins and into my core. I could feel that pool of energy in my center swirl and tumble, sloughing off ten times more ether than it could ever hope to absorb. The excess leeched back out of my body, pushing like a low-voltage current into the water.

Omega snorted and growled, doggie paddling behind us to catch up.

"I don't know...about this," Prometheus muttered as we approached the rift. Tactile waves of ether rippled off the glowing tear, my muscles twitching and spasming as they hit me.

I didn't know either, but one of the benefits of waking up with a crushed skull and brain damage was that I knew life was too short to look every time I leapt.

"What's the worst that could happen?" I asked as the rift's pull doubled in strength. I was moving through the water then, and no longer had to kick or pull myself alone. It felt uncomfortable like my spine wanted to push out through my belly button.

"Nothing good ever happens when you ask questions like that," Prometheus muttered, just as I felt my body contact the rift.

My body became a flashpoint of hot and cold, light and dark. Then everything folded around me and I tumbled, instantly regretting taking seconds at breakfast.

CHAPTER 34: THROUGH THE FUNHOUSE MIRROR

I rolled forward, turned sideways, and was promptly pulled inside out, all at the same time. Then I staggered forward, fell to my knees, and lost my cookies. Which was strange because I didn't remember eating any for breakfast. But yes, I literally watched chewed-up cookies come out of my mouth...amongst other things.

A heartbeat later, Prometheus staggered next to me. He looked straight ahead, then down at me. It was almost terrifying how calm he looked, then he too pitched over and threw up.

When he straightened, I clapped him on the back, only to notice my hand. I only had four fingers. Leaning in, I focused and counted—four. But for some reason, I couldn't articulate which finger was missing.

"My hands...!" Prometheus gasped next to me.

"I know. Four fingers. And my skin looks so tan."

Looking up at my counterpart I keyed in on several other distinct differences. His eyes appeared to be bright green and his teeth looked far flatter than I remembered.

"We look weird. Like re-colored versions of us, with some odd tweaks."

Omega appeared last, revolving from a flash of intense, blue ether. Only the wolf was no longer a wolf. Prometheus chuckled as I stood and circled my animal companion. Omega wobbled for a moment but then started to lick and groom his legs.

He was maybe a foot and a half tall, with orange fur, black tiger stripes, and clumps of poofy fur on his neck, tail, and each paw. The wolf finally lifted his head to me and growled. Or, I think he tried to, except it came out like a strange, angry cat meowling.

"Dude, what happened to your wolf? He looks like a weird stuffed animal of a cartoon kitty," Prom said.

"Um, I'm aware. Are you okay, boy?" I asked.

I felt Omega's emotions clear as day. He was more than good. He was great. Although, animals were sapped with the same vain sense of self we were. At the same time, I think even he'd pause and do a doubletake if graced with a view of his reflection.

"You didn't really expect to just pass through a tear in space-time and come out unchanged on the other end, did you? You know how you look and move in your little universe. Well, now you are getting a sneak peek at how you would look in another," Ivory explained, with just a touch too much satisfaction in his voice.

"Did you look like a mass-produced stuffed animal version of an anime house cat before you crossed over?" I asked, *"Because that mental image would never get old."*

"Ha ha ha," Laugh all you want, hairless ape-boy. *Right now, you're the one that looks funny. I particularly like your purple eyes and four fingers."*

Trying to ignore the spirit wolf, Prometheus and I set out to scout the area—the whole point of us going through first. Despite the rift on our side being in the middle of a small lake, the tear on this side resided in a small, rocky valley. Bizarrely-shaped bluffs rose all around us, forming a jagged bowl of pure stone.

We moved up the slope and away from the rift, our surroundings changing with every step. Then we passed through the veil and the world resolved in all of its strange glory. The glowing rift was behind us, only it was orange on this side.

The rocks framing us in were a dusty red, not grey, and a quick glance up stole my attention. Stars and moons filled the canvas above, the space between filled with the gaseous expanse of...whatever solar system this world existed in. I focused on the closest moon, as it has not one, but two rings, and a colorful, striped atmosphere.

"This place is wild," Prometheus breathed, following my gaze.

We found a cave at the base of the rocky cliffs and picked our way through the darkness. It narrowed at the end, so we carefully slid through and out the other end.

I beheld a landscape unlike any other I had seen before. It was plants and streams, yes, but not how I remembered. Some plants shot fifteen to twenty feet into the air, their leaves like conical spires of colorful petals. Others grew like pine trees but appeared to creep toward sources of water on tall, branching roots.

A stream gurgled just ahead. The water was clear, but not blue. Instead, it reflected the sprawling star scape above.

"It looks clear to me..." I started to say, just as something moved atop a tall tree just over the stream and to our right.

I glimpsed spreading wings right before the massive creature took to the air and dove right at us. The bird, if that was what it was, gave a terrible shriek and opened its four grasping legs, revealing long and impressive talons. I was all about improving beast-human relations and making friends, but that was an unmistakable sign of hostility.

"Prom, this is you," I yelled and ducked out of the way.

The beast swooped down just over us, the wind from its passing body sounding more like a thunderstorm. Its shadow loomed as it flapped back up into the sky and only then did I fathom its actual size. The beast was enormous, with a wingspan easily twelve, maybe fifteen feet across. It had a long head, tapered to a point at the back, giving it a pterodactyl-look, if not for the large mouth of long, pointed teeth.

"This one is definitely not a friendly beast," Prometheus said and tracked it with his bow.

"*You hairless apes are adorable. It isn't aggression tied to emotion, as with your kind. Everything is—he hurt my feelings, or he offended me, or I don't like what he does, so I'm going to hurt him. It sees you as food, as prey. This is survival,*" Ivory said, invading my thoughts.

"That makes sense," I said out loud.

"What's that?" Prom asked as the beast turned for another pass.

"Sorry, just talking to the wolf in my head. Evidently, this flying beast sees us as food. It isn't...personal."

"Getting eaten feels pretty personal," my scout friend grunted, lurched behind a tree, turned, and loosed an arrow. The flying monster shrieked as the projectile passed clean through its wing membrane.

"Aim for its body," I said, loosening and tightening my grip on my katana.

Prometheus snorted, pulled another arrow free, nocked, and drew. "What do you think I was aiming at?"

Realizing he needed a more reliable flight path to track, I stepped out into the clear and raised my arms, screaming incomprehensible nonsense at the flying terror. It shrieked in response and pulled into a dive.

"What are you doing?" Prom hissed.

"Giving you the flight plan ahead of time. Now, don't miss!"

I watched the beast fly right at me, its four legs extended, and talons opened wide. But I fought the urge to run. I had to stay in the open as long as possible, otherwise, the beast might veer away suddenly.

"Anytime, Prom!" I hissed as it closed, moving far faster than I was comfortable with.

It passed between two trees, the wind disturbing the branches, and then it was over the stream. *Shit!* I took a breath to scream his name just as the bowstring thrummed. Ducking my head, I rolled to the side as the beast screeched, the noise followed by a surprisingly loud *thud* as his arrow hit home.

I jumped to my feet as the massive beast dropped out of the sky, crashing in a heap twenty paces behind us. Drawing my wakizashi for...emotional support, we stalked toward the downed beast, bow, and swords in hand.

Hera was standing over the flying beast's body when we arrived, the others arrayed around her. Our spear-wielding warrior was still a little green, and not just from her trip through the rift. Her hair was the color of moss and her skin a rich tan, but her eyes shone a rich gold, which made her look like an angry cat.

"How goes the...scouting?" she asked, her left eyebrow cocked.

"The landscape is beautiful but strange, the sky is awesome, but the airborne wildlife is evidently very hungry," I said.

Joan and her people fanned out to secure the area, while Prometheus, Hera, Anita, and I knelt next to the massive creature's body. It was impressive up close, with thick, scaly skin, bristly fur covering its neck and abdomen, and three separate sets of large eyes. I wanted to comment about its toughness until I realized that Prometheus' arrow had hit it in the head and punched clean through its skull—right between the eyes. Well, one set of them, at least.

"Not many creatures can survive a direct and traumatic introduction of an arrowhead to the brain. Good shot," Hera said, looking at our scout.

"I was aiming for its chest," he said, deadpan.

I waited for him to crack a smile or continue, but in his typical fashion, he just turned away and scanned the trees.

"Okay, well let's see what we've got here," Anita said and started unpacking her tools and scanner.

It was the work of almost half an hour before our researcher was done, but she'd logged the beast's dimensions, and notable traits, sketched it, scanned it, and measured every aspect of its body. Wow, she was thorough.

Once done, we took trophies. Not to say we were on a big game hunt, but it kind of felt like one. Besides, there was no telling when we'd see these particular creatures again, so, Anita took tissue samples of its hearts and organs, blood, and brain tissue. The last one she claimed from Prometheus' captured arrow.

We, on the other hand, took the beast's core—which glowed with a distinct orange light—its skull, and its impressive talons. I wasn't morbid or anything, but the skull alone was so unique and impressive that I couldn't stand the thought of leaving it behind.

Anita led us deeper into the space, stopping almost every ten feet to scan, inspect, sketch, or sample something. Meanwhile, our two collective groups huddled around her, feeling very much the part of private security.

"Is this what it feels like?" I asked Hera as we moved around the stream.

"What 'what' feels like?" she hissed back.

"Not always having to watch your back. Actually find trustworthy, friendly people?"

"Time will tell," she said, shrugging. "I'm a little more jaded. They are going to have to prove themselves during a time of adversity before I fully jump onboard."

I agreed to that and we continued. The space beyond the rift wasn't all that large, as we discovered a wall barely half a mile beyond the stream. Wall sounds misleading, too. It was more like the inside edge of a massive bubble, its sides opaque and somewhat reflective.

"So, what keeps this place from collapsing?" I asked as another of the large flying beasts took flight on the other side of the valley.

"We don't know. Or, if we do know, that is knowledge being hoarded by one kingdom or another. That is why I have been trying to get into these rifts for so long, to try and unearth some of the rifts' mysteries. The more we know about them, how they relate to our world, and the ether that binds them together, the better off we'll be."

We started moving down the right side of the valley when I noticed what looked like burrows dotting the ground all around. The holes were large, perhaps two and a half feet wide, with a silky coating of what looked like spiderweb covering the ground before them.

"Stay back, that looks like the mouth of a funnel web spider's lair," Anita warned.

"How big would a spider be that lives in a hole that size?" Joan asked. "You know what, never mind. I don't think I want to know."

We moved clear of the burrows, taking care to avoid the obvious traps spread out on the ground. Until I walked right through a thick and almost completely invisible line of silk.

A host of noises echoed out of the nearest burrow, and before we could so much as form a line, a single, horrifyingly bizarre creature slunk forth.

"Is that a...?" Joan gasped.

"No, but I thought it would be a spider?" one of her fighters answered.

Hera cursed and laughed. "Of course it is," she said, leveling her spear, as another beast appeared behind it.

They were the rat creatures from the zoo, or as I could best guess, their true form. The creatures weren't as large as they were when we first encountered them, but they were stranger. With the body of a rat, they had six legs covered in spines. A noticeable, chitinous exterior shone beneath their fur, and spider-like mandibles hung down over their mouths.

Their tails waved threateningly as the leading beast raised onto its hind legs, flashing its belly, and fangs, in an obvious threat display.

"Form up!" Ajax growled, lifting his hammer as a horde of the creatures spilled out of their burrows.

I activated <<**Enhanced Strength**>> and <<**Burst of Speed**>> just as a beast lunged forward and cast an explosive shot of webbing over half our group. Prometheus and two French fighters were rocked back into a tree and immediately stuck in place.

Hera screamed, lowered her spear, and charged, with Ajax next to her. Omega, the tiger-striped, fluffy kitten version, roared and joined them.

"Omega, no!" I yelled. At that size, he'd be snack-sized for these beasts. Especially in their numbers.

Hera hit a raider—get it, I merged rat and spider together—with her spear, the blade plunging into its body and pushing it back. Ajax brought his hammer down onto the next creature's head, the impact flattening it with a crunch. And Omega pounced, like an adorable kitten.

I dashed forward to help him, but even with my enhanced speed, I couldn't cover the ground fast enough. I watched in horror as my companion jumped at a frenzied beast. It screeched excitedly and opened its mandibles in anticipation, but Omega didn't hit like a poofy kitty cat but bowled the hungry monster over with all the weight and ferocity of a three hundred pound, savage wolf.

He clamped his jaws onto its chitinous hide and wrenched it in one direction, and then the other, snapping several of its legs in the process. I jumped in, stabbing the creature in the face with my wakizashi, and plunged my katana in right after, finishing it off.

Omega hopped down and circled me, meowing excitedly.

"This might just be the weirdest thing ever," I muttered and chopped at another raider.

Cutting and stabbing hard with both blades, the raiders waved their front legs in the air, but ducked and dodged, moving like an expert fencer around my blades.

"These things are quick!" I grunted.

"No, these things are smart. They have fast reflexes and know to watch your blades, not your eyes. That denotes intelligence. I am also picking up on a particularly large ether signature almost directly below us. It is moving upwards very slowly. If these things reproduce the way I think, it could be their queen," Ivory said.

"Oh, great," I said and activated **<<Blazing Slash>>**. The fiery cut missed, but the beasts retreated from the flaming trail.

Omega Kitty Paws and I retreated toward the others, who had circled up around Prometheus and were fighting to free those stuck in the webbing. Ten feet separated us, then six, and something cold and slimy hit my lower body.

I twisted around, only to discover that Omega and I had been hit with a sizable wad of sticky webbing. My wolf counterpart was hissing and biting at the threads, fighting to extricate me, but a quick tug confirmed that my legs were stuck fast.

"Shit!" I cursed as the beasts swarmed around me. Counting wasn't necessary, as it wasn't like knowing how many mouths were going to eat me mattered. Okay, what a lie. Twelve freaking beasts, with rat mouths open and spider-like mandibles clicking prepared to make Omega and I the main course.

An arrow streaked in over my shoulder and I just spotted Prometheus in my peripheral vision. He was half-free from the sticky mess, but Hera and the others fighting to help him were fighting their own battle, as yet more of the raiders spilled forth from the tunnels.

The arrow hit a raider in the shoulder and knocked it back, but all that did was buy me a few seconds.

"You are dumb. Use the special weapon Mike prepared for you. Or, were you waiting for an even more dire circumstance in which to wield it? Please don't wait. I do not want to die!" Ivory

screamed in my mind.

I chastised myself while opening the offending box and ripped the submachine gun free. Another arrow streaked in, hitting a raider in the face and dropping it like a giant sack of potatoes. That small delay gave me just enough time to fold the stock open, jam the weapon to my shoulder, flip the fire selector, and mash the trigger.

The gun fired a single round into the chest of the lead raider—as I'd mistakenly flipped it to semi and not full auto. But the results did not disappoint. The round hit the creature beneath the jaw and blossomed in a bright, orange flash of back-the-fuck-down you strange, rat-spider...things.

The escaping ether blew a hole in the raider's carapace, singing fur, and tearing its lower mandibles free. Smoke rolled up and over its face as it screamed and thrashed. Not waiting around for it to recover, I swung left, mashing the trigger a dozen times.

Ether-infused .45 caliber rounds peppered the beasts in the swarm, coming alive in a near epilepsy-inducing dance of flash and pop. Add that to the ringing in my ears, but when my barrage was done, four raiders were dead, and the others were understandably shaken and confused.

Something tugged at my legs and I turned around, pointing the submachine gun at the ground. Hera was chopping at the webbing, her new spear making quick work of the sticky gunk.

"Hey, thanks!" I said.

"I'm right next to you. You don't have to scream!" she yelled back, then turned, cut down, and skewered a smoking raider as it made for us.

I kicked one leg free, switched to a one-handed grip with the UMP, and used my wakizashi to cut my other leg free. Three quick slashes freed Omega, who purred and ran right at a raider. The beast was running in a circle, having a side of its face scorched by an exploding round.

A thunderous shriek shook me deep inside, just as a

massive, dark form streaked in from above. It hit a raider right in front of me, and with long, dark talons ripped the flailing creature right off the ground. I looked up to find more of the winged-terrors circling overhead, and without warning, two more dove right for us.

CHAPTER 35: SPACE INVADERS

"I think we've really stirred up the hornet's nest now," Joan hollered as the raiders responded to the new threat.

The strange, rat-spider beasts swarmed in frantic circles, screeching as they went. Although they didn't attack us. They flung webbing between trees, creating large barriers of sticky thread.

A winged creature swooped in and tore right through the barrier. It didn't capture its intended prey, but the webbing did change its flight path enough that it missed its target completely. We pulled together as a group as the pterodactyl-like creature flapped off, singing a morose song as it went.

Prometheus let an arrow fly at one flying creature as it swooped down over us, but the projectile hit a tree instead.

"We're kind of sitting ducks out there. What's the plan, Kenji?" Ajax asked.

I turned to Anita, who huddled securely in the middle of our large group. She looked from the scrambling raiders to the divebombing predators, and then back to me.

"I have gathered a lot of data, but need samples from those things," she finally said, pointing at the raiders. They were scrabbling up the trees and throwing webs up with impressive speed. As we watched, one of the winged creatures swooped in, grabbed a raider off a nearby tree, and promptly became snared in a net.

The other raiders swarmed up and over it, some driving their poison-filled mandibles into its body, while others began wrapping it in webbing.

The circling creatures above instantly responded. They shrieked loudly and dove. The forest around us instantly turned into a chaotic, beast on beast battlefield. We watched them fight, the beasts savagely tearing each other apart, and for the first time in a long while, I didn't know what to do. It was like we'd wandered into the middle of a massive gang war and inadvertently set off the next major conflict.

"Maybe we just back out of here real slow?" Hera whispered.

By not moving, we seemed to have been forgotten by the warring beasts, but I wasn't foolish enough to believe that would last forever. And if we did flee, would the winged creatures just use that as an opportunity to pick us off on the move?

The ground shook then, interrupting my thoughts. The trees groaned, the rocks shifted, and the sandy soil started to push up and split apart. I tucked the wakizashi under my arm and hit the magazine release on the UMP, before pulling it free.

I'd been liberal with ammunition in that desperate burst, but still had nine rounds left in the magazine. Pulling the loose rounds from my bag, I popped them into place and rammed it home in the receiver.

A terror-dactyl—as I spontaneously decided to call them —swooped in and grabbed a raider in its claws. But as it flapped to gain altitude something shot out of the nearest burrow and knocked it right out of the sky. Then the ground gave birth to the most terrifying creature I'd ever seen. Yes, I said "birth."

Emerging in a mass of long, spiny legs, a large dark form pushed its way out of the ground. This beast was even more arachnid than the raiders, yet parts of it were still definitively rat, like its head. Although, half a dozen mandibles surrounded its mouth, with venom dripping off the sharp fangs.

The queen raider finally pulled the rest of its bulk free and stood to its full height—twelve to fifteen feet off the ground once its legs were extended. She screeched and scuttled forward, pouncing on the downed terror-dactyl as it tried to free itself from her webbing.

We watched as she swallowed the winged beast hole. Then, with horrible, dark eyes, she turned right at us.

"Stay together!" Ajax roared as she charged, rat-like pedipalps reaching for us.

Prometheus fired an arrow into her body, but the big beast didn't seem to even notice. One of Joan's warriors fired a crossbow bolt right after, but it barely slowed her down.

I aimed, fired a controlled burst of two rounds, and lunged forward, using <<**Blazing Slash**>>. I was mid-move when I realized that I was just holding the short wakizashi. And in perhaps one of my most spectacular but flashy failures, I cut hard through the air almost three full feet short of the queen raider's front legs.

Style points didn't protect me from the leg that knocked me into a nearby tree. At least she didn't eat me.

"That was stupid," Ivory said, as I rolled over, favoring my ribs.

"Spears up front! Archers fire!" Ajax yelled, commanding our conjoined forces together.

I struggled to my feet as Hera and two others lifted their spears, while Prom and two crossbowmen raised their weapons and fired. The long, pointy objects and the sting of arrows and bolts brought the massive raider queen's charge to a halt.

I wavered, cycled my ether, and exchanged the UMP and the wakizashi for the nodachi off my back. The queen turned, flashing her rather thicc abdomen my way, and I froze. Just beneath the stubby coating of brown, rat fur, something glimmered in the diffused light. It was shiny but definitely wasn't her hard, chitinous shell. It almost looked like metal. I felt something pull on that knot in my belly then, like before, with the rift.

Omega sprinted between the queen's legs and charge right at me, then leapt barely six paces away. I watched as my ferocious wolf, kitty, tiger companion sailed right by me and hit an approaching raider.

"...stop standing around! Those things are surrounding you," Omega growled. I'd become so fixated, my vision so tunneled that I'd almost lost track of the threats around me.

Ajax and the others spread out to surround the queen, Hera leading the spear wielders to keep her back. I hefted the nodachi, activating <<**Enhanced Strength**>> and moved toward Omega.

Falling back on my kendo training, I quickstepped forward and then to the right, cutting down at the same time. The heavy blade caught the first raider on the shoulder, the eviscerating strike cleaving its head and pedipalps from the rest of its body.

Omega growled and hissed, biting through the raider's tough exoskeleton with more jaw strength than any beast his size should rightly have. Then again, I knew he wasn't really an orange and black striped cat.

I focused on my breathing and posture, falling back on my training. A distant voice formed in my head, punctuated by the staccato *snapping* of a bamboo stick. *"Feet, knees, hips forward, core tight, shoulders and arms."*

My nodachi cut down again, then snapped around on the follow-through. Omega downed another raider and I waded in and finished it off. Depleting a bit more of my reserves, I activated <<**Blazing Slash**>> cutting clean through two raiders and setting a third on fire.

"Duck!" Omega screamed and I dove for the ground. A tremendous rush of air hit me as I rolled, the shadow of a diving terror-dactyl darkening the sky.

But when I managed to get my head up again, I saw a

bright streak of orange and black clutched in the creature's claws.

"Omega!" I screamed, jamming the nodachi into the ground. I pulled the UMP free and jammed it into my shoulder, but I knew before getting the creature in my sights that it was well out of range.

"On your left!"

I swung and fired a single shot, the ether flash taking half of the lunging raider's face off. Strafing left, I fired again and again, each round hitting the big creatures as they came at me. Until the UMP clicked empty.

Slinging the empty submachine gun, I ripped my katana free and cut back and forth, holding two beasts back. But my eyes crept toward the sky.

*"Focus on **your** fight. Omega can take care of himself,"* Ivory seethed, but I wasn't so sure. The terror-dactyls were large and incredibly hungry.

Realizing that I couldn't stand forever on my own, I cut and stabbed to push the remaining crowd of raiders back, then sheathed my katana and ripped the nodachi out of the ground.

Fighting the urge to reload the UMP to kill the beasts before me, I retreated toward the team as they fought off the queen. Ammo was a precious resource and I'd already burned through one entire magazine. Although, the ground was littered with ether-scorched bodies as evidence of the weapon's effectiveness.

I turned and found my team. They were holding their own but couldn't seem to cause enough damage to wound or drive the enormous creature off. My gaze caught on the shiny spot on her abdomen and I felt Ivory shift.

"What is it?" I asked, once again feeling the pull on the scar in my belly.

"Honestly, I don't know. But I can feel it, too. Maybe it is what formed this rift. Maybe it caused the raiders, as you call them, to mutate and deform?"

"Or all of it," I suggested.

"I was just going to say that, hairless ape," the wolf spirit growled.

"So, maybe we should cut it out and see what happens!" I whispered and activated **<<Burst of Speed>>** and **<<Enhanced Strength>>** for good measure.

I kicked into a run and pushed a good portion of my remaining ether reserves into my legs, then leapt onto the raider queen's thicc rear. I caught a spine with my boot. My armor grated on another, but I felt one slip through and bite into my thigh. Grunting through the pain I scrambled up the strange creature's body.

She started to jump and shake, her considerable weight booming as it hit the ground. I grabbed onto a spine and held on. It felt like I was on a bucking horse, as the motion threw me out and then up into the air.

I landed hard, her spiny body jabbing and poking me, but I refused to let go. Using my augmented strength, I climbed higher, until finally reaching the shiny spot. My fingers pushed down through her bristly fur and hooked around something hard. I only had a moment to inspect it before several raiders jumped onto her body below me. But at that moment, I not only confirmed that the shiny object was metallic but also felt the tug on my stomach nearly pull my belly button free. It appeared to be lodged or fused into her exterior.

Grabbing a spine, I swung my feet up, just missing the grasping pedipalps of a lunging raider, then I kicked off and crawled higher. Luckily, the queen's abdomen leveled off at the top and I was able to find a sure footing.

*"Did you feel that? Whatever is lodged in her body **is** the source of the pull. If I were a betting wolf, I would put money on it being connected to the rift as well,"* Ivory said.

"A betting wolf?" I stammered and cut hard, removing the leg from one of the raiders. *"Did you just say, 'if you were a betting wolf'?"*

"Oh, get over yourself. You know that I did. Getting stuck in your head is changing me. I'm becoming more like you. Trust me, I

probably hate the thought more than you do."

A raider jumped at me from the side before I could dodge and the beast's weight crumpled me to the ground, err, the queen's abdomen. Its mandibles came down hard on my left shoulder, but my high-tech Kevlar armor stopped the fangs from penetrating. I jammed my katana straight up into its body as payment and kicked the beast.

Rolling free, I moved to lunge just as the queen shifted and the added movement sent me flying. Holding my sword out before me I crashed right into the last raider, the blade ramming right into its mouth and cracking through the back of its skull.

My armor snagged on a spine as the raider tumbled free but I could tell that the fight below wasn't going well. Ajax's voice was booming and he didn't sound happy. I had to do something fast and my best chance was the fragment lodged in her body.

Pulling free, the strap broke, letting my chest piece sag on the left side, but I ignored it and scrabbled to the shiny spot. I dug my fingers in again and pulled with all of my strength. The queen responded instantly and jumped straight up into the air.

"Oh shit!" I gasped as the movement and the pull on my core almost unhinged me on two levels. And yet, my hands did not move.

"Yes. That is it. Yes! Pull it free. Pull!" Ivory urged.

I pulled with my arms and pushed with my legs, but even with my enhanced strength, it wasn't enough. So, working my fingers to find the edge, I lined up my katana and drove it in next to the fragment.

The queen screeched and jumped back, the impaled blade the only thing holding me in place. I rammed it all the way in, then pulled it back, moved it down the artifact, and drove it in again. The queen dove at the ground and dirt flew up and over me.

"She is trying to burrow into the ground to protect herself.

Hurry!"

My katana stabbed in, again and again, the hard, chitinous shell cracking each time. Then I felt the artifact shift. I sheathed my sword, hooked my fingers under the edge, and pulled again.

Dirt hit my face and chest, getting into my eyes and nose. I coughed and spluttered but did not stop. The artifact shifted, moved, and stuck. My strength skill was wearing off but I pulled until muscles started to tear and tighten in my back and legs. We were halfway into the ground when the artifact gave way with a tremendous crack and I fell free.

The ground reached up and accepted me with a totally soft and not in any way covered in rocks and sticks, hug. The impact knocked the breath out of my lungs, but I maintained enough composure to not pee myself.

Rolling over and blinking through the grit, I saw dark shapes converge on me. My fighting instinct took over, but my arms were filled with the artifact, my blades were sheathed, and the large form was Ajax.

"You mad, stupid, crazy, and insane bastard," he cursed and hauled me off the ground.

"Most of those things mean the same thing," I groaned once I was finally able to draw breath. He grumbled something else but a host of additional voices washed it away.

They were all around me and we were moving in one direction, and with great determination, I might add. Eyes watering, I just managed to catch sight of the raider queen behind us, her body trapped halfway in the ground. She was shrinking, her exoskeleton simply falling off in big pieces. The remaining raiders were thrashing on the ground, too, a strange, orange mist rising from their bodies.

"What happened?" I asked.

"We were hoping you could tell us. Oh, and what is that?" Anita asked, appearing from behind Ajax. "We saw you on top of the queen, then she tried to dig to get away from...something, and then the trees and the pocket world simply started to fall apart. The rift is closing. Whatever you did, it is collapsing this place."

"Shit," I cursed and broke from Ajax's strong grip. I started to understand the truth of our dilemma as we ran.

The ground was shaking and jumping. Rocks were crumbling, and the peculiar vegetation and trees were uprooting and falling over. But the sky, that was the unsettling part. The odd, reflective bubble enclosing the pocket world was shrinking and consuming whatever it touched. The swirling colors shifted from orange to green, to blue, and finally gray.

"Wait! Omega! We have to find him," I said and looked around.

"He's gone, Kenji," Hera said and ran by me. "We saw that thing eat him whole."

I fought back a pang of anger but knew the truth of it. I saw the terror-dactyl scoop him right off the ground. Omega wasn't a large, fierce wolf in this world. He was small and...poofy. I'd let him down.

We ran down the valley, across the stream as the water shook and danced. I was halfway across when large bubbles of clear liquid started to drift up into the air, not unlike old videos I'd seen of astronauts playing with their food in zero-G.

Holy crap...is that a new memory, I thought, but stowed the revelation for later. That is, if we survived the imploding micro-verse calamity we were stuck in.

We made it up the far side of the valley and my thoughts stuck on the cave ahead—our narrow, rather treacherous path leading to the rift. If this world was collapsing, and judging from the sheer destruction all around us it was, then surely something that fragile would have been the first thing to go. Or, not...!

We approached and found the mouth of the cave intact. Joan filed in first, with everyone stuffing their bodies through the small gap with little regard for bumps and scrapes. What were a few abrasions compared to getting stuck inside a collapsing portal?

I went in last, carefully cradling the artifact in my arms. After bumping my head, both shoulders, both knees, my back, and then my head again, I stumbled out the far side. The team was sprinting ahead, moving as fast as they could toward the rift.

The swirling ether vortex was red now and intermittently swelling and contracting, like something preparing to explode. The team sprinted right at it, Prometheus and Hera disappearing inside it first. I followed, noticing that everyone was running clear of a dead terror-dactyl's body.

I gave it only a passing glance as I ran past. But something spun me around right before hitting the rift. The dead beast jumped and shook, then as I watched, its belly split open and an orange and black paw appeared.

"Doh...it's...you have to..." Ivory stammered, just as the wall of the rocky valley exploded, the pocket universe crumbling down upon us.

I shifted the artifact to one hand and lurched for the corpse, grabbed the first thing available—its head—and pulled it toward the rift. Rock and debris rained down all around as ether burst forth in violent arcs of swirling color and destructive potential. It melted a swath of ground where I'd just stood, then lanced up and turned a massive bolder to dust.

Activating <<**Enhanced Strength**>> I surged and pulled with all of my power and as the micro-verse imploded around me, tumbled back into the rift.

CHAPTER 36: INTO A ROUTINE

My tumbling, falling, and twisting just added to the strange rift-transiting sensation, which only grew more intense by the fact that the rift destabilized above us, then promptly exploded in a violent shower of venting ether. Oh, and going from dry forest to submerged in a freaking cold lake didn't help any, either.

Gagging and somewhat miserable, I slogged through the water, one arm clutching protectively to the artifact I had secured from our raider queen and the other dragging the dead terror-dactyl. I'd barely made it back to the rocky shore when the dead creature behind me jumped and twitched, then promptly exploded.

Omega emerged from the winged creature's stomach, his body morphing back to his true, wolf form in a glorious but gory transformation. He moved to shake but Hera screamed and simply pointed to the water. With ears down and tail between his legs, Omega jumped back into the water to get clean.

I staggered up the bank and plopped down onto a fallen tree, then took a few deep, cleansing breaths. Once everything stopped spinning, I lifted my head and looked around. Without the rift floating above the water, the sheltered cove was somewhat darker and less...magical. Maybe mundane was a better word, but there was a definitive reduction of spine-tingling energy radiating throughout the space.

And yet...The pull on my core was as strong as ever. I pushed the artifact out to arm's length to give it a first, real look. The pull on my core shifted with it. *Interesting.*

Anita sat down on the tree next to me and very nearly sprawled over the back. She wavered, covered her mouth, and coughed.

"That was horrible. That *one* was horrible. Oh my gosh," she whispered and swallowed hard.

"Harder than any of the others?"

"Truthfully," she said, laughing, "I have only been fortunate enough to experience several small rifts firsthand. And beyond that, I was never afforded the freedom to explore beyond without limitations. The transit in those was a little disorienting, but this was...well, you felt it, too."

"They never let you explore freely beyond a rift?" I asked.

"Is it really so hard to believe, given what I've already told you? This kind of knowledge, what you saw beyond that rift, and, ugh, what you're holding in your hands, is the single greatest commodity in the post-ether world. On those rare occasions where I was able to explore rifts, it was my money that made it happen. I saved and borrowed, then hired private security. They led me to the rift, and it all felt perfectly normal. But once we got through the rift, they changed—took over, claimed anything with value, and abandoned me. I don't think they believed me a threat, otherwise, they might have killed me. The second time, well, let's just say I should have learned from my first experience."

"Mercenaries," I sighed, recognizing that the people she'd hired were likely men and women like us.

"My cohorts and I used to be mercenaries once, too."

"Used to be? Joan, she made it sound like you were..."

"We were," I repeated. "Everything I've seen and heard

since waking up after losing my memories has convinced me that I want to be something else. Something that stands for more."

I'd been thinking about our lives—what we did, how we earned, and how other people viewed us since claiming the paperwork from Manfred's estate. Hans had us running errands all over Zurich. Most felt benign, some just lazy gopher jobs, but we'd almost killed his guards that night. Well, not to mention the Seneschal and his cronies. But they'd attacked us, so it was self-defense. The guards, however, were just men and women doing their jobs.

I was tired of being a pawn and running in circles for powerful schmucks just because they had leverage by violence or debt over us.

Peeling the artifact away from my chest, I watched as Anita's eyes darkened. I couldn't feel her emotions like with Omega but could read her response well enough. She thought I was going to stash it away. To not let her see or study it. Because...well, I was a mercenary and that was what all the mercs had done before.

"Let's look over it together," I said, and finally straightened my arms.

That simple act felt harder than it should, as my muscles weren't just cold, but tight as the energy radiating from the relic leached into my body. Everything I knew told me that it wasn't ether. But if it wasn't, then what was it?

With more difficulty than I cared to admit, I straightened my arms, pried my fingers apart, and laid the artifact on the ground. And now that it wasn't fused into a giant, monstrous raider queen's body, nothing was trying to eat me, and we weren't running to escape a rapidly collapsing pocket universe, I got a good look at it.

Roughly three feet long by two feet wide, the artifact was shiny and smooth, like black glass. Its surface curved gently around but ended in jagged, broken edges, indicating it had been part of a greater whole. An intricate gridwork covered its face, with odd runes etched inside the lines framing it all in.

"It doesn't look like anything I've ever seen before," I admitted, and with a single finger, picked up the nearest corner to inspect the other side.

The material looked the same on the other side, except there were no runes, only a wide, patchwork of what looked like prismatic scales.

"It looks totally alien," Anita breathed and leaned in for a closer look. "May I?"

I nodded and moved back, so she could handle the artifact. She lifted one corner to study the outside, then flipped it over to look at the other. My gaze crawled to her arms as I noticed that she didn't seem to have any difficulty holding it.

"Do you feel anything when you touch it?" I asked.

"What do you mean? Like associated energy or stored charge?"

I nodded, messaging my forearms. Ajax and the others were congregating on the bank, talking and wringing the water out of their clothes and gear. Meanwhile, Omega was doggie paddling around the lake, and he wasn't quiet about it.

"I only feel a tactile stimulus. A smooth surface, cool to the touch, with symbols cut cleanly into the material. Perhaps it is a language," Anita mumbled, continuing her observations. "What did you feel when you touched it? Something more than what I just explained?"

"My fingers, hands, and arms were tight. Like there was some form of energy leeching out of it and into me. And yet, it definitely wasn't ether."

"Well, let's see what we can find out," the researcher said and pulled out her scanner. She passed the device over the artifact in one direction, then slowly brought it back.

Heightened by anticipation, I felt my stomach drop as the small device showed no lights or made any sounds. The wrinkles on Anita's forehead deepened as she moved the scanner over the artifact in every direction, and at every distance conceivable.

"What does it mean?" I asked, when she finally sat back, obviously confused.

"Scientifically? Nothing. It is obviously radiating some form of energy. The screen on my scanner says as much, but you are right. It isn't ether, otherwise, we would get a color readout telling us its intensity. You can feel the energy when you touch it, which is good enough for me. We simply need to continue testing it until we unearth its secrets. I can say this..." she said, trailing off.

I watched her for a moment as her gaze unfocused. It was like her thoughts slid somewhere far into the distance.

"What is it, Anita?"

"Oh, sorry. I just started thinking and I tumbled hard down that rabbit hole." She bent over and swiped the scanner over the ground for a moment, lifted it to her face, and then turned it so I could see. The glossy screen showed a single line of text.

Domestic [Flux]Net: _-16 W/m²_

"What does that mean? 'Flux'?"

"Essentially it is Earth's energy. If you want to think about it in the simplest terms, it is the culmination of energy our planet is releasing combined with solar radiation and other cosmic energy sources. That is what the 'net' means. We came to think of this as Earth's lifeblood, or her energy. After the collapse and once ether became known by name, these scanners simply started targeting and naming Earth's energy as 'flux.' I don't know how, but the devices can make the distinction between Earth's energy and other forms. I told you all of that so you could appreciate this," Anita explained and then waved the scanner over the artifact.

As before, there were no lights or sounds, and when she turned the device to me, the screen showed what I thought was the same line of text. I read it three times before I caught the difference.

Domestic [Celestian]Net: +468 W/m²

$$Domestic\ [Celestian]Net: +468\ W/m^2$$

"Celestian," I whispered, reading the line for what it was.

"Yes," Anita nodded. "If this scanner can differentiate between Earth's domestic energy and that of other sources, then that tells me that this artifact, whatever it is, is from somewhere vastly different than our world. And this number," she said, pointing at the line, "is extremely high. The highest I have ever seen here, say the hottest day of summer, is around one hundred and eighty. And that is diffuse. This is concentrated in a relatively small artifact."

"As soon as I ripped this from the raider queen's body, the pocket universe beyond the rift started to collapse. But not just that, she actually started to crumble and disintegrate...like it had become an integral part of her. But how and why?"

Anita chuckled. "You sound more and more like a researcher the longer I am around you. The key to science is asking questions and then working to answer them. The artifact was lodged in her body. Perhaps she grew around it or it had been surgically implanted? Perhaps it was the source of her and her offspring's mutations? I am not one hundred percent confident in saying, but it is likely that it wasn't just the artifact, but the fusing of it into her body that resulted in the formation of that rift."

"Does that mean that beyond every rift is one of those creatures and one of these?" I asked, dipping the toe of my boot under the artifact and lifting it.

"Good question. You just formulated a hypothesis and the only way to test it and gather answers, is to discover more rifts and find out! Once we answer that question, perhaps we will have enough data to dig into some bigger ones, like, where did the artifacts come from and what happened to cause the rifts?"

We came together to briefly discuss our excursion, but once the initial excitement wore off, it was replaced by a general feeling of dissatisfaction and regret. We'd claimed loads of samples, yes, but only walked away with two cores —all from the terror-dactyls. The fight with the raiders began and ended so abruptly, that we didn't have any time to observe or collect anything.

Prometheus and Omega led us carefully out of the sheltered lake, but I hung back. There was no concealing energy boundary now and when I turned to give the small valley a farewell glance, even the massive cluster of crystals beneath the water was gone. The lake, for all intents and purposes, had returned to normal.

Before following the others, I fished my small scanner out of my bag. I was curious to see what my efforts lately had netted me, and more, to see if it showed any signs of my contact with the artifact. The pull on my core was constant now, so it had to show up as something.

A thread of ether pushed forth into the scanner and its outline glowed to life. But unlike before, it didn't just read and show me the results. The edge of the device always glowed with a faint, blue-green light, but this time it cycled to orange and back again.

The scanner took several moments before the screen came alive, but once it did, I recognized the display. [**Cultivation**] appeared at the top, with my vital statistics listed out on the right and the corresponding icons to their left.

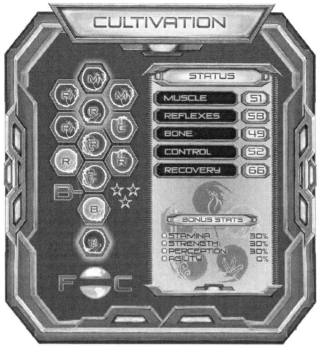

I whistled low, seeing how much of a beating I'd taken recently—muscle, reflexes, bone, control, and recovery were all down. My gaze crawled down and froze. A new icon glowed on the bottom of the screen.

"F and C," I whispered, recognizing that the two different colored halves of the icon created a globe. "Flux and Celestian energy. But what do the icons mean?"

I flipped over to the next screen, pulling up the **[Skills]** tab. Reading down the lists quickly, I surmised that nothing new had appeared. *Can't win them all.*

"Query," I said, "What is Celestian energy?"

Query returns:

{Celestian Energy} is a cumulative mass of non-Terran energies.

...

...

End—

The scanner's rather abrupt ending took me by surprise, although it was a device, so I didn't know what I was expecting.

"Why can I feel Celestian energy?"

Reason unknown---

Query error: Item: Celestian Energy data is still spooling. Records updating. Try query again at a later date.

"Try again at a later date," I said. "Well, I guess that is better than my typical rejections."

I started walking to follow the others as a host of additional questions started to pile up in my head. But they still didn't make sense yet. I landed on a single, simple question, and hoped it would supply answers.

"Query. Do I have Celestian energy inside my body right now?"

Query returns:

{Celestian energy} is present. Source is [unknown]. Concentration is [unknown]. Data is still spooling.

...

...

End—

"That answers that question. I can guess the location, but it would be nice to know more about what it is and why it is there," I said, rubbing the spot behind my navel.

Stowing the scanner away, I joined the others, quietly sorting through the unanswered questions in my head.

We worked our way carefully south from there, scouting and exploring, before finally approaching the heart of the zoo. The stadium came into view in the distance, with the castle and the sprawling ruins appearing in the trees to the west.

Per our already established plan, we avoided the stadium, as even from our distance, we could see signs of fighting. Several large columns of dark smoke were dotting the sky, with another fire blazing far off to the east.

We approached the ruins in silence. Prometheus scouted ahead and returned a short while later, his expression grim. Joan remained by my side as we crawled through the holes in the ancient compound's crumbling wall. The path led us into a courtyard, where we stumbled onto the obvious scene of a violent altercation.

Blood and entrails covered the ground near a small tree, with several large drag marks extending over the grass and through the archway leading deeper in. I stowed my katana in favor of the heavier nodachi. Joan watched me pull the big blade free and nodded her approval.

"So, what did you do before everything collapsed?" she asked, quietly.

Prometheus and Omega slunk forward through the arch ahead of us, while two of Joan's warriors, with crossbows held ready, followed.

"I can finally answer that question," I chuckled. "My father founded a dojo after he immigrated from Japan. He taught kenjutsu, or Japanese swordsmanship, aikido, and karate. Once I became old enough, I helped him teach. After a while, we moved away from the more traditional martial arts like kenjutsu and moved to kendo, which is more like fencing. People wanted the sport, the competitive element over the self-improvement Zen of the more traditional disciplines."

I stopped as we approached the next clearing. It wasn't lost on me how easily the information bubbled forth. I didn't have to fight or strain, the memories were just...there.

"*It's not random. That thing you pulled out of that big bug's butt did something to you. Although...I cannot tell exactly what. I can feel its energy, that Celestian energy radiating through you, all the way up here, in your mind palace,*" Ivory chimed in, speaking for the first time in a while.

"*I felt it pulling on my core, both when we approached the rift in the lake, and then stronger when the raider queen emerged from her lair. It makes me wonder where it came from, but also what it is a piece of...*" I replied, but Ivory appeared just as confused by the artifact as the rest of us.

"It makes me feel better knowing that you actually understand how to use that," Joan said, nodding her head at the nodachi. "I have met far too many mercs with machetes in my day. They are usually just as likely to hurt themselves as the person they are fighting."

The next clearing had been a room at one time but its ceiling fell in and rotted away long ago. Now it was just an open-air space, filled with scraggly plants, and bodies scattered everywhere. Well, just the parts of bodies the hungry something living in the ruins didn't want, that is.

Omega snarled and his hackles raised. Prometheus leaned into the next space and returned, shaking his head. I read his look easily enough—more of the same.

"Oh mon Dieu," Joan gasped, looking around. And she was right. *Oh my God.*

Judging from the volume of human remains, I guessed that no less than two teams had entered the ruins and never left. Judging from what we saw after first entering, and combining that with our snake run-in, at least four to five of the teams weren't going home.

"Is it always this bad?" Hera asked, creeping toward the next passage. She stopped just shy of the shadows, sniffed the air, and recoiled. "It smells absolutely rotten in there. This place gets a nope from me."

In the quiet, before anyone else spoke, I heard something reverberating from ahead. Stalking toward the shadows, I moved to the passage entrance and peered into the darkness. The air was thick, damp, and rank with rot. But also, I could just hear that low-frequency thrum, as if we were standing above a room full of large, buzzing insects.

"I don't want to go in there. Not with that smell and not with these bodies all around us. It is bad luck," one of Joan's fighters said.

"They didn't have our numbers," Ajax argued and thumped his hammer against his palm. "I say we go in, slaughter whatever it is, and move on. It is that or wait for something to sneak up on us while we're sleeping. And I don't know about the rest of you, but if I'm going to die, I want to do it while I'm awake, with a weapon in my hands, and my boots on."

Half of the combined team nodded in agreement, while a quarter of them shook their heads, and the rest simply looked unsure.

"Ajax is right," I said. "We don't have to stay here, but if we can kill the beast that ki—err, ate those teams, then we have one less thing to worry about when we camp tonight. We handled the raider queen back there. Every one of you held your ground and fought hard. If we do that again and watch our backs, nothing can stand in our way."

"Verdammt richtig," Ajax cursed. "If we divide, we'll end up just like those poor bloody bones over there. Let's march into this beast's hole, punch it right in the mouth, and show those arrogant, stuffy princes back at the castle what we're made of!"

"Right!" one hissed. And before I knew it, the whole group looked fit for a fight. Everyone save for Hera, who still eyed the doorway with a wrinkled nose.

"Spears first, then archers, and swordsmen in the back," Joan recommended as we massed before the doorway.

We crept through the next dark passageway, the air growing thicker and fouler with every step forward. And then we came to what had once been a great hall and Hera's fear made perfect sense.

Massive, three to four-foot long maggots covered the floor and ceiling, the rock slick with their secreted ick. Carcasses filled the space between—beasts and animals, all in varying states of decomposition and putridity. Perched on an immense egg sac, located centrally in the chamber, was the largest, most bloated fly I'd ever seen.

"That thing...killed those...? Bleh," Hera started to say but started to gag.

"Indeed," Ajax growled and eyed the slithering grubs.

I felt a tug on my core as Hera reluctantly joined the other spear-wielders at the front, but it took me a moment to realize that the walls all around us weren't just glimmering with secreted slime but shimmering, dancing ether.

"This chamber is a rift," Anita said from the back of our group.

"Then let's see what our fly friend is holding for us," I said, and tightened the grip on my sword. As memory served, the pestilential beasts hated fire. *Good.* I had a little bit of that to bring to bear.

"Prometheus, do you think you can put a few arrows in that thing's eyes?" I asked.

Our scout nocked an arrow and drew the string to his cheek, with a wicked smile forming on his lips.

"If I couldn't hit those huge things, I'd trade in my bow for a samurai sword," he said and fired.

"Perfect," I whispered back, activating **<<Enhanced Strength>>** and **<<Burst of Speed>>**. "As soon as I make my move, drill that thing in the eyeballs. I'll open the path for everyone else, so don't hesitate. Get in there and stick that bulbous thing as many times as possible."

I steeled myself, peeked around the corner one final time, and tried not to think about the large, pale squirmers. I'd always had a problem with maggots growing up—the way they moved, the sound, and their smell. My stomach was already bubbling and roiling.

Then, before I could talk myself out of it, I cut around the corner and sprinted right at the resting fly. The ether flowed out of my core like usual as I activated **<<Blazing Slash>>** but something tugged at my core as I did. A peculiar buzzing sensation filled my ears and the air all around me.

My muscles tensed as I coiled and brought the big sword around. Fire ripped forth from the blade, surging outward in a bright and blistering wave. The nodachi hit the first fly larva, cleaving clean through its soft body and I continued, but by the time I struck the second, the heat was so intense it vaporized a large swath of its skin.

Banishing the darkness, my ether fire rippled behind my blade, clearing a wide swath of the vermin. I'd never felt a skill connect with that much power before, and as Prometheus' bow string thumped behind me, I knew it had to be the relic, buzzing away in my secret compartment.

CHAPTER 37: THE PLOT THICKENS

Working together, our combined team fought like a group of inspired, savage gods, battling as if their hair were on fire and the world would end if they lost. Truth be told, I might have singed a few of them with my unexpectedly strong wave of blistering ether fire.

I apologized for that several times after the last of the stinking fly beasts fell. And oh, did they fall. Prometheus' aim was true, as he'd skewered the slumbering fly with an arrow in each eye. It could still see, mind you, but with nowhere the same acuity as before.

We set up camp in the highest, stable chamber of the ruins, after claiming cores, usable parts, and, to our surprise, and my disappointment, no new relics.

The "larva" as Hera insisted on calling them, were a bounty all on their own. Each contained a glowing, white core, although we had to make a special trip to wash everything after our collection was complete.

Even after a plunge in the icy water, I had that stink stuck in my nose. I watched Omega roll in the mud, sand, plants, and some less savory things as he tried to mask the stink as well.

I laid back in our camp sometime later and waited for sleep to claim me. I held the raider queen artifact in my right hand and watched the stars.

Anita had gone the relic again and again, but I tried to stay out of the way. She'd scanned and studied, jotted down notes, turned it over and over, and did it all while her tongue stuck out the corner of her mouth.

With the shard resting against my side and the stars shining bright above me, I closed my eyes. The pull on my core was twofold now, as the strange tickle behind my belly button fought to draw the strange relic to me. It was an odd sensation, but strangely, one I was becoming more comfortable with.

I opened my eyes a moment later, only to realize that I was lying in a soft bed of clouds, with the looming shadow of my mind palace high above me. *Shit.* I didn't even have my eyes closed for that long—fifteen, maybe twenty seconds. Had I been that tired? Or...

Moving to push off the ground, I realized that the relic fragment was gone. Okay, that surprised me a bit.

I set off down the cloud path, my excitement growing with every step forward. The clearing came into focus beneath the tower's entrance, the familiar koi ponds, benches, and nicely manicured plants exactly as I'd remembered them. Before reaching the stairs, I noticed Ivory standing off to the right, beyond the pond.

My gaze swept out over the water as I moved around to join the spirit wolf, but there appeared to be decidedly fewer fish than on my last visit. Yes, it was still well-stocked with colorful orange and white fish, but some were definitely gone.

"I am a wolf at heart," Ivory said as I approached. "You can't expect to keep a pond full of snacks around and have me not at least try a few. They don't taste particularly good."

"I could have told you that," I said, moving up next to him.

"Eaten a few koi fish, have you?" he asked, turning his large head my way. Damn, I hated the way he called me out like that.

Changing the subject, I turned to what the spirit wolf had been looking at and didn't bother hiding my surprise. A transparent version of our newly claimed relic hung in the air. It gently bobbed in the air, slowly revolving, as odd tendrils of energy popped in the air around it. It looked like they were emitting sparks, except there was no corresponding sound or heat.

"How long...?"

"It literally just appeared," Ivory said, interrupting my question. "I felt the ground shake and then *poof* here it was. Something happened in the tower, too. It sounded like something fell over or opened up, but I can't be sure. Maybe you claimed the souls of a couple house cats? It would be entertaining if those things were running all over your palace, knocking glasses off of tables, and pooping in doorways. I would find that highly amusing."

"Oh, you would?" I asked, extending a hand toward the relic.

The pull on my core returned in force as soon as my hand drew near, an invisible and strong wave of hot energy splashing against my palm.

"Yes," Ivory said, his voice almost bored. "I probably wouldn't eat them, either. I would just watch them run around and knock stuff onto the ground. Cats are so wonderfully chaotic."

"What do you think this is?" I asked. "I mean, beyond the obvious. That it is a fragment of something larger."

Ivory tilted his head—the equivalent of a shrug from what I'd learned.

"Does it matter?" he asked. "Well, yes, I guess it does. Since you asked, and all. Judging from what I can sense from it, I would say it is a fragment of something incredibly powerful. Or, something that *was* powerful. If possible, it was so intimately bound to the energy and its previous plane of existence, that the connection exists even now, as a tether that penetrates the barriers of time and space. But what do I know? I am just the spirit of a wolf bound to your mind."

"Yeah. That is what I was thinking, too," I said, lying, then threw Ivory a wink as he turned an irritable glance my way.

"Whatever they are, they are connected with whatever power is responsible for the creation of this palace. And wrap your head around this one, pale ape-man. They are not *of* ether or a source *of* it, but ether might be *of* it. I can't articulate it any better than that, so have fun untangling that riddle. Anyways, I am due for a nap. Those fish gave me indigestion."

"That makes sense, as *it* brought me here," I said as the wolf stood and stretched.

"Hmm?"

"I couldn't come here for the longest time, no matter how hard I tried. I was simply laying down, staring at the stars, with my hands resting on this thing, and when I opened my eyes again, I was here."

"Well, that is...something," he mumbled and trotted off.

I turned to watch him leave, shaking my head. Ivory had changed in so many ways since being trapped in my mind, and yet, in other ways, he hadn't changed at all. He was still irritable and moody.

Returning my attention to the floating relic, I moved in and around it. I braved the heat and tingling energy it emitted to get as close as possible. I was barely two feet away when I passed through a familiar distortion in the air.

Just like the veil surrounding the lake rift, the artifact was a pale and translucent outline one moment, and a solid, tactile thing the next. I shifted from side to side, even lifting my hands before me to shield my face from the waves of strong energy, but nothing helped. Squinting, I leaned to the right and realized the space beyond the floating relic had changed. A new path was forming, solidifying into something less cloud and more rock.

I didn't know what the artifact was forming or where

the path would lead, if it led anywhere, but I swore that I could see the faint outline of a swirling, blue rift revolving in the air.

No longer able to tolerate the stinging energy battering my face, and very eager to get inside my mind palace to look for new doors and skills, I stepped back. I passed back from the veil of cloaking energy and the world promptly tipped backward around me.

In the blink of an eye I was no longer standing, but lying on my back, with the expansive night sky sprawled out above me.

"Shit! No! Fuck!" I cursed and flailed from side to side.

I scooped up the artifact and pressed it to my side, then with my hands firmly clamped onto its glossy surface, closed my eyes. Focusing with all of my might, I tried to cast myself back into my cloudy realm. Stars greeted me when my eyes snapped open again.

Frustrated, I sagged against the ground and let my mind wander.

CHAPTER 38: APPROACHING THE END

The next days passed in a blur of routine—preparation, scouting, and a mixture of fighting and disappointment. As we discovered, the relatively easy rift areas had been picked clean first. I could feel the gentle and distant tug on my belly button as we entered each space, but it was clear that the rifts had long since collapsed, and whatever fragment powered it removed.

We had to fight our way into half of those areas and fight our way back out of the others. Anita hypothesized that the energy, the distortion, or the pull I experienced was drawing the creatures to those spots. A few of the creatures we fought or drove off were powerful, but the vast majority were relatively simple creatures. Some didn't look any different from regular animals.

We took cores from everything we could, took samples and meat from those that didn't have them, and scared away the ones that posed no real threat. All in all, we were happy with the haul, and Anita seemed thoroughly satisfied with the amount of data and materials she was able to collect.

It was dawn on the fifth day when I started to feel a definitive sense of urgency. Ajax, Hera, and I were cleaning up from breakfast. Some delightful pork belly we'd claimed from an enormous wild pig the day before. The thing took Hera's spear to the body and proceeded to push her almost a hundred paces in the wrong direction. It took all of us and half a dozen of Prometheus' arrows to finally bring the aggressive beast down.

"Nous avons besoin d'un plan," Joan whispered, staring out over the zoo. It was beautiful in the mornings, with the sunrise catching the fog and igniting it in spectacular shades of orange light.

"What is that?" I asked, moving up next to her.

"Oh, sorry. I was just talking to myself. We need a plan here. The way I see it, we have two paths remaining before us. Judging from the sounds of fighting over the last few days, whatever lives in the stadium is still alive. Or, people are in there fighting each other. The other is the castle. I watched it last night. Torches approached in the darkness, but none ever left. Not even this morning. That tells me that something incredibly powerful is likely living in there, ripe for the taking."

"Working together we killed the fly and its offspring. We could do it again."

"About that," Joan said, shifting, and turning my way. "That has been troubling me since we finished the fight. I do not believe that the fly was what had originally inhabited the ruins, not the one responsible for killing all those cultivators."

"What do you mean?" I asked as Ajax stowed his last pan and moved to join us.

"On our first day here and before we met up with you, we happened upon a most peculiar trail in the forest. Trees were broken and the ground was gouged from massive, spear-like feet. We followed that trail for a great while and found carcasses everywhere. Whatever made that trail was large and unfathomably hungry. We tracked a team from Stuttgart outside the stadium for a while. Whatever was in there overpowered them easily. They retreated into the woods and did not come back. We heard something tear through the side of the massive structure not long after. Birds and other animals took flight as the trees shook and fell. Another team arrived at the stadium shortly after, entered, and left, seemingly empty-handed. At least two teams died in the ruins, and yet the fly and her offspring were not strong enough to do that. I think she moved in after whatever killed those warriors left. Perhaps she was already there, hiding below, nesting with her eggs."

"That is quite the theory," Ajax chimed in.

"To be one hundred percent truthful, it is Anita's hypothesis. I didn't believe her at first but the longer I am here and the more I see, the more it makes sense. She calls it an 'extinction level' predator. One with an unparalleled appetite and no natural predators. Something like that could continue to feed and grow unchecked in an area, then simply move to an area with more food."

"And you think this thing is in the castle right now? Question two, is an extinction level creature something we should be going after?"

"I didn't sleep and have not seen any signs of it leaving. That does not mean that it didn't, but there is a strong chance that it is still there. You spoke of leverage. Even if we ignore the obvious bounty such a kill would garner, the kingdoms are all about reputation. Those responsible for slaying an extinction-level creature would be seen in a whole new light."

As if on cue, Omega growled and looked right at the castle. A flock of crows, previously roosting on the tallest tower, took flight, cawing loudly.

"Whatever we do, it will likely be our last here in the zoo. Hans recommended leaving plenty of time for extraction. I don't see any harm in scouting the castle and looking for Anita's supreme-level creature. We have a quality scout and a vicious, cuddly wolf at our disposal."

By now our two teams had come to an easy understanding. A thing was either going to get done or it wasn't. Strangely, no one had arguments about checking out the castle. Now, I held no delusions about what they would say once we got there. If this thing was there, and it looked unbeatable, then I expected them to be honest about the odds and our life expectancy. The point was getting out alive, after all.

We moved out of the ruins, taking a circuitous trail to forge a new route. We didn't want to retrace our path just in case anything had tracked us there. The fly's stench was easily strong enough to mask our scent, but the physical signs, well, we couldn't erase one hundred percent of our footprints, especially now that we were a larger group.

The historical significance of the landscape was not lost on me as we picked our way down the bluffs and through the woods below the ruins. This was old land we were treading on—the ruins of a ninth-century stronghold en route to its thirteenth-century replacement. Then when we were done with our time, we would return to Kruger and the others south of the wetlands. That was almost thirteen hundred years of humanity, living, fighting, and enduring. All done before ether forced its way into our world and changed things forever.

On the ridge above the castle, we found an abandoned camp and with it a stash of cores. Joan's people rifled through the bag excitedly, then counted out the haul. All in all, four small red cores and six green ones.

"Do you think they will come back for them?" Gaston, one of Joan's archers asked.

Prometheus leaned over the campfire, holding his hand just above the coals.

"This fire is cold. Maybe two days old. I'd say if they were going to come back, they would have done so by now," he surmised.

"Finders keepers," Hera mumbled, eyeing the cores, hungrily.

With no arguments about keeping the left-behinds, we pushed on down the bluffs. After waiting in the tree line for what felt like forever—or about fifteen minutes for us criminally impatient people, we moved in for the castle's crumbling portcullis.

Prometheus and Omega led, as our scout had come to not just tolerate the wolf's help with scouting, but now insisted on his presence. He ducked through, but appeared outside again, holding a small bag. He waved me forward.

"This was just lying on the ground inside," he explained.

Inside we found a healthy pile of small but incredibly clear crystals.

"Why is all this stuff just lying on the ground?" Joan asked.

"Who cares why," Hera answered, "It's not our problem that they can't keep their stuff secured. But it is ours now. Points to us."

I shrugged and we continued inside the outer wall. The castle was in surprisingly good condition, minus some crumbling spots on the top of the wall. The gates had also rusted into unrecognizable piles, the iron having stained the ground around it red.

The path leading to the main bailey was dotted with dropped items—small, white cores and crystals, leading me to believe that someone had evacuated the castle, perhaps with haste, and dropped their loot along the way. It was the narrative that best fit, at least.

Hera followed Prometheus and Omega across the open yard and through the next archway, scooping the items off the ground with almost child-like zeal. Honestly, I could almost picture her as a little girl in a white Easter dress hunting voraciously for plastic eggs.

Once inside, our attitudes became all business. Although, we found another smattering of cores down a dark corridor to the right. Naturally, Prometheus went that way first. The castle was quiet as we stalked through the first set of halls. We ducked around a caved-in section of wall, then bypassed an open doorway leading down and into the darkness.

Our path forward became more complicated after that, as we came across a collapsed hall, and then another. It was the better part of ten minutes, walking in silence before we found a route to the lower bailey. The keep loomed in the far back corner as Prometheus crept out into the sunlight.

Omega followed him, his hackles instantly rising. Then the wolf turned and trotted back to through the arch, his nose working over a scent on the ground. Half of our group was out from under the archway when the first loud *pop* fired off. I spun, sword in hand, as dust rained down from overhead.

Anita and most of Joan's team were behind me. My gaze flicked up to the archway. My instincts kicked in and I caught our researcher in the chest and pushed her back with all of my strength, then turned and dove into a roll.

"Get out..." Ajax hollered, as a dozen more *pops* fired in short succession.

The archway caved in, the large smooth stone crumbling in a deafening collapse.

"No! Marcel, no!" Joan screamed as I coughed and pushed up to my knees.

Dust filled the air around us but I could see enough to know that the archway we'd just passed through was simply gone. At least two of Joan's team, Omega, and Anita were on the other side— I hoped—while another, a spearman named Marcel, was pinned to the ground by a large pile of rock.

Ajax grumbled and coughed, walking in a circle, and Hera dove to Marcel's side, as she helped Joan try to free the captive fighter. I registered three things at almost the same moment— the distinctive bite of accelerant in my nostrils, like gunpowder, a strong, almost violent tug pulling on my core, and a deep, terrifying screech.

"Stand your ground!" Ajax roared, trying to organize the others.

Wiping at my eyes, I joined him, just as something moved toward us in the dust. Blinded by grit and tears I could only tell that it was large and moving fast.

"Prometheus. Arrows," I wheezed and pointed forward.

Our scout nocked and fired a single arrow before the hulking shadow reached us. I reared back and jumped forward, swinging the nodachi in a wide arc. The blade sang through the air and hit...nothing.

My momentum carried me forward and I staggered several wobbly steps. I planted and spun but felt something bite at my skin. The air around me was charged and hot, that strange pull yanking on my insides.

Someone screamed and I spun back in the other direction as the large dark creature moved by. Hera and two spearmen formed up and lifted their weapons high. I watched as the beast descended on them and ran to help, but by the time I arrived at Hera's side, the beast wasn't there.

I blinked again and again, but there was too much crap in my eyes to see properly. Was it that fast? Was it something else?

"You can't fight if you can't see, stupid. Use your ether to purge the debris from your eyes. You can use it to protect them from the dust. Use your brain!" Ivory snarled.

Cursing myself, I pulled a mass of energy from my core and focused, pushing it up to my face. An uncomfortable tingle rushed to my cheeks, then it grew hot, and settled in my eyes.

A cool, blue light washed over my vision as the ether expelled the tears and grit down my cheeks. The bailey emerged from the blur and only at that moment did I realize that most of the dust cloud had already settled. My eyes had truly been that bad.

Hera had most of the team arrayed in a defensive arc around Joan and Ajax, as they fought and clawed to pull Marcel from the rubble.

After swiping my face on a sleeve, I scanned the bailey. And yet, the wide courtyard appeared empty. A cool breeze blew in from over the crumbling wall, carrying the remainder of the dust cloud with it. But once it died away, we were left in a terrifying moment of silence.

"What the fuck is that thing? Did you see it? H-H-How did it do...that?" Hera growled.

"Do what? What did *it* do?" I asked, moving up behind them. I activated <<**Burst of Speed**>> and my brain toggled between <<**Razor's Edge**>> and <<**Blazing Slash**>>. But I didn't know what we were fighting, so the decision remained open.

"Honestly, Kenji. Sometimes I think your brain is asleep behind the wheel. You're telling me you didn't see that giant pra —" Hera started to say just as a bright blue flash of ether exploded between us.

We were alone and talking one moment, and standing in the shadow of a massive, praying mantis in the next. The beast spun, wings extended and legs stamping the ground. It was easily twelve feet tall, and twice that in length, with armored and barbed arms, bulbous, green eyes, and a fat abdomen.

I jumped back, avoiding its hooked feet as its arms lashed out with startling speed. One strike threw Hera's spear aside, another knocked a spearman off his feet, and then the beast chittered and came right at me.

Using my speed, I stabbed the nodachi right at its body. But I'd never meant for the strike to land, only deflect its grabbing arms long enough to spin away. And it worked...barely.

Thump-Thump, snapped its arms, the first knocking my heavy blade back, while the second clipped my shoulder and sent me into an off-balance pirouette.

I corrected and planted my feet just as the beast swept in on Ajax and Joan. It moved so fast I could barely track it. My big friend's hammer swung hard for a leg, but he missed, and the heavy weapon pulled him off balance. Joan screamed and lunged. Her sword caught the beast, or so I thought. Then it lifted an arm and pulled the weapon right out of her hands.

"Shoot that thing!" I screamed as the mantis bulled through Joan and latched onto Marcel.

Prometheus and the last remaining crossbowman aimed as the creature ripped poor Marcel out of the rubble, his body trapped in a spiny death grip. They fired just as the creature disappeared in a flash of fiery blue ether.

"Marcel!" Joan screamed, recovering her sword from the ground.

The beast reappeared atop the wall on the far side of the bailey, Marcel's screams echoing off the stone all around us. Then we watched helplessly as it brought the struggling man to its mouth, and he went quiet.

"How do we fight something like that?" Ajax asked, panting.

I spun on the spot, my mind a raging ball of panic and half-formed ideas. The mantis was armored, yes. It was massive and possessed a seemingly unquenchable hunger. But it also seemed to be able to phase in and out, or...teleport. Was that possible?

Truthfully, the flash of blue ether, the heat, and even the *popping* sound was eerily similar to what I'd experienced when transiting through the rift.

"Come together," I yelled, wishing Anita were with us. A host of weird, science questions were firing off in my brain and I didn't know how to answer any of them. Perhaps with her knowledge, we could find a way to fight the beast. But how could you kill something that was bigger, faster, and could simply vanish with a poof and bang?

The only answer I could produce was to run and survive. For now.

As a group, we ran down the bailey wall but could find no open paths out. So, we ran back in the other direction, flowing like a pack of scared animals. My insides shriveled up as I realized the truth of our situation. We were trapped.

I turned back as the mantis leapt off the wall, having finished the last few bites of poor Marcel. My gaze swept back to the archway we'd entered from, and if possible, my insides shriveled up a little more.

"My god. We followed a path of breadcrumbs right in here," I said, watching the mantis approach. "Someone led us to this thing and trapped us inside."

"Why would someone do that?" Ajax growled. But I saw him come to the same conclusion before anyone could utter a response.

Someone wanted us dead.

CHAPTER 39: COWARD'S BRAVERY

"Great. That's just fucking great! All this time, fighting and surviving, and I'm gonna get eaten alive by a giant, fucking praying mantis! No! No! That does not work for me!" Hera screamed.

"I'm not planning on having that thing eat me while I'm still alive. Spiders at least have the good graces to paralyze something with their venom first. But this..." Ajax responded.

"We're not dying today. This thing is just another beast. Yes, a really big, fast, and hungry one, with ugh...strange teleporting abilities, but in the end, it is just an animal," I said. "We can kill it, we just have to work together."

"It sounds like you have a plan. My hammer is too slow and that thing is too high for me to have any impact, so you tell us what to do, Kenji," Ajax said as the Mantis moved toward us.

I took a breath to speak, to tell them that I really had no idea how to fight it when my gaze locked on the beast's impossibly thin legs. Considering its height and girth, the legs looked cable-thin and had to be the weak point. It was my best guess, at least.

"Surround it and take out its legs. Bring it down so we can strike at its head and body. That is how we fight this thing. With your strength, one solid hit from your hammer should do the trick, Ajax."

I moved to pull out the UMP but changed my mind. The legs

were a relatively thin, moving target and I had limited ammunition. Yes, I could target the stumps where the legs joined the body, but the mantis' armor looked thick, and even that shot wasn't a sure thing. Better to save that weapon for contingencies.

"Surround it! Those with short blades go after its legs. Those with spears, use your longer reach to protect them," I said as the Mantis reached us.

Hera cursed and moved left, so I went with her, the other spear-wielders working to encircle the massive beast. Ajax huddled behind us, his hammer poised over his shoulder for a crushing blow.

My plan sounded solid in theory, but as soon as the beast was upon us, it became painfully evident that its twitchy, erratic movements would be the biggest obstacle. And worst of all, it seemed to understand that.

I used my strength skill and lined up a leg, activating <<**Razor's Edge**>>. The nodachi cut in hard from right to left, swinging off my shoulder with all the strength I could summon. And the mantis blipped—that's the only word I can think of to describe its motion—causing my blade to pass harmlessly through the air just beneath its barbed foot.

Hera stabbed at its face as the beast lunged for me, the sharp bladed tip of her spear hitting its clicking pincers and driving it back. Joan cut hard for another leg and scored a hit, but the blade reverberated off the limb like she'd hit a steel pipe.

"Ahh, merde! It is like chopping at a stone," she yelled.

I cut in, again and again, finally managing to score a hit on the third swing. My nodachi hit with a loud *ting*, as the impact reverberated up my arms.

This isn't going to work, I thought desperately just as the mantis disappeared in a bright, swirling flash.

It appeared to our right and we pivoted as a group, but the creature jumped into the air and disappeared in another flash. We swung left to face it as it reappeared, only to have it pop in and out in a dizzying explosion of light and color.

"My eyes! Trying to track this thing is giving me a headache," Ajax yelled just as the beast emerged from an ether cloud right on top of him.

Before we could react, the mantis snapped its arms down and scooped him right off the ground.

The pull on my core returned, my belly button being painfully wrenched toward the monster. The sensation grew in intensity, like the beast was preparing to...

"Prom! Shoot it, before it jumps away," I screamed as Ajax's hammer fell free. I fumbled my storage open and reached for the UMP, understanding it was my only option.

The scout was faster. With an arrow already nocked, he pulled and released it in a heartbeat. The projectile flashed in right below the beast's mouth and hit its green hide with a surprisingly loud *thump*.

Screeching, the monster swiped at the air with its left claw, while swinging Ajax around with the other. The burning in my core grew stronger, and the outline of the beast's body started to shimmer.

I found the UMP's handle but the buttstock snagged on the artifact stored next to it. With a desperate yank, they both came free—the submachine gun in my hand and the relic rattling to the ground.

The trigger squeezed—**bang, bang, bang.** Forty-five caliber rounds hit the mantis' body, my aim intentionally low. The resulting ether flashes popped like bright firecrackers. Three rounds hit near the front leg but the next few walked up the creature's body. Bits of shell cracked and flew off and in a moment of triumph, Ajax fell free.

I barely held off the trigger that last time, not firing the round that would likely have gone right through my friend. Prometheus loosed another arrow and scored a hit on the mantis' head. It reeled and screeched, gnashing the air with its pincers.

With pronged arms spread, the mantis tried to teleport away. Its outline grew fuzzy as ether clouded the air, but only half of its body disappeared, before reappearing a heartbeat later. It blipped but didn't go anywhere.

In response to the giant bug's twitchy, failed teleport, the artifact jumped on the ground and rang like a struck bell.

I watched it, dumbfounded for a moment as the mantis tried to teleport again. The artifact bounced, its surface ringing with a new high-pitched vibration every time.

"There! The beast is somehow bound to the relic. Perhaps it has one like it lodged somewhere in its body. Use it! That is the key!" Ivory chimed in.

I hooked Ajax under the arm and helped him to his feet. The monster's spiny arms had cut and poked him in more than a dozen places. He was bleeding, but it appeared that his armor had protected his vital areas.

"I am...okay," he groaned and staggered over to his lost hammer.

Scooping the relic off the ground, I threw my arm through the UMP's sling.

Hera jumped before me and brandished her spear as the mantis, blipping and screeching erratically, lunged in chaotic and unpredictable attacks. It was scared now, perhaps confused by its inability to use its power. I could feel it.

"The relic is the key. Form up! If we can knock it off its feet, we can strike at its body and head!" I yelled and looped around to the right.

Joan responded in French, organizing the remnant of her team to fill in around us. I held the artifact up like a shield and moved right at the mantis. It screeched and lunged at me, its grasping arms flicking forward in a blur. It hit me like a speeding car, the impact knocking me back two steps and ringing through my body. And yet, its arms never actually touched.

Resetting my feet, I moved in again and the mantis lashed out, but its arms hit the air just above me and rebounded. It couldn't touch the relic, or me while I held it! The artifact also seemed to prevent the beast from teleporting, as well.

"Shoot it!" I yelled and with the artifact held above my head, moved toward the monster.

"I am low on arrows. Four left," Prom shouted back as his shot and a crossbow bolt streaked in, both finding purchase in that soft spot beneath the beast's mouth.

Hera and the others jabbed their spears at its left side. I spotted Ajax in my peripheral vision, his hammer poised, so I moved in to draw the mantis' attention away.

Pushing the artifact forward, I activated **<<Enhanced**

Strength>> again for good measure and ran in. As I'd hoped, the Mantis squared up with me and blipped as it tried to teleport away.

Ajax, having waited for that moment, swung his hammer once the beast's outline stabilized, and struck its middle leg hard. The chitinous shell cracked loudly under the blow and the limb buckled.

The mantis screeched and scuttled left, working to protect the wounded leg, but moved right into Hera. With her spear held high, she thrust the wolf-bone blade right into its bulbous body. The long weapon, with all her strength behind it, did what our arrows before could not. It hit, bit, and plunged clean through the monster's thick hide.

"Hell yeah!" Hera screamed and ripped the spear back, a thick, gloppy shot of ichor pushing out of the wound.

The mantis swung her way, but Prometheus fired another arrow, this one hitting the beast right in the face. It hit with a *crack* and bounced away but forced the monster's arms up to shield its eyes.

"Three," Prom yelled and two spears stabbed in on either side, both scoring deep wounds on the mantis' body.

I pushed right through the creature's legs to stand beneath it, the artifact vibrating violently in my hands. Something inside the creature was singing a similar song. Its body started to roil and bubble inside, so I pushed the relic up as close as my strength would allow.

A massive stream of guts shot out of the wound from Hera's spear as the Mantis screamed, the noise drowned out by Ajax's hammer swinging in and breaking clean through one of its legs. In a moment of triumph, the enormous beast pitched sideways, its bulk almost crushing me on the way down.

"It's down! Kill it! Finish it off!" Ajax howled as the others moved in.

And yet, the mantis was hardly helpless. Its hooked feet and spiny arms thrashed and kicked, each enough to rip a person in half if they were foolish enough to get too close.

"Ajax...follow me!" I yelled and held the artifact out before me. It would provide us a safe path through the mass of dangerous limbs and his hammer would deal the killing blow.

The big man limped up to me, his face pale and drawn, and yet his eyes alight with fierce determination. Then without words, I led him toward the wounded mantis' head. It looked right at me, or at least I guessed that it did, who could tell with those freaky, compound eyes.

Holding the artifact with both hands, I pushed for the beast's head. It thrashed at me with its arms, but they rebounded from the relic. Ajax huddled right behind me, effectively shielded from its attacks.

We approached, the force pushing against the relic making my arms shake. Every muscle in my body burned and twitched, even with my strength enhancement. The mantis' head snapped forward, its pincers clicking and snapping like razor-sharp blades. They were even more dangerous than its arms, so it was up to me to give Ajax an opening and not get him cut in half.

I lowered the artifact a bit more, the pressure pushing the mantis' head forward and its pincers down. My back twinged and my shoulders screamed, but I didn't back off. We'd come too far and fought too hard to fail now. I heard Hera holler something and Joan screamed a heartbeat later, but I couldn't look up to see what they were doing. Managing another half-step forward, I choked on my next breath but got us in range.

"A-j-jax. Now!" I grunted, my teeth chattering together.

My friend pulled around me and lifted the hammer, just as something moved in my peripheral vision. It was small and dark, flying through the air. I watched as it hit the mantis' head and clattered to the ground before us—a shiny metal cylinder with a flat top.

I registered a change in air pressure around me, an uncomfortable burning sensation on my face, then...confusion, pain, and darkness.

I floated somewhere...that was all I could tell—I was weightless and in pain. My mind palace was just beyond the veil of darkness. I could feel it, that bit of structure keeping my thoughts from scattering altogether. Then I heard the voice.

"Pull yourself together!"

Recognition dawned. I knew that it was Ivory but I couldn't

see him, nor could I feel my body. Was I dead?

"No, you aren't dead! But you will be if you don't wake up...now!"

The wolf's voice tore through my mind so hard that it pushed me backward in the darkness, my ethereal form tumbling like a leaf on the wind. And it seemed to do the trick.

I was nowhere one moment and gasping for breath the next. The ground was beneath me—hard and cool, but I felt hot, my skin feverish.

Drawing on ether, I pushed it to every corner of my body, hoping it would both heal and protect me. It flooded up and over my face and eyes and my vision quickly cleared, revealing stone and rubble beneath me.

I rolled over, gasping down another breath, and found the artifact on the ground a dozen paces away. Ajax was to my left, and the giant mantis was further than that. Dark and indistinct forms moved around the large beast, pulling and pushing on it.

Did we do it? Did we succeed? But wha...what was the explosion from? Did the creature somehow explode? I thought, trying to put my muddled thoughts back together.

"Holy shit! You're alive!" someone said, as their form clarified from the blur.

I groaned as the man sauntered my way, then knelt next to the dropped artifact. Richter's rich blue jacket shone in the light, his Zurich standard practically glowing. His blue eyes were locked on the relic between us, although his face was still pointed at me.

"What a champ. You took that ether grenade full in the face. I've got to say, Takemi, you are one tough son of a bitch. Although, it looks like you're going to need a different haircut for a while. You are a little, ugh, singed," the Prime commando said, chuckling quietly to himself.

I watched as he plucked the artifact off the ground, turned it over in his hands, and smiled.

"I have to admit. I thought Alfred's idea was too simple to work on your team. But boy was I wrong. You and your team followed our trail better than I could have ever hoped. I said you were too smart to fall for something that stupid, but hey, thank you for proving me wrong. And you took that mantis down, too. So, double bonus for Prime and Zurich. We get the artifact from the

Mantis and the one from the lake, and I didn't have to fight either beast. It's really a shame you're not going to be alive to see Hans and Kruger's faces. Those two were so confident that you lot would survive this place."

"I am still...alive," I said, my throat scorched.

"Now, yes. But..." Richter said and turned back to the mantis. He shouted something to his team members who were cutting into the massive, dead creature. "We're just about done here, so, we're going to have to finish you and your team off. But hey, it's nothing personal. What happens at the Mêlée of Kings is strictly business."

"We need help," I said, forcing my thoughts to Ivory.

"No shit!" the wolf responded. *"Omega is looking for a way in. Stall him!"*

"Richter, wir haben es gefunden!" one of his men shouted as they chopped a large section of the beast's abdomen away. A dark, shiny piece of foreign debris came into view, the unearthed artifact fused into the beast's insides.

"Just take them and leave us...we won't stop you," I said, struggling to my hands and knees. My ether was cycling as fast as I could manage it, the spinning core trickling life out into my muscles. It was a Band-Aid holding me together. I was hurt bad, that much I could tell, but I needed to hold myself together for just a bit longer.

"Oh, you know, I wish we could do zat, Takemi," Richter said, clicking his tongue. "But you know, Zurich is poised on the precipice of change. Alfred started before we even left to come here. If Kruger and Hans were to leave here alive, they would return to a city cleansed of the Protectorate's power. You and your team have allied with them, so you must die as well. Besides, it is a bit of a melee tradition. Only the strong walk out alive at the end."

"We're mercenaries," I breathed and sat back on my rear. My hands were burned and although I couldn't see it, my face likely looked as bad. "We work for the highest bidder."

I stretched my neck and used that moment to find Hera and the others. They'd been pulled together into a group on the far side of the mantis, with their hands and ankles bound. They'd been far enough away from the blast, so they appeared to be okay. But Ajax was lying on the ground, and unfortunately, he wasn't moving.

"Hmm. That may be—" Richter started to say as his men cheered. I looked over his shoulder only to find one of the men hoisting the mantis' artifact high over his head.

"Sorry. I was going to say that may be true for mercenaries, but I do not believe that is true for you and your friends here. Again, this is nothing personal, but I cannot let you all walk out of here."

Richter brushed his hands together and stood, turning back to his team.

"Kill them all. And make it look like the beast did it."

"Since you didn't mention it, I'll take it you didn't find the other artifacts," I said, trying a new tactic.

"Oh? Which ones? Because we ambushed several teams before you and took what they found. It's a pity these zoos are so wild, so dangerous. The beasts, they do kill so many people. I hope their families mourn them well," Richter said.

I fought down a stab of anger, but mastered it, understanding that we would only survive if I could find a way to keep him talking. My temper would only expedite the inevitable.

"Not them," I grunted, feigning weakness. My strength was returning, as ether flooded my body. That didn't mean I wasn't in pain, however, as my burned skin and ruptured eardrums sucked. "I mean, the artifacts we buried before coming in here. I was worried about traps and didn't want to carry everything with us."

Richter accepted the artifact claimed from the mantis' body as his team started to mass around him. I tried not to fixate on the stolen treasure, but its pull on my core and eyes was undeniable.

"...and what artifacts would those be? We possess those claimed from the stadium rift, the graveyard beyond the old church, and the Olympic village. With yours, and if memory serves, that is most of the known rifts."

Ajax shifted and groaned. I chuckled, not just mocking the arrogant Prime commando, but hopefully trying to draw attention away from my wounded friend. The less he knew and the more he doubted, the better.

"You must not have found the cave at the base of the bluff," I said, then pulled the snake's core out of my bag. "It led to a tunnel and then an underground river. We found a rift there and a surprisingly large snake living beyond. It didn't give up its artifact easily, either."

"What snake? What cave?" Richter asked, looking to his team.

The members of his team all shrugged and looked at one another.

"Willst du mir damit sagen, dass sie etwas gefunden haben, was wir nicht gefunden haben? Ihr Ficker seid wertlos," Richter shouted at his team.

"I'll show you where we hid it if you let my team go."

"There is no deal you can offer that I will trust, Takemi. But I will leave one of your teammates alive. They can take me to this stash, and if it is true, we will escort them out of the zoo and let them go. One person of your choosing, of course."

"You're going to make me pick?" I asked. "That is fucked up."

A flood of emotions washed over me then—anger, fear, and pain. Omega was coming.

"I guess that's what sets us apart, Richter," I said. "You would probably stab any one of your teammates in the back, but us? We stick together."

"Holy shit, this is going to be awesome. Get back!" Ivory screamed into my mind, just as Omega sprinted in from the right and hit one of Richter's commandos mid-stride.

"Kill the fucking wolf!" Richter shouted and turned, pulling his longsword free.

Omega bit, pulled, and shook, savagely removing the man's head from his shoulders. The Prime commandos spread apart and moved to encircle the wolf, just as the stag barreled in behind, its antlers skewering two men at once.

I performed a rather ungainly roll backward to gain space as the stag raised its head, lifting the impaled men right off the ground. Omega took the opportunity to pounce on another man, clamping his jaws onto his arm and pulling him to the ground.

"No!" Richter snarled and ripped something off his belt. I recognized the small object but had no time to do anything but scream.

"Get back!"

The Prime commando tossed the ether grenade at Omega's general direction, but thanks to our link, the wolf understood that it meant danger. He reared up and jumped away, just as the strange explosive flashed bright, creating a hot cloud of expanding ether.

I spun away, covering my already damaged eyes and face with my arm, but the wave of heat still hurt. When I'd finally managed to turn back, Richter was sprinting away across the bailey, flinging ether grenades into the path behind him.

CHAPTER 40: ONE SNAKE, TWO HEADS

Ajax coughed and spluttered as I limped to him, his lips covered in dark blood. He opened his eyes, too, but they were filled with broken vessels. His beard was singed and his eyebrows were just gone.

I helped him roll over so he could breathe, then looked up and spotted Anita and the last member of Joan's team running from the northern wall. Omega circled, growling and snorting, while the stag shook its head, fighting to remove the bodies impaled on its antlers.

"Don't move," I whispered to Ajax, "I'll be right back."

I pulled my wakizashi and ran over to Hera and the others, quickly cutting her bindings first, then releasing the others. They exploded into action around me, all fists and rage, but it became clear that they didn't know what to do with it.

Hera joined me at Ajax's side, her eyes flipping between our sturdy friend's many wounds. We'd seen him beat up and bloodied before, but this...this was different.

"Can you walk?" she whispered.

He took a breath, grunted, and nodded. "I will...try."

Hera and I helped Ajax off the ground, but it became clear by how much of his weight we had to support, that he wasn't going to be moving under his own power anytime soon. Joan and Gaston appeared at our side.

"Did you hear him?" I asked.

"Just a little," Hera admitted.

"We weren't the only team they've ambushed. Prime waited for the others to finish a fight, then swept in and took them out. Richter admitted that it was Alfred's directive. Hans and Kruger are in danger. I don't know what story they would use, but we were never intended to leave the melee alive."

"You have to get back and warn them," Hera gasped. "Ajax can't travel on his own. We'll help him. Take Omega and go!"

I turned and managed a half step before turning back. Part of me couldn't stomach the idea of leaving them to navigate their way out of the zoo on their own, but she was right. They could help Ajax if they stayed together. In a group, they were safe. But we would never get back in time if I traveled with them.

"Be safe and watch your backs," I said, pulling Hera into a hug. "And take care of our boy here."

Ajax managed a weak smile through his grimace.

"Go, Kenji. Give that...prick a walloping for...me."

"I will," I said and squeezed his arm, then turned and quickly moved off.

Omega loped up next to me, his almost lazy gait helping him easily overtake me. I could run, but it hurt. Ether would help, but I would have to manage my supply along the way. The last thing I wanted was to get back to the camp and collapse from exhaustion, especially if there was a battle to be fought.

"Show me the way out of here, boy! Lead me and track that weasel-faced fucker down," I said to Omega. "Go!"

The wolf growled happily and accelerated, his nose hovering barely a foot off the ground. I narrowed my focus and activated <<**Burst of Speed**>> and at once felt the draw on my ether reserves. I would have to reactivate the skill several times and just hoped my body would hold out.

Omega led me to the far wall, where he thankfully slowed. I caught up to him just as he slipped through a large crack. It was barely wide enough for me to pass through walking sideways, but that fact didn't prevent my claustrophobia from kicking in.

The narrow path was dark, save for a bright light at the far end. Rocks crumbled and fell as I pushed through with bits of sand and old mortar raining down from above.

"Please don't collapse. Please don't collapse," I mumbled in a mantra.

I stumbled and almost fell halfway through, and by the time I pulled myself free on the far end, my back and legs were on fire. But the fresh air had never felt better. Omega growled at me as I leaned over on my knees to catch my breath, the wolf perched on the hillslope twenty paces away.

"I just need a moment..." I said and pulled a small handful of crystals free but he snarled loudly and flashed his teeth. He was right. There was no time for breaks.

I kicked off and ran to follow him, focusing on two things— absorbing ether and breathing. My supply of both ether and air was disappointingly low. A third sensation caught my attention and I used it to keep my focus off of everything I was lacking. The pull on my core was still there but getting weaker by the moment.

"Work with what ya...got, Kenji," I said under my wheezing breath and ran. And ran. And ran.

I'd known runners that always told me that stopping was the worst thing a person could do while running distance, that they needed to allow their bodies to find equilibrium. They called it catching their wind. Evidently, my wind had ADHD and wasn't in the mood to be caught, because I felt like I was dying.

Omega led me by the stadium but the massive structure loomed large and quiet above me. My imagination filled it with all manner of beasts, but for once I was more than happy to pass right on by unnoticed.

A small group of rat creatures tried to spring a trap on Omega when we reached the woods beneath the bluffs. The wolf picked up the first creature in his mouth and shook it like a toy. I limped in right after and pinned another to the ground with my katana. The rest scurried away into the trees.

I picked up on fresh footprints at the base of the bluffs and stopped to look up the dangerous switchback. It was an excuse to catch my breath and let my heart rate slow, but considering the strange weapons Richter had used, it did make sense.

A yell echoed out from somewhere above, the sound

bouncing down the bluffs around me. Omega yipped and kicked forward again, sprinting up the switchback. He hadn't growled or snarled but yipped in what strangely sounded like "move."

"God, you are a savage," I breathed, dropped an empty crystal, and followed him. The first few steps were stiff but my legs loosened after.

Something exploded in the trees as I neared the top. A faint, blue cloud and smoldering leaves were raining down as we stepped off the trail.

"How many of those things does he have? He has to be out by now, right?" I asked Omega. The wolf cocked his head to the side and whined, then ran off into the trees.

"You're right," I whispered. "He's always got one more."

Fighting to breathe as quietly as possible, I ducked off to follow the wolf. My breathing, as it would turn out, was the quietest part of my travel through the underbrush. Everything swished, cracked, or groaned around me. *Shit! Shit!* I thought as every step forward brought another noise.

I almost fell over Omega as we neared the end of the woods and spotted the wall and gate. Richter was just ahead, talking to men standing on the battlement.

I fought the impulse to sprint ahead and drive my katana through his back, especially once one of the men produced a long, brass horn and gave it an impressive blow.

Omega moved to howl as the instrument blared, but I wrapped a hand around his shoulder and gently muzzled him. He growled and tried to break free, but I held tight.

"Shhh, boy. We don't want him to know we're here."

A few moments later, the gate cracked, groaned, and started to open. I watched Richter slide through once it was open and waited. Omega growled and tried to run, but I held him back.

"No, boy. We want him to think he is home free," I whispered but struggled with the same impulse.

Hoping he was well clear of the wall and on his way back to the tents, I led Omega back through the woods a bit and pushed out onto the trail. Then, trying to walk as casually and naturally as possible, I moved toward the wall.

I was almost to the opening before the horn sounded again.

When the tone faded away a man on the other side yelled, "Exiting now is Takemi, the wolf of Zurich. Sponsored by the Protectorate. Congratulations, warrior. You have survived the Mêlée of Kings."

An impressive ring of heavily armed soldiers greeted me on the other side, their armbands sporting a host of different standards. If only they knew that the man they'd let leave before me was likely responsible for the deaths of their friends or family, they might have taken care of Richter for me.

"Yes, and then they would have claimed the artifacts on his person and you would look like a fool. Try again," Ivory sighed in my mind.

"How did I ever think that you were hard to get along with?" I replied. *"And did you hear that, he called me the 'Wolf of Zurich', it sure has a nice ring to it."*

"He was talking about the literal wolf next to you. Get moving. I think Richter is running now."

Letting Ivory's last comment go, I kicked forward into a faster walk, but once we were well away from the wall and its corresponding crowds, I started to jog.

Soldiers were stationed sporadically along the wetland trail, but it was a fraction of what had been there before. I passed a group of women lighting torches along the way as the eastern sky was already starting to darken.

A cold breeze blew past me as I crossed over a small footbridge and far off in the distance, thunder rumbled. I passively considered the horizon, taking note of the large thunderheads. Judging from their speed and how the wind had picked up, it would be raining soon.

Despite the rapidly cooling air and the breeze, I was sweating by the time we reached the tents. I ducked behind an outhouse and pulled the UMP out from under my wolf-pelt cloak, released the magazine, and inspected the contents. I had four rounds left.

Sliding the magazine back into the receiver, I slid it behind my cloak and set off for the Zurich tent. Burning braziers crackled and popped in the wind as I approached, but I could hear voices from inside. Hoping I wasn't too late, and with Omega at my side, we pushed inside.

Kruger was standing at the map table in the middle of the

large space, while Hans Gruber stood to his right, a pipe clutched tightly between his teeth. They both turned as I walked in. The normally composed men stopped talking, their eyes going wide.

"Takemi, you're...here. The horn. What happened to you? To your face?" Hans asked, stepping clear of his cloud of pipe smoke.

I reached halfway to my face but stopped when Omega growled. There wasn't time.

"Prime ambushed us inside the zoo. They took out most of the other teams, too, and claimed their loot as their own. Richter bragged about how the Protectorate was going to fall and none of us were going to make it back to Zurich to warn..."

Someone started to clap loudly as the tent flap on the other side pulled open. I watched as smug-faced Alfred walked in, with Richter right behind him. Omega bristled as more Prime commandos filed in behind us.

"Well, isn't this cozy? And what nice timing, too. We were worried that we'd have to run you down separately, Takemi. Now we've got, oh how do they say it? All of our eggs in one basket. Jawohl. Excellent."

"Guards!" Kruger yelled, but in a surprising display of speed, Richter drew a blade from inside his armor and brought it to the Protectorate leader's neck. Alfred moved behind the two men, lazily inspecting the map laid out on the table.

"They are gone. And if things are going well back home, by the time we've returned from this stinking armpit, all of the Protectorate will be expunged from our fair Zurich."

"That is rather ambitious of you, Alfred," Hans said, after pulling the pipe from his mouth. "It appears I have underestimated you. You aren't just a sniveling weasel, after all. You're a backstabbing one, too."

Damn, even then, with armed men surrounding him threatening death, he had a twinkle in his eyes.

"We placed our forces on alert before leaving. Once your sell swords botched the assassination attempt on Mistress Müller of the Brewers Guild. We tracked the men back to the Builder's League. And I imagine the coin to hire them was funneled through the House of Coin?" Kruger asked, lifting his neck away from the blade. "Did Herr Meier jump out of his trousers at the opportunity to lick the King's ass? Or in his typical lazy fashion, did he have your Prime commandos do it for him?"

Alfred chuckled. "You would be surprised by how many came forward with the promise of tearing you two down from your pedestal."

"Came forward? Or were motivated by Otto and the promise of money and new stations?" Hans asked.

"Does it matter?" Alfred asked.

"Where is our fair King these days?" Hans asked and threw me an almost imperceptible wink.

"You don't think he would stick around for all of this...uncomfortableness, do you?" Alfred asked. "No, our fair leader has much more pressing affairs to deal with back in Zurich. Namely to root out your supporters that are in hiding. Once he finds Herr Schmidt and Catherin Müller, and with the destruction of the Protector, he can finally take back sole authority. As it was always meant to be."

I felt a blade poke into my back as another man settled near Omega. The fourth commando, including Richter, moved in to Kruger's left.

"Do not worry," Alfred continued. "King Otto will erect a magnificent statue in your honor. Songs will be sung of Takemi's exploits here in the melee, and the Protectorate will become the necessary villain the King needs to make real change. In the end, it will be like all the stories, Jawohl? Everyone will live happily ever after."

Hans smiled and turned toward the commando standing guard over him. He took a long pull on his pipe and blew the smoke into his face. The soldier moved to wave it away and coughed.

I activated <<**Burst of Speed**>> just as Hans knocked the man's blade aside and stabbed the lip of his pipe right into his eye. Kruger bent back and just managed to keep the knife from slicing open his neck, but the other soldier closed fast, his longsword poised and ready.

Using every bit of speed I could muster, I wrenched my cloak aside and pulled the UMP forward. The blade bit hard into my back even as I squeezed off the first shot. The bullet hit the swordsman in the shoulder, the subsequent ether eruption blowing off his arm.

Omega tore into the man behind me and I felt his blade grate against my armor. I swung the UMP over at Richter and the commando promptly tossed the blade to the ground.

"Scheisse! He has a gun. Don't kill me! I was just doing what they told me to do," he said and tried to back away from Kruger.

"Fool me twice," I said, and unloaded the last two rounds into his chest. The rounds blew him back into Alfred and they both tumbled to the ground.

He screamed and pushed free, tearing something off the dead commando's gear. I recognized the cylinder and let the UMP fall, reaching for the handle of my katana.

"You all die," Alfred screamed and grabbed the pin. Omega, feeding off my emotions, lunged over the table and caught his arm. The King's magister reeled, with the immense strength of my wolf preventing him from moving his arm to pull the pin.

I'd already felt the sting of one of those weapons and only survived because the artifact shielded me. I knew better than to rest on hope.

"Get off of me you...stupid," Alfred snarled as I ran forward.

The magister looked up just then, his cold, hate-filled eyes opening wide as my blade flashed across. Omega let go, the ether grenade falling free, and Alfred staggered back. He mouthed something, then reached for his face, as his head tipped cleanly off his neck.

"Sehr gut," Kruger breathed and I looked over as he fell back into a chair. He dabbed at his neck, where Richter's blade nicked him, but the wound didn't look back.

Then everything caught up to me at once—the fight with the mantis, getting blown up, the marathon run from the zoo and this. My back abruptly flashed hot, then cold, and everything tilted.

I reached for the table as my head went fuzzy, but it was farther away than I thought. My katana blade caught the ground and I almost sliced through my neck as I fell. Omega's warm, wet tongue was on my face then as someone rolled me over.

Hans Gruber knelt above me, fumbling with my armor, panic filling his normally composed face tight. I tried to understand what he was saying, but my ears were fuzzy. Then I fell again, tumbling into a cold and empty darkness.

CHAPTER 41: DONE YOUR PART

I only sank into the darkness for a moment before a violent and profound tug yanked me back out again—by the belly button. Air rushed into my lungs and I jumped, or flopped, and opened my eyes.

I groaned, finally finding my voice as the increased pressure in my core expanded. The movement ignited a pain in my back as something painful pulled tight.

Voices whispered, but they sounded far away.

I blinked. I was in a tent and struggled through a moment of panic. People were moving and talking beyond the fabric walls but I couldn't hear any signs of fighting.

"Relax. No, you didn't time travel back to that tent on the battlefield. And yes, your head is still intact," Ivory said, his voice downright warm and friendly.

"That's good," I sighed and let my head rest against the pillow.

"You'd best be careful, freund," someone said and I snapped around to find Hans Gruber standing in the corner. He'd been there the whole time and I hadn't noticed him.

The movement made the pain in my back flare again.

"It feels like I've got a hot coal burning in my back."

"Well, it should. That commando's blade slipped right through the gap in your armor. It missed the artery by less than a fingerbreadth," Hans said, stepping forward.

"That would explain the pain," I grunted.

"But that is not what you should be careful of," he continued, staring down at me. "You showed some real grit, mein freund. And you saved Kruger's life. He is not used to being in that position. I think you made an impression, as he is starting to like you."

"Like me? When is that a bad thing?" I asked.

"Kruger is like all the faction leaders in Zurich, polarizing. Befriending one naturally means that you've marked yourself as an enemy to those that oppose him."

"Ahhh," I groaned.

"Now me? I already liked you, so now I just like you a little more," Hans chuckled.

"Just a little?" I asked and he nodded, his blue eyes sparkling.

I started to roll over to sit and the Protectorate captain helped. Once I was up, the pain faded a little.

"Alfred? Prime? Do we head back to Zurich now and confront Otto?" I asked.

"Return to Zurich? Yes. But not you, I'm afraid."

"I don't understand," I said.

Hans settled onto the cot next to me and sighed.

"Kruger and I will marshal our forces here and return to Zurich. Then we will start sorting out the tangled mess Otto has brought down on the city. But you and your capable friends, well, I'm afraid to say, you're getting a promotion."

"A promotion?" I asked. "I thought this was a one-and-done deal—serve Zurich at the melee, and if we lived, our debt and alleged crimes would be forgiven."

"Yes, and yes. But also, no. I think you saw and heard enough from Richter to know that things are far more complicated than you probably ever realized."

"The rifts? The convergence?" I guessed.

"Jawohl," Hans nodded and pushed off of the cot. Then I watched him stride purposefully to the other side of the tent, grab the corner of a white sheet covering a long table, and pull it free.

Artifacts covered the table. Two I recognized and the rest were new. Some were small enough to fit into my palm, while the largest, the one Richter's team pulled from the mantis, was easily three feet tall by two wide.

"You've probably guessed by now that these are the true purpose of the melee. The kingdoms covet and collect them, horde them in their vaults, and employ teams of specialists to try and unlock their secrets. With the chaos in Zurich, we cannot bring them back with us."

"To understand the convergence?"

"Some, yes. But others? They seek to use the artifacts to unlock power for conquest and glory. As you can guess, Otto belongs to the second group," Hans admitted.

"If they can't go back to Zurich, where will they go?"

"When I said you are getting promoted, I did not say it lightly. The Protectorate has no interest in a military coup. We do not wish to rule Zurich, but that may be unavoidable at this rate. At least for a while. Independent and free rulers have kept this region in peace for a long time and we wish to maintain that balance. Kruger would like to elevate you with that idea. Have you ever heard of Montebello Castle?"

I shook my head. Then again, I was still stuck on the idea of Kruger elevating me within a system of free and independent rulers. What did that mean, exactly?

"Wait, are you giving me a castle?" I asked.

"Jawohl. Precisely," Hans said, his smile widening. "Up until ten years ago, the Protectorate garrisoned troops in the castle, but the in-fighting in Zurich required us to pull our forces back. Sadly, the castle and the village supporting it have suffered. My last report indicated that it is badly in need of repair and a little...oh, how do you say it in English? Tender loving care? Jawohl. That is it. Take these artifacts and keep them safe. Repair and maintain the stronghold and help *us* continue to serve Zurich's interests. It is that simple."

"Nothing is ever that straightforward," I said, watching him.

"You are right, of course. If you accept this posting and title, you will be allying yourself with the Protectorate. That means our interests become yours, and so will our allies and enemies."

"Title?"

"Lord of the Castle. Or 'master' if you fancy that more. It is up to you."

I chewed on the idea for a moment. It didn't feel like my goal of distancing myself further from the stuffy, arrogant, and pretentious nobles. Hell, it would mean that I would become one of them.

"I'm sorry, Hans, but I..."

"Talk to your people before you answer either way," he interrupted. "They have been itching to see you and I think you will find their input on the matter quite helpful."

Before I could argue further, Hans moved to the tent and pulled the flap aside. Hera, Prometheus, and Ajax poured inside. The big man came in last and gingerly, at that. I forced my way off the cot and before anyone could speak, I threw my arms around him.

Ajax grunted and returned my embrace. Hera and Prometheus crowded around us, joining our hug.

"We need to stop meeting up in medical tents," Hera sniffled after we finally pulled away.

"Right?" Prometheus laughed.

A moment later a large dark blur launched in through the tent flap and almost bowled me over. Omega bathed my face with kisses, his tongue hot and wet. The others helped me to push him back and down. The licking hurt more than anything, as my ether-scorched skin ached to the touch.

"Where have you been hiding?" I asked the wolf while scratching between his ears.

"In Joan's tent of all places," Hera offered. "You'd better be careful. I think you might have some competition there."

"You wouldn't leave me for her, would you?"

Omega cocked his head to the side and growled.

"I would. She is prettier and smells better," Ajax laughed.

"How are you feeling?" I asked after the laughter died down.

"Crispy," Ajax chuckled and held his gut. A large bandage had been wrapped around his midsection and another covered his left arm. "But my beard will grow back. Besides, as bad as I feel, you look worse." He reached up and rubbed the stubbly beard covering his chin.

"Thanks, buddy."

"It's sad that we've got to almost blow you up to get you to trim your beard," Hera said, gently jabbing the big guy.

"I might have if you'd asked nicely."

We talked for a while longer, catching up on what happened after we'd separated. They already knew most of it—Richter and Alfred dying, and Otto fleeing back to the city. But it felt good to tell them. Hell, it felt good just to see them all okay.

Anita appeared in the doorway then, her pack on one shoulder, and a walking stick in the opposite hand. I waved her in and her eyes immediately fell to the artifacts covering the table.

"They offered me a castle..." I started to say but Hera cut me off.

"We know. Hans talked to us. And we all discussed it while you were out. You should do it, Kenji," she said.

"Just like that? I figured you of all people would be advising me to run the other way, especially after everything that's happened recently," I said.

"I know. I know," she said, waving me off. "And that was my first impulse—"

"Actually, her first words were, 'no fucking way, asshole!'" Ajax said.

Hera turned a scowl his way.

"What? The tents are made of fabric and you talk really, really loudly."

"I do not!" she shouted, then seemed to realize it, and blushed. "Okay. Yes. I yell. But just hear me out. Yes, we want to get away from all the scheming and the conflict. But the way I see it, we'll find that no matter where we go. We've all got one thing in common: we want to build a home. And in this crazy, turbulent world, what safer more secure home can we ask for than a castle? Besides. Joan wants to discuss a treaty and we could provide Anita someplace where she can study the convergence and feel...safe."

Hera turned her gaze to the researcher then and the two women's eyes locked. More than a little color warmed both of their cheeks.

"We make real change to the region, Kenji," Prometheus said when Hera didn't continue. "Bring in people to plant and grow crops, raise livestock, recruit craftsmen, and use our strength to provide them all a safe place to live."

"And where else are you going to be able to keep your ever-increasing pack of animals? That stag followed us out of the zoo. You've got Omega here, and don't forget about the bear," Ajax said.

"Yes...that," I said, petting the wolf again.

I studied my friend's faces for a moment. Yes, I was surprised by how willing they all seemed to take Hans' deal and tether our little group to the Protectorate, but then again, the more I considered the idea, the more comfortable it felt.

My gaze slid past them to the table full of artifacts, their combined presence creating a steady pull on my core.

It would give us a defensible space—check.

The ability to recruit the people we wanted to live with for a change—check.

And just maybe, help provide answers to some long-nagging questions—double check.

"All right. Let's go claim our castle!" I nodded and winced, the movement having irritated my burned skin.

"I can't wait for you to tell Layla!" Hera whispered.

"Why?"

"The women down there speak Italian!"

Printed in Poland
by Amazon Fulfillment
Poland Sp. z o.o., Wrocław

34942617R00242